True Freedom

LIGHT *in the* EMPIRE

TRUE FREEDOM

CAROL ASHBY

CERRILLO PRESS

TRUE FREEDOM
Copyright 2019 by Carol Ashby

Publisher's Note: This novel is a work of fiction. Names, characters, places, and incidents are either products of the author's imagination or used fictitiously. All characters are fictional, and any similarity to people living or dead is purely coincidental.

Scripture quotations marked CSB have been taken from the Christian Standard Bible®, Copyright © 2017 by Holman Bible Publishers. Used by permission. Christian Standard Bible® and CSB® are federally registered trademarks of Holman Bible Publishers.

Scripture quotations marked (ESV) are from the Holy Bible, English Standard Version, copyright © 2001, 2007, 2011, 2016 by Crossway Bibles, a division of Good News Publishers. Used by permission. All rights reserved.

Scripture quotations marked (NIV) are taken from THE HOLY BIBLE, NEW INTERNATIONAL VERSION®, NIV® Copyright © 1973, 1978, 1984, 2011 by Biblica, Inc.® Used by Permission of Biblica, Inc.® All rights reserved worldwide.

Scripture quotations marked (NKJV) are taken from the New King James Version. Copyright © 1982 by Thomas Nelson, Inc. All rights reserved. Used by permission.

Scripture quotations marked (NLT) are taken from the Holy Bible, New Living Translation, copyright © 1996, 2004, 2007. Used by permission of Tyndale House Publishers Inc., Carol Stream, Illinois 60188. All rights reserved.

Cover and interior design by Roseanna White Designs
Cover images from Shutterstock.com

ISBN: 978-1-946139-10-8 (paperback)
      978-1-946139-11-5 (ebook)
      978-1-946139-17-7 (hardcover)

Cerrillo Press
Edgewood, NM

For I know the plans I have for you," says the LORD. "They are plans
for good and not for disaster, to give you a future and a hope.
Jeremiah 29:11 (NLT)

Greater love has no one than this,
than to lay down one's life for his friends.
John 15:13 (NKJV)

And we know that for those who love God all things work together
for good, for those who are called according to his purpose.
Romans 8:28 (NKJV)

To my children, Paul and Lydia,
for their love, support, and encouragement.
To Andrew, gifted wordsmith and true brother in Christ,
who helped so much as I was writing every novel
from The Legacy *to* Honor Bound.
And especially to my husband, Jim,
who embodies the best of every hero in these stories.

And most of all, to Jesus.

Soli Deo gloria.

A Note from the Author

Freedom—something we long for, something we cherish when we have it.

But there are times when life closes in upon us, forcing us into circumstances we don't want now and futures we dread. It can seem impossible for all things to work together for good when life goes totally wrong.

I've known loss, but I've never lost everything. I've had to do what I didn't want, but I always knew it was only for a season. I know God loves me beyond measure and wants only what's best for me, but how many times have I questioned the events in my life because they weren't what I wanted? It can be hard to remember in the moment of trial that all things work together for good for those who love God.

Sometimes I act as if I know better than God what is best for me, but I only see in part, not the whole. If I stay open to what God is trying to show me, I can learn the truth, and it is truth that sets me free.

Each time I come through the storm and look back, I can see His loving hand. And each time I do, it's easier to remember while the lightning is still striking all around me that the rainbow will appear after the thunderstorm. When I stop trying to control everything, I'm free to relax and enjoy the ride.

In *True Freedom*, Dacius's life in a loving Christian family is ended by the Roman army that kills his parents and makes him a slave. He loses everything except his faith in God and his salvation through Jesus. But even though he's treated as an animal, he knows he's still a man. He chooses to do what pleases God as much as he can as a slave. And when he risks everything to obey Jesus's command to love, all things work together for good.

True Freedom is a story of faith when the future seems hopeless, love to the point of sacrifice, and the power of faith and love to bring true freedom to all involved

I hope you enjoy the story of Dacius and Julia and how his faithfulness ultimately frees them both. May we always remember that our own faithfulness in the times of trial can open the way to a better future than we ever thought possible.

Characters

JULIUS SECUNDUS FAMILY AND SLAVES

Tiberius (52): ex-consul of Rome, now proconsul (governor) of the province of Sicily

Tiberius (32): Tiberius's oldest son, married and living at one of the estates outside Rome

Manius (25): Tiberius's second son serving as tribune in a legion stationed in Britannia

Antonia Alba (25): stepsister of Julia, wife of Titus Flavius Sabinus, mother of Flavia and Sabina

Aulus (18): Tiberius's third son

Julia Secunda/Calantha (16): youngest child of Tiberius

Trebonia Procula (deceased): Julia's stepmother, Antonia's mother, Tiberius's second wife

Dacius/Leander (23): Enslaved in Dacia at 11, Christian, litter slave for Julia

Gallio (mid-40s): steward of the Julius Secundus family

Primus: litter slave who hates Dacius and blames him for the kidnapping

Taurus: bodyguard and Julia's litter escort

Glyptus: cook and friend of Dacius

Verres and Capellus: litter slaves who join Primus in lies about Dacius

CLAUDIUS DRUSUS FAMILY

Lucius Fidelis (36): father of Marcus Drusus

Lucius (20): oldest son, a tribune near Rome but about to transfer to Judaea

Marcus (18): Aulus's best friend

FLAVIUS SABINUS FAMILY

Quintus Flavius Sabinus: ruthless Roman power broker; political enemy of Tiberius Secundus

Octavius Flavius Sabinus (19): Quintus's son

Titus Flavius Sabinus (31): nephew of Quintus Sabinus, husband of Antonia Alba

Flavia (6) and Sabina (3): children of Antonia and Titus, Julia's nieces

Titus Flavius Titianus (21): nephew of Quintus Flavius Sabinus, tribune in XI Urban Cohort

AT THE LUDUS BRUTI

Marcus Antonius Brutus (32): wealthy equestrian owner of gladiator school, Ludus Bruti.

Africanus: Brutus's favorite gladiator as bodyguard, sparring partner, and good friend

Rufus: another of Brutus's favorites as bodyguard

Lanista Felix: head trainer over the Ludus Bruti

Fortis: gladiator used as a trainer of young men by Brutus

KIDNAPPERS

Gaius Faltonius Callidus (43): ex-legionary turned kidnapper

Gnaeus Aelius Bassus: childhood friend of Callidus (thin kidnapper)

SEMPRONIUS RUTILUS FAMILY AND CHRISTIAN FRIENDS

Gaius Sempronius Rutilus (50): Christian farmer who shelters Julia and Dacius outside Rome

Marcella (50): Gaius's wife

Publius Aelius Mestrius and wife Lucillia (40): taberna owners, members of Gaius's house church

Quintus Sertorius Festus and wife Petronia (23): poor farmers, members of the house church

Sextus Valerius Genialis (45): Gaius's best friend; widower, member of the house church.

Servilia (45): Christian shopkeeper who hides Julia and Dacius from kidnappers

OTHER IMPORTANT CHARATERS

Claudius Ursus: Very wealthy son of an imperial freedman of Emperor Claudius

Metilia Neposa (16): Julia's best friend; grieving the death of her brother/Julia's betrothed.

Cities and Towns

Stadia: Roman units for distances: 1 mile=8.7 stadia; 1 km=5.4 stadia
Mille passus (pl. *milia passuum*) Roman mile=0.92 English miles=1.48 km

Alba Longa: town south of Rome in Alban Hills
Ardea (1) : town on coast south of Rome
Castrum Novum (2): near present-day Giulianova
Carnuntum (3): legion headquarters on Danube east of present-day Vienna
Cosa (4): ruins in southwestern Tuscany
Cyrene (5): city in Africa, near present-day Shahhat, Libya
Dacia (A): Roman province, present-day Romania
Dyrrachium (6): port city on Adriatic Sea, present-day Durrës, Albania
Fidenae: town north east of Rome
Lacus Albanus: present-day Lake Albano in the Alban Hills of Lazio
Liternum (7): town on coast north of Neapolis (present day Naples)
Luna (8): coastal town in northern Italy, present-day Luni
Mare Nostrum (B): "our sea", the Mediterranean
Neapolis: present-day Naples
Ostia (9): older port town on Tiber River serving Rome
Pisae (10): present-day Pisa
Ponninia Superior (C): Roman province, present-day Austria
Portus (9): newer port town on Tiber River serving Rome
Puteoli (11): major port on west side of Italy
Roma (12): present-day Rome
Sarmizegetusa (13): capital city of Dacia
Tibur: town east of Rome, present-day Tivoli
Trebula Mutuesca (14) : town northeast of Rome
Tusculum: city south of Rome in Alban Hills

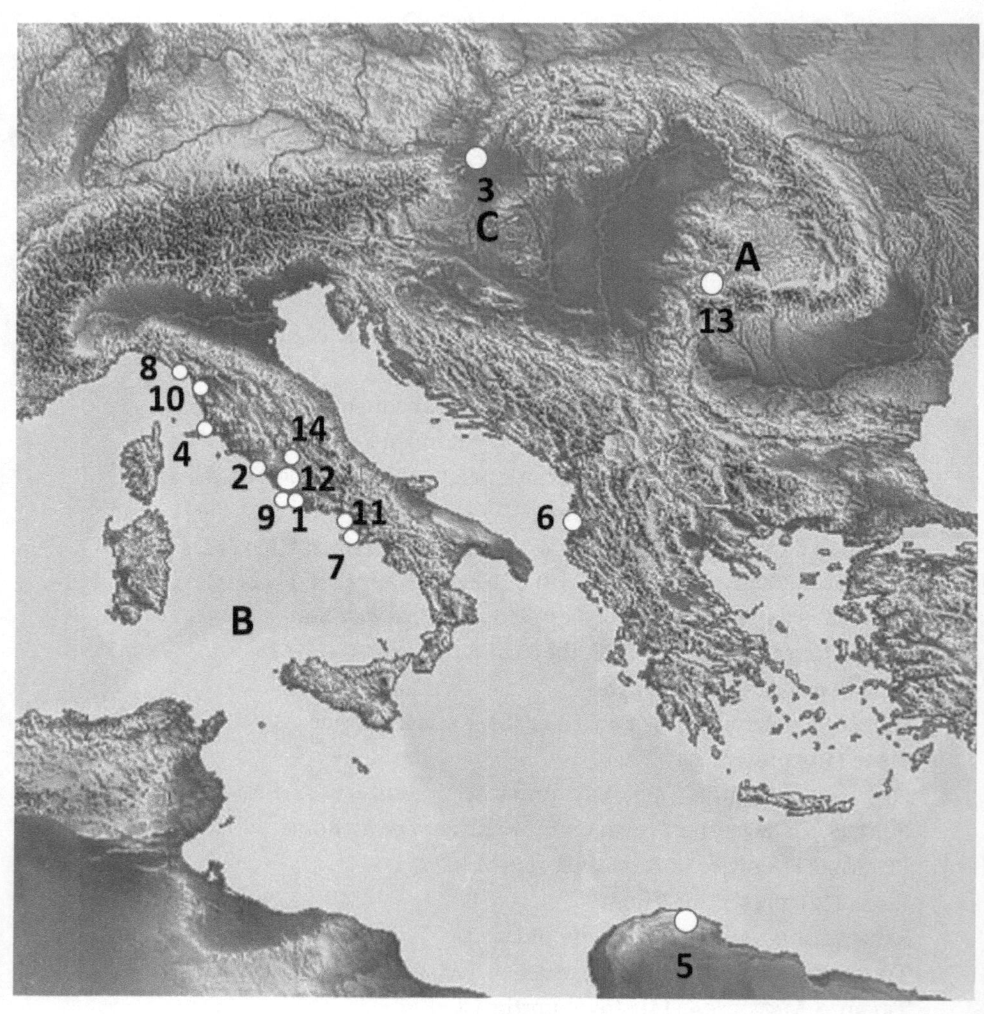

3
C
A
13
8
10
4
14
2
12
9
1
11
7
B
6
5

Chapter 1

READY TO HELP

Rome, AD 118
The Secundus villa, Day 1

The woman's scream ripped into Dacius. He dropped his shovel of manure and sprinted into the stable yard.

Flames danced in a pile of straw three feet from the grindstone. The fire was small, but it transformed the skittery young stallion the master's son had just bought into a thousand pounds of lunging, rearing, kicking terror. The horse had ripped its lead rope from the stable boy's hand and run for the open gate in the eight-foot masonry wall—just as the young mistress returned on her litter.

She blocked its escape, and the stallion was determined to get out, even if it had to go through the litter where Mistress Julia sat screaming. Its flailing hooves knocked the right rear bearer to the ground.

With no one holding the pole, the litter tipped, and the still-screaming mistress tumbled out, not five feet from the horse's hooves.

Dacius stripped off his tunic as he ran toward them. The stallion reared, and as its full weight came down on the bearer's head, it crushed the man's skull.

The mistress tried to stand, but she tripped on her long tunic and fell even closer to the terrified animal.

Her shrieks fueled the stallion's panic, and it started to rear once more. Dacius leaped, caught the lead at the halter, and pulled its head down and sideways, away from her.

As the hooves came back to earth, he flipped his tunic across the

1

horse's face and pulled it snug. The stallion froze, trembling, when the fire disappeared from view.

He led the horse into its stall and stood with it, stroking its neck. "Calm, boy. Steady, boy."

The fear drained from the trembling stallion as Dacius's voice and hand caressed him. After the horse calmed, Dacius released his tunic and lifted it from the stallion's eyes.

"Good boy." Two soft slaps to the horse's shoulder, and he left the stall.

The litter escort, a tall, muscular German, was carrying the limp form of Mistress Julia into the house. Dacius's brow furrowed. He would have sworn he'd pulled the horse away before he struck her.

A boy of about eleven stood with his back pressed against the wall, his eyes flicking toward the overseer like he was hoping not to be noticed.

Dacius slipped along the wall to stand beside him. "Is the mistress hurt?"

The boy shook his head. "No. She fainted. She can't stand blood."

"Well, I don't really like it myself." Dacius tousled the boy's hair and smiled at his worried face.

The boy tipped his head to look up at Dacius. "You ran up to that horse. Why weren't you afraid?"

Dacius shrugged. "He was only panicked by the fire. I knew he'd calm down as soon as he couldn't see it anymore."

The boy's eyes shifted from Dacius to the overseer, and Dacius's followed. The overseer strode over to the slave who'd been sharpening the hoes and swung the bronze knob on the handle of his three-cord whip into the side of his head, knocking him to the ground.

"Stupid son of a donkey! Didn't you see the sparks going into the straw? Move the grindstone over there." He pointed to the wall farthest from the straw and hay.

The slave stood, rubbing the side of his head. He bowed. "Yes, overseer."

Dacius stared at the whip as the overseer hung it back on his belt. The bronze was polished, the leather supple, as if frequently oiled. The overseer was proud of that whip, and that could only mean one thing.

He liked to use it.

The overseer nudged the trampled bearer with his foot to make sure he was dead. "Move this litter out of the gate." He turned to one of the other bearers. "You. Get this body out of here."

The man bowed. "Yes, overseer."

The overseer swung and pointed at Dacius. "You. Clean up that blood so the mistress won't see it again."

Dacius dipped his head. "Yes, overseer."

He drew a bucket of water from the cistern and poured it on the blood that had pooled on the paving stone where the man's head had been. The red diluted and faded in the expanding circle of water, but some had soaked into the stone.

He'd seen war, and he knew too much about cleaning up blood. It would take soap and hot water and scrubbing to remove most of it. And even then, a faint shadow would remain. The water had washed away enough that the mistress shouldn't notice it, but he would always know a man had died there.

Dacius sucked a breath between his teeth and shook his head as he released it. In Roman eyes, not a man. A slave had died there, his body now gone, tossed aside like a piece of broken furniture and just as easy to replace.

The steward had gone to the slave market yesterday to buy him for stable work. He'd be going tomorrow to get another slave for the mistress's litter.

After replacing the bucket by the cistern, Dacius returned to the dirty stall. As he scooped up one more shovelful of manure and straw, he sighed. *Slaves, obey your earthly masters with respect and fear and sincerity of heart, just as you would obey Christ.* That was what Apostle Paul had commanded. *Serve with your whole heart, as if you were serving the Lord, not men.*

He hadn't even been in this household a full day, and it was already clear it would be a place to sorely test him as he tried to serve Jesus, his Lord.

Julia awoke in her bed chamber as her lady's maid wiped her cheeks and forehead with a cloth dampened with rose water. Her eyelids drifted open as she threw up her arm to rest the back of her hand on her forehead.

Apicula dropped the cloth in the blown glass bowl. Its blue and green swirls caught the light to make a dancing pattern on the wall as she set it aside on the small table by the bed. She pushed an escaped strand of graying hair behind her ear. "Are you revived now, mistress? What happened?"

Julia started to sit up, then flopped back on the bed. "Not quite. The room is still spinning. That horrible horse my brother just bought—it killed one of my bearers and almost killed me. Someone pulled it away, and then I saw the crushed head. All the blood—you know what that does to me."

She tried to sit up again, and this time she succeeded. "Am I ever going to grow out of this? I feel so stupid when I faint over the smallest amount of blood. A Roman woman shouldn't be so squeamish." She touched Apicula's arm. "I'm glad you weren't walking beside the litter today. You might have been killed as well."

Apicula offered her hand to help Julia back to her feet. "I'm glad, too. Who did the stallion kill, mistress?"

"I don't know. Whoever was standing at the right rear. I didn't notice who was there earlier, and I couldn't bear to look at him all bloody."

"I'm glad someone reached that horse before it hurt you. Who was it? Perhaps he would like something extra to eat tonight. You could have some of the leftovers sent out to him."

Julia raised her shoulders and arched her back after she stood. Her dizziness was gone. "I like that idea. It must have been one of the stable slaves, but I don't know which one. I didn't look at him before I saw all the blood and then... Gallio can find the right one. I would think our steward knows all the slaves, even if I don't."

Julia pressed her palms to her cheeks and pulled them off sideways. "I'm planning to go to my sister's house tomorrow morning. It's been almost a week since I went there and played with her little girls."

Five steps took her to the dressing table. Her hair was still tidy, and the reflection in the polished silver mirror showed her color had returned to normal. "I promised Flavia I would do her hair up pretty like mine the next time I came, and I don't want to disappoint her. I need a box to take some of my hair ornaments. I'd better take enough to do Sabina's as well, since she's three now and likes to mimic her older sister."

"Shall I get the box now, mistress? Do you feel well enough for me to leave you?"

"Yes. That's over. Let's pack now so I have everything ready. They're such precious children, and I want to go early."

Apicula smiled her agreement. "You'll make a wonderful mother yourself, mistress. When your betrothed returns from Britannia, perhaps the gods will smile on you and give you a child during your wedding week."

"Wouldn't that be wonderful? I don't remember much about Metilius Nepos, except he's handsome. I was only twelve when we celebrated the betrothal at the Nepos townhouse, and we didn't talk alone."

Her stomach fluttered. In a few months, she'd marry the man her father had chosen. But that was the Roman way, and Father loved her too much to pick someone unsuitable.

"Metilia says he's such a dear, kind brother. If she thinks he'll be a wonderful husband and father, I'm sure he will. In only a few more months, I'll find out."

As Apicula left the room to find a box, Julia began selecting the ornaments she was sure the little girls would love.

The Baths of Trajan

Aulus walked up the marble steps of the cold-water pool at the Baths of Trajan. The bath slave handed him a towel, and he wiped his face. He moved away from the pool edge before toweling his hair. His eyes were closed when something hard rammed into his stomach.

"What the—" He stepped back as he tossed the towel aside. A man muscled like an ox stood before him with a hinged wax tablet clutched in a hand large enough to crush a melon.

"Aulus Julius Secundus?" His voice was a low growl.

A shiver ran up Aulus's spine. "Yes."

The man thrust the wooden frame of the wax tablet into his stomach again. "Take it."

Aulus snatched it from his hand and stepped back again.

With spread legs and crossed arms, the thug glared at him. "Your brother-in-law's cousin, Octavius Sabinus, let you continue to gamble on promise of prompt payment. Four months paying nothing is too long, and his father is calling in the debt." He dipped his head toward the tablet and held out a stylus. "Read and sign."

Aulus flipped the tablet open and scanned the text.

> Tiberius Julius Secundus owes Quintus Flavius Sabinus 10,000 denarii for debts incurred by his son, Aulus Julius Secundus. Unless other arrangements are made, Ti. Julius Secundus will pay in full within thirty

days of his return to Roma at the end of his governorship of Sicilia.

A wide finger tapped the wax below the text. "Sign." Two more taps. "Now."

Aulus rolled the stylus between his fingers as his stomach churned. He'd lost money that wasn't his to lose. Everything he treated as his own was legally Father's as *paterfamilias*. And every debt he owed was a claim against his father.

Father's red face on the pier in Portus swirled in his memory. Father's anger at him betting too much on the Red faction to win in the Circus Maximus was seared into Aulus's brain. He'd promised Father he wouldn't do that again while his father was away from Rome. And he hadn't...he'd bet on the Greens, and they almost always won.

He'd been money ahead until that dinner party at his step-sister's house.

He planned to pay the debt, but to sign a legal promise committing Father to pay as soon as he returned...

The thug's mouth turned down. "If you don't sign now, I will come back." His scowl turned into a cruel smile. "But you don't want me to."

His fist hit his open palm, then twisted slowly.

Aulus clenched his jaw and hoped that was enough to hide his fear. Better another tongue-lashing from Father than a beating from a gladiator.

He pressed the stylus into the wax, concentrating on keeping his letters from wiggling and betraying him.

With a snap, he closed the tablet and handed it back to the brute.

"Wise choice." The thug smirked as his gaze raked Aulus from head to foot and back. Then he spun on his heel and disappeared into the crowd.

"What was that about?"

Aulus jerked at the quiet voice of his best friend, Marcus Drusus.

He ran shaky fingers through his hair. "I'm in big trouble. I was at my step-sister's villa a few months ago, and I gambled with her husband's cousin. I lost 10,000 denarii, and I don't have the money to pay." He rubbed the back of his neck. "Octavius said that wasn't a problem, that he'd give me time to pay him. But now he's told his father, and his father is demanding the money...from Father."

"Your father's rich. He can pay that without even noticing it."

"That's not the problem. Sabinus and Father have been political enemies for years. Sabinus will try to use this to hurt him."

Marcus's brow furrowed. "Your father seems more than a match for anyone."

"But I wasn't supposed to be gambling. Not at that level, anyway. I hadn't planned to, but they had this great Falerian wine. I drank too much of it before we started." His shoulders drooped. "Father's going to kill me when he comes back to find I've exposed him to his enemy like this. Octavius's father is Quintus Sabinus."

"Quintus Sabinus?" Marcus sucked air through his teeth. "He wanted to marry my aunt Claudia right after Grandfather died. Mother fought with Father for saying yes before Aunt Claudia ran away and Sabinus married someone else."

His eyebrows lowered, then relaxed. "I can ask Father to give me the money. Ten thousand isn't much for him. He'd do anything for his best friend." Marcus nudged Aulus's arm. "He'll let me help mine."

Some tension drained from Aulus's shoulders, but not all. "But what if he won't?"

"Then we'll figure out another way to get it." A twisted smile curved Marcus's lips. "I know. We can fake your kidnapping to get enough ransom money to pay the debt." The smile turned into a chuckle. "But Gallio already took away your key to the strongbox after you bought that stallion that's too jumpy to ride. Maybe he won't want to pay that much for you."

Marcus slapped Aulus's shoulder. "We can fake Julia's kidnapping instead. Gallio would pay any amount to get her back."

Aulus chuckled. "He would." He punched Marcus's arm. "I can always count on you to come up with a good plan." The last of the tension vanished. Marcus's father would help, and his own father would never know.

Chapter 2

A Bad Idea

The Secundus villa, Day 2

Dacius had almost finished feeding and watering the horses the next morning when the steward entered the stable yard with the overseer.

The overseer nodded as the steward spoke. "The young master's stallion created a problem, Vilicus. She wants to go as soon as she finishes her breakfast, so I need one the same height. There isn't time to go to the market. Do you have one you can spare?"

Dacius emptied his bucket into Niger's water trough. The steward's request shouldn't affect him. He was the only slave working in the stable. There had been another, but yesterday Vilicus sent him into the garden to help dig a new reflecting pool. No sign of him this morning, so Dacius had to do the feeding, grooming, and cleaning alone. He couldn't be spared from the horses.

He patted the young stallion's neck before fetching another bucket of water from the cistern.

Vilicus didn't like a slave to look directly at him, so Dacius kept his eyes down. Since he tried to serve as if serving the Lord, he never avoided work. But it was obvious why the other slaves tried to be invisible when this overseer came near. He'd jerk a man off one task to do another. Later, he'd curse and sometimes strike him for not completing the first task. It was a chaotic place to serve.

As Dacius poured the last bucket into the stallion's trough, he heard the guttural voice. "You."

He turned and bowed his head. "Yes, overseer."

"Go stand by the litter."

He froze his eyebrows to hide his shock. Was Vilicus planning to leave the horses untended? But no matter how foolish the command, he had to obey.

Three bearers already stood by the litter, so he joined them.

Satisfaction lifted the corners of the steward's mouth. "He's the right size. I'll take that one for today. Have him wash to get rid of the stable smell and put him in a litter tunic. She'll be wanting to leave in perhaps half an hour."

Vilicus tipped his head. "Yes, steward." He watched the steward enter the house before spinning on Dacius. "You. Wash that stench off. Then dress for litter work."

Dacius lowered his eyes. "Yes, overseer."

The overseer strode through the small archway that connected the stable yard to the garden, and Dacius sighed. It was a good thing he'd risen early. Otherwise, the poor animals would have gone without. He'd barely finished placing the feed and water in the last stall, but Vilicus didn't know that when he ordered him to litter duty.

He scanned the stable yard as he headed to the cistern to draw some water. The horses needed grooming. The stalls needed cleaning. If he were a betting man, he'd bet the work would still be waiting for him when he returned, and Vilicus would yell at him because he hadn't finished.

Slaves, obey your earthly masters with respect and fear and sincerity of heart, just as you would obey Christ. He'd reminded himself at least ten times yesterday. Another sigh escaped. He'd probably hit twenty today.

The Drusus townhouse

When Marcus entered his father's library, Lucius Drusus Fidelis had a hinged wax tablet open before him.

"Good morning, Father." Marcus lowered himself into the second chair by the desk.

His father closed the tablet. "A letter from your brother."

Marcus raised his eyebrows to feign interest. "How is he?"

"You know your brother. It's impossible to tell. He never complains, no matter what his situation." Father's lips tightened. "I went to some trouble to get him a good tribune posting near Rome, but he's decided to apply for a posting in a frontier province. He's going to ask for Britannia, Dacia, or Judaea. He hasn't decided which."

Marcus pasted on a smile. "That sounds like Lucius. He'll want to go to the most dangerous place where no one else would volunteer to serve, so I'd bet on Judaea."

Father drummed on the tablet with a silver-tipped ivory stylus. "You're probably right. Your brother would put the needs of Rome above his own self-interest. Someone needs to serve there, but I'd rather it wasn't my son."

Marcus picked up a brass stylus and rolled it between his fingers. "There's glory to be found in battle. Lucius probably wants some excitement while he's tribune."

"Judaea isn't like Germania before it was pacified. The Germans fought you like warriors. They didn't stick a knife into you as you were going down the street and then keep walking as if they'd done nothing. Lucius might get himself killed by some zealot and left like the bodies the Urban Cohorts gather after they were murdered during the night. There's no glory in that." Father rolled his eyes. "But Lucius is too much like his grandfather, so he'll probably volunteer for the most dangerous place."

Father placed the stylus atop the closed tablet and leaned back in his chair. "But you didn't come to discuss your brother." His eyes warmed as they rested on Marcus. "So, why have you sought me out so early?"

Marcus stopped rolling the stylus. "I need 10,000 denarii."

Father rested his elbows on the desk and steepled his fingers. "What for?"

"To help a friend."

"Aulus Secundus? What sort of trouble has he gotten himself into this time?"

"He was gambling when he'd drunk too much, and he lost more than he realized."

His father laughed. "I'm not surprised. Aulus tends to act without thinking, and when the wine flows in, his sense leaks out. I'm glad my own sons are smart enough to keep their drinking and gambling separate."

Father's eyes narrowed. "Why didn't you stop him before he lost too much? He always follows your lead."

"I wasn't there, or I would have. You've taught me what a man should do for his best friend. His father told Aulus not to gamble to excess while he was governor in Sicilia, and except for that night, he hasn't."

Marcus leaned forward. "Will you give me the money so I can help him before his father finds out?"

"Of course. My best friend helped me more than once so your grandfather wouldn't know. Marcus Corvinus and I were closer than brothers at your age. We still are. That's why you carry his name."

"Thank you, Father. Sabinus sent a gladiator to the baths yesterday to make Aulus sign a document committing his father to pay the debt within a month of his return. If Aulus clears the debt now, his father will never know."

Father's head pulled back. "Why would Aulus's brother-in-law use a gladiator?"

"He didn't lose to Antonia's husband. It was her husband's cousin, Octavius."

"Quintus Sabinus's son?"

The edge on Father's voice raised Marcus's heart rate. "Yes."

"Did it say Secundus owed Quintus?"

"Yes. Why?"

His father rubbed his mouth. "That changes things. Secundus and Quintus Sabinus have been political enemies for as long as I can remember. Secundus is an honorable man, but Sabinus...Let's just say he's not a man to cross."

Father rested his elbow on the desk as he rubbed his forehead. "You were only fourteen and living with your mother when he wanted to marry your aunt Claudia. She ran off to Titus in Thracia to avoid that, and Sabinus was ready to kill me over the embarrassment that caused him.

"He spared our family because he found another girl to marry with better political connections. It's been four years, but I still feel the venom in his gaze."

He tightened his lips until they vanished. "If it were anyone else, I'd give you the money, but I'm not going to get between the crocodile and his prey."

"But—"

Father held up his hand. "This discussion is over."

Marcus froze his face to stop the frown. "As you wish, Father." While he could still control his irritation, he turned and left the room.

Aulus was waiting for him in the peristyle garden, sitting on the low wall by the pool.

When Marcus entered, he shot to his feet, smiling. "So, do we go to Octavius or his father to settle the debt?"

"Neither. Father said he'd give me the money; then he backed out when he heard you owed Quintus Sabinus." He spat. "I never took Father for a coward before."

The blood drained from Aulus's face. "What am I going to do?"

Marcus's placed his hand on Aulus's bicep and squeezed. "I'll think of something." A slow smile crept across his face. "I guess we need to plan a kidnapping."

"I thought that was a joke." Aulus bit his lip. "We can't actually do it."

Marcus rubbed his chin before the half-shrug. "Why not?"

Chapter 3

Invisible Man

The Secundus villa

Dacius stood by the right rear pole of the litter, cleaned up and dressed in the blood-red tunic with cream banding along the lower edge and around the armholes. He stood and waited. Waited while he looked at the horses that needed grooming and the stalls that needed cleaning. No one had been told to do either. Nothing was being done while he stood doing...nothing.

He glanced at the other three bearers. They all appeared content to simply stand there. He turned to the man at the left rear pole. "Does the mistress usually come soon after the call for the litter, or do you think we'll be waiting for a long time?"

The left rear man shrugged. "Does it really matter? Either we stand here and wait or we stand at her friend's house and wait. I just hope we're going to one of her friends who lives nearby. Or maybe her sister's where we get to sit in the shade while we wait."

It mattered to Dacius. The other three had nothing to do but carry the litter, but he had horses waiting for him to care for them. The sooner they took her, maybe the sooner they would return. Then he could get his real work done.

He heard girlish laughter and turned his eyes on the door to the house. He was curious to see what the young mistress looked like when she was conscious. He hadn't yet seen her face.

She and her maid stepped into the sunshine, and he was not disappointed. Mistress Julia was a pretty young woman of sixteen. Her nutbrown hair was braided and wrapped at the back of her head, held in place with gold picks decorated with butterflies, and she wore a crown of curls made of slave hair that matched her own.

As she walked toward the litter, she moved with such grace that she almost seemed to float across the paving stones. Her green tunic draped and wrapped her form in a way that left no doubt that she was no longer a mere girl. Her light brown eyes brightened with the sweet smile she directed at her maid, who walked beside her with a box decorated with ivory inlays and carvings of flowers.

She reached the litter, sat down, and swung her legs in—all without even glancing at him as he stood within three feet of her by the right rear pole.

It was no surprise that she didn't. In fact, it would have surprised him if she had.

He was a man you could pass in a crowd and never realize he was there. He was well muscled but not more than other farm slaves, and neither tall nor short. Not ugly, but not so handsome a woman's eyes would be drawn to him. No one would mistake him for a gladiator or a charioteer with their aura of arrogance that drew women like moths to a flame.

Reddish blonde hair in the ragged slave haircut, gray eyes that were almost always calm, eyebrows and mouth that were usually at rest, although the trace of a smile that lifted the corners of his mouth a little was unusual on a slave. He was not someone you would notice unless you looked deep into his eyes. Concern for others, born of his love for Jesus, shone there, so out of place amidst the cruelty of Rome. But who bothered to look deep into the eyes of a slave?

He'd never been a house slave, where the master or mistress might actually know his name and call him by it. He had no expectation of any friendship between owner and owned that might grow and lead to freedom. The most he ever expected was that the overseer might call him by name, but even that was unlikely in this household, where everyone was simply "you."

Her escort, a tall, blond German muscled up like a gladiator, approached. "Mistress, where shall we take you?"

"To my sister's."

The escort bowed. "Yes, mistress." He stepped back and signaled the bearers. "Ready the litter."

Dacius knelt like the man across the litter from him and placed his shoulder under the pad on the pole.

"Lift." At the escort's command, all four stood.

Dacius placed his left hand on the pole to steady it. It felt odd to have so much weight pressing down on his shoulder and against his neck, but it wasn't too much different from carrying a sack of grain. Like the left rear bearer, he hoped they wouldn't go too far today. He was muscular and strong, but he wasn't used to carrying unbalanced weight on one shoulder. He'd be sore tomorrow if they went too far.

The escort walked to the head of the litter. With a flick of his hand, he commanded the men to move out.

◆

Julia settled in against the backrest cushion as the litter passed through the gate. Apicula walked beside her, carrying the carved chest of hair ornaments.

She leaned forward and patted the seat cushion. "You don't need to be carrying that heavy thing, Apicula. Put it here."

Her maid obeyed, turning the box to give Julia the most room for her legs beside it.

"I think Flavia will be surprised by what I'm bringing. Now that she's six, she's ready to start her own collection of hair ornaments. I packed some that her mother gave me when I was little. I'm planning to let her keep them. I'm sure Antonia will love seeing what she gave me on her own little girl."

A smile curved Apicula's lips. "I think so, too, mistress. She always liked doing your hair when you were Flavia's age."

"I know her husband was disappointed that both their children have been girls, but I'm glad. Little girls are such sweet treasures, although I do hope the new baby will be a boy. I'm sure I'll love their son, too."

Apicula's smile faded. "A son to carry on the family name is important. Some men get discontented if they don't get one."

"For Antonia's sake, I hope her Titus isn't one of those." Julia shifted against the backrest. "I wonder what my first baby will be. Another six months, and Metilius Nepos will be home. I wonder how long after our marriage I'll have to wait for my own little one."

"If the gods look on you with favor, perhaps less than a year, mistress."

"I can hardly wait. Metilia says her brother will make a wonderful father. I hope I have a son first to make him happy. Then I want a girl for me."

◆

Dacius trudged along with the weight of the ornate litter and the mistress pressing down on his shoulder. It was good she was a slender woman. His quarter of the total weight was more than the sacks of grain he was used to carrying, and they'd already traveled more than a mile without stopping.

Hopefully, the steward would buy the replacement for the dead man that afternoon. This was not a task he'd want every day, but at least it had proven interesting. He'd never been this close to one of his owners for so long, and some things he'd learned about the young mistress were pleasant surprises.

As she chatted with her maid, she never said a single unkind thing about anyone. Not at all what he'd expected from a Roman noblewoman. She also spoke with her maid as if she were a friend, not a slave. He'd heard that happened with some house slaves, and now he could say he'd seen it.

Finally, the escort led them through a gate into a walled courtyard. He stopped, then spoke. "Down."

Dacius knelt in sync with the other bearers until the legs of the litter rested on the ground. He tipped his shoulder and stepped sideways as he rose. He reached across his chest and massaged his left shoulder and neck. His muscles appreciated the break after carrying her for almost an hour.

If she visited long, most of the day would be gone before he returned to the stable. He took a deep breath and blew it out. If the overseer hadn't seen fit to put someone else working there, he could be working past dusk to finish what must be done.

He watched the mistress's maid pick up the box. Then the legs of the mistress swung out of the litter. Legs with smooth, womanly curves drew his gaze until he flipped it back onto the box.

Her maid offered a hand to steady her as she rose from the seat. Without a glance toward him, the mistress strolled toward the entrance of the house, still chatting with her maid. His eyes drifted from the box to her. Her shoulders floated, like her feet weren't even moving beneath the flowing tunic that swept the ground.

No man could help enjoying the way the mistress moved, not even a slave. He forced himself to turn his eyes away and stop that train of thought. Thinking about the beauty of the mistress wasn't the right way to serve as if serving the Lord. He turned and followed the other bearers to the benches under a tree to await the command to carry her back home.

Dacius pushed the handcart of straw over to the stallion's stall. A day of sitting and waiting had ended exactly as he expected. No one had been told to clean the stalls, and the overseer ordered him to get it done before he could join the rest of the slaves for the evening meal.

As he pitched the first forkful of straw into the stall, the steward marched into the stable yard.

"Vilicus."

The overseer's domineering stance relaxed into subservience. "Yes, steward. What do you wish?"

"The slave you put on Mistress Julia's litter this morning. Did he perform well?"

"I think so. Taurus didn't say there was a problem."

"If her escort is satisfied, that's good enough. Master Aulus spent too much on that useless stallion that killed the last litter slave. I don't want to waste more money buying a replacement. I'll be selling the other three when Mistress Julia marries in six months, anyway."

Dacius forked more straw into the stallion's stall. The steward and overseer weren't even six feet from him, but he was invisible.

"If you can spare that one she used this morning, I'd like to keep using him on the litter when she needs him. He can do other work when she doesn't."

Dacius's jaw clenched. *God, once wasn't bad, but all the time?* He tossed another forkful into the stall.

"Good idea, steward. I can spare him without any problem. He doesn't do anything special that another slave can't do when he's carrying."

Dacius glanced down the row of stalls. Maybe another slave could, but Vilicus hadn't bothered to assign one today. Would he next time?

The overseer stood close enough that Dacius suppressed the sigh. Nothing he did with the horses was appreciated. But he took pride in serving as if serving his Lord, and the horses needed him.

If he must, he'd start rising an hour before dawn to make sure they at least got fed and watered before he ate breakfast himself. It shouldn't be more than six months. After she was gone, his work load should go back to normal.

Chapter 4

No Better Alternative

The Drusus townhouse, Day 3

Aulus leaned over and drew his fingers through the water of the pool in the peristyle of the Drusus house.

"I don't know, Marcus. I thought about asking my oldest brother for help, but he's too much like Father. He never got himself into any kind of trouble. If I told him, first he'd give me a lecture on being more responsible, and then he'd send a letter to Father about what I told him."

Marcus wet his fingers and flicked the water in Aulus's face. That usually made him smile, but not today.

"My brother Lucius wouldn't tell anyone if I asked him not to. He might even have the money. He's getting the tribune's pay of 1500 denarii a month, and he's probably not spending much since he doesn't like to gamble. He'd help me with most things, but never if I told him the truth about what we need it for." Marcus's nose twitched. "He'd keep telling me you should tell your father right away because it was the honorable thing to do. What about Manius?"

"He'd help if he was serving in Rome, but he's off in Britannia right now. Even if I could get a message to him, he'd never be able to get the money back to me in time to pay off Sabinus before Father gets home."

A sly smile tugged at the corners of Marcus's mouth. "I know! We can drug Gallio long enough to get the strongbox key. You can get the money and slip the key chain back around his neck before he wakes up."

Aulus gave Marcus a light shove. "We couldn't drug him without him knowing, and when he counts the money in the box, like he does at least once a week, he'd know it was missing."

Marcus shoved back. "I was joking, Aulus. But I have been thinking about that kidnapping idea. We could stage one and get Gallio to take the 10,000 denarii out of the strongbox himself. It really is the best way to get it, given the lack of alternatives."

Aulus furrowed his brow. "Well...maybe. What exactly did you have in mind?"

"I don't have fixed plans yet, but suppose we send Taurus on some errand, then have Julia go somewhere with someone we pick as the escort. We could have her kidnapped from there, held until we get the ransom money, and then have her sent back home."

Aulus rubbed his neck. "It sounds simple, but how would we find the ones to do it?"

Marcus's smile drifted toward a grin. "Just leave that to me."

Aulus stood. "I don't know. It sounds risky to me."

Marcus also rose. "Think on it a while, and you'll like it better. Let's go to the baths, then dinner at your house."

With Marcus's arm draped across Aulus's shoulder, the pair headed for the door.

The Secundus Villa

Dacius swung the pick into the ground and jerked it toward him to loosen the hard-packed dirt enough to shovel.

He fought the sigh. First, he got dragged away from the stable by litter duty, and now Vilicus had decided he should help dig the reflecting pool. He wasn't sure which was worse: heavy labor where at least he was doing something, or hours of boredom waiting for the mistress to decide to go home.

As he set the pick aside to grab the shovel for loading the handcart, the voices of Master Aulus and his best friend, Marcus Drusus, drifted over his shoulder.

"I wish we'd gone to the Baths of Titus today instead of Trajan's. That gladiator who works for Sabinus wouldn't have been there. The way he 'accidentally' knocked me into the wall before mumbling something about men paying debts with money or blood..." A shudder jerked Master Aulus's arms into his side as they passed Dacius.

Drusus rested his hand on the young master's shoulder as they walked toward the house. "He was only bluffing. He'd never dare to attack a governor's son with so many people watching. The baths are too public for anything like that."

"Maybe, but we walk to the baths, and there are too many places where he could do something between the baths and our homes."

Drusus stepped away and punched Master Aulus's arm. "I'll protect you. I always carry a dagger, and I know where to cut a neck to kill even the biggest man before he can make a sound."

Dacius scooped the first load of dirt into the handcart as the pair disappeared into the house. He'd seen enough of Marcus Drusus to believe he'd kill to protect Master Aulus. There was something about Drusus's eyes. If Dacius were a betting man, he'd even bet Drusus would enjoy it.

◆

Julia bit into the sweet pastry and let the fruity flavor of the strawberry filling flow across her tongue as she lounged on the dining couch. Dinner had been delicious, but something didn't feel right.

She glanced at Aulus, only to find him watching her again. But he wasn't simply watching her; he was contemplating her. And every time she caught him doing it, he flipped his gaze away from her and said something to Marcus.

Marcus was his usual smooth self. His words were always friendly, but the warmth in his voice often didn't match the coolness of his eyes. She never had been able to read his thoughts, and maybe that was a good thing.

And there was that flattening of Aulus's mouth as the corner twitched. When Father was home, that usually triggered a question about what Aulus had been doing. What followed wasn't always the truth. Father was extraordinarily good at catching the whiff of a lie coming from anyone, and he was especially good at sniffing out one of Aulus's.

"Why are you watching me, Aulus?"

"Watching you? I'm not watching you. Why would I? You're only my sister."

"No, you've been watching me all dinner. Like something's wrong."

"You're my sister, and if I want to watch you, that's my right." Aulus swung his legs off the couch and stood. "Only Father has the right to tell me to stop doing something. Not you."

He balled up his napkin and hurled it at the couch before striding from the dining room.

Julia's head bounced back, and she stared at the door through which Aulus had disappeared.

Marcus also rose. "I'm sorry, Julia. His stomach didn't feel well this afternoon, and I think he isn't better yet. Please excuse me. I'll go take care of him."

"Of course, Marcus. He's lucky to have you as his friend."

A not-quite-genuine friendly smile curved Marcus's lips as he tipped his head to her before heading out the door.

Julia shook her head. Something was wrong with Aulus, and it wasn't his stomach. Her lips tightened. It would be good when Father returned. He'd get Aulus straightened out as soon as he got home, and that couldn't be too soon for her.

The Secundus villa, Day 4

Dacius stood by the right rear pole of the litter, waiting for Mistress Julia. He glanced at the row of stalls. Patience was a virtue, but a lot of work waited for him. If only she'd hurry. The sooner they went, maybe the sooner they'd return.

The thuds of trotting hooves drew his eyes to the gate. Marcus Drusus passed through and reined in.

Dacius left the litter and hurried over to take the horse's halter before the rider dismounted. "Shall I stable your horse?"

Drusus swung his leg over the horse's neck and slid off. His eyes flicked toward Dacius, then away. He took a step before replying.

"No." With quick strides, he entered the house.

Dacius led the horse to the water trough. It drank deeply before lifting its head. Water dribbled from its muzzle as it turned alert eyes onto him. The Drusus horse was a stallion his father would have been proud to have in their herd. But it wasn't as fine as Niger, even if only Dacius could handle the young master's horse...yet. Any horse could be gentled, if you knew what you were doing, and he did.

He tied the reins to a ring attached to the wall and returned to stand by his assigned pole.

Primus put his hand on Dacius's shoulder and shoved. "Don't be so eager to serve. You're on litter duty, and Aulus's friend can tend to his own horse."

Dacius raised an eyebrow. "I was bought for the stable. Until they buy someone to replace me, the stable is still my task."

A snort accompanied Primus's sneer. "You're just trying to impress Vilicus. An overseer's favorite gets special treatment."

"Special treatment? I've already got that." Dacius's mouth curved up on one side. "He calls me 'you' and tells me to finish the stable work before I can eat when Mistress Julia stays out all day. When the mistress doesn't go anywhere, he gives me time off from the stable to grow stronger digging that pool."

Dacius swept one hand toward the stalls, the other toward the garden gateway. "Three tasks and no evening meal until I finish them...I'm clearly one of his favorites." A chuckle escaped. "If you'd like to join me in that elite group, I can tell him you'd like three tasks instead of one, too."

Primus's eyes narrowed, but he turned away without another word.

Dacius had scarcely turned to watch the door for the mistress when Master Aulus and his friend came out. He left the litter and approached the pair.

"Which horse today, master?"

The master didn't even glance at him. "The gray."

Dacius still dipped his head. "Yes, master."

He fetched the gray mare from her stall and tossed her saddle onto her back.

As he cinched it, the master's friend spoke. "Let's not go to the races today. You shouldn't risk losing more when you've already got that debt to Sabinus."

"But I might win enough to pay part. I've got to do something."

Across the mare's back, Dacius caught the tightening of Drusus's mouth. "I already told you what we should do. Little risk and certain reward."

Master Aulus shrugged. "Your plan sounds good, but if Father ever found out..."

"He won't. If only you and I know, the secret is safe."

Dacius handed Master Aulus his reins and fetched his friend's horse. The two mounted and rode out.

Primus's glare greeted him as he returned to the litter. He'd barely reached it when Mistress Julia and Apicula came through the door. Now if the mistress would only make her visit a short one today.

◆

Julia thumbed through the codex of poetry as she and Apicula entered the stable yard. "I'm glad Calpurnia likes the same poets I do. This new codex I got last week is the perfect gift."

She handed it to Apicula, who ran her hand over the cover. "It is. The binding is so pretty, too."

Julia sat on the edge of the litter. "I think it's disgraceful how the others are shunning her because her father must drop from equestrian order. It wasn't his fault that he lost his ships in those storms and then had his warehouse burn. If his wife hadn't decided to divorce him and take her dowry back, he'd still be equestrian. But even though he isn't, that's no excuse for hurting Calpurnia. A friend should stay true in the hard times as well as the good."

She swung her legs in. "Well, I won't abandon a friend just because her family lost its wealth. Aulus said her father had to sell their estate just north of Rome to pay back the dowry. He bought a townhouse on the Viminal Hill. Gallio found out where it is for me. It's not in the best neighborhood, but Taurus said it's in a safe enough part of Rome and close enough that we can go often." She held out her hand for the book. "She'll be so surprised when we visit."

Her smile drifted into a frown. "A true friend would never drop someone just because they lost too much money to stay equestrian. If the girls we both thought were friends shun her, how can I be sure they wouldn't do the same to me someday?"

Apicula reached behind her and fluffed the pillows. "You can't, mistress. But your father is a senator, and his wealth is safe in the estates. Those can't get lost like ships or burn up like a warehouse, so you'll never have to find out."

Julia leaned back on the pillows. "Calpurnia always said her father was the best of husbands...faithful, kind. She wants a man just like him. For a wife to leave the man she should be devoted to just because he's no longer as rich as she wants...well, that's just wrong."

◆

Dacius knelt at Taurus's guttural "Ready the litter" and stood at the escort's "Lift." After several times carrying her, the litter no longer felt too heavy on his shoulder. With a flick of a hand, her burly Germanic bodyguard started their trek.

As they passed through the gate, Dacius's usual slight smile broadened. The mistress's betrothed, whoever he was, would be a fortunate man when they married in six months. A loyal wife was a blessing beyond measure.

The corner of his mouth twitched up. And he'd be a fortunate man to get off litter duty and back to the stables.

Then he suppressed a sigh. His own father and mother had been one flesh, like God said they should be. Either would have willingly given up anything for the other. As a child, he'd always expected a marriage like theirs, but it was best not to think about what could never happen. A man must accept what was impossible to change and somehow find contentment with what must be.

Chapter 6

Too Much to Ask

Day 5

With his sandal, Dacius traced circles and squares in the dust at his feet as he sat on the bench at the Sabinus villa. An hour's fast walk brought Mistress Julia to visit her step-sister and nieces. For the mistress, the highlight of her week. For him, another boring day of hurry up and wait...and wait...and wait while his horses went untended.

But at least Vilicus wasn't there, swearing at the men he thought moved too slowly, cuffing their heads to speed them up.

It was peaceful under the shade tree. Serving as if it was for the Lord wasn't hard when that meant carrying the mistress to play with the children she loved.

The musical laughter of Mistress Julia blended with the giggling of her step-sister's daughters as the little girls frolicked in the mosaic-lined pool surrounding the dolphin-shaped fountain. Squeals of delight came from the little girls, and he raised his eyes to watch them. The mistress was sitting on the low wall beside the pool, scooping up handfuls of water to splash them.

The smaller girl took the mistress's hand and tugged. "I want to ride the dolphin. Help me?"

"Of course. Let me fix my tunic, and then we'll make him your mount for a race with Neptune."

She stood and shortened the length of her tunic by tucking it into the silver chain that wrapped around her waist and chest several times, making the most of her womanly form. With her legs free and bare, she stepped into the pool.

"It's slippery, Sabina. So be carefu—"

The mistress's arms flew out as she fell backward, and the splash as she hit the water soaked both little girls.

A chorus of giggles that included her melodious laughter told him she wasn't hurt. But when she stood, her green linen tunic clung to her, magnifying every curve and revealing more than a man's eyes should see.

He turned his head away.

Flavia clapped her hands. "Look who wasn't careful."

"That's a lesson for all of us. Come, Sabina. Let's put you on the dolphin."

Primus's elbow rammed into Dacius's right side. "Take a look, Dacius. That's a sight you don't see every day. I'd like to spend some private time with that." Primus glanced at the other bearers sitting to his right. "Verres and Capellus might want a turn, too."

Capellus grinned, but Verres frowned. "Don't let Taurus hear you talking like that, or you'll be on the auction block."

Dacius kept his face turned. He held back any words, but his jaw clenched.

Primus rammed his shoulder into Dacius, almost knocking him off the end of the bench. "What do you think? Wouldn't time with her feel good?" Another shove, but this time Dacius had his foot braced and didn't move.

An elbow into Verres's side drew a soft grunt. Primus grinned. "He probably wouldn't know what to do with her."

Dacius's nostrils flared. "Stop it, Primus. It's not right to talk about the mistress that way."

Primus's mouth curved down. "I see how you watch her. You're no different than the rest of us."

"No man could fail to see she's pretty, but thinking about lying with her is wrong."

Primus's frown flipped into a leer. "You were a farm slave. I hear the masters put farm slaves together to make slave babies. If I had that chance, I wouldn't be thinking about the mistress. Did you get some of that?" The leer turned into a sneer. "Or didn't they think you were good enough to have one of the women?"

Dacius kept his voice calm. "It wasn't that way on the Crassus estate. We weren't treated like livestock. Women aren't just for making babies and giving a man pleasure. If I ever have a wife, I want it to be because we truly care for each other."

Primus's nose scrunched. "That doesn't happen."

"That's how it was for my mother and father." Dacius shrugged.

Primus crossed his arms as his eyes narrowed. "But they were free. You'll be a slave until you die. Better to take what you can get whenever you can get it. You're a fool if you expect anything more."

"It's true that my body isn't mine, but the *familia Secundi* doesn't own my mind. Like any man, I can still choose to do the right thing."

Primus's head bounced back. "A man? You won't be a man as long as someone owns you." His voice softened. "None of us will. We're only animals in any master's eyes. We'll work like one, and we'll die like one." He rose and walked away.

Dacius turned his eyes on the other bearers beside him. Verres shrugged and looked away. Capellus hung his head and stared at the ground.

"He's wrong, you know." But the defeat in their eyes showed they didn't believe him.

Dacius set the pick aside, filled the shovel with the dirt he'd loosened, and tossed it into the handcart. He'd hoped for time in the stable when the mistress came home early from her sister's, but no. Vilicus was in the stable yard when they carried the litter through the gate, and it was instantly "You. Go dig."

The mistress had been under the arbor, reading some poetry to her maid, but that made her thirsty. As Apicula walked through the doorway to fetch her a drink, Master Aulus came out.

The young master stopped by his sister. He took a deep breath. "I just heard some news you won't like."

Mistress Julia's spine straightened. "Is it Father?"

"No. Nothing that serious. Well, not for me, anyway. It's Sextus Nepos. He's dead."

Her breath caught. "How?"

"A fever."

Mistress Julia's shoulders drooped. "Oh, Aulus! That's terrible. Metilia always said what a good, kind brother he was. She thought he'd make the finest husband. I was only a child the last time I saw him, but Father said Nepos was a fine man, too."

She closed the codex resting in her lap. "It might be too hard for her if I visit today. She loved Sextus dearly, and seeing me...well, it was going to be so wonderful being sisters, and now..." She bit her lip. "I don't want to make it even more painful for her. Maybe a letter now, and I'll go see her in a couple of days. I need to write my condolence to his parents, too."

She rose and squared her shoulders. "Well, Father will be back in a month and a half. He thought it would be an excellent marriage, but I suppose he'll arrange something equally appropriate when he returns."

Dacius's eyes followed the mistress as she walked into the house with her head bowed, the slight smile that was almost always there now absent. Her fingertips wiped the corner of her eye as she disappeared from view.

Sextus Nepos would have been a lucky man to have her as his wife. Primus was right that she was an attractive woman that any man might dream about. He'd made a mistress box in his mind and kept her in it so her pretty face and womanly figure wouldn't tempt his thoughts where Primus's had gone. But she was much more than a beauty.

The mistress had a kind heart. A cruel husband would crush that.

God, please let her father find her another kind man.

He traded shovel for pick. As he drove the point into the ground once more, he sighed. Another kind noble Roman. Maybe that was too much to ask.

Chapter 7

TIME TO WARN HER

Day 6

Dacius swept the brush down Niger's neck, and the stallion's whole body relaxed.

"Feels good, boy, doesn't it."

The black horse reached out to snag some grass from the manger, then shook his mane. His graceful neck turned sideways, and he fixed calm eyes on Dacius.

"You're a handsome one; that's what you are. I'd love to take you into the country for a gallop, but..." He sighed. He was still the only one who could mount Niger, but Vilicus would never trust him to take the horse for a run and return.

But at least the overseer hadn't been in the stable yard when they returned from the baths with Mistress Julia, so he'd been able to catch up on some of the stable chores instead of dig.

Two sets of hoofbeats entered the gate, and Dacius made one final sweep down Niger's side. Time with his favorite was over.

"Where's your stable slave?" Suspicion tinged Drusus's voice.

"Who knows." Master Aulus's voice was relaxed. "Vilicus puts him where he wants each day. Most of the time, no one's here."

The master was in for a surprise today. Dacius took a step toward the stall door. Before he could take a second, Drusus spoke.

"Like I keep telling you, you can get the money to pay Sabinus if you have the courage to do it. No one will suspect you when she's kidnapped for ransom."

Dacius's foot froze in midair. Then he crept deeper into the stall and hid behind Niger. If they discovered he'd heard, he was a dead man.

"Maybe not, but what if the kidnappers are careless, and she over-hears my name?"

"She won't." Drusus's arrogant chuckle raised the hairs on Dacius's neck. "I can make the arrangements through someone who won't be careless or maybe do it myself. If you're so worried about her revealing our role in it, we could have them sell her. A pretty virgin like her—she'd bring several thousand denarii."

A hand slapped a shoulder. Then the young master spoke. "Leave it to you to plan something to really get us in trouble if we're caught." His tone was light, as if he thought it funny!

"But we won't be caught." A pause, then Drusus spoke. "Are you certain no one's here?" The nervous edge on his voice raised Dacius's heart rate. Would they search the stalls?

"He'd have come as soon as we rode in if he was. Just put your horse in one of the empty stalls. Someone will take care of him some-time."

The hinges on the stall next to Niger's creaked, and Dacius forced his breathing to slow. If his own fear made Niger restless, they'd surely look in.

A slap on a horse's rump, then Drusus's voice just outside. "Surely you can see how it's the perfect solution to your problem. As soon as Gallio pays the ransom, we can go to Octavius and find out how to ap-proach his father to get back that promise of payment you signed. He got you into this mess when he told his father about the debt. I think he'll be willing to help you get out of it."

Master Aulus's profile appeared, and he rested his arm on the stall's half-door. "I'm still not sure we should do it. What if something goes wrong?"

Drusus's head was framed in the opening. "What could go wrong?" The indifference in his voice chilled Dacius. "Men face their problems, Aulus. They consider the options, and then they act. It's time to decide."

"Maybe you're right. Maybe I'm worrying over nothing. It should work like you say."

A slap to a back, then Drusus's voice. "We should hurry, or we'll miss the first race."

Their voices faded away as they headed toward the house.

Dacius's breath came faster as the horror of what he'd heard wrapped around his heart. Mistress Julia's own brother was planning to kidnap her, maybe to sell her into the hellish life that awaited pretty young slaves—like his sister Ariana. Roanna, too, if she'd lived long enough to grow into a woman.

He'd been looking forward to Mistress Julia's marriage. When she joined her husband, he'd be freed from carrying the litter. He'd rather be with the horses, but he would miss watching her play with the children and laugh with her friends. If her brother took Drusus's advice, she would never have her own children or see her friends again.

He massaged his neck. Was there anyone he could tell who'd believe him? It would be his word as a slave against a noble son of Rome.

But if he warned her himself, at least she could be on her guard. She'd know whom she could trust to protect her. She'd never spoken a word to him, but that didn't matter now. He had to warn her, even if that meant speaking to her first.

With jaw clenched, he squared his shoulders. He'd take the first chance to tell her when only she would hear. Only God knew if Master Aulus had accomplices in the household. People who would choose to help him, not her, when the choice came.

Marcus popped the last pastry into his mouth, and the juice of the fruit hidden within oozed across his tongue. A satisfying finale to an evening of watching their target.

"Julia, is something wrong? You've been so quiet tonight. Can I help?"

"Something's wrong, but nothing can be done to fix it. Metilia's brother died in Britannia, and I'm worried about her."

"Why?"

"She hasn't been to the baths for several days. Actually, no one has seen her since the news came. She hasn't even answered the letter I sent the day Aulus told me."

Julia nibbled her lip. "I stopped by the house to see her on the way home from the baths this morning, but only her father was there. She and her mother have gone to their villa to get away from all the condolence visitors. He promised to let me know when she returns. He thought it would be at least two weeks and more likely three."

Marcus glanced at Aulus, whose face was placid as he picked up another raisin, tipped his head back, and dropped into his mouth. Either his friend was an excellent actor, or he failed to see what her words meant.

"It must be hard to wait for a chance to cheer her up. I know you'll drop everything and go to her the moment she's back."

Julia's smile was sad but warm. "Yes. I love her like a sister. Just like you and Aulus would do anything for each other; that's how it is with Metilia and me."

Marcus wiped his mouth before folding the napkin and placing it on the couch beside him. "Maybe it won't be as long as her father thought. Maybe she didn't even see your letter before she left. Surely, she'll let you know as soon as she gets home."

"That can't be too soon for me." She swung her legs off the couch. "I think I'll retire now so you two can enjoy each other's company. I'm rather tired."

As she left the room, Marcus clapped his hands once. All the slaves serving the diners snapped to attention and turned their eyes on him. "Leave us, and don't come back to disturb us."

With small bows, they filed out.

He listened to be certain their footsteps faded away. He even rose and checked at the door before turning to Aulus. "Fortuna just smiled on us. I know what we should do, and I can start arranging it this week, if you'll agree to it."

"I guess you're right." Aulus's shoulders sagged. "It's probably the best way."

"No." Marcus walked back to his couch and sat on the edge. "It's the only way."

Aulus ran his hand through his hair. "Maybe, but only the ransom, not the sale. I can't do that to her. I don't need extra. I only need enough."

"Whatever you want, that's what I'll arrange. Enough for the debt and to pay whomever we hire."

Marcus poured more wine into his silver goblet. "The greatest success comes to those who take risks." He raised it toward Aulus. "To risk and reward."

Aulus lifted his own goblet. "And no surprises."

They both tossed back their heads and drank deeply of the ruby liquid.

Marcus slapped his knees and stood. "I feel like a few games of tabula."

Aulus rose as well. As they entered the atrium and headed toward the library, he punched Marcus's arm. "But no high-stakes betting. I've learned my lesson."

Chapter 8

SERVING TOO WELL

Day 6

Dacius swept the sweat from his brow with a grimy arm. He'd undoubtedly left a veneer of mud behind, but it was either wipe it or have the sweat get in his eyes again.

It was a hot, muggy day, and he'd stripped his tunic off to work in just his loincloth. Digging the new reflecting pool wasn't so bad when the moist air formed broken clouds that gave short respites from the summer sun. But today's mix of unbroken sunshine and humidity made the drizzle of the day before that had coated the hard-packed earth with a slippery skin seem almost pleasant.

He swung his pick several times to break the hard surface before trading it for the shovel. If only it was straw and manure instead of clods of clay that he heaved into the handcart. But his task for the day wasn't his to choose, and Vilicus had ordered him into the garden right after breakfast.

To his right, a string of curses was followed by Vilicus slapping the back of Rusticus's head for not working fast enough.

Dacius tossed another shovelful into the handcart. As boring as it was to spend the day waiting by the litter, today he would welcome a summons to the stable yard to clean up for litter duty.

He would escape another grueling day with pick and shovel, but that wasn't why he wanted to hear Taurus's guttural voice summoning him. He might get a chance to warn Mistress Julia about her brother's plans.

She'd never said a word to him that would allow him speak to her. She'd never done more than glance at him before sitting on the litter and swinging her legs in. But God might make today different so he could protect her from his sisters' fate.

Her kindness to her nieces and friends revealed a good heart, no matter how she treated him. Twelve years as a slave had taught him to expect nothing from Roman masters, and she was only living up to his expectations.

The handcart was full enough to satisfy even Vilicus, and he trundled it over to the growing pile that would soon be terraced to make a new rose bed. With knees bent, he positioned the handles on his shoulders and stood, tipping the cart so the dirt tumbled out.

Rusticus struggled to do the same beside him.

"Let me." Dacius crouched between the handles.

As he dumped the handcart, Rusticus glanced at the overseer. Vilicus stood with fists on his hips and his back toward them. The corners of Rusticus's mouth twitched up; then the old man's shoulders sagged.

His voice cracked, even as he whispered. "Thank you, but don't let Vilicus see you help me. That would be bad for both of us."

Dacius shrugged and patted Rusticus's arm. Then he gripped the handles of his own cart and pushed it back to where his pick and shovel waited. He was about to step into the shallow pit when a movement under the grape arbor caught his eye.

Mistress Julia was reading a codex...alone and only thirty feet away. There could be no better opportunity to warn her with no one else listening.

He glanced at Vilicus, who was now holding his whip, playing with the three leather strips as the men he was watching double-timed their digging.

Nine quick steps and he stood before her. "Mistress, I—"

Fear flashed across her face. She sprang from the bench and slipped behind the arbor post. "Stay away from me!" Panic made her voice shrill and loud.

"I mean no harm, mistress, but your brother's dangerous. He plans to—"

The brass knob of Vilicus's whip slammed into the side of his head. The first explosion of pain was followed by a second, dropping him to his hands and knees.

"Mistress..." He tipped his face toward her. Surely she knew one of her litter bearers would never hurt her. But no sign of recognition lit her eyes.

The first lash struck his back, and he felt the flesh tear. The mistress's hand flew to her mouth as she gasped.

Vilicus's foot to his ribs drove the breath from him. He gulped some air before he could lift his face again and speak. "Please, mistress…"

Her cheeks turned ashen as she stared at his back. Then she spun and ran toward the door.

Three new lines of pain shot across his back as the lash struck the second time. He braced for another strike as the first trickle of blood ran down his side.

"Vilicus. Stop that." Gallio's voice froze Vilicus's arm midswing.

The overseer turned toward the steward. He drew his fingers down the first leather strip and flicked the blood off before cleaning the second and third.

"Isn't that one of the litter bearers?" Gallio stood with arms crossed, glaring at Vilicus.

"Yes, steward."

"I don't want him damaged too badly to carry her. Why are you whipping him?"

"He spoke to Mistress Julia and frightened her."

Gallio's gaze met Dacius's and held for a moment before flipping back to Vilicus. "I doubt he was going to hurt her. Taurus says this one is the best of the lot."

His eyes focused on Dacius again. "Go to Glyptus and have him put something on that. You'll probably be needed for the litter tomorrow, so don't do anything to make it worse the rest of today."

Dacius rose. "Yes, steward."

He took careful steps as he walked toward the kitchen, but the cuts from the lash still triggered ripples of pain with each movement of his back.

Gallio's voice was harsh behind him. "Think before you make one of the slaves that serve Mistress Julia bleed. At least he's at the back so she won't see much of him. If the cuts ooze some when he's carrying, it shouldn't show with the red tunic. Not enough to make her faint, anyway."

Vilicus mumbled his apology.

If his back and head didn't hurt so much, Dacius might have laughed. Saved by the steward, not because he disapproved of lashing slaves who'd done nothing wrong, but because the mistress might faint if she saw his blood.

Well, he'd tried to warn her. He wouldn't do that again. Next time could be a beating or a full whipping instead of only two lashes. He could only pray for her now. Maybe her brother wouldn't actually do what his friend was planning.

As Dacius entered the kitchen, Glyptus swept a pile of chopped vegetables into the stewpot and placed it atop the stove.

"Glyptus." The cook glanced over his shoulder. "I need some help."

Glyptus's head bounced back when he turned. "What happened to you?"

"Vilicus, but Steward Gallio stopped him before he got more than two strokes in." He started to shrug, but that triggered a grimace. Then his face relaxed into an ironic smile. "Gallio didn't want me damaged too much to carry the litter."

"At least it's not as bad as the last one I had to treat. When Vilicus gets drunk, he loses count." He dragged his fingers across Dacius's chest and wrinkled his nose at the sweat and dirt on his hand. "We need to clean you up first."

Glyptus snapped his fingers, and a kitchen boy trotted over. "Take a clean bucket and get fresh water from the fountain in the street." As the boy scurried away, Glyptus rested his hand on Dacius's shoulder and leaned in close to look at the cuts. "Could be worse. We'll wash the mud off you, pour some wine on the cuts, and smear them with honey. They usually don't infect when I do that. Sit over there." He pointed to the slaves' regular table. "Lepus runs like a rabbit. He'll be back quick."

Dacius took a seat. With elbows on the table, he rested his forehead against his hands and closed his eyes.

God, I know You let Gallio buy me, so I'm probably here for some reason. I'm trying to serve as if I'm serving You, but Vilicus makes that so hard. He filled his lungs and blew the air out between pursed lips.

He startled when Glyptus's hand settled on his shoulder again. "Lepus is back. It will only hurt more if we wait. Lean over."

The water pouring across the cuts didn't hurt much. The soap hurt more, and the wine burned as Glyptus dribbled it repeatedly along each cut.

With eyes scrunched, Dacius sucked air between clenched teeth.

Glyptus tousled his hair. "Cleaning is done. Now the honey to protect and heal. Rest your chest on the table."

When Glyptus finished smearing honey into each cut, Dacius straightened in the chair. He opened his eyes to find Primus leaning against the doorframe, sneering at him.

"So, what did you do to get a lashing?"

Dacius swallowed the retort before it escaped his lips and said nothing.

Primus took a step into the room. "Did the lash hurt your ears as well?"

Glyptus glared at him. "Vilicus doesn't need a good reason to whip anyone, so you should watch your tongue, Primus." He fixed his gaze past Primus. "Isn't that right, overseer?"

Primus's eyes saucered, and he spun. A frown pulled his mouth down when he turned back. "Very funny, Glyptus."

One of the house slaves stuck her head in. "How's your back, Dacius?"

"It's been better, but it could be worse." Dacius managed a smile.

Primus faked a concerned frown. "Why did Vilicus do this?"

She shrugged. "Mistress Julia was frightened when Dacius got so close and told her Master Aulus was dangerous, but who knows why Vilicus decides to hurt anyone."

She withdrew, and Primus's sneer turned into a smirk. "Trying to protect her from her brother? That's maybe the stupidest thing you've done here."

Dacius's jaw clenched, but he forced his voice to remain calm. "A man should try to protect any innocent person if he possibly can."

Primus spat. "No rich Roman is innocent. I don't care about any of the ones who've owned me. In their eyes, I'm not a man...and neither are you. We're only work animals to them, and they're nothing to me."

He sauntered from the kitchen, but his chuckle drifted back into the room.

Glyptus's mouth curved down. "He's right, you know."

"About them seeing us as property, yes. About us being animals and not men, that's a choice we make, not them." His mouth relaxed into a slight smile. "And I choose to be a man."

Glyptus squeezed the top of his shoulder. "Go find the laundress. I need cloth strips to wrap your chest. Tell her I said to give you a clean tunic, too."

He turned back to the stove and stirred the stew. Dacius headed out the door, then turned back to watch his friend.

Men like Glyptus would always be men, no matter what their Roman masters thought.

That evening, Dacius entered the empty stall where he usually slept and leaned his shoulder against the wall. Morning would come early, and he'd have to rise before dawn to feed the horses before his own breakfast. And then...Gallio expected him to carry if the mistress wanted to go somewhere, but at least the steward had told Vilicus not to put him digging until his back healed.

God, please let her decide to stay home tomorrow. But if she doesn't, let it be a short trip.

As he straightened, he felt every stripe. *Please heal me fast. Help me bear this until You do.*

A deep breath was followed by a deeper sigh. He'd made it through twelve years as a slave without a single lash mark. How ironic that he didn't get these from failing to serve. He'd tried to serve too well.

He winced as he lowered his chest to the ground and raised his arms so he could rest his head on his hands. He'd sleep on his stomach until his back stopped hurting. With his neck twisted sideways to get his nose clear of the straw, he tried to relax.

For a moment, deep regret surged through him. Why had God let the Crassus estate sell most of its racehorses...and him? Life had actually been good there.

Then he shoved it out of his mind. No point in grieving over what was gone. Somehow, he would manage to serve in this chaotic household under an incompetent overseer with a mean streak. Maybe it would get better when the master came home. Surely a man who could run a province could make his own estate run properly.

He closed his eyes and slowed his breathing. If sleep would only come, it would quiet the pain.

Maybe, if God chose to show him special mercy, he'd be sold again to only work with horses, like he loved. Until then...

God, some days it's so hard here. Please give me strength to serve this household as if I were serving You.

Chapter 9

The Next Step

The Drusus townhouse, afternoon of Day 7

Marcus eyed his father as he popped the last dried date into his mouth. This lunch was the first step in his plan.

It can be hard to find a partner in crime when you don't know any criminals. But even a senator or equestrian occasionally needed someone to take care of a problem in a less-than-legal way. The most ruthless person Marcus knew was his father. Father had hired men to drag Aunt Claudia back from Thracia when Quintus Sabinus was determined to marry her four years earlier. Perhaps that wasn't kidnapping since Father was her guardian, but the same kind of men were exactly what he needed.

Marcus swung his legs off the dining couch. "Aulus is busy this afternoon, so would you like to play a few games of Mercenaries?"

The smile on Father's face was exactly what he expected from a man who loved strategy games.

"My afternoon is free as well." Father stood and swept his hand toward the door. "Go set up the board, and I'll be right there."

In the library, Marcus arranged the beige and blue rondels of sliced bone and the king pyramids on the wooden board. His finger traced several of the swords in the intricate battle scenes carved along two edges of the grid.

When Father entered and sat at the desk, Marcus lowered himself into the second chair.

"You go first, son." One corner of Father's mouth turned up. "To give you a better chance at beating me."

Marcus turned on a grin. "With what you've taught me, almost no one but you beats me now. No one wants to bet with me anymore."

"I had that problem myself at your age."

Marcus moved his first piece, and they settled into a companionable battle. As the game neared completion, he deliberately chose a move that left him open to attack. The corner of Father's mouth twitched as Marcus opened the way to victory.

"Father." His father's gaze shifted from the board to his face. "Have you ever had to hire muscle for something?"

"Malleolus usually hires guards for transporting money through Brutus's *ludus*."

Marcus picked up a captured rondel. "That's not quite what I meant. When Sabinus sent the gladiator to give Aulus that demand for payment, where would he have found such a man? Someone willing to threaten the son of a senator in the middle of hundreds of people at a public place like the baths?"

Father chuckled. "Sabinus probably owns his own gladiators who enjoy that kind of work. Making a barely veiled threat isn't a problem for a man like him, no matter how public. Most of the magistrates either owe him a favor or are afraid to cause him any trouble."

Marcus leaned back in his chair. "What if it wasn't just a threat? What if he wanted someone to really hurt a man?"

Father rubbed his chin. "He might not use his own slaves. They'd break under torture if brought to trial. I think he'd hire free men for that, citizens if he could find them. He can buy anything in Rome, even the death of someone who's in his way."

"Where would he find such people?"

Father's eyes narrowed. "Why are you asking all this? You don't need muscle to remove someone...do you?"

Marcus raised his hands and summoned what he hoped was a natural-sounding laugh. "Not me. I'm not old enough to have made that kind of enemy yet. I was just curious."

He moved his piece, putting Father's king in danger. His father immediately countered the move, and Marcus lost some men.

He forced a sigh. "You were supposed to be distracted enough by my questions that you didn't see that."

Father grinned. "There's no point in trying that with me. I'm a master at recognizing danger and moving before it can reach me."

Marcus massaged his temple. "Well, I can see there's no way I'm going to beat you this game, so why don't I concede? Then we can start a new one."

Father's eyebrows relaxed, and he leaned back in his desk chair. "Set it up."

The Secundus villa

A satisfied smile curved his lips as Dacius polished the last silver medallion on Master Aulus's bridle. God had answered his prayer for a day of rest. Mistress Julia's friend had come to her, so he'd spent the day with his horses. Some light brushing for each and extra time with Niger—it had been a good day for all of them.

But it was time for Glyptus to check his back, so he hung the bridle on its hook and headed to the kitchen.

Glyptus stirred the pot before turning. "Sit at the table, and let's see how it looks."

After removing Dacius's tunic, Glyptus unwrapped his bandages. "Rest your chest on the table. Time for more wine and honey."

The wine hurt less than the first time, but Dacius still held his breath as Glyptus dribbled it into every cut. After applying more honey, Glyptus rewrapped his chest. He dropped the tunic over Dacius's head, and Dacius slipped his hands through the armholes.

"Fortuna is smiling on you." Glyptus rubbed his jaw. "I've treated a lot of lashings, and you look much better than I expected."

Dacius grinned. "Not Fortuna. I've been asking my God to heal me quickly. It's His power, not Fortuna's smiles, that heal."

Glyptus snorted. "Maybe you should stop those prayers. It's less painful now, but Vilicus will put you back digging sooner."

"A small price to pay for healing quicker." Dacius's shrug triggered a grimace.

"Looks like your god doesn't like you shrugging."

"Perhaps." The corners of Dacius's mouth turned up. "But He won't mind me cutting up carrots for the stew while I can't do much else."

Glyptus handed him a knife and waved him toward the waist-high cutting table where Lepus was chopping purple carrots.

The speed of the boy's knife drew Dacius's whistle. "You'll have yours all done before I cut up my first carrot."

His praise lit Lepus's eyes. "But I could never stop a wild stallion like you did. I'd love to work with horses, but I'll probably never leave the kitchen."

"Cooking a good meal—that makes the day better for all of us. It's much more important than taming a horse so Master Aulus can ride it."

When Lepus grinned up at him, he tousled the boy's hair. Then he lifted a carrot from the stack and cut his first slice.

Day 9

God had given Dacius the day to heal that he'd prayed for plus one more, but the third morning found him dressed in the red tunic, standing by the right rear pole. Mistress Julia had decided to visit her nieces.

Chatting with Apicula, the mistress came out the door in a pale blue tunic...like the one she'd worn when he tried to speak to her. He shifted his weight to one leg, and the lash cuts complained. Glyptus had insisted on treating them with wine and honey right after breakfast. The wine hurt; the honey helped. The surprise on his friend's face over how quickly he was healing had triggered a chuckle, even if Glyptus rolled his eyes when Dacius said it was God's doing.

The mistress sat on the litter. "Antonia said last time that the baby should quicken any day. I hope it has. I liked feeling her girls kick."

Taurus strode through the garden gateway. "All is ready, mistress. Still your sister's villa?"

Mistress Julia glanced at him. "Yes." Then her focus returned to her maid.

She rested a hand on her own stomach, and her eyes turned wistful. "I hope Father finds me another good husband as soon as he comes home. I don't want to wait years to feel my own little one."

"Babies often come quickly to new brides, mistress." Apicula's smile drew a sad one from Mistress Julia. "You'll be a wonderful mother."

The mistress swung her legs in, and Taurus moved toward the gate. "Ready the litter."

Dacius bent to place his shoulder under the pad. The pain sharpened.

"Lift."

He stood and rested his left hand on the pole. The lifting slapped a sheet of pain across his back, but once he was up and bearing the weight, it wasn't so bad.

God, don't let her have us set the litter down until we get there.

Taurus led them through the gate.

Each step jarred a little, and he felt each jolt. But the pain wasn't as fierce as the day before. He could bear it for the hour or so to reach her destination.

Soon, they'd gone about a quarter of the way. Each step triggered a little pulse of pain, and walking so fast made it worse. He was already tired.

God, could she maybe see a friend and stop to talk?

Taurus stepped aside and let the litter pass him. He fell in beside Dacius. "Problem?"

Dacius tightened his lips and shook his head. "I can keep the pace."

One curt nod, and Taurus started toward the front.

"Taurus?" The mistress's quiet voice slowed her escort's stride. "Is there a problem?"

"One of your bearers was hurt three days ago, but it's not a problem."

"There's no hurry to get to Antonia's. We can go slower while he's recovering."

Taurus dipped his head. "Thank you, mistress." He dropped back beside Dacius. "Set a comfortable pace."

Dacius's grateful smile drew a quick tip of Taurus's head. He slowed the pace to about two-thirds, and Taurus walked ahead to lead once more.

As Mistress Julia and Apicula resumed their conversation, Dacius's mouth curved into a smile. He hadn't expected her concern, but it was just one more sign of her kind heart.

His smile faded. *God, please protect her from her brother until her father comes home.*

When they passed through the stable-yard gate, two small girls sprinted toward them.

Before Taurus even said "Down," Flavia had taken the mistress's hand. "I thought you were never going to get here."

"We walked slower today." Mistress Julia swung her legs out. She glanced back at Dacius, and a smile flickered across her lips. His head bounced back. Was she going to speak to him? Was this a second safer chance to warn her?

But she turned away without a word, and Sabina wrapped her arms around the mistress's waist. Mistress Julia scooped the little girl into her arms and balanced her on one hip. Flavia slipped her hand into her aunt's and swung their arms as they headed toward the house.

She was totally focused on her nieces, the men who'd carried her forgotten. But he didn't expect more. It was enough that she'd wanted to spare him some pain.

Primus's voice came from behind him. "Well done, Dacius. You've gone from trying to be Vilicus's favorite to getting special favors from the mistress."

Dacius ignored the insinuating tone and headed for the bench.

Primus bumped his shoulder, then slapped him hard on the back. As his back arched away from the pain, Primus dropped his voice so only Dacius would hear. "Maybe she'll play in the fountain with the little girls. I wouldn't mind watching her get wet again."

Another slap to the back, and Dacius sucked air through his teeth. Primus's hand settled on his shoulder, and Dacius swatted it off.

That drew Primus's chuckle. "Maybe she'll slip, and she'll let you help her up." He bounced his eyebrows. "Maybe—"

Taurus's giant hand gripped the back of Primus's neck and jerked him away.

"Stop now, Primus. If I see you doing anything else to slow Dacius's healing, I'll see to it that you get some of the same from Vilicus."

Primus's eyes widened "I beg pardon, Taurus. I wasn't thinking. I meant the slap only as a sign of friendship."

Taurus snorted. "No, you didn't, and don't do it again."

Primus hurried to sit on the end of the bench farthest from Dacius's usual spot. Verres took the seat next to Dacius but kept his eyes down and said nothing. With pinched lips, Taurus turned and walked back to resume his conversation with Antonia's escort.

Dacius relaxed toward a slouch, then straightened. Letting his back curve pulled too much on the cuts. He filled his lungs, then released the air slowly. Sitting at attention like a legionary minimized the pain, but at a price. No matter how long the mistress visited, it was going to be a long day.

Chapter 10

An Honest Man

Ludus Bruti, Day 14

Marcus Drusus handed the *gladius* to the armorer of the *Ludus Bruti* and snatched up a towel to wipe his face and chest. It had been a good session with his usual trainer, and the workout left his muscles pleasantly tired. The baths would open to the men in an hour, and he would enjoy the hot soak in the *caldarium*, a swim, and a massage.

M. Antonius Brutus, equestrian owner of the ludus, joined him. "I was watching you today, Marcus." Brutus toweled his face, hair, and neck. "You've improved a lot in the last couple of months." He wiped his chest. "You might be ready to move up to sparring with Fortis."

Marcus grinned. "And after Fortis, maybe Africanus?"

Brutus chuckled. "No, my young friend. You're nowhere near ready for my favorite sparring partner." He slapped Marcus's arm. "But you might get there before you take your first tribune posting. Your brother Lucius did."

Marcus cringed inwardly but didn't let it show. Comparisons to his older brother galled him.

Brutus tossed the towel into a basket. "How is Lucius liking his first posting?"

"Not enough. He wrote Father that he's planning to request a transfer to the frontier. Britannia, Dacia, maybe Judaea."

A broad smile curved Brutus's mouth. "It's good to hear when one of the young men I trained chooses service to Roma over an easy posting." Another slap to Marcus's arm. "I expect you'll do the same when it's time."

Marcus smiled as he nodded. Not likely, but better if Brutus didn't know that.

"Fortis." Upon hearing the head trainer's bellow, the gladiator backed away from the middle-aged senator with whom he was sparring.

A flick of Lanista Felix's fingers brought Fortis to him at a trot.

Felix crossed his arms. "This man is asking about joining the ludus. Get him a gladius. I want to see some friendly sparring before we talk more."

Brutus rested his hand on the top of Marcus's shoulder and squeezed. "Another ex-soldier wanting to contract with me as an *auctoratus*. Watch and learn. You'll see the military fighting style where the goal is a quick kill, not a good show."

Brutus placed one arm across his stomach and rested his elbow on it. As the ex-soldier exchanged strikes and thrusts with Fortis, he rubbed his chin.

After a few minutes, Brutus strolled toward the fighters. Marcus grabbed his purple-striped tunic from the bench and slipped it over his head. He positioned the dagger scabbard at his side, and fastened his belt. Watching the soldier had been instructive, but he was ready to leave.

When Brutus stood beside Felix, his lanista spoke. "That's enough."

The soldier placed the gladius in Fortis's outstretched hand.

Brutus crossed his arms. "I'm Antonius Brutus. This is my ludus."

The man stood at attention. "Gaius Faltonius Callidus."

"Where have you served?"

Pride lit Callidus's eyes. "I enlisted in the XIV Gemina at seventeen and served in her twenty-five years. I've just come to Rome from the legion fortress in Carnuntum."

Brutus's signature smiling frown appeared. "So, you served Roma in the Dacian war?"

"Yes. I even saw the head and hand of Decebalus when they were brought to Emperor Trajan."

"Many settle where they retire, yet you came back to Roma?"

"I expected to find my father and take over his *taberna*." Callidus's jaw muscle twitched. "He's dead, and the taberna is gone." Anger simmered in his eyes. "So, I need work. I'd rather train and fight than... many other things."

Brutus's mouth turned down. "You have good skill for a legionary, but to fight in the arena here in Roma..." He drew air through his teeth. "My standards for my ludus in Roma are very high. Higher than where you are now. Maybe higher than you can reach. Your first fight in Roma will likely prove fatal for you."

Callidus pulled a deep breath. As he released it, his shoulders sagged. "Battle is what I know."

Brutus's brow furrowed. "The arena in Roma would kill you, but in the smaller towns, you might still compete. There's a ludus that might suit you just east of the amphitheater in Luna. That's north and west of here up the Via Aurelia and Via Aemilia Scauri. The lanista is an honest man who won't arrange a match to get you killed for the dead gladiator price at the end of your contract."

"How far is that?"

"By sea, three days. By horse, six to seven. Walking, probably twice that."

Callidus tightened his lips, then nodded once. "That's not too far. Thank you for telling me."

Brutus slapped his arm. "It's my pleasure to help a man who has served Roma well. Ask for a four-year term on your contract and 1200 denarii for your signing fee. He should agree to that."

That drew a smile from Callidus. "Vale, Antonius Brutus. May Fortuna smile upon us both." He walked, head high, into the stairwell that would take him outside.

Marcus raised a hand in farewell to Brutus and followed Callidus up the stairs. It had been nine days since Aulus agreed that a fake kidnapping was the solution, and he'd made no progress on finding the right accomplice. But Fortuna had just smiled on him. Anyone desperate enough to sell himself into the arena should leap at the offer of a year's wages for a few days waiting for a girl to come and a few hours keeping her locked away.

When he reached the street, Callidus had disappeared into the crowd.

Marcus rubbed his neck. Left or right? Right would take him toward the arena, left toward a street of tabernae where a frustrated man might find a drink to drown his disappointment. He went left.

His hunch paid off when he caught sight of Callidus turning into a door half a block ahead of him. He picked up his pace and entered in time to see Callidus sink into a chair in the back corner.

Fifteen steps, and he stood before the man who might be the solution to his problem. "May I join you?"

Callidus's brows dipped. "Why?"

"I heard you talking with Brutus, and I have a proposition for you."

Callidus's hand swept toward the empty chair. "Sit."

Marcus moved the chair so his back was to the wall. What he was about to say wasn't something he wanted some stranger walking past to hear.

"Might you be looking for work other than as a gladiator?"

"I'm open to anything, as long as it's honest work." Callidus shrugged.

"Oh, it's honest. It's to help someone convince a woman who's taking too long to agree to marry him." Marcus raised his hand to summon one of the girls serving the tables. "Let me buy you lunch, and we can talk."

The corner of Callidus's mouth turned up. "I'm not married myself, but I wouldn't mind helping someone else marry."

When the servant came, Marcus ordered two servings of wine and pointed to Callidus. The ex-soldier ordered a bowl of pork stew and fresh bread.

"You told Brutus you fought in Dacia." Marcus leaned his arms on the table. "What was that like?"

Callidus eyed him. "You wear purple stripes. You'll be a tribune?"

Marcus nodded. "In two years."

Callidus snorted. "You'll never see war like I did. When the legion advances, shields side by side, blood on our gladii…nothing can stand against us. You feel most alive in the company of death." His eyes veiled. "It's not something a man can explain to a boy." He rubbed his mouth. "What do you want me to do, and what will you pay?"

"My friend wants to marry a certain girl right away, but she's in no hurry." Marcus lowered his voice. "But if she thinks he'd do anything for her, that would change. We think a fake kidnapping where he comes to rescue her would win her over. She'll be so grateful she'll want to marry him on the next possible auspicious day."

"What would you want me to do?"

Marcus scanned the nearby tables. No one was listening. "Nothing dangerous. Just hold her hostage at an empty house in Subura for a few hours. We'll get the gladiator bodyguard who's her regular escort out of the way. One of my own slaves will escort her litter. You'll hold both of them hostage until my friend comes. Then you'll fake a fight, and when it looks like he's beating you, you'll run away."

Callidus chuckled. "A simple plan. It should work. What will you pay me?"

Marcus leaned in. "Three hundred denarii. That's almost a year's wages for a few days of your time, with 150 before she comes. I'll meet you with the other 150 the day after my friend rescues the girl."

Callidus's mouth curved into a tight-lipped smile. "That's acceptable. I wouldn't expect to be paid the entire 300 up front by someone who doesn't already know I'm an honest man. Where's this house?"

"I can take you there after you eat. It's an empty rental, so you can stay there until we finish this. It might be a couple of weeks before we do it." He reached into the purse hanging from his belt and pulled out a handful of coins. "Here's ten denarii to hold you. I'll bring the rest of the 150 when I come to tell you which day she'll be coming in her litter."

Callidus's broad grin revealed several missing teeth. "Sounds like an excellent plan to me."

The servant girl delivered the food and drink, and Marcus leaned back in the chair. As his unwitting partner in crime shoveled the stew into his mouth and bit off chunks of bread, he sipped his wine, silently toasting the solution to his best friend's problem.

The Secundus villa

Julia heard the anger in Gallio's voice long before she stepped into the atrium. He stood, arms crossed, lips compressed, glaring at her brother.

"Your father left me in charge, Aulus. Serving him well can mean making hard decisions. I made the mistake of assuming you were mature enough to make all your own choices. That black stallion in the stable is proof you aren't. Before you buy another horse, you check with me first."

"You're Father's steward, but I'm his son." Aulus's voice rose. "Father often buys racehorses, and that stallion was a bargain at what I paid."

"It's too wild to ride, too young to breed, and it already killed one slave. If I hadn't bought that new stable slave the day before, it might have killed your sister. It won't even let you close enough to mount it."

"But that slave you bought has gentled it a lot. He said it would be ready for an expert rider before Father returns. You know how much Father likes a spirited animal. He's going to love it."

"That might be, but I'm not giving you money for another stallion until he returns. You can ride one of the mares." He dropped his arms to his sides. "I have business to attend to, but this discussion is over, anyway."

With a slight dip of his head, Gallio strode toward the exit.

Aulus rammed his fists into his hips and scowled at the door through which Gallio had passed.

Julia approached from behind. "Aulus?"

He spun, eyes wide. "Don't sneak up on me like that."

"I didn't mean to." She offered a smile. "I heard what Gallio said. I don't think he's being fair. It's not your fault someone started a fire and scared that horse." She placed her hand on his arm. "He gave me money for jewelry when Metilia and I went shopping just before she left town. I didn't find anything I wanted, so I still have the 400 denarii. You can have it for a horse."

He brushed her hand off and stepped back. "I don't want your money. I can get anything I want from Marcus."

Two fast blinks, then lowered brows magnified his frown before he followed Gallio out the door.

Julia's brow furrowed. Aulus had been acting strange for a couple of weeks, but why did he get angry when she only tried to help? They used to get on so well, but now... It would be good when Father got home and took him in hand. Maybe Father could bring the old Aulus back.

Chapter 11

NOTHING TO WORRY ABOUT

Subura, Day 16

With his back against the wall, Callidus sat in the taberna two blocks from his unnamed employer's rental house and nursed a cup of cheap wine.

It had been two days since the young nobleman hired him, and no message had come. But that wasn't a problem. The longer it took for the kidnapping to start, the longer he had a free roof over his head. The longer he could wait before heading northwest to Luna and selling himself into combat for another four years.

Combat, not for the growth of the Empire and the glory of Rome, but for himself and the money that would let him open a taberna like the one in which he sat. Like the one that had been seized to pay his father's debts after he died.

His jaw clenched. The judge should have contacted him and given him a chance to pay them. For twenty-five years, he'd served Rome and her emperors, and that judge had seized and sold his birthright before he even knew his father was dead.

He gazed into the cup and swirled what was left of the wine.

"Callidus?"

He raised his eyes and focused on the thin man across the table. "Who's asking?"

A thin man about his own age faced him. "Gnaeus Bassus. Don't you remember me?"

"It's been a long time." A smile crept across Callidus's face as he recognized his childhood friend. "Many years and many miles. It's good to see you, Bassus." He pointed to the empty chair. "Sit."

Bassus settled into the chair. "This is a surprise. I thought you were in a legion up on the Danube."

"I was. The XIV Gemina. Fought in Dacia with Trajan. I just retired and came home to join Father in the taberna."

Bassus's brow furrowed. "But he died at least six months ago."

Callidus's mouth turned down. "So I just learned. I come back to find I have nothing."

"Didn't the legion give you retirement pay?"

"Yes, in land. But not where I'd ever want to live."

Bassus signaled the servant girl. "Two cups of wine for me and my friend."

He rested his elbows on the table and leaned forward. "What are you going to do?"

The girl returned with a cup for him and a pitcher of wine to fill both cups.

"I've been a soldier so long; fighting is all I know." Callidus rubbed the back of his neck. "I have a quick job for some senatorial son who wants to fake a kidnapping so the girl will marry his friend. Then I'll be heading north to hire myself into a ludus. Four years, and I'll have the money I need to start a taberna somewhere."

Bassus sucked air through clenched teeth. "Four years in the arena? How many survive that?"

Callidus shrugged. "I'll get food and a place to live and at least 1200 denarii when I finish. That's enough to start over."

"If you don't die first." Bassus rubbed his chin. "What if you could make more than that without the risk? Interested?"

Callidus's brow furrowed. "How?"

Bassus glanced over his shoulder, then moved to the chair beside Callidus to put his back to the wall. He lowered his voice. "This girl... young enough she'd be a virgin?"

"Probably. The one who hired me won't be a tribune for two years. His friend's probably young, too."

"Good." Bassus's voice softened more. "Then we can make at least three times what you'll get from the ludus if we sell her...and I know where to do that."

Callidus's head bounced back. "Selling a girl from a senator's family? I'm not sure that's a good idea."

"That judge who cheated you out of your father's taberna is a senator. It's only right you use a senator's daughter to get back what a senator took from you." The corner of Bassus's mouth pulled sideways.

"You fought in Dacia. You turned thousands of women and girls into slaves, and some of those came from noble families. How is this any different?"

Callidus opened his mouth to explain; then the logic of Bassus's point struck home.

"I guess it isn't." His nose twitched. "Noble Romans sold once-noble Dacians like cattle. The generals and the emperor got the money from those sales."

His friend interrupted. "And we'll get the money from this one." Bassus's twisted smile grew into a grin. "This is the chance to get both of us enough to start fresh." He lifted his cup. "To that young son of a senator and Fortuna's smiles."

Callidus lifted his cup as his own broad smile broke free. "To chance meetings with old friends...and Fortuna's smiles."

The Secundus villa, Day 17

Dacius made the final sweep of the brush along the back of Master Aulus's gray mare. So far, it had been a good day with his horses. Mistress Julia's sister had chosen to visit her, and he could hear the children's laughter through the garden gateway.

It was eleven days since the lashing, and his back had healed enough that carrying the litter had moved past bearable to almost comfortable again. Glyptus rolled his eyes every time he told his friend it was God's doing, but Dacius knew the truth.

He'd even healed enough for Vilicus to put him back digging the pool, but Mistress Julia was in the garden with her nieces today. Perhaps the overseer or, more likely, the steward didn't want him where Mistress Julia might see the slave who frightened her again. Whatever the reason, he gave thanks to God that he was off pick-and-shovel duty for now.

Master Aulus and Drusus strolled onto the portico, and the master summoned him with a flick of his fingers.

He trotted over. "What do you wish, master?"

"Saddle the gray and fetch Marcus's horse."

"Yes, master." With a quick dip of his head, he took a step back before turning to walk back to the mare.

The master and Drusus settled into two chairs and resumed their conversation.

Dacius caught occasional words, enough to know they were going to Drusus's house for dinner. Both with legs stretched out and Drusus with his hands on his head, fingers laced, they looked like two men without a care in the world. That seemed strange, but it was a big improvement. Yesterday Master Aulus had been tightly strung, like a bowstring ready for the hunt.

He tossed the saddle on the mare, and his smile broadened as he tightened the cinch. Perhaps his prayers had been answered, and they'd found a solution to the master's money problem without having to kidnap his sister.

He opened the stall next to Niger's, where Drusus had put his gray stallion. As he led it out, Niger stuck his head out the stall door. His nostrils flared, and a scream proclaimed his displeasure at having another stallion in his stable yard. The Drusus stallion swung to face Niger, rising a few inches off the ground with a front-leg kick and an answering scream. Dacius grabbed its halter, pulled down hard, and hurried it away from the stalls.

It was time to shuffle the mares to fill that stall so Drusus would have to put the older stallion in the stall farthest from Niger. He scooped up the gray mare's reins and led the horses toward the portico.

His gaze fell on the master and his ruthless friend. Had the danger they posed to the mistress passed? Or was this only the quiet before the storm?

If only what men might do was as easy to predict as horses.

He rubbed his chin. Maybe there was nothing to worry about. It had been twelve days since he heard Drusus pushing the young master to kidnap her. Wouldn't they have done something already if it was more than talk? Besides, he, Taurus, and three other bearers were there to protect her when she wasn't at home, and not even Master Aulus would be foolish enough to stage something at their house. The mistress's refusal to listen to his warning probably wouldn't matter.

He reached back and drew his finger along one of the freshly healed cuts. He'd carry the scars for the rest of his life, but he'd still do it again. Like he told Primus, any man should try to protect the innocent, and a man who served Jesus should be willing to risk everything to obey his Lord's command to love.

Circus Maximus, Day 18

Marcus leaped to his feet as the chariots swept past with the Greens holding a commanding lead. He'd placed no bets so Aulus wouldn't be the only one in their party not betting. It was enough that the team he would have backed had won.

He settled back onto the seat beside his friend as the winner took his victory lap. "I met with someone today, and it's set for tomorrow."

Aulus's back straightened. "I hope we made the right choice." He ran his fingers through his hair. "It's not too late to find another way."

Marcus slapped his friends back. "You worry too much. I have it all arranged. The problem should be solved and everyone home by this time tomorrow, the next morning at the latest."

Aulus's eyes focused on his feet; then his gaze shifted to Marcus. "You're right. A man faces his problems and takes action to solve them." The corner of his mouth turned up. "Without risk, there's no reward."

Chapter 12

SOMETHING SPECIAL

The Secundus villa, Day 19

The young stallion's nose bumped Dacius as he poured the last bucket of water into his trough. He turned and rubbed the stallion's blaze. "That's all for now, boy. Maybe they'll give me enough time in the stable today so I can give you a good brushing."

He slipped past the horse and latched the gate. His gaze swept the stalls where his horses were contentedly eating what he'd just given them. It was worth getting up before the crack of dawn to make sure he could feed and water before the slaves were given their breakfast.

Dacius was the last one in line as Glyptus dished out the morning porridge.

The cook plopped a ladle of the runny gruel into Dacius's bowl. "You work too hard. No one appreciates it, and Primus hates you for it. You make everyone else look lazy."

"I can't let the horses go hungry. Besides, I'm just one more "you" to Vilicus. I doubt he even knows my name, and he's never there to see what I do before dawn. Now my back has healed, I can't predict whether he'll put me in the stable, carrying the litter, or digging the pool. The grooming and cleaning can wait, but I can't rely on him telling someone to feed if I don't."

Glyptus ladled a second serving into the bowl. One corner of his mouth rose as he shook his head. "Fortuna never smiles on me, but she smiled on the horses when Gallio bought you."

One of the housekeeping slaves scurried through the portico and approached the litter escort. "Taurus, Master Aulus wants you in the library."

As Taurus followed her into the house, Glyptus's brows rose. "That's different. Still, if Master Aulus needs Taurus today, at least you shouldn't end up taking the litter somewhere. So, what do you think, stable or garden for you?"

The corners of Dacius's mouth lifted into smile. "Stable. When I prayed last night, I sensed God has something special for me today."

Glyptus's laugh was more of a snort. "You always expect the best from your god. You'd still be free in Dacia instead of a slave in Rome if your god had any power. Better to worship many gods so maybe one of them will smile on you." Sadness filled his eyes. "But the gods don't care about slaves."

Dacius rested his hand on Glyptus's arm. "My God does. To Him, there's no difference between slave and free, Roman and Dacian, man and woman. He cares about us all."

Glyptus's gaze locked on Dacius, and he opened his mouth as if to say something. No words came out before he closed it. Then he took a deep breath. "I would like to hear more about your god. Sometime when it's just you and me."

Dacius's grin reflected his delight. "Any time you think is good."

Before he could say more, Taurus strode back into the room. "Dacius, Master Aulus wants me to take the bay mare to Marcus Drusus's house right away."

Dacius set his bowl down. "I'll saddle her for you."

Taurus frowned. "No. I'm going to lead her."

"Lead her? That will take half a day for you to get there and back."

"That's what Master Aulus told me to do." Taurus shrugged. "She's probably too small for a man my size, so walking is better."

"Let's go get her." Dacius looked back at Glyptus as he followed Taurus toward the stable yard. "I'll be right back for my porridge."

Dacius tightened his lips when Taurus wasn't looking. What was Marcus Drusus going to do with his little mare? Anyone who could tell a brother to sell his sister to protect himself wasn't the kind of man he wanted to have control over any of his horses. He sighed. But no matter how much he cared about them, they weren't really his. Nothing was really his.

The corners of his mouth lifted into the trace of a smile that set him apart among the slaves. Nothing on earth, anyway. He had great treasure in heaven, and that was all that really mattered.

Dacius hummed softly to himself as he brushed the back of the black stallion. When he finished, the horse turned his head and nickered.

"I know, Niger. It feels good, doesn't it? But I need to brush the others too." He stroked the horse's nose. "You'd love a good run, but you have to let Master Aulus mount you before you can have that." He slapped the stallion's shoulder. "You'd be safe with him."

But not if you were his sister. Dacius's eyebrows lowered.

He slipped out of the stall and closed the gate. Niger sauntered over and hung his head over it to watch as he moved to the next horse.

In less than three weeks, he'd turned the skittish stallion who jumped at his own shadow into a calm animal. He could still kick and bite if startled, but not with Dacius. He was almost ready for the young master to ride. That triggered Dacius's smile. The Crassus overseer would have given him a reward for that. Here...nothing.

He mentally kicked himself. Apostle Paul had taught about speaking and acting to please God, not men. Only God's approval mattered. God had gifted him with his way with horses. He should be thankful that at least part of his work let him use that gift.

He was about to enter the next stall when Vilicus's guttural voice stabbed him. "You."

He turned and bowed his head. "Yes, overseer?"

"Get cleaned up for litter duty."

Dacius froze his eyebrows. Litter duty? When Taurus was gone? He suppressed the sigh. "Yes, overseer."

At least he wouldn't be digging, and he'd had some time with Niger. Maybe that was the special thing he sensed last night. Apostle Paul had learned to be content with whatever he might have and wherever he might be. He would do the same.

Dacius stood by the litter, waiting as patiently as he could manage. Mistress Julia finally came through the portico...without Apicula. Instead, a silver-haired man he'd never seen before walked beside her.

As he stood by the right rear pole, he watched her face. The sweet smile that usually graced her lips when she walked with Apicula was missing.

The old man spoke as they reached the litter. "No one else has been able to lift her spirits, but Mistress Metilia should be so much better after she sees you."

"I'm glad you were sent for me as soon as she returned. I'll do all I can to cheer her."

She sat on the litter and swung her legs in. Dacius and the others knelt and put their shoulders against the pole pads.

The old man spoke. "Lift."

Dacius stood, raising his corner of the litter shoulder high. The elderly escort walked to the head of the litter, and the bearers followed him out the gate.

Chapter 13

TRAPPED

Subura

Dacius had been carrying the litter for less than three weeks, but he'd often carried Mistress Julia to the Baths of Trajan to visit with friends. When the elegant buildings and gardens rose before them, he expected they'd be meeting her distressed friend there. Instead, they walked past and turned down a street that led off the Oppian Hill, where the Baths sat overlooking the city.

He hadn't yet carried her to all friends' houses, but something seemed very wrong about the part of town into which they were walking. This was not an area of villas or elegant townhouses with lush gardens behind masonry walls. It wasn't even a decent neighborhood with smaller houses like the one where Mistress Calpurnia lived. As they trudged down the slope, the buildings became shabbier, the streets narrower and dirtier.

As they passed loitering men, his neck itched as if a bug crawled upon it. Too many stared at the mistress. His lips tightened. Lust lit too many eyes. Carrying her through this area with Taurus as escort—that would be safe enough. No one would dare try anything and risk a fight with Taurus. With this elderly man? The mistress herself looked more intimidating.

The escort stepped aside to let the front bearers pass. He loosened the ties holding the curtains back on the left side and let the fabric fall.

Mistress Julia sat up straight. "What are you doing?"

"We have to pass through an area unfit for your eyes, mistress."

He walked behind Dacius and moved past him on the right side to

61

release the remaining curtains. Once she was hidden, he resumed his place ahead of the litter.

Dacius's tension drained away. It hadn't been the fitness for the mistress's eyes that bothered him. It was the leering men who weren't fit to see her.

The escort finally led them into a small stable yard. Dirt and dead leaves overlay the paving, and no horses stood in the stalls.

Why would her friend want to meet her at an abandoned house?

A brawny man rose from a faded chair on the portico and strode toward the escort. He moved like a soldier, not a servant. His shifty eyes and swagger bespoke scoundrel, not slave.

"Your mistress is expected inside." Not a trace of deference in his tone.

Too many things were not what they should be. Dacius's teeth clenched.

The escort opened and tied back the curtains on his side. "We're here, mistress."

As the mistress swung her legs out, the two men exchanged glances. The escort's mouth twitched, and the other nodded almost imperceptibly.

Dacius's heart rate ratcheted up. These two knew each other, and that wasn't a glance of friendly recognition, like he often shared with his fellow slaves in the Secundus household.

The escort gestured for Mistress Julia to follow the man into the house. As she walked ahead of him, he turned back to the litter. "Go home. She'll return in my mistress's litter."

With legs spread, fists on his hips, Dacius watched the old man until he disappeared through the doorway.

Verres and Capellus were already down on one knee. With his shoulder under the left rear pole, Primus glared at him. "Dacius, let's go."

"No. The mistress didn't tell us to go. We should wait for her." He ran his hand through his hair. "Something's not right."

◆

Julia followed the big man through the *vestibulum* into the atrium. It was filthy, as if no one had cleaned it for weeks, if not months.

"Where's Metilia?" She cast her eyes around the room as her whole body tensed.

A wry smile twisted the big one's lips. "There's another litter coming. Metilia didn't want anyone to follow you to where she is, and changing litters is the best way to avoid that."

The old man's back straightened as his head jerked back. "I wasn't told that. I was told she was only supposed to stay here for a few hours, maybe overnight." He glanced at Julia. "With Mistress Metilia."

The wry smile twisted into a sneer. "There's been a change of plan. My friend and I want more than we were promised after we release her. A pretty virgin like her will bring top money in the market—at least thirty times what the man who hired us was going to pay."

As he spoke, a thin man entered the atrium from a side room.

Julia's eyes saucered, and her gaze circulated between the three of them. She swallowed hard and backed up toward the escort. The other two stepped closer.

The old man shook his head. "That wasn't part of the plan, and I'm not going to let you do it."

A cruel laugh rumbled up from the brawny one who'd met the litter. "You can't stop us."

He grabbed her arm.

The escort stepped forward and seized her other arm, trying to pull her away from the thug.

Julia pulled free from the escort and slapped the kidnapper, and for an instant, his grip weakened. She jerked her arm free and stumbled back closer to her only protector.

The thin kidnapper rammed his fist into the old man's temple, and he dropped. As he tried to rise, the thin one kicked his arm, and he collapsed back to the floor. He tried to rise again. Two kicks to the head snapped the old man's head back, and he flopped back on the floor, limp as a rag doll. He didn't move again.

The brawny one wrapped her in iron-band arms. She gulped a deep breath before her scream rent the air. Thin man slapped his palm across her mouth, muffling the sound and crushing her lips against her teeth. He pulled a grimy cloth from inside his tunic. He jerked back his hand when she tried to bite him and shoved the rag into her mouth before she could scream again. When she tried to push it out with her tongue, he shoved it deeper until she started to gag.

"Hold her while I get some rope from the garden. There's a sack there big enough to shove her in. No one will know what we're carrying." He drew his finger along her jaw, and she jerked away. "She's small enough anyone would think she's a pig."

As the thin one left the atrium, Julia thrashed and kicked. Each time her sandaled feet struck the big one's legs, he squeezed her tighter until she could barely draw a breath.

His foul breath assaulted her nostrils as he nuzzled her neck. "You smell good. I'd keep you myself if you weren't going to sell for top money. Virgins bring more, but maybe we will keep you...for a while."

Sheer panic flooded her. Her struggles weakened as his constricting arms pulled tighter still. Thrashing became wriggling. She pushed back on the dizzy feeling, but she was losing the battle as she fought to remain conscious.

Chapter 14

A Place to Hide

Dacius's head snapped back. From somewhere within came the cry of a woman, quickly muffled.

"She's in trouble. Follow me." He trotted toward the door. As he reached it, he looked back. The other three still stood beside the litter.

"Come on." Verres and Capellus looked away, while Primus rested his fists on his hips and shook his head.

He sucked air through his teeth. Whatever had to be done, he would have to do alone. He stepped inside and crept to the doorway between the *vestibulum* and the atrium.

His eyebrows lowered. The prostrate form of the escort lay face down on the dirty mosaic floor. No blood, but the frost-blue eyes were open, unblinking.

With his back toward Dacius, the kidnapper held a wriggling Julia beside the scum-coated pool, her arms pinned to her side by the iron bands of his brawny arms. A rag had been shoved in her mouth to muffle her cries.

A quick glance around the atrium revealed no one else, but others might be in the small rooms that opened to the side or in the peristyle beyond.

No time to lose. Dacius took a deep breath...and launched himself at the kidnapper.

The impact of his shoulder on the man's spine loosened his grip on the mistress, and she wriggled free. Dacius drove his fist into the man's cheekbone, snapping his head sideways.

"Run to the litter!" He hissed at her, lest someone in an adjoining room should hear.

Instead, she backed up against the wall and froze.

He slammed his fist into the kidnapper's jaw, and the man staggered back.

"Run!" He spoke louder, harsher. She still stood pressed against the wall, like a rabbit frozen as a snarling dog circled it.

The kidnapper swung at him, but he ducked. As he rose, he rammed his fist into the bottom of the man's jaw, and the kidnapper crumpled.

As Dacius stood over the unconscious man, something rustled behind him.

He spun and threw up his arm to block the knife plunging toward his heart. With a twist and a shove, he deflected it, but it still pierced his chest just below his right collar bone. The kidnapper pulled the blade out, but before he could stab again, Dacius pummeled the side of his face and jaw. The man went down.

The mistress still stood frozen at the wall. He grabbed her right hand with his left and pulled her with him as he ran back through the vestibulum. He burst through the outer door with her trailing behind.

"Ready the litter!" He shouted as he dragged her toward it. The front bearers knelt by the poles, but Primus just stood staring at the blood that had already soaked the shoulder of his red tunic.

"Kneel, Primus!" Left rear did as ordered.

When they reached the litter, Dacius pulled the mistress past him, twisting away from her to block her view of his blood. "Get in, mistress. We must leave—now."

She swung her legs in as he stepped back by the pole.

Dacius knelt, then yelled, "Lift." The litter rose to shoulder height. "Run."

The men began trotting, but their steps were out of sync. The litter was bouncing erratically. The mistress shrieked as she almost fell out before she lay back and grabbed onto both railings by the backrest.

"Together. Step. Step. Step." Dacius called out the cadence, and the men settled into a synchronized trot.

◆

As the bearers synchronized their steps, Julia was no longer pitched around as if the litter were a gale-tossed ship. It still bounced up and down, but it was rhythmic, not erratic, and she let go of the railings.

A violent shudder coursed through her as memories of the attack assaulted her mind. The old man dead on the floor, the kidnapper shoving a rag in her mouth, the arms squeezing the breath out of her, her heart racing as fear of what was coming crashed in on her.

Then, out of nowhere, one of her bearers hurling himself into the man and fighting to rescue her. He'd won and then...the second thug with the knife.

Another shudder as visions of the knife leaped before her eyes. She would have sworn the knife went in, but her view had been blocked by her slave's body. He couldn't have been badly hurt. He'd still knocked down the second kidnapper and run, pulling her behind him.

Now he was trotting with the litter as if nothing was wrong.

But the front of his tunic was already wet when he pulled her away from the wall. Wet only on the right side, so it couldn't be sweat. And he hadn't gone near the scum-coated pool.

Her stomach flipped. It had to be blood. Could there be that much if the wound was almost nothing?

◆

Dacius tried to keep his eyes focused forward, but even a quick glance revealed the expanding wetness on his tunic. The blood stain ran down to his stomach, where it spread across at the belt line. He had to get her far enough away that the kidnappers wouldn't catch up, but how long would he be able to hold up his pole?

The excitement of the fight had given him strength even as bleeding drained it away, but now the blood loss was winning. His strength was flagging, but only three men couldn't carry her. Maybe he should have had them run with her and leave the litter behind.

He felt the stumble coming, but how many steps before it hit?

"Hold on, mistress."

She made no move to heed his words.

When it came and he fell, the litter tilted sharply to the right before his pole hit the ground. The mistress tumbled onto the pavement.

The other bearers stopped and lowered the litter.

Dacius staggered to his feet. "Your bearers will get you home. Tell Steward Gallio what happened. Have Taurus guard you from your brother until your father returns."

Wide brown eyes flecked with gold and trembling pink lips on an ashen face held his gaze as she knelt before him. He stepped toward her, offering his left hand to help her up.

The hair on his neck rose. He spun to see why...in time to spy the thin kidnapper with an arrow nocked and aimed at the mistress.

He swallowed hard. The mistress was pagan. Eternity in hell waited for anyone who didn't believe in Jesus.

The fingers released, and the missile began its deadly flight.

He steeled himself for the pain...and stepped between her and the arrow.

It pierced his thigh, and he almost fell. Sheer will kept him on his feet.

He yelled at Primus and the others, "Take her and run."

They obeyed part of his command. They ran.

Dacius hauled the mistress to her feet and shoved her through the litter to get her out of the sightline of the archer. He stepped through behind her, keeping his body between her and the kidnapper.

God, how do I protect her now? Help us.

He pushed free of the litter curtains and found the answer to his prayer. A narrow passageway lay open before him, blocked from the kidnapper's view by the litter.

Thank you, God!

With his left hand, he grabbed her right and dragged her into the passageway.

He stayed ahead so she wouldn't see the blood-soaked front of his tunic and faint on the spot. He'd never be able to carry her if she did.

The arrow still in his thigh made each step agony, but he stumbled on, pulling her with him. It wouldn't take long for the kidnapper to reach the litter and find the passageway. He had to find someplace to hide her before he collapsed or the kidnapper caught up.

If he were a betting man, he'd bet the collapse came first. Then who would protect her from being taken and sold?

God, please give her an escape.

The passageway opened onto a street lined with small shops, many with their displayed wares encroaching into the walkway. His eyes were drawn to the first one on the left. On the post supporting the awning, he saw the fish. Two curved lines, touching at one end, crossing each other to form the tail. Just inside the shop, a large basket about three feet tall stood open and empty with a lid resting against it.

She would fit.

"Mistress. The basket."

He pulled her past the brick counter and into the shop. He bent his knees so he could wrap his good left arm around her thighs, set her on his uninjured shoulder, and lift her high enough for her feet to go in.

She gasped and grabbed his head as his arm wrapped around her and he began to lift. Lightning bolts of pain shot through his leg, and it almost buckled. Determination alone steadied it as he stood with her sitting on his good shoulder.

"Put your feet in."

She obeyed, and he lowered her in. Then he pressed down on her shoulder. "Hide."

She crouched, her terrified eyes looking up at his, and he placed the lid on top. "Stay quiet, mistress."

The shopkeeper, whose silver-threaded hair framed a face that testified to the passage of more than forty years, froze as she stood staring at him. He stumbled to the counter and traced the fish shape with his finger.

She nodded and gripped his upper arm. After pushing open the door to her living quarters behind the shop, she shoved him in before closing it again.

Dacius's strength was spent, drained from his body by the blood still oozing from his shoulder and thigh. He sank to his knees and pressed his left hand against the stab wound. Fierce pain shot through him, and he jerked it away. Crimson drops trickled down his palm and dripped to the floor. He pressed his hand into the wound again. Pain or not, he had to slow the bleeding.

Thank you for guiding me to a sister. But what do I do now, Lord?

He hung his head.

He couldn't take the mistress to her home. Her brother would certainly try again. To her sister? That would be the first place her brother would look. If she showed up there, he couldn't get the ransom money. He'd have to try again. To her friends? Which one might hide her until her father returned? Could any of them do it secretly enough that her brother wouldn't find her?

God, I need to protect her, but how am I going to do that like this?

He started to sway, and he shifted his left hand to the floor, leaning on it to keep from collapsing. *God, help me. Please...help us both.*

Chapter 15

Help from a Sister

Servilia pulled the door shut behind the wounded young man, then scooped up two folded rugs and placed them atop the lid of the basket. She stepped back to the counter just as two men emerged from the passageway. With angry faces and a quiet exchange of words, they split up, one going each way. The thinner one sprinted past her and down the street.

She lifted a folded blanket from her counter, shook it open, and refolded it. Then she walked to the basket and placed it on top of the stack.

She spoke in a near-whisper, "Two men are looking for someone. Stay in the basket. Make no sound until I tell you all is clear."

She stacked another folded rug on the basket lid. Then she stepped into the back room and closed the door.

The young man was down on his knees, leaning on his left hand. She knelt beside him.

"Can you stand?"

He shook his head. "My shoulder, leg...lost too much blood."

She slid her hands under his arms. "Try, and come away from the door. I want to cover you up. Two men came through the passage, I think hunting you. If they look in here, we don't want them to see you."

With her help, he stumbled deeper into the room, away from the doorway.

"Lie down. Let me cover you."

He dropped to his knees and rolled on his back. His eyes locked on hers. "Don't let them find her."

She took the blanket from her bed and spread it over him.

"She's well hidden. As soon as I see where they went, I'll tend to your wounds." After a gentle pat on his uninjured shoulder, she stepped back outside.

She resumed her post at the loom when she saw the thin man who'd chased the young couple hurrying back up the street. At each stall, he was asking something.

Finally, he stood where she and her nearest neighbors could hear. "Listen, all of you. I'm looking for two people—a girl in a green tunic with fancy hair and a man who's hurt. They're runaway slaves who stole jewelry and clothes from their mistress. They came through there." He pointed at the passageway that opened by her shop. "Have you seen them?"

Servilia held her breath. At least one of her neighbors must have seen her help them.

Then the shoemaker with the shop directly across from hers spoke. "There's another passage to the next street right over there. They went that way."

Without a single word of thanks, the man disappeared down the narrow passage.

The shoemaker smiled and nodded at Servilia, and she mouthed her silent thank you. Then she went inside to help the young brother before he bled to death.

◆

As Julia cowered in the basket, the shopkeeper's footsteps came closer, then paused.

"I think they're gone, but stay in the basket. I'm going inside to care for your young man. I'll be back soon."

The calmness of the woman's voice helped to slow her racing heart.

She waited in silence for the woman to return—waited and waited and waited...

It was only a short time, but it seemed like hours that she'd been hiding in the basket. After crouching for so long in such tight quarters, her thigh muscles screamed for relief, and she could scarcely feel her toes.

The longer she remained there, the more likely it seemed the kidnappers would find her. With each slap of sandals on the pavement outside the shop, her heart pounded. With each sudden sound of a man's voice, a shiver raced through her. What if the lid were jerked away to reveal the leering face of the brutal man who reeked of rotting teeth and sweat?

Her wounded slave was somewhere inside, bleeding and maybe dying. He wouldn't be there to stop anyone this time.

She could stand it no longer. With her heart pounding in her ears, she pushed the lid up enough to peek out. She saw no one but the shoemaker across the street, and his back was turned as he bent over his workbench.

She stood, balancing the basket lid so the stack of rugs wouldn't fall. She placed one hand on top of the stack and the other inside the lid so she could tip it and set everything on the ground without making any noise.

The lip of the basket was too high to step over, so she crouched down and leaned against its wall. It flopped over, and she crawled out.

She cast a furtive glance at the shoemaker. Surely he must have heard the basket hit the ground, but his back was still toward her. She crawled out, straightened the basket, and replaced the lid and rugs without standing up. If the kidnappers came back, they mustn't think the basket had changed. Then she crawled through the half-open door into the back room.

Her slave was lying in the back corner, stripped to the waist with his red tunic on the floor beneath him. His left arm lay across his bare chest, his hand holding a pad against the stab wound.

Her breaths came too fast, and she fought to slow them. How much of that red was blood?

The shopkeeper knelt beside him. "The arrow twisted when you were running. If I just pull it, it's going to tear too much coming out. The tip is almost through anyway, so I can just push it the rest of the way. Then I can break the shaft and pull it back through."

"Do what you must, Servilia." He pulled over a corner of a blanket, made a fold, and placed it in his mouth. Through clenched teeth, he spoke. "Do it now." His voice was thick with pain.

Julia's hands flew up to cover her eyes. Then she spread her fingers to peek after she shifted to where the shopkeeper's body blocked her view of his bleeding leg. Now was not the time for fainting.

His back arched up as the shopkeeper shoved the arrowhead through his skin, but he made no sound. A soft grunt escaped as his back settled again on the tunic. He arched once more as she snapped the shaft and pulled it back through his thigh.

Servilia looked over her shoulder at Julia. "It's good you came in.

I need help with his shoulder. You can press on that cloth to stop the bleeding. He's not strong enough to do it."

Julia swallowed hard and took three steps toward him. Servilia lifted his left hand from the cloth pad and tipped it up, exposing the wound that was still oozing blood.

"Come over here and press on this pad."

Julia froze. How could she be expected to touch him with all that blood and him being a half-naked man with a hairy, muscled chest and brawny biceps? She closed her eyes trying to shut out all the red as she swayed a little.

Servilia grasped her hand. "There's no time to waste. He needs you now." She pulled Julia to her knees beside him. Then she placed Julia's palms on the pad and pushed on the back of Julia's hands. "Keep pressing on it like this."

Julia leaned her weight on him. He winced, and her breath caught as she jerked her hands away. "But I'm hurting him."

Servilia took her hands and put them back on the pad. "A little pain won't kill him, but if you don't keep pressing, he's going to bleed to death."

His eyes had been squeezed shut, but they opened.

For the first time, she looked deep into his smoke-gray eyes. Past the pain, there was a calmness that shocked her. How could he be so calm when he was terribly hurt and they were being hunted?

The lips that had been squeezed tight a moment earlier relaxed into a slight smile. "Please do it, mistress. The pain doesn't matter."

She leaned into his wound. His eyes squeezed shut, and his jaw clamped. She fought against tears. The pain did matter, but she had to hurt him to help him.

She kept her gaze locked on his face and tried to push all the blood out of her mind. He needed her help, and she must not faint.

What would have happened if he hadn't been carrying her today? That horrible man who reeked of sweat, the crushing pressure of his filthy arms so tight around her chest, the salty taste of the dirty rag shoved in her mouth—the terror of those moments surged through her again. Hopeless terror...and then he came out of nowhere and rescued her.

Julia chewed her lip as Servilia finished bandaging his thigh.

"Your leg's not hurt so bad. My husband served in the XIII Gemina, and you're not the first man with wounds like yours that I've cared for. I've seen much worse on men who were back in battle in less than three months. You might not even limp when it's fully healed."

Her gaze shifted from him to Julia. "I'll take over on that shoulder now."

Those were the most welcome words Julia had ever heard. She rose and stepped back. Servilia lifted the blood-soaked pad away and placed a fresh one against the stab wound. He reached across and held it in place. Then she helped him sit up and began securing it with wrappings over his shoulder and around his chest.

Julia fought the urge to look at her hands and lost. They were covered with red she knew was blood. The room started spinning, so she moved farther away from him and sat down on the shop floor where there wasn't any. She drew her knees up and rested her head against them, eyes closed.

When the light-headed feeling passed, she turned her eyes back on him. His face seemed too pale, but at least his eyes were open. He wasn't clenching his jaw like he had been, either.

Servilia glanced at the wood-framed rope bed. "Do you think you can get up on the bed?"

Her slave shook his head. "No, but I always sleep on the ground. Here is good."

Servilia wrapped her arm around his shoulders. "Then you should lie down."

She supported him as he collapsed back onto the tunic. "How did you get hurt like this?"

Julia felt as much as saw his eyes focus on her. Then they shifted to Servilia. "I overheard the mistress's brother and his friend talking about kidnapping her and claiming he paid ransom to get the money to pay his gambling debts."

Julia's mind reeled. Aulus was a terrible gambler, and he'd been acting strangely, his anger flaring for no reason. But he'd always been a kind brother. How could he do such a horrible thing? Something certain to hurt her?

"Someone just tried to kidnap her. I stopped them, but they're probably nearby and still looking for her. His friend told him to sell her to get even more money."

Julia's stomach churned, and she fought to keep everything down. Her own brother was willing to make her a slave?

"They killed her escort, so they need to find her. They can't leave a witness. I'm not sure they know they hurt me so bad I couldn't take her far." His eyes turned toward Julia, then back to Servilia. "If they come here...it might be too dangerous for you to harbor us. Don't risk yourself. If they threaten you, give me to them, but please tell them my mistress kept running after I fell. Please keep her from them."

Julia stared at him. Let himself be taken by the murderers to protect the shopwoman? Didn't he care what happened to him?

Servilia patted his uninjured shoulder. "Of course I'll keep her safe, and I won't give you to them, either. Helping you is not too dangerous for me. I've been close enough to battle to hear the war cries of the legionaries as they attacked during Trajan's campaigns, and I'm certainly not afraid of some kidnappers."

His mouth curved into a full smile. "I can't thank you enough, Servilia. May God bless you for hiding us. Can you help with one more thing?"

Servilia's eyebrows dipped. "I'll try. What is it?"

He drew a deep breath and released it slowly. "I need someplace safe for Mistress Julia where her brother can't find her until her father returns in a month. Do you know someone who could take her in for a while and keep her safe?"

Julia's gaze remained riveted on his face. Why was he only asking for her, not himself?

Servilia smiled down at him. "I do. I can send both of you out to a farm with a brother. He delivers vegetables and chickens twice a week when the wagons move into Rome at night. God's hand is surely upon you; he's coming today. He can take the two of you out of the city in his wagon. I'm sure you'll be welcome to stay with him and his wife until you're well again."

His whole body relaxed as the smile turned into a full-blown grin. "Nothing could be better. God's kind hand truly is upon me."

Julia wasn't sure when she'd last seen such a happy face on a man. If ever. Why would he be so delighted to be taken in by a farmer who was the brother of a woman he'd barely met?

Servilia pushed his tawny hair back from his forehead and ran her fingers through it a few times. "You need to rest and regain your strength for the ride. I'll take care of you until Gaius and Marcella take over."

His grin faded, leaving a trace of a smile.

The shopwoman took his left hand and stroked the back with her thumb. "There's a little bread and a pitcher of watered wine on the shelf over there. Try not to make any noise my customers might hear.

I'll mostly be out front at the counter. I might have to leave for a little while, and someone else might be outside the door then. Don't leave this room unless I tell you."

The corner of his mouth lifted into a wry smile. It broadened as Servilia lifted his head and slid her own pillow under it.

"I'm not planning to go anywhere without your permission."

Her fingers swished through his hair again. "Try to rest, and don't worry. I'll take care of everything to get you safely out of Rome."

She turned to Julia. "Watch over him. Give him something to drink if he asks and apply pressure if he starts bleeding again. If he starts to bleed a lot, peek out to make sure I'm alone before you tell me."

"I will...and thank you." It took several fast blinks to hold back the tears.

Primus and his fellow bearers had run about a quarter mile when he stopped. Verres and Capellus caught up and stopped beside him.

Verres grabbed his head. "We shouldn't have left her. Vilicus will wear that whip out on us when he finds out. What are we going to do?"

Primus raised both hands, palms toward them. "We're going to agree on a story that will keep us out of trouble. If we all stick to it, who's to say otherwise?"

Capellus rubbed the back of his neck. "But what will we say?"

Primus's gaze bounced between the two men. "Dacius was bleeding like a stuck pig even before the arrow hit him. He's probably dead by now, and she's probably been taken by the ones who shot him. Let's put any blame on him."

Verres crossed his arms. "Gallio will come to see where everything happened. Vilicus is stupid enough to fool, but not Gallio."

Primus drew a deep breath and held it before blowing it out. "So, we'd better go back to the house and see what's there. I'll figure out something that even Gallio will believe."

As they retraced their steps, the corner of Primus's mouth curved. Dacius had always served without complaining and been quick to help anyone he could. Even in death, he was going to get them out of trouble. How fitting that the one he'd heard Taurus say was the best of them all, the one who presumed to think he was still a man, would be remembered as the one who betrayed the mistress he was bought to serve.

Chapter 16

But Why?

The shopkeeper closed the door when she left. After Julia's eyes grew accustomed to the dim light leaking in through the small window above the door, she could see her slave. He lay with his eyes closed and mouth tight from the pain as she sat in silence near him.

She didn't want to look at him. There was too much red she knew was blood, but her eyes were drawn against her will. He'd been horribly hurt rescuing her...but why?

Apicula would have risked anything to save her, but she was a friend, not just her slave. Taurus would, too. But he'd trained as a gladiator, so he probably liked to fight. This man...he was only one of the nameless slaves who did whatever was needed. He had no reason to protect her when it might cost his life.

She bit her lip. Who was he, that he would do that? He'd been serving her for a while, but she didn't know his name.

He'd just saved her from a horrible fate. He risked dying when he came to save her, and she didn't even know his name.

She moved over where she could reach him and rested her hand on his upper arm. "What's your name?"

His bicep flexed as her touch startled him. Even when it relaxed again, it felt hard.

He dragged his eyelids open. "In your household, mistress, I'm called Dacius." His eyes drifted shut.

A shudder ran through her as images of the kidnapping flashed through her mind. She'd always thought it was safe travelling in the litter. Taurus and her bearers would protect her. But Taurus hadn't been there, and all the others had abandoned her. Only Dacius had come for her. Only Dacius had stayed to defend her.

The others probably ran home. They shouldn't have deserted her, so they'd probably lie and say he was one of the kidnappers.

But he was in danger even if the others told the truth. Her own brother had planned the abduction, and Aulus would be furious that one of their slaves had thwarted his plans. He'd report Dacius as a runaway who kidnapped her. The punishment for that could be some wild animal ripping him apart in the arena…or crucifixion. Another shudder coursed through her.

Her lips tightened as she raised her chin. But Dacius was her father's property, not her brother's, and he was serving her just like Father would want him to. No one would ever punish him as a runaway if she had anything to say about it.

Her gaze stayed fixed on his face. He looked so ordinary. Tawny hair tending toward red, but not much different from Taurus and the other three bearers. Unevenly cut, like most of the slaves. Nothing remarkable about his chin or nose or eyebrows or ears.

But there was something special about his eyes. So calm when she looked into them for the first time today, like he wasn't frightened at all, even though his words proved he saw the danger. Yet he only asked protection for her, not him.

Why such concern for her? He could only have carried her since the stallion killed her bearer…less than three weeks. The dead man was at the right rear. Dacius was there today, reaching to help her up after she fell out when he dropped his pole.

He'd stopped to look behind him and then…he stepped in front of her just before the arrow struck him. He deliberately took that arrow so it wouldn't hit her, but why would he do that?

Her gaze drifted down his body, and her breath caught. Barely healed lash marks wrapped around his side a little below the bandage. Her litter slaves did nothing except carry her, and they were never whipped. She'd gone to Antonia's right after breakfast the morning after her bearer died. Too early for Gallio to go to the market and buy a replacement, so he would have told Vilicus to pick another slave who was the right height and strong enough.

Maybe a garden slave? The corners of her mouth drooped. Dacius must have been the filthy slave who came too close and then said Aulus was dangerous. He'd acted like he expected her to listen to him, like she should recognize him. If he'd been carrying her, he might expect she would.

He'd frightened her when he came so close that morning. That muscled bare chest, those brawny arms—he stunk of sweat, too. Who wouldn't have told him to get away?

But he'd been knocked down and whipped for simply speaking to her. She cradled her cheeks as she stared at his closed eyes. Why didn't she stop that instead of hurrying inside?

Her eyes drifted to the lash marks again. He was only trying to protect her from Aulus. She should have stopped Vilicus and let him speak, but the blood on his back from the first stroke made her head spin.

His jaw clenched, drawing her attention back to his face.

Slaves weren't always working on the new pool. Where was he then?

Her hand shot to her mouth. That horrible morning when her brother's new stallion trampled her bearer—a stable slave had jumped between her and the horse's slashing hooves, thrown a cloth over its head, and led it away. But everything started swirling when she saw the blood on the dead man's face, so she hadn't really seen the one who saved her.

She shook her head as she bit her lip. If Dacius had been in the stable yard when Gallio told Vilicus to find a replacement, he'd be the first one the overseer saw. If he'd take a knife and an arrow for her, he'd take on a terrified stallion, too.

Twice he'd come to help her, even though she'd paid no attention to him. He'd only been a slave dressed in the blood-red tunic her bearers wore. Only a slave doing whatever someone ordered him to do. An invisible man playing his part in their household, unnoticed...and unappreciated.

Until today. Today he abandoned his post by the litter to fight two armed men when she cried out. Today he came and saved her.

But why?

The sound of men shouting and cursing came from beyond the door. She swallowed hard and stared at the door until she was sure no one was coming in.

She'd never been out in the city alone. Taurus and Apicula had always been there to protect her.

His quiet sigh drew her gaze back to find his teeth clenched and eyes squeezed shut.

If Dacius should die, what would she do?

She shouldn't go home. Who knew what her brother was still planning? He could have more thugs watching for her, ready to grab her again if she tried. She could maybe go to her sister or one of her friends, but surely Aulus would look for her there.

The litter curtains had been closed, so she had no idea where she was. But even if she did, she wouldn't know how to get to her house or anyone else's. Taurus always took care of that.

If Dacius wasn't with her, would it still be safe to go with the farmer to hide in the country until Father came home? How would she ever get back to Rome after he returned?

How could she know whom to trust...except Dacius?

She chewed her lip as she gazed at the haggard face of the man she'd never bothered to see before. Even with his sun-darkened skin, he seemed pale. How much blood could a man lose before it killed him? If he'd lived this long, did that mean he was going to make it?

His breathing paused, and his closed eyes scrunched. They relaxed as he released the breath.

She blinked several times to stop the buildup of tears.

His wounds were all her fault. If she'd run when he broke the first thug's hold, they might have been out of the house before the man with the knife could stab him. They might have been gone before the archer shot him.

So much blood lost and so much pain...and all for her.

He blurred, and she wiped the tears away. He should never have been hurt like this. He had to recover. He had to.

She watched his chest rise and fall. Now and then it stopped as his jaw clenched. The start of a moan, but he silenced it so no one outside might hear. Then his chest started rising again.

For what seemed like hours, she sat alone with him, listening to him breathe, watching his pain, and wondering why he had done what he did...for her.

Chapter 17

Not What They Expected

The Secundus villa

Aulus stood with arms crossed, but he kept his face passive. He'd managed to convince Gallio to keep the black stallion until Father came home, but that could change if the steward thought he was gloating over his victory.

Running footsteps echoed in the atrium as they approached the steward's office. Both men turned their eyes on the boy as he burst through the doorway.

"Steward, Mistress Julia's bearers just came back to the stable yard without her. They said Mistress Julia has been kidnapped."

Gallio leaped to his feet, knocking his desk chair over behind him. He strode past Aulus, and his arm swept the boy out of the way as he jogged toward the stable.

Aulus followed, pausing only long enough to stick his head into the library, where Marcus was setting up the board for Mercenaries. "Follow me."

His eyebrows lowered as he trotted behind Gallio. The first notice of the kidnapping was supposed to be the ransom note Marcus had arranged to have delivered later that afternoon. The escort was supposed to have sent the litter home because she would return in Metilia's litter.

When Aulus entered the stable yard, Vilicus stood beside a grim-faced Gallio. Three litter slaves cowered before the pair. Taurus had just walked through the gate, and he hurried to join the others.

Gallio's fists rammed into his hips. His glare focused on the left-rear bearer. "What happened, Primus?"

"The old man who came for the mistress, he led us into Subura, where we'd never gone before. When we got to the stable yard of an empty house, someone came out and said Mistress Metilia was waiting for Mistress Julia inside. The escort told us to stay with the litter. Then he tapped Dacius on the shoulder and told him to come with them. Dacius started to grin, then squashed it. That seemed odd, but I never expected…"

Gallio scowled. "I don't care what you expected. What happened?"

"There was some noise inside, like a scuffle or something. Then everything got quiet. Too quiet. We waited a few minutes and still heard nothing. Then I told Verres and Capellus she might be in trouble, so we went inside."

Primus rubbed the back of his neck. "We found the escort dead in the atrium. There was no sign of Mistress Julia, Dacius, or the man who came out to get her."

His eyes darted to the other two bearers, then back to Gallio. "We came back to tell you as soon as we could. It looks like Dacius was helping the kidnapper since he disappeared, too. He must have known the man before you bought him, and he helped set the trap so they could take her. Now he's run away himself."

His gaze shifted to the ground, then returned to Gallio. "Dacius liked to watch the mistress too much when she was at Mistress Antonia's villa. Maybe he wasn't content to just watch anymore."

Taurus snorted. "Dacius wouldn't do such a thing. He's the most reliable man I've ever had carrying her litter."

Primus bristled. "Are you calling me a liar? He'd be with us right now if he wasn't running away."

Vilicus's nostrils flared as he looked down his nose at Taurus. "If right-rear is so reliable, where is he now? And why weren't you with them?" He fingered the handle of his whip.

Taurus's eyes spit fire as his eyebrows plunged. His shoulders squared, as if ready for a fight.

Vilicus pulled the handle of his whip from the hook holding it on his belt. His knuckles whitened as he gripped the brass-tipped handle.

Taurus drew a deep breath, held it, then released it with a shrug. "Think what you want, overseer."

Aulus stepped forward. "I'd asked Taurus to take the bay mare to Marcus's house. He had nothing to do with this."

Gallio focused on Taurus. "Get swords for you, Drusus, and Aulus."

Taurus nodded and headed for the weapons cabinet in the room where Aulus's father received his clients during salutation.

Gallio's eyebrows dipped as his gaze returned to Primus. "Take us to the house. Vilicus and you two." He pointed at the other bearers. "Come along."

Taurus came from the house with three gladii in scabbards. Aulus, Marcus, and the escort draped the straps across their chests, and the party hustled through the gate.

Aulus's throat was too dry for a good swallow. Something was going wrong...very wrong. What did that mean for Julia?

The walls of the Baths of Trajan soon rose above them. A short distance, and they left the Oppian Hill and began their descent into Subura, the rough-edged part of Rome that only a fool would travel after dark without an armed bodyguard.

Traveling at quick-march speed was no problem for Aulus, Marcus, and the litter crew, but Gallio was soon breathing heavily and Vilicus was huffing.

Primus led the way, at first quickly, but as they got deeper into Subura, he began to hesitate at street crossings. Each time, he consulted Verres and Capellus, and between the three, they picked a direction.

As the troop started down a narrow street, Marcus nudged Aulus and mouthed "wrong way." He tipped his head toward a narrow street they'd just passed.

"Stop." Aulus's voice brought an instant halt. "Are you certain we're going the right way?" He glanced back over his shoulder and down the side street. About a block away stood a litter. "There's a litter down there."

Taurus turned back and peered at it. "The cushions and canopy are the color of ours." He spun on Primus. "Why is Mistress Julia's litter there?"

Primus swallowed. "We didn't want to leave it at the house where someone might steal it, so we were trying to carry it back. I wasn't strong enough to carry both poles any farther."

Taurus's eyebrows shot up and disappeared under the thick fringe of blond hair covering the top of his forehead. "You expect me to believe you carried half a litter by yourself? Who really carried it this far with you?"

Aulus strode past Taurus. "Stop discussing things that don't matter. We need to get to the house as quickly as we can."

Marcus trotted up beside him, and the rest followed.

Another two blocks, and Marcus pointed at an open carriage gate. "Is that the stable yard?"

As one, the three bearers nodded.

Marcus drew his sword, and Aulus and Taurus did the same before entering.

Dead leaves crunched under Aulus's feet as they approached the door that would lead to the atrium. At the doorway, Marcus signaled for Taurus to go first, and the former gladiator stepped noiselessly inside the vestibulum, sword poised to kill. He crept along the wall and peered into the atrium.

"All clear." He entered the room but kept his sword drawn as he knelt by the limp form of the old man. He twisted to face Gallio, who had entered silently behind them. "Broken neck."

His eyebrows scrunched as he stared at the dirty floor. He pointed to a place where something had disturbed the coating of dust that was uniform closer to the wall. "There was a fight here. Someone was knocked down." He touched a crimson spot where dirt had turned to mud. "And someone lost some blood." He stood and pointed to a narrow strip clear of dirt near the wall. "Her tunic might have dragged there."

Gallio swept his arm toward the small rooms on one side of the atrium, then the other. "Search all the rooms for any sign of her or that slave."

A thorough search of all the rooms, including the second floor, revealed nothing.

Gallio grabbed his head with his hands. Then he straightened and squared his shoulders. "They took her. Time to report her abduction to the Urban Cohort." He rubbed his forehead. Then he fixed misery-filled eyes on Aulus as his shoulders sagged. "How are we going to tell your father?"

Panic surged within Aulus like ocean breakers and tossed him on the rocks. His breath came faster and faster.

Then Marcus rested his hand on Aulus's upper arm and squeezed. A tightlipped smile and his nod reminded Aulus to slow his breathing, and the panic slipped away.

Marcus turned to Gallio. "The only good reason I can imagine for someone taking her is to get ransom money. With the escort dead, they probably thought it safer to wait for that somewhere else. We need to return to the house so we'll be there when the ransom demand is delivered."

Gallio drew a deep breath and straightened. "Let's go."

As they trudged back up the street, they came once more to the litter.

Aulus stopped beside it and stroked the cushion where Julia usually reclined. "We need to take this home. She'll need it when we get her back."

Gallio nodded. "Vilicus. Take Dacius's pole."

Vilicus's jaw dropped, then snapped shut into a scowl. "I'm overseer. Taurus should carry it."

Gallio raised his hand, silencing him. "He's too tall. You're the right height. You can carry it this time."

Fury flamed in Vilicus's eyes as his jaw clenched. "Yes, steward." His tone oozed anger.

Taurus tightened his lips and froze his face. "Ready the litter."

Vilicus joined the other three down on one knee.

"Lift." Taurus walked to the front of the litter. When Vilicus could only see his back, his smile leaked out. With a flick of his hand, the big German started them home.

Aulus glanced at Marcus as they marched beside Taurus. The serenity of his friend's face was inexplicable, unless he'd made special plans with the kidnapper in case something unexpected happened. The escort wasn't meant to die. Marcus was right that the man they hired couldn't keep her there with a dead body, so maybe he'd only taken her somewhere else for a while. Somewhere safe, and maybe he'd have her back at the house at the agreed-upon time for Aulus to rescue her.

He fought to swallow. Then again, maybe not.

Servilia's shop

Dacius had been dozing fitfully, finding blessed relief from the pain in the short periods of sleep. As he awoke once more, his mind drifted back to his prayer time the night before.

One corner of his mouth curved. His conversation with Glyptus at breakfast seemed so long ago. When Taurus left, he'd thought the day might be special because he'd get to spend it with his horses. Or maybe because Glyptus was asking about his god and he'd finally get to tell his friend about Jesus. Would that ever happen now?

Or maybe...

Was all this the special thing You had for me, Lord? A chance to save Mistress Julia from her brother?

Maybe the special thing was the end of his life as a slave...freed by death to enjoy true freedom forever with Jesus. Lord Jesus himself had said to follow His teaching. Then he would know the truth, and the truth would set him free.

I've loved her like you commanded, Lord, enough to give up my life for her. I know Your truth. Are You setting me free?

He waited for an answer with his eyes closed. God's warm presence embraced him, even in the midst of his pain, but no answer that he could understand came.

His eyelids cracked open, and his gaze fell upon Mistress Julia.

But if I die now, who will care for her until her father returns? Please, God, let it be Your will to leave me here to help her get home.

Her gaze met his. "Did you want something, Dacius?" Even whispering, her voice seemed musical.

The mistress was watching over him? He managed a smile.

"A drink, mistress. If you please." What he really wanted, only God could give him.

She rose and glided over to the pitcher of watered wine. She poured some in the cup and returned to kneel beside him.

"There's a roll, too. Would you like half?"

He kept his eyebrow from rising. "Thank you, mistress, but you should eat it."

Her warm hand slid behind his neck and raised his head. She placed the cup against his lips, and he rested his own hand on hers to guide it as he drank. It smelled of roses, and its softness felt good against his calloused palm. He looked into her eyes, and the gentle kindness there made him glad he'd saved her, no matter what it cost him.

He finished the cup, and she lowered his head to the pillow.

"Thank you, mistress." It was easy to remember to whisper so no one outside would hear. It took too much effort to do anything else.

"Rest now, Dacius. You need to get your strength back for the trip tonight."

"Yes, mistress." He closed his eyes and once more asked God to dull the pain and give him sleep.

Chapter 18

THE RANSOM

The Secundus villa

Lunchtime passed, and the ransom demand had not arrived. Aulus sat beside Marcus in the peristyle, watching Gallio pace.

The steward rubbed the back of his neck. "It's been hours since she was taken." He glared at Marcus. "Maybe we should have stayed and searched the neighborhood. Someone must have seen something when they took her away from the house."

Marcus frowned. "Maybe, but I can't believe that would have been a better choice. It took almost an hour for the slaves to get back here, at least that long for us to get down there. Plenty of time for them to conceal her somewhere well away from where they seized her. Any low-class person can disappear in that part of Rome, and no one is going to tell an equestrian or senator where one of their own is hiding." He ran his fingers through his hair. "Not without money changing hands, and anytime you pay someone, they're as likely to lie as not just to get that money."

Gallio's shoulders sagged, and he rubbed his mouth. "But we've got to do something to find her and soon. What if they didn't take her for ransom?"

Aulus's breathing sped up, and he fought to slow it down.

Marcus's lips tightened. "I suppose that's possible, but they could never sell her for as much as they can get as ransom. It would be stupid to try. They must know she's the daughter of a former consul. At least that litter slave did. Surely they expect they can get a small fortune from you to get her back. She'd never bring more than three or four thousand denarii as a slave, if even that."

"Steward Gallio!" The rapid slaps of sandals echoed in the atrium before the door slave burst into the room. "A boy just delivered this." He held out a hinged wax tablet.

Gallio snatched it from his hand and opened it. His eyebrows plunged as he read it.

Aulus rose and strode to his side. "What does it say?"

"It's asking for 12,000 denarii for her safe return...with her escort." Gallio's mouth curved down. "How can they offer the safe return of a dead man?"

Aulus opened his mouth but closed it without speaking. Marcus had written the note and arranged its delivery before everything started going sideways.

The steward's frown deepened. His eyes flipped between Aulus and the tablet as he scanned the rest. "It says you must bring the money alone, all in aurei and in two cloth sacks."

Gallio drew a deep breath and blew it out slowly. "I have that much in the strong box." His brow furrowed as he read on. "You're to wear no toga or cloak so you can't hide a weapon. It says to start from the Baths of Trajan in three hours and walk down the Clivus Suburanus. Keep walking toward the Forums. Somewhere along that route, someone will take the money. Then she and the escort will be released and sent back to us within two hours."

The steward ran his fingers through his hair. "It says if anyone follows you or tries to interfere, they'll slit her throat and toss her body in the Tiber."

With tightened lips, Aulus nodded. "We'll do exactly what it says. No amount of money is worth Julia dying, and I don't care if we catch the kidnappers as long as we get her back safely." He bit his lip. "So, that's about 500 coins. That's less than, what...ten or fifteen *librae*? I can carry that with no problem. We can have her home in no more than five hours."

Gallio's lips disappeared when he tightened them. "If they intend to keep their word after killing the escort." One deep breath, and he forced it out through his nose. "But I don't see that there's any choice."

Aulus's throat tightened at those words. Marcus had planned to meet him somewhere along the route to get the ransom and take it back to his house. Then Marcus would meet the man he'd hired to pay the second 150 denarii and tell him to send her and the escort home. But with the old man dead and her not being at the empty rental house that belonged to Marcus's father, where could she possibly be? Would the man still meet Marcus to get the second half of his payment and tell Marcus where she was so he could go get her?

His stomach twisted. What if the man didn't appear at all and something terrible happened to her?

He focused his eyes on Gallio, hoping the steward didn't see the guilt there. "Get the money ready." He turned to Marcus. "Go with me as far as the baths. I know I must go the rest of the way alone, but until I start down into Subura..."

Marcus slapped his arm. "I know. Some things are best done with a friend."

In almost no time, Gallio returned with the money divided into two plain cloth bags and a gladius.

Aulus took the money but held up his hand when Gallio offered the sword. "No. He might not approach me if he sees I'm armed."

Gallio held out the gladius again. "It's for Marcus so no one will rob you before you get to the baths."

Marcus took the sword and slung the strap across his chest. "We can ride to my house, and I'll walk you to the baths from there."

Aulus squared his shoulders. "Let's go."

The two men strode to the stable. Marcus had left his stallion saddled and in the empty stall farthest from the gate because no stable slave had appeared when he arrived. Aulus saddled the gray mare himself since the stable slave was still absent.

Side by side, they trotted out the gate, heading for the Porta Esquilinas, the closest entrance through the city wall. As the gate closed behind them, Aulus's heart rate ramped up. "What if he doesn't meet you? What if he's done something horrible to Julia already?"

Marcus shook his head. "He seemed like an honest man. He's probably just moved her somewhere to get her away from that corpse. I'll lock the money in the strongbox in my room. Then I'll go to the agreed place right away and wait for him. There's no reason to assume the worst."

Aulus's head snapped back. "No reason? The man you hired was willing to break Roman law by holding her hostage. He's already killed her escort. Why do you think he won't break his word to you and not show up?"

Marcus's face turned grim. "I have to hope I'm right until we know otherwise." His jaw clenched. "If I'm wrong...then we'll hunt until we find her."

"But where? We have no idea where he and that litter slave could be."

"No, but I'll figure it out." He rested his hand on Aulus's shoulder. "Somehow, we'll get her back."

Aulus rolled his eyes and took several deep breaths until he could respond calmly. "We'd better, Marcus. How can I live with myself if I've killed my sister?"

"I'm sure she's alive. They wouldn't have killed her. There's no advantage to them in that." He squeezed Aulus's shoulder before lowering his arm. "And against the two of us, an old, retired soldier and a slave don't have a chance."

Aulus's shoulders sagged. "I pray to the gods you're right."

Chapter 19

STILL HER PROTECTOR

Servilia's shop

The afternoon dragged by. With her arms wrapped around her legs and her cheek resting on her knees, Julia tried to doze. But every time sleep crept up on her, Dacius's breath would catch, and the whispered groan as he released it awoke her.

A blade of light sliced into her eyes, and Julia turned her head away from the door. Servilia stepped inside and pushed the door mostly closed before coming to kneel beside Dacius.

The shopwoman rested a hand on his arm. "Dacius?" Her voice was a near-whisper.

His eyelids cracked open, and a slow smile appeared. "I haven't tried to leave without asking you."

She rested her palm on his forehead before running her fingers through his hair. "That's good." Her smile came quicker than his. "How are you feeling?"

Julia felt the tears trying to escape again. Her fingertip swept the corner of her eye before the moisture there could betray her.

But his eyes still swiveled from Servilia to her before he answered. "Maybe a little better."

Servilia's eyes turned on her as well. "Has Julia given you everything you need?"

His eyes started to drift shut, but he blinked a few times, and they stayed open. "Yes. Everything."

Servilia stroked his cheek with her thumb. "It's only a few more hours until Gaius comes, and a couple more after that until you'll be at the farm. Marcella knows how to take care of wounded young men. You'll feel much better after you get to her."

He drew a breath and blew it out through pursed lips. "Looking forward to that."

She patted his arm. "Rest now. It won't be long."

One corner of his mouth turned up. "God's kind hand is still upon me." His eyes drifted closed.

Julia's hand shot to her mouth, and her eyes asked Servilia the question she was afraid to speak aloud.

The shopwoman smiled and patted her arm as well before rising. Then, without a word, she left the room and closed the door.

The faint light coming through the small window faded to dusk. A low rumble came through the doors, punctuated by angry male voices. That drew Julia's smile. The wagons were starting to move through Rome. Soon the farmer should come, and someone who knew how to care for his wounds would help Dacius.

The door opened half-way, and Servilia made several trips carrying stacks of folded rugs and blankets.

Finally, the shopwoman stood beside Julia. "I'm going to lock up the shop with you inside. Then I'll go find Gaius. As soon as I can, I'll bring him back here to get you."

Her gaze settled on Dacius, and her smile dimmed. "No need to awaken him until it's time to go."

She rested her hand on Julia's shoulder and squeezed. "It won't be long now.

Julia glanced at Dacius. "I hope so. He needs help as soon as possible."

After one more squeeze and a smile, Servilia left the room, leaving the door partly open behind her.

◆

Dacius grew dimly aware of some motion around him. He heard the distant voice of Servilia as she told Julia where she was going. He was fully awake to hear the iron rods sliding into the rings of the shutters as Servilia closed her shop for the evening.

He turned his head to find the mistress watching him. He swept his left hand to encompass what lay around them.

"I beg pardon, mistress...for all this. I wanted to get you to a friend who'd protect you." His hand fell back to his side.

"None of this is your fault. I don't know what would have happened to me without you today. You're the only one who came to help me."

"I should protect you until your father returns." He shook his head once. "I might not be able to."

"Yes, you can. We'll be at the farm soon, and we'll be safe there. After you heal, you'll protect me again."

His ears caught the quaver in her voice.

He took a deep breath and released a deeper sigh. Even in the darkened room, everything looked…sparkly.

God, is this what it feels like to be dying? He focused on her frightened face. *I'm ready to be with You, Jesus, but…what will happen to her when I die?*

◆

Julia's heart raced. He should have said "yes, mistress" or something, like he always had before. His silence drove daggers of fear into her. His eyelids started to drift shut.

"Dacius." His eyes focused on her again. "You will heal there, and you will keep taking care of me." She tried to sound commanding, but the tremor in her voice ruined it.

"I'll try, mistress."

They were quiet words. Words like slaves say when they don't want to upset the master. He didn't look like he thought he could do what she told him.

"No. You're not going to try. If I want it done, you're going to do it."

One corner of his mouth turned up. He still didn't say "yes, mistress."

His eyes closed. She swallowed hard. What was going to happen if he didn't get better, if he couldn't take care of her?

She wrapped her arms around herself. What would happen if he died?

Chapter 20

NOT ACCORDING TO PLAN

Subura

Once they passed through the city gate, Marcus and Aulus took the shortest route to the Baths of Trajan and past them to the Fagutal district on the western end of the Oppian Hill. When they rode through the gate into the Drusus stable yard, two slaves scurried over to take their horses.

Marcus swung his leg over his stallion's neck and slid to the ground. He flipped his reins to the slave and waited for Aulus to dismount. "First a small matter in my room."

Aulus followed him into the house. Marcus waved Aulus into his room ahead of him, then closed and latched the door. In the corner stood a cabinet carved with hunting scenes. He retrieved a key from a hidden ledge under his bedside table before opening the cabinet doors to reveal a small chest built into the bottom.

He knelt to unlock it and held out his hand for the money bags. He placed them inside, rearranged the contents so the lid would shut and lock, and returned the key to its hiding place.

"That part's taken care of. Now we get Julia."

Aulus shifted his weight from foot to foot. "But how do we do that? Nothing's gone according to plan yet."

"That's not quite true. The ransom note was delivered, and Gallio gave us the money."

Aulus threw his hands up. "But Julia's gone! Where is she? How do we get her back? Not one part of what was supposed to happen to her has gone like we planned."

"No, it hasn't." Marcus rubbed his forehead. "But that doesn't mean it won't work out. I told her kidnapper you'd come to fake a fight with him at the house. He'd pretend to run away and then come get his second payment from me. Maybe he's still expecting that to happen." He massaged his neck. "So, you need to go to the house, and I need to go to the taberna where we were to meet."

Aulus's breaths came fast. "But the escort wasn't supposed to die, the litter slave wasn't supposed to be in league with the man you hired, and he was supposed to keep her at the house."

Marcus placed his hand on Aulus's upper arm. "True. Maybe it would be better if I go with you. Julia won't be surprised to see me helping you, and him running at the sight of two of us makes more sense."

Aulus's fast nods...those were all Marcus needed to see Aulus's fear start to fade.

He slapped his friend's arm as he took his hand away. "Let's go get her."

As they left the house and headed for the Clivus Pullius, the shortcut from the baths atop the hill to Subura in the valley below, Marcus kept his face optimistic. But inside, the serpent of doubt twined around his mind and tightened its coils.

Aulus kept them at quick-march down the hill and through the narrowing streets. As they reached the place where Julia's litter had been abandoned, he gripped Marcus's arm and froze. His own arm shot out, his finger pointing at a red splotch on the pavement.

"Was that there before?" He grabbed the back of his neck with both hands. "It looks like blood."

"I didn't see it." Marcus knelt and drew his fingertip across the patch. He sniffed his finger and rubbed it with his thumb. "Whatever it is, it's been here long enough to dry. Might be blood, but it might not."

"What if it's Julia's?"

Tightened lips accompanied the shake of Marcus's head. "It's not. Her bearers said they carried the litter here after they found she'd disappeared."

"That's what they said, but how do we know they told the truth? Taurus didn't think that was possible."

"Why would they lie about it? I know slaves lie all the time, but usually it's for a reason. Gallio's not blaming them for what happened. They don't gain anything by lying."

Marcus stood. "Let's go."

Another couple of blocks and they entered the stable yard. Marcus's hand gripped the hilt of his gladius as they entered the vestibulum. He crept forward to peek into the atrium. Then he stepped through the doorway, motioning Aulus to follow.

The body was gone, so the Urban Cohort must have already examined the scene and taken it. But had Julia and her captors returned?

"Let's see if they're back or if they left us a message about where she is." Marcus's voice was scarcely above a whisper.

They searched the peristyle garden and the rooms off it, then climbed the stairs to search the rooms off the atrium balcony. With each dust-coated and empty room, Aulus's heart sank lower.

Back in the atrium, Aulus picked up a wadded-up cloth by the wall where Taurus had said something had swept away the dirt. "Julia would never use something this dirty. It must be his." He crunched it in his hand and hurled it away from him. It landed in the scum-coated pool.

He held his head between his palms and pushed until his head hurt. "Oh, Marcus! What are we going to do?"

Marcus raised his palms. "Calm down, and let's think about this. He would have taken her away from here, but probably not too far. No way for us to guess where that is, so no point in us looking right now. He has your slave to leave guarding her, so he can still meet me for payment." Marcus squared his shoulders. "So, it's time for me to get to the taberna and wait for him, and time for you to go home—"

"And do what?"

"Let me finish. Go home and tell Gallio someone met you to get the ransom and told you a message would come about where to get her back."

Aulus rolled his eyes. "No message will come, and you know it. Maybe the Urban Cohort can find them if they know his name."

Marcus's lips tightened. "We didn't exchange names. I thought it safer that way." His hand gripped Aulus's upper arm. "And we must not tell anyone we hired the man, or we'd be charged as kidnappers ourselves."

"We are kidnappers now that she's disappeared!" Aulus took several deep breaths. "But I can see you're right. I've never seen him, and neither of us know his name. Nothing we could tell them would help."

He closed his eyes and rubbed his forehead. "I trusted you to pick the right man."

"I know, and I failed you. But we'll figure this out, and we'll get her back. Right now, I need to get to that taberna." Marcus's hand squeezed his arm. "It's a shorter walk back to my house if you come along. It's on the Vicus Sandaliarius, so you can take the short route past the Amphitheater and up the stairs to the baths."

"I could wait with you at the taberna."

"No, it's better if you go back to Gallio to wait for a message."

Aulus's eyebrows shot up. "But no message is coming."

"I might send one. I'll join you later, after I've met with the man and found out how to get Julia back. If I can fake the rescue myself, I'll get her and bring her home."

"And if he doesn't show?"

"Don't assume the worst until it happens."

Marcus started walking, and Aulus fell in beside him.

He kept telling himself not to assume the worst, that things might turn out better than he hoped. But no amount of optimism would save his sweet sister from the fallout of their stupid plan if the man who had her now was everything he feared.

A taberna near the Ludus Bruti

Marcus scooped the last bite of pork stew from the clay bowl. For a low-class taberna, the taste hadn't been too bad. He took another bite from the wedge of bread that came with the stew. It wasn't the fine bread he was used to, but it, too, was edible.

For three hours, he'd been waiting for Callidus to come and tell him where Julia was. Long enough for him to be forced to order two cups of cheap wine and then the stew if he wanted to keep sitting at the table in the back.

The sun was getting low. If he waited much longer, it would be dark enough to be dangerous to be in that part of Rome alone.

He stood with a sigh. Callidus wasn't coming, and he'd have to report to Aulus that Julia wouldn't be coming home that night.

His jaw clenched. And maybe never. He shook himself mentally. No, they would hunt, and they would find her. Callidus needed money. The only good reason to keep her would be to sell her, and if he did, there would be some trail of where she went.

He walked briskly until he reached the Amphitheater and started up the stairs to the Fagutal. A laughing group of drunken men jostled each other on the stretch just ahead. Hand on his gladius, he stepped aside to let them pass.

It was deep dusk when he reached the Drusus stable. A snap of his fingers and pointing at his stallion made the stable slave scurry to get the horse ready. The moon would be close to full. Plenty of light for a ride to the Secundus villa.

For a moment, he considered waiting until morning. That would give one more chance for him to check the taberna to see if Callidus would show or at least leave some message for him.

But that was a fool's dream, and he was no fool.

He jumped to toss his leg across the stallion's back and trotted through the gate.

Real men made decisions and then took action. Callidus had played him and betrayed him. It was time to face Aulus with the bad news and then figure out what to do next to get Julia back.

The Secundus villa

Aulus sat across from Gallio, drumming on the ransom tablet with a stylus, while Gallio sat with his elbows on his desk, face buried in his hands.

The steward turned desperate eyes on Aulus. "It's been hours since you paid the ransom. When was that message supposed to come?"

Aulus massaged his neck. "He didn't say exactly. Soon."

Gallio stood and began to pace. "It's already long past soon."

The slap of sandals in the atrium drew both set of eyes. When Marcus strode into the room, Aulus's breath caught. A single small shake of Marcus's head, and Aulus's heart spiraled down toward black despair.

"Any message yet?" Marcus settled into Gallio's empty chair and placed his palms on the desk.

Aulus's eyes saucered. He opened his mouth, then shut it when Marcus lifted his fingers and palms from the surface and offered a fleeting smile.

Gallio returned to the desk and leaned on his fists. "No. I need to contact the Urban Cohort immediately and tell them the kidnappers took the ransom but didn't return her."

Marcus stood and motioned for Gallio to take his own chair back. As the steward dropped into it, Marcus's face turned grave.

"It's definitely time for that." He turned to Aulus. "I need to put your father's gladius back. Join me."

As they entered his father's office, Aulus grabbed Marcus's arm and spun him to face him. "What am I going to do?" His heart pounded in his chest. He lowered his voice to a whisper. "I've killed my sister, Marcus. For 10,000 denarii, I've killed my sister."

Marcus placed his hands on Aulus's arms and gave him a quick shake. "No, you haven't. They aren't going to kill her. That soldier needed money, or he never would have taken the job. He'll sell her, and that means we can find her and get her back."

"But how? Neither of us knows anything about the slave trade. Where would we even start to look?"

Marcus's hands moved to Aulus's shoulders. "You and I don't know anything, but we don't have to. We know someone who knows the underbelly of Rome better than we ever could. It's time to talk with Brutus."

Chapter 21

HAND-OFF TO GAIUS

Servilia's shop

The faint light inside the room dimmed until Julia felt the darkness smothering her. Only the soft in and out of Dacius breathing gave her comfort. Her only way back to Father was still alive.

She sat close enough to touch him, even though she didn't. She had her feet tucked up under her floor-length tunic and her arms wrapped around her knees as she sat beside him. Even as weak as he was, knowing he was close to her in the darkness made it a little less frightening.

She finally heard the scratching of a key in a lock and the iron rods being drawn aside to free the door in the night shutters. The pale light of dusk burst into the room as the inner door swung open.

Servilia entered and pushed the door partly closed behind her, blocking the view of Dacius from outside. She knelt beside him and rested her hand on his uninjured shoulder. When he didn't stir, she shook him a little.

"Dacius? Time to wake up. Gaius is unloading now. Then he'll bring his wagon here. Do you think you can walk to it?"

She had cast Julia a quick glance and then ignored her while she spoke with her slave. That still felt odd, but Julia was relieved to have someone besides herself take charge.

Dacius's breathing quieted as he shook off the last remnants of sleep. "I can try, if someone helps me."

Servilia patted his arm. "Gaius is not so young anymore, but he's strong. Between the two of us, we can get you to the wagon."

Dacius rubbed his left hand across his eyes. "They might still be hunting my mistress. Any men out there you don't know? We can't let them see her. I couldn't stop anyone from taking her now."

She turned her gaze on Julia. "I already thought about that. I'll give her one of my tunics. She'll look like Gaius's daughter in it, not the noblewoman they're hunting. I have one of my husband's tunics for you, too. Yours smells too much like blood. It could betray you even in the dusk. I'll wash and mend it and send it out to you later."

"God bless you for all your help today."

"I'm glad He led you to me so I could." Servilia rested the back of her fingers on his cheek. "When you get to Marcella, tell her I wasn't able to clean your wounds. She'll take care of them better than I could here."

She rested her hand on Julia's knee. "Marcella will take care of both of you."

She opened a chest and drew out a plain woman's tunic and a pair of unadorned sandals. "These should help you get out of the city without being recognized."

◆

Dacius turned his head so he could watch the mistress. She looked more like a frightened little girl than a grown woman. She sat with her arms wrapped around herself, rocking slightly, as if she needed someone to hold her and tell her everything would be all right.

For the moment, he was the only someone available.

She stared at him with fear-filled eyes, eyes that begged him to take care of her. She made no move to take the tunic Servilia offered. It was not his place to tell Mistress Julia to do anything, but tonight she needed him to.

"Mistress, would you like to change now so we can go as soon as Gaius comes?"

She startled at his words, then shifted her eyes from him to Servilia and back. "Yes. Where should I go? I don't see any place...private."

He understood. He was a slave, but he wasn't a eunuch. A proper Roman maiden would never disrobe where one of her male slaves could watch.

He took the tunic Servilia had given him and draped it over his face. "The whole room is private now, mistress."

Servilia stood and offered Julia her hands. "Come over to the corner. I'll help you change quickly. The cart shouldn't stand in front of my shop too long. Just in case."

Dacius heard the rustling of fabric as Mistress Julia changed. Since the first time he carried her litter, he'd tried not to notice what a pretty woman she was. It was hard sometimes. She was willowy and moved with the grace of a dancer. The fine linen and softest wool of her tunics draped her elegant curves in a way that fired a man's imagination too much. And that day she slipped in the pool... It should be much easier once she was dressed in the rougher fabric of a working woman.

Anything that would help him keep her in the mistress box was welcome. His wounds had drained his strength, but God had spared his life...so far. If infection didn't kill him in the next few days, he'd have to stay close to protect her for almost a month.

He would never betray his Lord by yielding to sexual temptation, but it would be much easier if she were a homely old woman. There was no way to avoid looking at her pretty face when she spoke to him, but it should be easier to ignore the rest of her in a drab, loose-fitting tunic.

Servilia's voice reached his ears. "You can look now, Dacius."

He pulled the tunic down. Mistress Julia was dressed in a plain tunic of undyed wool, but it hadn't helped a bit. It draped her figure just as well as the fine linen. She actually looked better without the towering crown of curls made from slave hair. Her nut-brown hair flowed in waves across her shoulders, tempting a man to wrap it around his fingers and sniff the sweet perfume that always wafted around him as she rode the litter. She was still much too pretty. It would be a tempting month...if he lived.

That was beginning to seem more likely. The sparkles were gone, and he felt a little stronger than he had before Servilia locked them in.

Servilia came over and knelt beside him. "Now let's get you dressed." She slid her arm under his shoulders and helped him sit up. The room shifted as he tried to focus on the tunic in her hands. He looked down and closed his eyes. *God, I can't do this alone.*

"Reach up." Her voice slipped farther away. He wanted to obey, but his body didn't.

The voice came again. "Julia, come help me. Guide the tunic over his head and hands."

Rustling told him she had come to help. Servilia guided his right arm and he guided his left to a position where Mistress Julia could line up the openings with his head and hands and drop the tunic over them.

A man's voice forced his eyes open. "Servilia, are they ready?"

"Almost, Gaius. Come help me with Dacius."

A wiry man with gray hair stepped through the door. His face was wrinkled from long hours in the sun, which made it hard to tell if he was forty or sixty. He strode across the room and knelt on the other side of Dacius.

"I'm Gaius Sempronius Rutilus. Servilia told me you need a place to heal, so you're coming home with me. Let's get you and the young lady into the wagon, and we can be home in a little over an hour."

Dacius picked up his belt with his left hand and flipped it around his back. When he tried to use his right hand to fasten it, pain ripped through his shoulder. His teeth clenched.

Gaius rested his hand on Dacius's forearm. "I'll do that."

"God bless you for helping us, Gaius. My mistress needs a place to stay until her father returns to Rome in about a month. Can you shelter her that long?"

"You're both welcome to stay as long as you need." Gaius slid his hands under Dacius's arms and lifted him to a standing position. "Put your arm across my shoulder, and let's go."

With Gaius's arm wrapped around his back and a shoulder to lean on, he was able to take a step. But how many more to get to the cart? He wasn't good for too many. Some of the sparkles had returned.

God, please give me enough strength to at least get her safely out of Rome.

◆

Servilia went out the door first to make sure no one was watching. Julia was right behind her. A four-wheel *plaustrum* with a team of mules stood before her. The back panel of the wooden box had been lifted and set aside for her and Dacius to get in.

After folding the blood-stained rug, she placed it on the wagon bed to soften the ride over the stone roads. Julia turned and hopped up to sit on the bed. Then she swung her legs in and scrambled forward to rest her back against the front wall.

Dacius had almost reached the wagon. She bit her lip as she watched him hobbling toward her with Gaius as his crutch. With each step, his head dipped lower. When they were only a few steps away, she patted the bed beside her.

"Put him here with me so I can cradle his head in my lap. He can lie on his side then to keep off his shoulder and thigh."

Dacius raised his eyes to hers. "You should be up on the seat, mistress. I shouldn't be in your lap."

"Hush. I'm your mistress, and I'll decide how we should travel. I'm staying back here to make sure you don't get hurt more."

She caught the twitch of Gaius's mouth. He probably thought it was funny for a slave to tell his owner not to take care of him. Well, he could laugh if he wanted. Dacius was hers, and after what he did today, it was only right that she look after him at least this much.

Servilia leaned across the wagon wall to whisper in her ear. "You want to be more careful, Julia. Don't talk about him being a slave where anyone can hear. You don't look like his owner anymore, and someone might try to take him from you. They could get a good reward for turning him in as a runaway. He'll die for certain if that happens. Don't tell anyone who you are, either. Someone tried to kidnap and sell you once. There might be another waiting to try again. Too many will do anything for a few denarii."

Julia's eyes widened, but she didn't speak. She hadn't thought about the danger to them both of just being where someone might hear her words for the next month.

Servilia handed Julia the sack of her own clothes and a blanket. "He's lost a lot of blood, so you should cover him and keep him warm. You can send the blanket back with Gaius when he no longer needs it. I'll wash the blood from his tunic and send that out to you."

She patted Julia's arm. "I'll be praying for you both."

Julia nodded her thanks, but what could praying do?

The men reached the wagon, and Gaius turned so Dacius could sit on the bed. As Gaius climbed into the wagon, Dacius's shoulders slumped, his chin dropped to his chest, and he started falling sideways. Gaius caught him before his head hit the sidewall.

Julia's hand shot up to cover her mouth. "Is he dead?" Her voice wavered. She held her breath.

"No. He's only passed out."

She blew the breath out. "Give him to me." She patted her lap.

Gaius pulled him up beside her and rolled him onto his left side. He shook out the blanket, and draped it over him. "It's better for him this way. The ride can be rough. It takes a little over an hour to get to the farm."

Gaius clambered out of the wagon, reloaded several empty chicken crates, and replaced the back gate. He climbed up onto the driver's seat and slapped the reins. With a jolt, the trip to their safe haven for the next month began.

As Julia cradled Dacius's head in her lap, she touched his cheek with her fingertip. He didn't stir. After the first light touch, she stroked it. It was prickly with stubble. There was something fascinating about the feel of him. She'd never been this close to a man who wasn't her father or brother before. And he was a man, even if he was a slave. He wasn't just a piece of furniture or an animal.

She'd treated him as nothing more than that since Gallio bought him. What could make a slave take the risk he had when she hadn't even let him speak to her? When she'd been repelled as if he were something disgusting? When she'd let the overseer lash him when he'd done nothing wrong? What inspired that kind of loyalty to someone who'd never even looked in your eyes and called you by name?

She pulled the blanket up a little to tuck it closer to his neck. Loyalty like his deserved a great reward, and she'd start by doing whatever she could to ease his pain on the way to the farm.

Chapter 22

Almost to Safety

With so many carts and wagons clogging the narrow streets, a snail might have beaten them in a race. Julia's nerves were stretched tighter than a lyre string before Gaius merged with the traffic on a broad street heading northeast.

He looked back over his shoulder. "We're on the Vicus Patricius now. This will take us straight to the Porta Viminalis. It will be slow until after we get through the city wall there. Then we'll make better time." Gaius faced forward when a string of curses erupted from the ox driver ahead of them.

Julia twisted to see what was going on. A wagon crossing the road at the side street ahead of them had lost part of its load of hay, and several men were helping the driver toss it back into his wagon bed.

Gaius turned back to her. "How is he?"

She pulled the blanket closer to his chin. "He hasn't awakened." Her gaze flipped from Dacius's shuttered eyes to Gaius. "Should he have?"

Gaius's mouth turned down, but he shook his head. "Not necessarily. Servilia said he lost a lot of blood. That makes a man sleep. As long as he doesn't start bleeding again, he could be fine."

"Could be?" Julia swallowed the lump she couldn't keep from forming.

Gaius shrugged. "Servilia and I are praying for him, and God can heal anyone."

The crack of the ox driver's whip started the team ahead of them, and Gaius turned back to his mules. A snap of the reins, and they resumed their crawl toward the Porta Viminalis and the safety beyond it.

When they finally passed through the city wall, the view opened before them.

Gaius swept his hand toward the north. "That's the training field of the Praetorian Cohort. Ahead is the Castra Praetoria. Hadrian isn't in Rome, so many of the Guards are with him, but there are plenty left to keep things under control. The Urban Cohort is headquartered there, too."

As they drew closer to the towering gray walls of the Praetorian fortress, Julia couldn't keep her eyes off the many sepulchers that lined the road. Some were buildings of marble with ornate carvings, like that of the Julii Secundi off the Via Appia. Some were simple markers that proclaimed how someone loved the dead enough to erect a monument that might have cost more than they could afford.

Her gaze settled on Dacius's face. It looked peaceful with him sleeping. No clenched jaw, no scrunched eyes that had proclaimed his pain that afternoon.

A shadow passed over him, cast by a mausoleum with columns modeled after a Greek temple, a fitting memorial to noble ancestors.

But there were people who left no one who cared behind. For most slaves, their bodies would be burned, their ashes treated like trash and tossed away.

That might have been his fate before, but not now. She wiped at the corner of her eye. She'd make certain Father placed his ashes with those of her family and had a small plaque carved to preserve his memory as a man willing to give everything to save her.

She squared her shoulders. But it shouldn't come to that. He was going to survive this and take care of her. He would get her home to Father, and she'd make certain he was rewarded for his loyalty.

The wagon passed by the fortress and a stretch with more sepulchers. Finally, they were free of the reminders of death. A scattering of small buildings lined the road. Fields and vineyards stretched out beyond them.

Gaius turned on the seat. "The slow part is over. We're almost half way home. We'll take a side road off this one soon, and then it won't be long."

Julia offered him a weary smile. "Thank you for everything, Gaius."

He shrugged. "It's nothing. I'm glad Servilia came for my help." He turned his back and slapped the reins. The mules picked up the pace, and Julia was left in the silence with her thoughts.

Dacius awoke to the jolting of a wagon rolling over paving stones. That drew a smile. The long hours of darkness and pain were over...the darkness, at least. The moon was close to full.

Nothing hurt less, but at least they were on their way to a safe haven for Mistress Julia until her father returned. His left shoulder and thigh were bouncing on a hard surface, but his head rested on something warm and soft. A pillow—one more thing to be grateful to Servilia for.

And then it moved.

His eyes shot open. The mistress's lap. That was the last place he wanted his head. He tried his best to avoid thinking of her as a woman. That was hard, and resting his head on her lap made it even harder.

He shifted his left arm under him until he could push himself up to a sitting position.

"What are you doing?" Her words sounded more censure than question.

"I beg pardon, mistress. I didn't mean to touch you. I don't know how—"

"I had Gaius put you there when you passed out. The road's rough, and I don't want you hurt more."

"But it isn't right for a slave to rest his head in his mistress's lap."

"Lie back down. You need to rest." Her voice has softened to the tone she used with her nieces, but that just made it worse. She was escaping the mistress box.

"It's not right, mistress." She opened her mouth as if to argue. He needed a different reason. "I need to sit up. I should be watching for the kidnappers."

She closed her mouth and tilted her head. "I'm not sure that's necessary. We've come a long way from Servilia's shop."

A quick glance around him revealed fields past small buildings scattered along the road. "Yes, mistress, but what if they set a watcher at the city gate and saw you?"

Her eyes widened. "I hadn't thought of that." The pitch of her voice rose. "Would they do that?"

He hadn't meant to frighten her. "Probably not, but just in case...I want to watch."

"Then I guess I should let you sit up. If you feel well enough, that is."

Just pushing into a sitting position had drained his energy, and shifting to get his back against the cart wall drove daggers into his leg and shoulder. Feel well enough? Not at all, but the alternative was having his head in her lap, and that made her seem too much like a pretty woman instead of the mistress. He'd rather fight pain and exhaustion than temptation.

A faint scent of roses still surrounded her, and his side that was near her felt warmer than the side farther away. She was too close, too much like a woman sitting right next to him.

As he leaned back against the front of the wagon, he tried to keep his eyes open. Open and looking away from her. For a few minutes, he succeeded. Then his eyes started drifting shut. He tried shaking his head a little, but he didn't dare shake it as much as needed for fear she'd notice. The jostling as the wheels rolled across the paving stones helped, but not enough.

His eyes closed; his chin lowered to his chest.

When he jerked awake, his head was on her shoulder. "I beg pardon, mistress. I didn't mean to touch you."

"It only happened because you dozed off. You're not watching at all."

"I beg pardon. I'll try harder to stay awake and watch."

"No, you won't. It's ridiculous for you to be sitting up when you need to sleep. Lay your head back in my lap."

"But—"

"Don't argue with me, Dacius. When I tell you to do something, you're supposed to just do it."

He drew a deep breath. She was right. Despite the temptation from lying in the lap of a pretty young woman, he had to obey his mistress... as long as what she commanded didn't put her in danger. His head in her lap wasn't a danger to her, only a temptation for him.

"Yes, mistress."

She shifted her legs to make a better lap, and he lowered himself into it.

She pulled the blanket back over him. "Now, close your eyes and sleep like you need to."

He obeyed. His breathing slowed as he relaxed. This was no worse than sitting close beside her. Even sitting, she'd seemed too much woman, too little mistress.

Then she began playing with his hair, as if he were a lap dog.

He'd forgotten how good that felt. In the days before Rome ended his childhood, his sister Ariana used to do it. She was only five years older than him, but she liked to mother him anyway. When he had trouble getting to sleep and sometimes even when he didn't, she would sit on the bed beside him. Her fingertips made spirals and circles on his temple, and she would run her fingers into his hair as she hummed.

The smile those memories brought drooped, then vanished.

Ariana—he never saw her again after she and his younger sister Roanna were dragged off with the other girls to be sold.

On the slave ship to Rome, he'd longed to know where she was, what she was doing. When he was sold to his first owner, that changed. He saw firsthand what happened to pretty young slaves in that household. Longing turned to dread. And now, twelve years later, all he could do was pray that somehow Ariana and Roanna had found their ways to kind masters. It was possible...no matter how unlikely. Roman men were almost never kind.

He opened his eyes to gaze up at the mistress. *Thank you, God, for letting me spare her from my sisters' fate.*

She actually smiled down at him. "Close your eyes. I want you to sleep. You'll get better faster if you do."

"Yes, mistress." His eyelids shut, as ordered. Her fingers kept brushing his forehead and temple and pulling through his hair. The kindness the mistress showed her nieces was for him tonight, and he relaxed as the soothing fingers kept moving.

God, please heal me so I can get her safely back to her father. I couldn't help my sisters. Let me finish helping her.

He drifted off.

◆

Julia heard his breathing slow and felt his weight settle into her lap as he dozed off.

Her friends would be appalled to see her cradling a litter slave, stroking his hair to comfort him. Menial slaves were nothing more than living furniture in their households.

That was what he'd been to her before that morning. Just a slave who did what she needed without speaking or intruding more than was necessary. She was aware of a common slave's absence sometimes, but almost never of his presence.

But that was different now. Dacius had rescued her.

He was all that stood between her and her horrible brother until Father came home. Only he knew how to get her home after Father returned.

Servilia said Gaius's wife knew how to care for him. Good, but she would take care of him, too. He had to get better. Everything depended on it.

Her hand moved to his bristly jaw. Her thumb stroked his cheekbone, but there was no sign he felt it.

She blinked back tears as she gazed on his plain face with its slightest trace of a smile. He had to get better, but it wasn't only because she needed him. Someone as brave and loyal as he was shouldn't have to die because he came to save her.

Chapter 23

Safe at Last

Gaius's farm northeast of Rome

The moon bathed the countryside in silver as the wagon finally followed the dirt track into a farmyard. For the first time since Julia had entered the filthy atrium behind the kidnapper, the last trace of tension drained from her body.

Safe at last.

Then her eyes turned down onto the man who'd made that possible. "Dacius, we're here."

He didn't move, and her neck muscles tensed again. She rested her fingers on his cheek and patted. His deep breathing turned shallow, and his eyes opened.

"We're at the farm."

"That's good, mistress. You'll be safe now."

"We'll be safe now."

One corner of his mouth turned up.

As Gaius climbed down, the door of the cottage flew open, and a woman with a lamp stood in the doorframe. Gaius started toward her, and she hurried over to meet him.

"You're so late. I was starting to worry."

Julia's eyebrow rose. The woman's voice carried no worry in it.

Her smile seemed worry-free as well. "God gave me a sense that something wasn't right, and I've been praying that all would be well."

Gaius placed his palm on her cheek. "All is well with me, but Servilia needed my help for a young couple. It took a while to get to her shop and then out of town. Julia needs a place to stay for a month or so, and Dacius is hurt."

With her arm threaded around her husband's, the farmer's wife approached the wagon, smiling at Julia. "I'm Marcella. Welcome to our home."

Marcella's sharp intake of breath when she looked over the wall and saw Dacius sent Julia's heart rate higher.

Gaius's wife turned to him. "We need to move a bed into the main room. He'll need close watching."

"I'll move one of the girl's beds in there now." Gaius headed into the house.

Marcella reached across the wagon wall to place her hand on Julia's arm. "I'm going to help him get the bed set up." Her gaze dropped to Dacius's face. "Let him rest until we're ready for him." She walked back to the open door.

Dacius shifted his left arm under him and started to push himself up.

Julia's gaze returned to his face. "Don't do that. You're not to move until Gaius returns to help you."

"Yes, mistress." He dropped his head back in her lap and closed his eyes.

She nibbled her lip. He'd objected to lying in her lap both times before, so why no argument this time? But maybe he'd only decided she was going to make him do it, no matter what he said.

The blanket had fallen from his shoulders when he tried to rise. She tucked it back around him.

It was only a few minutes before Marcella returned with Gaius in tow. As he was removing the back gate and then the chicken crates, Marcella stood beside Julia.

"Is he your husband or betrothed?"

Dacius opened his eyes and then his mouth.

Julia patted his cheek. "Don't try to talk." She paused before answering herself. Servilia had warned her not to tell anyone who she was. She didn't know what Servilia might have considered safe to tell Gaius. Gaius's wife probably posed no danger, but...

"No, but we live in the same neighborhood, and he always takes care of me when I need help. He got hurt rescuing me from kidnappers, and I'm afraid to go home yet."

Marcella's welcoming smile made her caution seem rather foolish. "You can stay as long as you need. It will be some time before he can travel back to Rome."

Servilia had stressed one thing that the farmer's wife must be told.

"Servilia told me you should know she wasn't able to clean his wounds. She said you'd know what to do."

"As soon as we get him inside, I'll take care of that."

Gaius led the mules as close to the house as he could. Then he scrambled into the wagon, slipped his hands under Dacius's arms, and lifted him to his feet. Marcella moved to the rear. Three small steps, and Gaius had him at the edge. She lifted his legs as Gaius lowered him to sitting on the wagon bed. She steadied him as Gaius hopped out. Then he got Dacius's left arm wrapped around his shoulder again and served as the crutch as the two men moved slowly toward the open door with Marcella right beside them.

Julia's hand flew to her mouth. That had been hard for Dacius when they loaded the wagon. It looked like sheer misery for him now.

She scooted to the edge of the wagon and hopped out. By the time she reached the entrance, they had Dacius lying on a narrow bed along the wall across from the door. His eyes were closed, but a slight smile showed he was conscious. Maybe it hadn't been as bad as it looked.

Marcella sat on the bed beside him. "I'm sorry, but we have to clean those wounds before you can sleep."

That half smile appeared as his gaze focused on Gaius's wife. "Do whatever you must. It's not going to make my day any worse than it already has been."

A kettle of water was steaming over the fire. Marcella carried it to the rough wooden table and poured some into a basin. She'd already placed some soap and wash rags, a pitcher of wine, and a small canister beside it.

"First your shoulder, then your leg." Gaius supported Dacius in a sitting position. She started unwrapping the bandage Servilia had applied, but she turned at Julia's footsteps. "You can help me by holding the basin while I wash around the wound."

Julia swallowed hard. She'd almost fainted helping Servilia, but he must have stopped bleeding long ago. "Just tell me what to do."

As the last wrap fell away, Dacius reached across and held the brownish red pad in place. Julia turned her eyes away.

"Spread that towel behind him. I want him on his back for this."

Julia managed to avoid looking at his shoulder as she complied.

Marcella brought her the basin of warm water and dipped a rag in it. Then she began wiping the area near the wound with the wet cloth. Between wipes, she dipped it in the basin.

At first, Julia kept her eyes on the bowl, but each dip put swirls of blood in the water. Her head started to swim, so she squeezed her eyes shut. Then curiosity drove her to look again. Swirling ribbons of blood were a problem, but there was enough in the basin that it was a uniform red now. That wasn't so bad.

Then she made a huge mistake. Her gaze shifted from the bowl to his shoulder. It had started bleeding again with the cleaning. The whole room started to spin. She barely got the basin set on the floor without spilling it before she dropped to the floor and sat with her head resting against her knees.

Dacius turned his head toward her. "Are you well, mistress?"

"Yes. It's just the blood. It always does this to me, especially when I haven't eaten in a while."

She locked her gaze on his calm gray eyes.

Understanding filled them. "Don't try to help if it's too hard."

Marcella looked at her. "You can do this, Julia. He needs you to. I need more than two hands here."

Dacius's gaze never moved from Julia. "I can help."

Marcella shook her head. "You shouldn't even try. She can do it. It will get easier as she does." She held a hand out to Julia. "Come on, dear. I need you back here."

Julia rose and picked up the basin. She stepped back over beside Marcella and averted her eyes. As long as she stared at the ceiling, she was fine. There was no blood up there.

Marcella looked up at Julia. "You can put the basin on the table until I tend his leg. But first..." Her gaze returned to Dacius. "Some wine for cleaning and honey to start the healing. I'm afraid the wine will hurt."

His jaw twitched "I've had water, wine, and honey on wounds before." He blew his breath out through pursed lips. "Sometimes it takes more pain to start the healing." He forced a smile at Marcella. "The sooner you start, the sooner it's over."

Julia looked away. The stripes from when Vilicus lashed him—they were her fault, too. She heard him suck air between his teeth as Marcella dribbled wine into the knife wound. A deep sigh released that breath.

"Finished with the honey. Now I just need to rewrap you, and then I'll do your leg." Marcella's calm voice brought Julia some comfort. The arrow had pierced both sides of his leg, but at least a third of the cleaning was over.

As Marcella treated his leg, Julia again held the basin and counted the knots in the planks that made the ceiling. Relief surged through Julia at Dacius's next deep sigh.

"All finished." The relief in Marcella's voice matched her own.

Gaius had gone to attend to the mules when Marcella started on the leg, and he returned as his wife finished. As he bolted the door, Marcella embraced him with her smile. "It's so late. You must all be hungry. Bread and cheese tonight, but I'll feed you well tomorrow." Her hand swept toward the table. "Sit."

She withdrew some hard cheese and bread from a cupboard as Gaius and Julia settled into the chairs.

The sight of the crusty bread and cheese fired Julia's appetite more than a banquet at home. She'd eaten nothing except Servilia's small roll since breakfast, and her mouth watered at the prospect of quieting her murmuring stomach.

Marcella cut some cheese slices for Dacius and carried those and some bread to his bedside.

His eyes opened when she sat beside him and offered him the bread. He took it in his left hand. "Thank you." After he took the first bite, his eyes closed. His chewing slowed, then stopped.

Marcella tapped his uninjured shoulder. "Dacius. Stay awake."

His eyes reopened with several fast blinks. He started chewing again, only to have his jaw slow and stop. With a jerk, he awoke and swallowed.

She took the bread from his hand. "You need rest more than food at the moment. I'll give you a good breakfast in the morning."

He nodded, and she spread Servilia's blanket over him. Then she ran her hand lightly through his hair and rested her palm on his cheek.

Julia's brow furrowed. Just like Servilia, Marcella was showing him affection like a mother would her own son, even though he was a total stranger.

Marcella placed her palm on his forehead. "Dear Lord, keep Dacius in Your loving care this night. Take his pain and give him rest. Thank You for bringing him to us in this time of need. Please heal him quickly, and restore him completely. We ask this in the name of Your Son, our Lord Jesus. Amen."

Gaius's "amen" came from beside Julia, and Dacius whispered the word as well.

Julia's breath caught. Marcella and Gaius were Christians. So was Dacius. She knew the emperor didn't approve of them, but she knew only a little about them herself.

At a banquet with Aulus's friends, there had been mocking comments about how they were willing to die in the arena for some dead carpenter all because they didn't want to honor a living emperor with a little incense.

Someone had teased Marcus Drusus about his grandfather becoming a meal for the lions when he became a Christian. Marcus responded with scoffing remarks about them picking up exposed babies to raise as their own and not as slaves. He mocked them for being so stupid when they helped sick neighbors and even strangers when they could sicken and die themselves. His grandfather was a fool for becoming one, and his father was right for turning him in.

But Aemilianus claimed they were harmless. He didn't see why the emperor and some of the provincial governors were so hostile to them. Sabinus had argued they were dangerous fools whose rebellion couldn't be allowed, no matter how harmless they were as individuals.

Her jaw clenched, then relaxed. It was good that Christians picked up abandoned babies and helped sick people. These Christians had welcomed her wounded slave and her when they needed it most, no questions asked. She would never let anyone say anything bad about Christians in her presence again.

After Marcella settled into the chair between Julia and Gaius, she glanced at Dacius's sleeping form. "I'm thankful today was your trip to Rome, Gaius." She touched Julia's hand. "Thankful, too, that you found Servilia."

"Fortuna smiled on us when she took us in."

Marcella patted her hand before withdrawing her own to take the slice of cheese that Gaius offered her. "Not Fortuna, dear. God."

Julia smiled and said nothing more while Marcella and Gaius ate and talked.

When all had finished, Marcella rose. "You can sleep in what was our daughters' room before they married. Let's get you settled in. You must be tired."

Julia dredged up a weary smile. "Very."

Marcella led her into a short hallway and directed her into a room on the left that was no more than five feet wide and only a little deeper. A small window high over the single bed let the moonbeams dance on the wall. "Sleep well."

Julia bit her lip. "Will Dacius be all right?"

Marcella took her hand and squeezed. "The worst is over, and God will take care of him." She freed a curtain from a hook at the side of the door. "He'll take care of you both now."

As the curtain fell into place behind Marcella, Julia turned back the covers and lay down on the bed. She pulled the sheet up to her chin, and closed her eyes. It had been the worst day of her life, but somehow things would turn out all right. Dacius was still there to protect her, and he would get her home.

Chapter 24

CALANTHA, NOT MISTRESS

Day 20

Dacius still hadn't awakened when Julia scraped the last spoonful of breakfast porridge from her bowl.

"He needs to get some food in him." Marcella rose from the table. "I'd hoped he'd wake up on his own, but I guess I need to wake him."

She moved over to sit beside him on the bed. "Dacius. Time to wake up and eat."

Marcella ran her fingers through his hair several times before his eyes finally opened. "Ready for some porridge now?"

His smile came slowly. "I should be, but..." His voice started soft and faded away to silence.

She rested her hand on his cheek. "I know you're still weak, but I'll help you."

"I'll wait a while, if you don't mind." His eyes drifted shut again.

Julia's eyes moistened as she watched. He should have been stronger, not weaker than yesterday. He'd never get stronger if he didn't eat. But he was hers, and even if he wouldn't eat for Marcella, he'd have to eat for her.

She rose and scooped an ample serving from the pot. With the full bowl and a spoon, she walked to the bedside.

"Dacius, you won't get well if you don't eat. Marcella's porridge is very tasty, and I'm going to feed you a bowl of it."

Marcella rose and swept her hand toward the bed, inviting Julia to take her place.

His eyes opened wide when she sat beside him, and his lips parted as if to speak. She placed her finger across her lips.

"Hush. I know what you're going to say, and I'm not going to let you say it. You belong to me, and if I want to take good care of you right now, you shouldn't be telling me it's not something I should do."

She ran her fingers through his hair, as she had just seen Marcella do.

That trace of a smile appeared, and his eyes warmed as she did. "Yes, mistress."

"That's better." Julia scooped up a spoonful and held it to his lips. They parted again, but this time it was only to receive the spoon.

◆

If anyone had told Dacius two days ago that Mistress Julia would not only be looking into his eyes but caring for him herself, he would have asked if they'd broken into the wine stores. She was always ready to help her little nieces, but to help him like he was a man who mattered—that was beyond imagining.

Yet there she was, sitting beside him, her lips parting slightly with every spoonful she held to his lips, smiling at him as he swallowed each one.

He was dreadfully tired and not hungry at all, but he ate the whole bowl...for her.

Dacius had just swallowed the last spoonful when the shadow fell across him. A man was standing in the doorway. The stranger's eyes narrowed, and his gaze swept first Dacius and then the mistress. The smile that lifted the corners of his mouth was more leer than greeting.

Mistress Julia set the bowl on the floor and adjusted his blanket.

"Don't you feel better now you've eaten something? It's always best when you o—"

"I've had enough. You can go now."

◆

Julia's back straightened and her eyes saucered at his harsh tone and words of dismissal. No slave had ever spoken to her like that before.

"Rutilus?" The voice behind her was more growl than greeting.

Julia jerked as the surprise shot through her and transformed into fear. She twisted to stare at the man. His gaze swept over Dacius, lying helpless on the bed. Then his eyes scanned her and lingered as his gaze shifted from curious to lecherous. A shudder followed the cold chill that ran up her spine.

She scooted back on the bed until she felt Dacius's thigh against her hip

Dacius raised himself up behind her and rested his left hand on her shoulder. "What do you want with Rutilus?"

"I came to look at a ram, but that's a very pretty one. Is she for sale?"

"No, and she's never going to be."

Julia turned wide eyes on Dacius's face. His voice was forceful, his jaw set, his eyes serious. He'd been so weak a moment before; where had that strength come from?

The man hesitated as his eyes shifted between Julia and Dacius.

Marcella stepped through the door and slipped past the stranger to stand between him and the bed.

She greeted the man with a smile. "Can I help you?"

The stranger pulled his gaze away from Julia. "I came about a ram Rutilus has for sale."

Marcella swept her arm toward the door. "Please. Go ahead of me. I'll take you to Gaius."

After scanning Julia once more, he turned and led Marcella out the door.

◆

Dacius collapsed onto the pillow. It had taken all he had to bluff the stranger who'd threatened the mistress.

"I beg pardon for touching you that way, mistress." His voice was weak enough that Mistress Julia leaned over to hear his words. "I meant no disrespect. I had to make him think you belong to me. He'd come back otherwise."

"I know. You only protect me." She bit her lip. "He felt...dangerous."

"He might be. We must be more careful. What we say in front of Gaius and Marcella doesn't matter, but we are in hiding. Calling you mistress in front of that man, even acting like I'm your slave, could put you in danger. The wrong person could learn we're here, so I must stop. But I won't forget you're my mistress, even when I don't speak it."

Even those few words drained what little strength he had left, but he pressed on. "You shouldn't use your real name. Pick one for while we're here. Something common, not noble."

"I hadn't thought of that, but you're right." Julia rested her palm on her cheek. "Not noble? So maybe something like the name of Metilia's old nursemaid? Calantha. She's a freedwoman now, but does that sound too much like a slave name?"

"No, mistress. Calantha means beautiful flower. Free Greeks are named that, too."

His eyes focused on her face. She truly was a beautiful flower among her friends. So pretty, but also kind. Calantha was a good name for her.

"Free but not noble is good, don't you think?" She didn't wait for an answer. "It seems so odd to be changing my name. It's going to be hard to remember to answer to my new one."

"It's not hard. I expect a new name when I'm sold. A few days, and it seems like your own." He drew a deep breath. Talking so much had exhausted him, but for her own safety, she needed to know what he'd told her. He closed his eyes.

"So you haven't always been called Dacius?"

He struggled to open his eyelids. She wanted a conversation? She was the mistress, so...he must try.

"No, mistress."

"What else have you been called?"

"Diegis." *So long since I last heard it...through Ariana's sobs as the soldiers dragged her away.*

"That's an odd name, not Greek or Latin. Where does it come from?"

"Dacia."

"So that's why we call you Dacius?"

He nodded once.

"Have you always been a slave?"

"No."

"When did you become one?"

"When Trajan captured Sarmizegetusa...our capitol."

"You couldn't have been very old then."

"Eleven years." *Old enough to remember everything...but it's better not to.*

"Have you had many owners before my father?"

"Three."

"Were you a litter slave for your last mistress?"

"No."

"What were you before we bought you?"

"I trained horses and mules...on a large estate."

"So you were the one who calmed my brother's stallion when it killed my litter slave."

"Yes."

"The special food I sent out to reward you, did you like it?"

He nodded once. No need for her to know it was never given to him. It wasn't her fault if Vilicus ate it himself.

"Were you anything different before that?"

"Free."

Silence.

Please. No more questions. Let me rest. Even one-word answers had dragged the last shred of energy out of him. His eyelids drifted shut.

His last answer caused her discomfort. Conversation about things long past that could never be again pained him as well.

He forced his eyes open. Two fast blinks to keep them that way didn't help much. She wanted his full attention when she spoke to him, but try as he might…

"I beg pardon, mistress…I mean Calantha…I'm trying…but I can't stay awake."

He drew the deep breath he needed to continue. "But I do thank you…for helping me eat."

◆

Pity tugged at Julia's heart. With each blink, his eyes stayed closed longer.

"You saved me, Dacius. Of course I'm going to help you." His eyelids opened halfway. "If I change my name, we should change yours, too. What should I call you now?"

"You pick something…I'll answer…to anything you choose." His eyes didn't open after the next blink.

She gazed down at his ordinary face. Before yesterday, he'd been invisible to her. Now his unremarkable features were burned into her memory. Fatigue and pain were etched there only because he'd risked his own life for hers. He was so brave, fighting those horrible men to save her.

"I think Leander. Like a lion. That's how you fought for me. It fits you."

His eyes flickered open as the corner of his mouth twitched up. "Leander it is." Then they shut again.

She gazed down on him as his breathing slowed and he drifted off to sleep.

Leander. Yes, that fit him very well.

Chapter 25

The Stupidest Thing

The Secundus villa, Day 20

Aulus swallowed his mouthful of dried dates and swung his feet off the couch when Gallio entered the dining room. "Any news?"

Gallio's mouth turned down as he massaged his neck. "The tribune of the XI Urban Cohort is supposed to come first thing this morning. He'll be in charge of the effort to find Mistress Julia and catch her kidnappers."

Marcus rose from his couch. "I think Aulus and I should go see Antonius Brutus. Maybe he'll have some ideas about where someone might take her if they wanted to keep her hidden...or sell her when they don't have legal papers on her."

Gallio's jaw clenched. "I hate to think that's happened already, but we can't assume it hasn't."

"Brutus will want to help us find her if he possibly can. Not much happens in Rome that a ludus owner can't find out."

Gallio's shoulders drooped. "Go."

As Aulus walked toward the stable beside Marcus, his brow furrowed. "Why did you tell Gallio that?"

"He'd wonder why we left and where we went. Now he won't be asking questions we might not want to answer when we get back." He placed his hand on Aulus's shoulder. "Besides, we really are going to see Brutus. Never tell a lie when the truth serves the same purpose."

The ride to the Drusus house was quicker than Aulus expected, and they hurried down the steps from the Fagutal to the Amphitheater, then on to the Ludus Bruti.

Since both Aulus and Marcus trained there, the door slave barely glanced at them as they passed. Up the steps to the balcony overlooking the training arena, then down to the sand to talk with Brutus.

Stripped to the waist, Brutus and Africanus struck blow after blow with dull-edged gladii, each parrying with the sword or deflecting with a shield.

Marcus leaned over and spoke softly. "That's how I want to fight... good enough to stand against Africanus."

With sweat-soaked hair clinging to his head, Brutus stepped back, and Africanus did the same. As Brutus wiped the perspiration from his brow with his forearm, his gaze settled on Aulus and Marcus.

"Not your usual time, boys."

Marcus stepped forward. "No. Can we talk with you in private?"

Brutus handed his sword to Africanus and snatched a towel from the stack on the bench by the wall. He toweled his hair, face, and chest before tossing it in a basket.

"Follow me."

He led them down the hall by the weapons room and into his office. Marcus came last and closed the door behind him.

Brutus's eyebrows rose as Marcus slid the bolt. "What's wrong?"

Aulus glanced at Marcus, who nodded. One deep breath, and he forged ahead. "I made a horrible mistake. I wasn't supposed to be gambling for high stakes, but I got drunk at my step-sister's house and lost more than I should to her husband's cousin."

Brutus spread his legs and crossed his arms. "It takes a fool to be high-stakes gambling with any Sabinus and an even bigger fool to be doing it drunk."

Aulus ran his fingers through his hair. "I'd lost too much betting on the races, and Father ordered me not to gamble too much before he left for Sicilia. I obeyed him. But friendly gambling with close friends and extended family wasn't the sort of thing Father meant to forbid. Antonia's cousin by marriage should have waited for me to pay him. He shouldn't have told his father about it."

"Quintus Sabinus?"

Aulus nodded, and Brutus sucked air between his teeth. "I'd never want to owe Sabinus anything. It's often not money he demands to square the debt. Too many sacrifice their honor to pay what he demands."

Aulus's mouth turned down. "I know. Father never compromises his honor, and that's made Sabinus his political enemy for years."

Brutus stroked his chin. "How much did you lose?"

"Ten thousand denarii."

A shrug accompanied Brutus's smiling frown. "That's nothing, given your father's wealth. What's the problem?"

Aulus stared at his feet before raising his eyes to Brutus. "Losing the money wasn't the stupidest thing I did. I didn't want Father to be angry with me, and I knew if I asked Gallio for it, he'd tell Father, and Father would be furious."

Brutus's eyebrows lowered. "What did you do, Aulus?"

Aulus looked at Marcus, whose nod told him to continue. "We thought we'd fake Julia's kidnapping to get 10,000 in ransom, then use it to pay the debt before Father ever knew."

With his head tipped back, Brutus rolled his eyes. "Nothing good ever comes from a lie, and no man should ever lie to his father."

"We know that now. The man we hired to hold her for a few hours yesterday...well, he and one of the litter slaves kidnapped her for real."

Brutus's mouth fell open, then snapped shut. "Who did you hire? Where did you find him?"

Marcus moved forward. "I found him right here."

Brutus spun on Marcus. "Here? Impossible."

Marcus took one step back. "Remember when that old legionary was asking about joining your ludus? The one you told he'd die if he tried to fight in Rome?"

Brutus's brow furrowed. "Yes."

"Well, I followed him and asked him if he'd like to make 300 denarii helping us."

Brutus pressed his palms against his temples. "By all the gods, why would you think you could trust a stranger like that?"

Marcus raised his chin. "You seemed to think he was a good man. You even told him where to go to find a ludus that might contract him without getting him killed."

With a deep sigh, Brutus sank into his chair and placed his elbow on the desk. He rested his jaw on his hand.

His lips tightened as his gaze flipped between the boys. "I always treat our retired soldiers with respect. They sacrificed twenty-five years of their lives for the good of Roma. That doesn't mean I trust any of them." With a closed fist, he rubbed his forehead, eyes scrunched. "Until I know a man is honest, I withhold my full trust. And even a man I thought was honest...I wouldn't put a young woman under his power."

Marcus hung his head, then raised it to fix his gaze on Brutus's eyes. "I know I made a huge mistake, but we need your help to undo it. We think maybe he sold Julia, but we don't even know how to start looking for her."

Aulus leaned forward. "Please, Brutus. Help us find her. You're the only one we know who knows about the dark side of Rome where they could sell her."

Brutus stood and rested his palms on the desk. "I'll help you. I do know enough men who know the dark side that there's a chance we'll find her. But the places you'll go looking are dangerous for boys like you. You'll need a bodyguard." He rubbed his mouth. "A man wise enough to know whether to use words or weapons. Africanus."

He turned a frown on Aulus. "For the moment, what you did is best kept secret. We're more likely to find her if no one suspects you." Brutus tapped Aulus's chest with two fingers. "But the moment your father returns to Roma, you and I are going to tell him everything. Nothing is more important than honesty between a father and son, and I won't be party to you hiding anything from him."

Aulus's shoulders slumped. "I know. We wouldn't be here now if I'd just told Gallio from the start and paid the debt before Quintus Sabinus heard of it."

Brutus rested his hand on Aulus's shoulder and squeezed. "The past can't be changed. Let's work on getting Julia back so she can have a future."

Chapter 26

THE DARK SIDE OF ROME

Brutus seated himself and swept his hand toward a chair by the wall. "Bring that over and both of you sit. This will take a while." Marcus settled into the chair already by the desk as Aulus dragged the extra one over.

Brutus leaned on one elbow and rubbed his mouth. He picked up a brass stylus and rolled it between his fingers.

"Since it's been a day and Julia hasn't found her way home, one of two things has probably happened to her."

He focused on Aulus, whose expectant gaze made it harder to speak the next words. "She might be dead." Anguish replaced hope in the boy's eyes. "There's no reason to assume that's happened yet, but we have to face the possibility. If they killed her, then someone will find her body. When...if that happens, the Urban Cohort will be notified. They gather all the dead of Roma each morning and take the bodies to their headquarters in the Castra Praetoria. They hold them for a few days so relatives or friends have a chance to identify them and claim the body."

Aulus's throat moved as if he was struggling to keep breakfast down.

"Aulus, you can ask your steward to send someone every morning to see if she's there." Brutus leaned across the desk to place his hand on the boy's shoulder. "I don't think they will find her. Dead, she's worth nothing. Alive, she could be worth several thousand denarii. I think the only way she'd be dead is if they killed her by accident. It's hard enough to kill someone deliberately, so I suspect she's still alive. But just in case, that visit to the castra should be made until we find her."

Aulus relaxed, and Brutus withdrew his hand.

"It's more likely that they're planning to sell her. There is a market for unspoiled young women like her, but it's not out in the open. The regular slave market has imperial inspectors on site checking papers to make sure only legally enslaved people are offered for sale and certifying the sales that are made."

He massaged the back of his neck. "I only make legal purchases, so I have no personal experience with the special dealers who are not so particular about whether papers have been forged. But I know some people who can direct us toward those dealers. It might take me several days to learn who they are and how to approach them to find out what special offerings they have at the moment."

The blood drained from Aulus's face. "Several days? But what's going to happen to Julia between now and then?"

Brutus raised his palms. "I suspect not much. If they do anything to her, the price they can get for her drops to normal slave prices. Anyone clever enough to stage her kidnapping is probably not stupid enough to risk that if money is their goal."

Marcus leaned forward. "When we find her, how do we get her back? Buy her? Take her by force?"

Brutus leaned back in his chair and crossed his arms. "There's no one answer to that. It depends on who has her and where. Some might claim they thought she was a legal slave and were fooled by the men pretending to own her. They'll be willing to release her immediately for what they paid. You might be able to threaten to report them to the authorities and get her for nothing, but I wouldn't risk that. She could vanish before you returned."

He bounced his closed fist on his lips. "Others are more dangerous. They might try to get rid of you permanently as soon as they realize why you're there. That's why I'm going to send Africanus with you and maybe one more of my men. He can tell when a viper is about to strike, and he can cut off its head before it does. And he's wary enough to know which kind of men you're dealing with before they try something."

Marcus settled back in his chair. "So, is there anything Aulus and I can do today that might help?"

Until Brutus talked with some people, there was nothing the boys could do. But Aulus's eyes begged for something, anything. "It's not likely you'll find her, but it's still worth a visit to the slave market, just to be certain she's not already there. If you see anyone offering cultured young women, you might ask if they have any others that they'll be bringing to the market later. Or if they have special sales rooms for unique slaves." He shrugged and offered Aulus an encouraging smile. "Who knows? Fortuna might smile on you, and she'll be there."

He stood. "I need to clean up before I visit some people to see what I can learn. I'll send word as soon as I know where to start the search. Probably tomorrow or the next day."

He walked around the desk and rested a hand on each of their shoulders. "Don't despair. Roma is big with many places to hide. But it's money they want, and they have to come out of the shadows to get it. When they do, we'll find her."

Aulus's face brightened. "And we'll hunt until we do. Thank you, Brutus."

Brutus nodded, and his lips curved into his typical smiling frown. "We will. Check the market before you go home. Send me word if you find her. Otherwise, you'll be hearing from me soon."

As the boys headed for the exit, the frown overcame the smile. They would hunt, but what would they find? Only the gods knew what waited for them on the dark side of Rome.

Chapter 27

The Reason Why

Gaius's farm, Day 21

Leander drifted upward from the soft, dark place into the brightness. When he opened his eyes, the deep exhaustion of the day before was gone. The pain was still there, but it was more penetrating than piercing—not good, but better.

But he had a new worry. He felt too warm. His wounds might have infected before Marcella had a chance to clean them.

He rested his left forearm across his forehead as he stared at the ceiling. *God, please don't let a fever take me, not now after I made it through losing so much blood. Mistress Julia still needs me to get her home.*

He turned his head to see Mistress Julia, elbow on the table, chin in her hand, watching him. She rose and glided to his side. After adjusting the blanket, she sat on the edge of the bed. Her head tilted, and she graced him with the smile he'd seen her give her nieces so many times.

Just like her nieces, he couldn't resist smiling in return. His first thought—how good it felt to have her look at him that way. His second—he shouldn't be feeling like that. She was the mistress, not his aunt, not his friend. His smile faded.

"Are you feeling better, Leander?"

"Some, mistress."

"You're not supposed to call me that. Remember? I'm Calantha for the rest of the time we're here." Her smile teased him. "You need to practice. Say it."

"Calantha."

Maybe it had been a bad idea telling her he shouldn't call her mistress. It was too tempting to think of her otherwise when he didn't say it. Especially when she sat at his side smiling like that.

"Much better. Now, would you like something to eat or drink?" She gestured toward some bread and dried fruit on the table. It was almost like a dance move.

Lord, why does she have to be so graceful?

"Marcella's doing whatever she usually does. She said I should feed you, but I'm supposed to get her or Gaius if you need more than that. Do you?"

"No, mis—Calantha, but I could eat a little."

She rose and disappeared down the hall to where she slept. She returned with a pillow. Before he could say anything, she slid her arm beneath his shoulders and lifted. She placed her own pillow behind his back to prop him up a little for eating.

The bandage kept her arm from touching the skin of his back, but her hand resting on his bare left arm sent tingles to his spine. Her closeness drove his heart rate up.

She's the mistress, only the mistress.

But that was so not true. She was a woman as well. A kind, beautiful woman smiling at him as if she saw a man, not a slave. Her hair was loose, hanging halfway to her waist. It fell forward and brushed against his cheek as she was lifting him. So soft, still with a hint of roses.

Only the mistress taking care of me because I'm her property and she needs me to get home.

But her eyes gazed into his as if he mattered, as if he wasn't merely a voiced implement, a talking animal of importance only because he served her.

She walked to the table and returned with a clay bowl that held a large wedge of bread and raisins. Once more, she sat beside him.

He reached across his chest with his left arm and picked up the bread. As he raised it toward his mouth, her small hand wrapped around his, halting its movement.

"That piece is much too big. Let me tear it into bite-sized pieces for you."

"I can manage it, m—Calantha."

Her eyes flicked up to catch his. That smile and nod...he'd used the name she wanted, but he'd rather call her mistress when no one else would hear. Much easier then to keep her in the mistress box he'd made in his mind to keep from thinking of her as a pretty woman.

"Perhaps, but Marcella told me I should feed you today, and I intend to." She tore off a bite-sized piece and placed it against his lips. He opened them, and she slipped it in his mouth, smiling at him as she fed him like a small child.

Her fingers brushed his upper lip, and heat shot through him. *Didn't expect that, Lord. Don't want her to do that again.* The problem was, part of him did. He opened his mouth wider the next time to avoid the touch.

He watched her face as he chewed. Some raisins, some bread—she alternated until he'd eaten it all. Her own lips parted a little each time she offered him a bite.

Soft, womanly lips. *No. The lips of a mistress, that's all.*

The smile she wore when she started feeding him faded with the last few morsels. Her eyes changed from almost teasing to serious.

Does she suspect I struggle to see her only as mistress? That she stirs me as a man?

She set the empty bowl aside. "I have to ask you something, Leander. Something I need to understand, so answer me truthfully."

"I would never lie to you." *Mistress.* She wouldn't let him say it aloud, but he could keep saying it to himself to keep her smiles and kindness from taking his thoughts where he didn't want them to go.

"Why didn't you just leave like the escort said? Why did you come find me and fight for me?" She drew a deep breath. "Why did you risk dying to save me?"

An easy question. "I'm a Christian, mistress." His muscles that had tensed anticipating her rebuke relaxed.

The "mistress" slipped out, but she let it pass. Maybe she didn't notice because his answer really was important to her.

"What does that have to do with you saving me?"

"Jesus tells me to pray for those who persecute and abuse me. He tells us we have to love our enemies." His gaze flicked away from her, then back to her eyes. "I try, but it isn't easy. I should even love the Roman soldiers who killed my parents and took my sisters away to...I'll never know."

She was the virgin daughter of a noble family. Maybe she already knew, but he chose not to be the first to tell her what lustful men liked to do to unspoiled girls like her.

Her head snapped back. "Do you think I'm your enemy?"

"No, mistress!" He shook his head vigorously. "No, but I'm supposed to serve willingly and well even a master who is, even if he treats me like nothing more than an animal. I'm only property in your father's house. I know what that means. I couldn't let you become someone's property. Not if I could stop it. Women slaves are usually...well, I wanted to spare you from what happened to my sisters."

The ugly image of the mistress's terror and pain when her owner came to her the first time—he shook his head to drive that away.

"I know the life you'll have if your brother sells you. How could I face my Lord Jesus if I did nothing when I had a chance to save you from that? If your brother kills you, you'll spend eternity in hell, and I don't want that for you, either."

"Is that why you took the arrow meant for me?" She swallowed as if there were something in her throat. "You might have been killed."

"Death holds no terror for me or the terrible fate it does for you. It will only take me to be with Jesus forever. My life isn't my own, anyway. I'll always be the property of another man. Work animals like me don't earn their master's favor and freedom." His mouth curved into a subdued smile. "But my spirit is still free, even if my body isn't. It was my free choice to save you, even if I die because of it."

Her blinks came quicker. He hadn't meant his words about death to frighten her.

With her fingertip, she wiped the corner of her eye. "Anyway, you're hurt, but you're not going to die. I want you here with me. I did name you after a lion, but I don't think you're an animal. If you're going to serve me well, you have to get better. Promise me you will."

Her barely contained teardrops—they must only be from fear of being all by herself. They couldn't really be for him. As kind as she might be to her noble friends, she couldn't care that much about a talking animal whose name she only learned two days ago.

"I'm in no hurry to die...but I won't make a promise I might not keep."

The fever was burning hotter, and he had no doubt what that meant. He'd survived the blood loss, but the infection...only God knew if he'd make it past that. But if he were a betting man, he'd bet against it.

"But you are going to keep it." A tremor crept into her voice as the fear grew deeper in her eyes.

His mouth twitched. He had no power of life and death over himself. "If it's God's will, mistress."

He closed his eyes. He couldn't promise what she wanted, and he didn't want to watch her panic because he couldn't.

God, if she needs me that much, please leave me here to help her.

Chapter 28

GOD OF LEANDER, PLEASE!

By evening, Leander's fever was running high. His leg pulsed with pain, so the infection probably started there, but it didn't really matter. It had a strong hold on him now. His face too hot even while he shivered. His heartbeat a trotting horse, not a walking one. If he turned his head too fast, the room swirled for a moment.

He'd watched a man die on the Crassus estate when he'd been flogged for running away and his shredded back infected. It hadn't been quick, and for most of the several days it took for him to die, the man was raving or unconscious.

If he were a betting man, he'd bet this infection would kill him, too.

He watched Mistress Calantha glide across the room. She was caring for him herself, wiping his face with a wet cloth, trying to cool him.

It wasn't working.

His mouth turned down. The mistress was depending on him. How much longer before his mind clouded and he'd be no use to her?

She had no idea how to take care of herself. She wouldn't know how to get back to her father if left to figure it out on her own. Only he knew who she really was. Only he knew where she lived. Only he knew how to get her safely home...and he wouldn't be alive to do it.

◆

Calantha came back with a fresh bowl of water and sat down beside Leander. She wrung out the cloth, folded it, and drew it across his forehead. His eyes were staring at her when the cloth moved past and she could see them again.

Her breath caught. Those eyes radiated a hard brightness far different from the fevered dullness that had been worrying her.

"Listen carefully to what I'm about to tell you." His voice was forceful. "You must do exactly what I say."

Her eyes popped. He'd stopped calling her mistress, but to speak like he was the one in charge? He'd only done that when the man came to buy the ram and wanted her instead.

"Wait two weeks longer than when you think your father should be home, just in case he's delayed. Go back to Servilia. Tell her your father's name, and she'll find out where your house is. Ask her to find someone who can go to your father and tell him—and only him—that you want to meet him at one of the public baths where your friends don't go. I always carried you to Trajan's, so maybe go to Titus's.

"Don't go in your own clothes. You don't want anyone you know recognizing you. You don't know who you can trust. Maybe Servilia can go with you like she's your mother. No one from the noble orders will pay attention to a low-class mother and daughter. If your father hasn't come home yet, come back here. Ask Servilia to send you word when to try again."

Her spine straightened. "Why are you telling me this? You're going to take me back yourself when it's time."

◆

Fear flared in her eyes.

Leander longed to tell her he would, but he couldn't. The blood loss hadn't killed him, but the infection probably would.

His forehead felt too hot even to his own hand. "I don't think so… but you'll be safe if you do what I'm telling you."

Her breaths came faster. "Yes, you will. You belong to me, and you have to do what I tell you. You're going to get better and take me back yourself." Her lip quivered as her eyes swam in tears.

"I'll try."

"You won't just try. You'll do it." Her voice dropped to a whisper. "Please, Leander. Don't leave me alone."

She slipped her hand into his, and he could feel it trembling. He tightened his grip around it. The trembling stopped.

His heart clenched. *I don't want to, but it's not my choice.* Her rapid blinks betrayed the terror lurking near the surface. She'd never had to face any problem alone. She couldn't handle the truth about what he expected to happen. *Please, God, if there's any way it can be Your will, heal me so I can take care of her and get her home.*

He managed a weak smile. "I'll do what I can, mistress."

He closed his eyes, and his smile faded. His gentle grip on Calantha's hand relaxed, and his hand fell away. Calantha dipped the cloth in the water again, wrung it out, and wiped his flushed face one more time.

Why had he called her mistress again? He was talking like he wasn't going to obey her, like he was ready to give up and die.

With her other hand, she brushed away the teardrop that had escaped and trickled down her cheek.

You can't die. You just can't. She stared up at the ceiling. *Please, god of Leander, don't take him from me. I need him more than you do.* Her gaze locked once more on his shuttered eyes. *He's such a good man. Don't let him die because of me.*

It had been many hours, and his fever still burned. Calantha still wet the rag and wiped his face, but he hadn't opened his eyes in the longest time. She watched his chest rise and fall. It stopped for a moment, then it began to move again.

What if it stopped for good?

Her chin started to quiver, and his face blurred. First one, then another teardrop trickled down her cheeks. Her chest jumped once, then twice. She fought against making any noise as the trickle turned into a steady stream.

She jumped when Marcella placed a hand on her shoulder. "It's time you take a break for a little while. I'll watch him."

Calantha's voice was scarcely above a whisper. "No. I can't leave him. He needs me to help him get better."

Marcella took her hand. "Come outside. I need to tell you something."

Calantha tipped her tear-streaked face to look at Marcella's warm eyes. "But he needs me here."

"He can spare you for a moment. He'd want you to take a short break." She gave a gentle tug, and Calantha rose.

Marcella led her outside, then turned to face her. "I've done all I can. You've done all you can. Dacius is still alive, and God still might heal him, but you need to accept that it might not be God's will for him to live. He belongs to Jesus. His death will take him to be with Jesus forever. He wouldn't want you to be broken-hearted over that."

Before Marcella could say another word, the dam broke, and hiccupping sobs shook Calantha. Marcella drew her into her arms and held her until the torrent subsided.

Calantha stepped back and fixed anguished eyes on the kind woman who'd taken them in, no questions asked. "It's all because of me. My brother hired kidnappers, and when they grabbed me, Dacius came to save me. He's only here dying because of me." A few more tears trickled down her cheeks. "He fought to free me, and they stabbed him and they shot him and he still kept protecting me...and I didn't even know his name until after all that."

Marcella's eyebrows shot up. "You didn't know his name?"

"No! I only saw him as a slave who carried me around the city. I never spoke to him. I never looked into his eyes. I couldn't even have told you which place he stood by the litter. And now he's in there dying because he came to save me."

Marcella's eyes softened as she pushed a strand of hair behind Calantha's ear. "And it doesn't matter to him that you didn't know his name then. He'd willingly do it all over again if he had the choice. Jesus tells us to love each other as we love ourselves. He said there was no greater love than to lay down your life for another."

Calantha's voice quavered. "But I don't want him to die for me. I want him to live."

"I know, and he still might."

Calantha bit her lip "What am I going to do if he doesn't?"

"You'll grieve, and you'll go on. It's all any of us can do."

"But I don't know how to go on. He was going to take care of me until Father returns."

Marcella drew her back into her arms. "We'll take care of you until you know how. He hasn't left you all alone."

She whispered into Marcella's shoulder. "But I want him to live."

"And he still might. While he breathes, there's hope. I keep praying for his healing, and God can heal anyone of anything, even death itself when it fulfills His purpose."

Marcella eased Calantha to arms' length. "Now, let's have no more tears. They don't help him at all. If he wakes to see you've been crying, he'll be worrying about you, and that won't help him heal. You need to take a short break. Wash your face, walk a little, and then you can sit with him again."

Calantha nodded. Marcella squeezed her hand before turning to go inside.

She wiped the tears from her cheeks and swallowed the lump still rising in her throat. *Please, god of Leander, heal him, like Marcella says you can.*

She squared her shoulders and headed toward the well.

Chapter 29

It was a quarter of an hour before Calantha's walking calmed her enough to return to Leander. The door stood open, and she found Gaius and Marcella kneeling beside his bed. Gaius's hand rested on his ankle, Marcella's hand on his forehead.

Gaius's words reached her. "We give you thanks and praise, Father." Then both said, "Amen."

Calantha remained in the doorway until they rose. When they turned at the sound of her footsteps, her head bounced back.

Leander lay dying on the bed. How could their eyes and smiles look joyful?

Her gaze locked on his motionless form. Then his chest rose and fell, and her frozen breath released.

Marcella wrapped an arm around her shoulders. "You can go rest now. He'll be fine."

"But he's so hot. He needs me to cool him."

Marcella left her arm around Calantha as they walked to his bedside. "It isn't his time to die. God is healing him. The fever has broken, and he'll recover." She squeezed Calantha. "You can help me take care of him while he does, but you need your rest for that."

Calantha laid the back of her fingers on his forehead. Still warm, but the fiery heat of the fever was fading.

Marcella rested her hands atop Calantha's shoulders and turned her toward the hallway. "To bed with you. He'll awake in the morning, and he'll want to see you looking well when he does."

Calantha paused at the door to her room. Back by the table, Gaius held Marcella in his arms. Peace surrounded them. And for some reason she couldn't explain, that peace wrapped around her as well.

They called their god "father," and he heard and answered their prayers. And maybe the god of Leander had listened to her prayer, too.

Day 22

Calantha came from her bedroom to find Marcella stirring the porridge. But it was Leander who drew and held her gaze.

"He's fine, just sleeping." Marcella held out a bowl. "You can watch over him for me when he awakens. I have work to do in the garden."

Calantha took the bowl and sat at the table. "I've never cared for a sick person before. How long until he wakes up?"

"Whenever he's rested enough. I have some bread and fruit there for when he's hungry. You'll only need to give him food and drink as he asks. Anything more, come get me or Gaius."

Gaius came through the door and walked to Leander's bedside. "On the mend." A smile curved his mouth as he settled into his chair and took the bowl Marcella offered.

When Marcella joined them, the couple bowed their heads and closed their eyes. Calantha copied them.

Gaius spoke. "Thank you, God, for this food and this new day. Thank you especially for healing Dacius. Let him soon join us at this table. In Jesus's name, amen."

If someone had asked her what herbs had seasoned the porridge, Calantha couldn't have answered. Her thoughts kept following her eyes to rest on the man who'd risked his life to save her own.

It was some time since Marcella and Gaius left the cottage. Leander had begun to stir, but his eyes remained closed. He was close enough to awake, and Calantha couldn't wait any longer.

She sat on the bed beside him. Then she rested her hand on his cheek and stroked his stubble with her thumb. He no longer felt hot. She ran her fingers through his hair until his eyelids parted and she could see his quiet gray eyes.

"It's gone, Leander." Joy bubbled up and curved her lips. "Your fever's gone. Marcella said your god could heal you, and he has." She took his calloused hand in hers and held it against her cheek. "You're going to live."

His lips curved to mirror her own. "It appears so, mis...Calantha. You won't have to try to get home alone. It's almost a month before your father returns. I should be healed enough to take you back then."

She hadn't planned it, but she couldn't resist. She dropped her head to his chest and slipped her arms around him. "I'm so glad you didn't die because of me. I can never thank you enough for coming to save me."

His chest was solid with work-hardened muscles, and she felt the rhythm of her own heartbeat blend with his. Each th-thud lifted her spirits a little higher. After watching him hover so close to death, to feel the life beating within him made her heart dance to its rhythm.

◆

The slow sweep of Mistress Calantha's fingers through his hair had pulled Leander out of the dream. As good as the gentle stroking felt, he was sorry. It had been years since he'd dreamed about his childhood with his sister Ariana.

In the dream, Ariana was singing to him before she rested her hand on his cheek and whispered, "May God give you blessed sleep, Diegis. I love you." Her eyes, blue-grey like the sky of a cloudless dawn, glowed with love for him. She leaned over and kissed his forehead. As she straightened, her eyes shifted from blue to light brown, and her tawny hair darkened until it was a shimmering nut brown. Her face blurred, then refocused. It was no longer Ariana but Mistress Calantha smiling down at him.

He cracked open his eyes, only to discover it really was Mistress Calantha, not Ariana, running her fingers through his hair.

Her eyes sparkled as she told him the fever was gone and he would live. When she lifted his hand to her cheek, he was too stunned to move it away.

The corners of his mouth lifted into a smile. *Thank you, God, for letting me stay to help her. Now she'll get home safely to her father.*

No reason for her to be afraid any more. She knew it, too. Her joy at him telling her that he would get her home lit her whole face.

Then she shocked him.

Leander's pulse leaped when Mistress Calantha rested her warm, soft cheek against his chest and slid her hands across his skin until she had him wrapped in her arms. It was the last thing he expected...and the last thing he wanted her to do.

It was a big problem, and the biggest part of the problem was that part of him was thrilled to have her so close, touching him as if he were a free man who was dear to her.

It took all the self-control he had not to wrap his own arms around her and hold her in a gentle embrace. Instead, he placed his hands on her upper arms and pushed so she would sit up.

He couldn't let her get in the habit of touching him like he was anything more than a slave. If her father were to suspect that he saw her as a kind, beautiful woman instead of the mistress who owned him, the master would never believe he was only a loyal slave fulfilling his duty to protect her. He'd believe the lies about him being in league with the kidnappers and think he took her because he wanted her as a woman. Vilicus would enjoy using that whip before he was sold...or worse.

When he'd only carried her litter and watched her from a distance as she played with her sister's children, he'd managed to control his thoughts and keep her in his mind's mistress box...for the most part. But she'd been so kind as she helped Marcella care for him, and that had changed everything. In his weakness, it was impossible not to see her as Calantha, the gentle woman who saw him as a person, not property.

But now that his fever had broken, she wouldn't have to help him as much, and he'd be able to see her once more as a noble mistress instead of a lovely woman who cared for him.

At least he'd try. *God, please give me the strength to do it.*

◆

Calantha sat up when he put gentle pressure on her arms. He'd been so strong when he lifted her into the basket. He seemed so weak now. He couldn't lift her if his life depended on it...or hers. Father would be back in a month, but how fast does a man recover from almost dying?

"It will be wonderful to get back to Father, but maybe we should wait for a couple of weeks after he's supposed to be home, like you said I would need to if I went alone. You might not be ready for such a long trip in only four weeks. If you aren't completely well then, we'll wait until we can do it without it being hard for you."

◆

Calan—no, Mistress Calantha ran her fingers through his hair. Leander was torn between knowing he should tell her to stop and wanting her to do it again.

"I'll be ready to take you back as soon as you want me to."

How kind she was to put what was better for him above her own eagerness to return to living as a noblewoman with her father in Rome. His smile warmed as she ran her fingers through his hair one more time.

Then it cooled. It was becoming much too easy to think of her as Calantha without the Mistress. The thought of a few days longer with her pretending to be an ordinary woman and him a free man gave him too much pleasure. This was only play-acting. It couldn't last, and he'd better keep that at the forefront of his mind. When he took her back, everything must be as it was before he ran into the abandoned house and saved her.

He shut his eyelids so she wouldn't see the deep regret in his eyes. She mustn't ask him what was wrong. How could he ever explain what it meant for a man who'd tasted the sweetness of freedom to once again have to live as a slave?

Chapter 30

Officer of the Law

The Secundus villa, Day 22

Marcus watched Aulus cross the library for what seemed the five hundredth time. He rolled the scroll he'd been reading and placed it back in the cubicle.

"Aulus, sit. We can play tabula or Mercenaries, or you can join me reading. But you're driving me to distraction with that pacing."

Aulus flopped into the desk chair. "Brutus said he'd send us a message today, but where is it?"

"No, he said he'd start asking around and he might learn something yesterday or today. But that also means he might not."

Marcus lowered himself into the second chair by the desk and pulled the wooden gameboard between them. He picked up the inlaid wooden box that held the game pieces and tipped back the lid. He'd just placed the first set of blue and blond bone rondels on the board when the slaps of scurrying sandals came from the atrium.

The slave that Gallio had sent to the Castra Praetoria entered and bowed to Aulus.

Aulus's spine straightened. "Well?"

"Good news, Master Aulus. The mistress wasn't there."

Aulus relaxed in the chair. "Good. Go find Gallio and tell him as well."

The slave hurried away, and Marcus's mouth relaxed into a smile. "Looks like Brutus was right that she's likely to stay alive until we find her."

Aulus rubbed the back of his neck. "But I can't relax until she's back home."

Marcus moved his first piece. "She will be."

Muted voices drifted in from the atrium, then the door slave appeared. "Tribune Flavius Titianus of the XI Urban Cohort and his guard are waiting for you in the first room left of the vestibulum, master."

Aulus's hand froze above the board. "Bring the tribune to me and fetch Gallio as well."

Marcus scooped the pieces off the board and dropped them back in the box. Aulus's eyebrows rose.

"Titianus is a friend of Lucius. We don't want him to think we're playing games instead of worrying."

The click of hobnail sandals on stone announced the tribune's arrival before he entered.

Tribune Titianus strode into the library, metal body armor gleaming and a brass helmet with a red horsehair crest under his arm.

His eyebrow rose as his gaze settled on Marcus. "Drusus. I didn't expect you here."

Marcus offered a friendly smile. "Aulus Secundus is my best friend. When he has trouble, I'm going to be with him."

Titianus's smile proclaimed his approval. "Lucky man. I haven't seen Lucius for several weeks. I trust all is well with him."

Marcus kept the smiling mask in place. "He just asked for a transfer to Judaea to be an aide to the governor in Caesarea."

The corner of Titianus's mouth turned up. "I'd wondered if serving near Rome would offer enough challenge to satisfy Lucius. I'd rather be with a frontier legion myself, but my father's health makes it necessary for me to stay near Rome. I'd prefer battle with barbarians to being a policeman, but duty to my family is more important than satisfying my own desire to serve in a more exciting place."

Titianus's head turned toward Aulus. "I don't believe we've met before, Secundus, and I wish it were under more pleasant circumstances. But finding the men who dared to kidnap a senator's daughter and recovering her is the most important assignment I've had, and you can rest assured that nothing will stop me from bringing the kidnappers to justice."

Aulus's eyes widened and flicked to Marcus. "I...I'm glad to hear it."

Titianus's brow furrowed, and Marcus shifted in the chair to draw Titianus's eyes back upon himself. "Nothing could be more reassuring than that promise."

Gallio stepped into the room, and Marcus swept his hand toward him. "This is Gallio, steward of the Julius Secundus household."

Titianus squared his shoulders, any hint of familiarity gone. "Tribune Titianus of the XI Urban Cohort. I've been assigned to find your missing mistress."

Gallio's face remained grim. "Anything we can do to help, just tell us."

One quick tip of his head was Titianus's response. "I need you to tell me everything you know and anything you suspect that might help in the search for Julia Secunda. Were there any signs that something was going on before this abduction happened?"

The steward drew a deep breath. "Nothing at all. Mistress Julia had been very worried about Metilia Neposa after her brother died. When a slave appeared claiming to have been sent to get her because Metilia had just returned home after two weeks' absence, no one was surprised. He was supposed to escort the litter to meet Metilia somewhere. Instead, he led the bearers into Subura and was killed."

Titianus nodded. "I inspected the body from the Subura house. A couple of bruises, but very little sign of struggle. Broken neck."

Gallio's frown deepened. "I contacted Metilius Nepos after we found the escort dead and the mistress missing, only to discover his daughter had not yet returned and no one had been sent for Julia.

"I'd bought a new litter slave about three weeks ago, and he went into the house with her and the man who met the litter in Subura. Her other bearers became worried when the new one didn't come back out promptly. They went in to see if Julia needed their help. When they discovered she'd vanished and the escort was dead, they came home to tell us. They can provide you more detail and a description of the kidnappers they saw. That slave is now a runaway as well."

Another slight nod by the tribune. "I'll speak with them after I hear about the ransom demand."

Gallio glanced at Aulus before speaking. "We went to the house as soon as the bearers got here. By the time the ransom tablet was delivered, we'd already seen where she was kidnapped and discovered the dead escort. The instructions were simple. Master Aulus was to walk down the Clivus Suburanus alone and unarmed with 12,000 denarii. Someone would meet him and take it."

He rubbed his mouth. "I thought it odd that the tablet promised the release of Julia and the escort immediately upon payment of the ransom. The escort was already dead. But I hoped the note had simply been written before the murder and no one bothered to change it."

He picked up the tablet from the desk. "Here's the tablet, if you want it."

Titianus took it, inspected it inside and out, and handed it back. "Keep it here. If I need it, I'll get it later."

His gaze locked on Aulus. "Tell me all you can about the delivery of the ransom and the man who took it from you."

Aulus's eyes flicked toward Marcus, who moved to stand beside him. "I was with Aulus for the first part."

Aulus took a deep breath. "We rode to Marcus's house, and Marcus went with me as far as the baths. Then I walked alone and unarmed into Subura, as instructed. A man approached me from behind and told me not to turn around, so I didn't. He took the two bags with the ransom money and said a message would come telling us how to get Julia back. If anyone tried to follow him, they would kill her and dump her body in the Tiber. So, I didn't try to see what he looked like in case that would make them kill her, too."

His teeth clenched. "But that message never came."

Titianus had been standing with a wax tablet open and stylus ready, but he didn't write down anything. "Is that all you can tell me?"

Aulus's jaw twitched. "Yes."

A frown pulled Titianus's mouth down, and he snapped the tablet closed. His gaze moved from Aulus, to Gallio, to Marcus. "If there's nothing else the three of you can tell me, I'm ready to speak with the litter slaves."

Gallio's hand swept toward the door.

With eyes that seemed to see too much, Titianus stared at Aulus until Aulus looked away. Then he turned his eyes on Marcus. "Please give my regards to your father and send Lucius my greetings in your next letter to him."

Marcus summoned a smile. "I will."

The tribune's eyes snapped back on Aulus. "I'll keep you informed of my progress." He spun to face Gallio, who stood behind him. "Now those slaves."

Gallio looked over his shoulder as he led the tribune through the door. "Follow me."

Aulus listened to their fading footsteps, then stepped to the door to make sure they were out of earshot. He turned to Marcus. "What do you think?"

Marcus rubbed his jaw. "I think we'd better find a certain retired soldier before Titianus does and make certain the tribune of the XI Urban Cohort never gets a chance to ask him questions."

Aulus's eyes widened. "You mean—"

"Yes. Anyone who would take Julia to sell her deserves to suffer Roman justice, and I want to be the Roman delivering it to him."

Aulus's mouth squeezed into a narrow line. "I want my part in that, too."

Marcus slapped his friend's arm. He would do his best to bring Roman justice to Callidus...before Roman justice could come after him.

Chapter 31

Worth Thanking

Gaius's Farm, Day 22

Calantha sat at the table, watching Leander's chest slowly rise and fall. After so many desperate hours fearing he would die, nothing was more satisfying than seeing that tiny trace of a smile that always seemed to linger at the corners of his mouth.

The sunshine streaming through the door was blocked when Marcella entered the cottage and stood behind her. "It's good to see him sleeping peacefully."

"But he's still so weak."

Marcella rested her hands by Calantha's neck and squeezed. "That might last for a week or two, but with plenty of rest and my cooking, Dacius will be back to full strength before you know it."

Calantha tipped her face up to see Marcella's eyes. "Dacius isn't his name anymore."

Her friend's eyebrows rose. "It's not?"

"No. He's Leander now. I renamed him because he fought so bravely to save me. And Julia won't be my name while I'm here. He was worried someone might hear my name and then tell someone about us. He said I should use something else in case there were listening ears, and I chose Calantha. He said it means beautiful flower."

"Gaius and I will call you whatever you choose." Marcella walked over to his bedside and smiled down at him. "I'm certain he appreciates the new name you gave him. He certainly earned it. And I like the one you chose for yourself." Her smile turned on Calantha. "It fits you."

She reached to run her fingers through his hair but stopped before touching him. "Once a week, we have a small group of friends gather here."

Calantha's quick breath drew Marcella's gaze.

"You don't have to worry. None would reveal you're here if we ask them not to, but we'll use your new names with our friends as well."

"He'll think that's wise. He's so protective of me."

A smile tugged at the corner of Marcella's mouth. "We all need someone to protect us. God blessed you with him."

She walked into the small storeroom directly across the hall from where Calantha slept and returned with some dried figs, cheese, and bread. "Gaius should come for his lunch soon." She flashed a smile at Calantha. "It gives me such pleasure to take good care of my man."

With her elbow on the table, Calantha rested her chin on her hand. "The loom in the corner...what are you making?"

"A new winter tunic for Gaius."

"Leander's wearing a tunic that belonged to Servilia's husband. His own got soaked with blood, so she said to leave it and she'd send it out after mending and washing it." Her gaze shifted to Leander, then back to Marcella. "But it's the red tunic our litter slaves wear. I don't want him in that. May I do some weaving while we're here? He's going to need a tunic and cloak, and I'd like to make them for him. I'd also like to make something you could sell to pay some of what it will cost for us being here."

Her words drew Marcella's smile. "We don't need to be paid anything. Helping the two of you gives us both pleasure, and it also pleases God. But it would bore me to tears to have nothing to do for a month, and you have to stay almost that long. Did you want to make the tunic or cloak first? I'll ask Gaius to set up the right loom for whichever you choose."

"Maybe I should make his cloak first since he doesn't have one. But first I need to get enough wool and spin the yarn."

Her brow furrowed. "I know how to spin, but I've never had to spin all my own yarn. I simply got what I needed from the spinners at the estate. If I wanted some special yarn, I bought it. How long will it take to spin enough for a cloak?"

Marcella placed the food on the counter and began arranging it on a tray. "I've already spun enough for a new tunic for me and for an elderly neighbor whose hands are crippled. That should be enough for his cloak. After you finish weaving you can replace what you use. We have plenty of fleece from this spring's shearing."

Calantha turned her eyes back to Leander. "Don't tell him who I'm making it for. I want it to be a surprise when I give it to him. I want to thank him for all he did, but he'll keep telling me a mistress shouldn't be weaving for her slave." Her smile turned into a grin. "But after I have it finished, I'll simply tell him he has to wear it and enjoy it because that's what I want him to do."

"Gaius is like that, too. Always telling me I shouldn't go to a lot of work to do something special for him. He doesn't realize how much pleasure it gives me."

A shadow was cast over Calantha when Gaius blocked the sunbeams. "How much pleasure what gives you?"

Marcella walked to his side and wrapped her arm around him. "Having you as my husband. God truly blessed me with you."

His lips brushed her cheek. "Not as much as He blessed me with you."

She patted his arm before fetching the tray of cheese and dried figs and placing it on the table. She pointed at an empty chair. "Sit, dear."

As Gaius seated himself, Marcella brought over three cups and the small pitcher of watered wine.

As soon as Marcella settled in her chair, Gaius lowered his head. "We give thanks, Lord, for this day and this food and for the joy of eating it together. In Jesus name, we pray."

The "amen" that Marcella spoke was echoed by Calantha. She glanced at Leander. His god, the god of Marcella and Gaius, was definitely a god worth thanking.

The aroma of pork and onions and carrots and something savory he couldn't identify teased Leander's nostrils as he opened his eyes.

Gaius stood at his bedside, smiling down at him. "Awake just in time for one of Marcella's specialties. How are you feeling?"

Leander felt his smile grow to match that of Gaius. "It's been a while since I could say this, but hungry for a big helping of anything that could smell that good."

With his left arm, he pushed himself to a sitting position. That took more than he expected, and he gauged the distance from the bed to the chair. Eating at a table again would be good, but...

Gaius rested a hand on his uninjured shoulder. "You're not quite ready to join us, but maybe tomorrow."

Although he fought it, Leander's back still slipped from straight to slouched. "I guess you're right."

Gaius stacked his pillow with the mistress's pillow from the foot of the bed. Then he slipped his arm around Leander's shoulders and eased him back against them.

When Gaius stepped away, Mistress Calantha stood behind him, carrying a steaming bowl of stew and a wooden plate holding some bread.

"You don't have to feed me, mistress. I can do it now."

Her gaze moved from the bowl to the plate to his eyes. Her lips tightened but only because they were holding back a smile.

"Just how do you intend to balance a bowl of stew and handle a spoon while reclining on a bed with only one good arm? You don't want to spill and make a mess for Marcella."

He opened his mouth to speak, then closed it. He'd never even reclined to dine with two good arms.

Her lips relaxed, and the smile leaked out. "I knew you'd see I should help if you thought about it for a moment."

She sat beside him and, with arched eyebrows, offered him the first spoonful.

A taste that put the aroma to shame filled his mouth as he chewed, then swallowed. "Thank you for helping me, mistress."

"Mistress isn't helping you. Calantha is." Her voice and eyes took all the sting from the rebuke. "My fearless lion should be able to remember that."

He nodded as he chewed.

As she presented spoonful after spoonful, pausing for him to take bites of bread, he watched her face. Beautiful flower...she'd chosen the perfect name for herself.

It wasn't his place to decide which name to call her...or himself. Dacius, Leander, fearless lion—he would be whatever the mistress wanted until it was time to take her home.

Chapter 32

READY TO BRING HER HOME

The Secundus villa, Day 23

Aulus tried, but he couldn't stop his eyes from drifting to the couch where Julia reclined when they ate together. The hot, rosemary-laced bread the chef had prepared for breakfast tasted like sawdust, and the drop of wine the slave had spilled while filling his silver goblet looked too much like the dark stain where the litter had been abandoned. No matter what Marcus said, it must have been blood. But whose?

Marcus swung his legs off the couch across from Aulus. "What shall we do today?"

Aulus forced out a heavy sigh. "I only want to do one thing...find Julia."

Rapid footsteps drew nearer, and both men stared at the doorway.

One of the house slaves stepped into the dining room and bowed. "A message from Antonius Brutus, master. He said to come right away and bring good horses."

Aulus scrambled to his feet. "Go tell someone to saddle the gray mare and Marcus's stallion." The young boy started to bow. "Now!"

Still bent at the waist, the boy scurried from the room.

Marcus's mouth curved into a satisfied smile. "I knew Brutus would be able to find her."

"I hope you're right. But wouldn't he have said if he had?"

Marcus's eyebrows lowered. "Well, yes, but he must at least have a lead for us to follow. That's a good start." He slapped Aulus's arm. "The sooner we get to Ludus Bruti, the sooner we find her and bring her home."

With Marcus striding before him, Aulus headed toward the stable. Bring good horses? A strange instruction if Julia was in Rome. And if she wasn't, where could she be?

Ludus Bruti

When Aulus and Marcus rode through the gate into the stable yard at the ludus, two quality horses stood saddled and waiting. Big horses, ready to carry big men.

A slave scurried over to take Aulus's mare as he slid off. "Master Brutus is waiting for you in his office."

Marcus walked at his side as they passed through narrow hallways lined with cells and training areas to reach Brutus's office.

When they entered, Brutus looked up from a wax tablet that lay open on his desk. His hand swept toward the two chairs that sat opposite his own. "Take a seat, boys."

Aulus scooted to the front of the chair as soon as his seat hit the wood. "Did you find her?"

Brutus's smiling frown was more smile than frown. "Perhaps."

Aulus leaned closer. "Perhaps? Either you did or you didn't."

"I might have found where she was, and I have an idea where she might be if I'm right."

"Where?"

Brutus closed the tablet and leaned back in his chair. "Remember I told you there were private dealers who handled special slaves at special prices? Some are scrupulously honest, and some are not. I did some shopping yesterday at some I suspect of occasionally accepting forged papers for unusual slaves."

Brutus looked past Aulus toward the door. "Come in."

Aulus turned to see Africanus and Rufus, another of Brutus's top fighters, enter and take positions against the wall.

"I was shopping for a pretty young woman educated to be able to converse with equestrians and senators on many topics and with manners that would make her suitable as a companion at a formal banquet. I found one."

Aulus could scarcely stay seated. "Was it her?"

"I don't know. The dealer said those were very hard to find, and he'd just sold the only one he had the day before."

Aulus's shoulders slumped; then he straightened. "But we can get her from whoever bought her."

"Perhaps. At first, he didn't want to tell me who that was, but I offered him a pass to join my fighters at the next dinner I hold the night before the games." The corner of his mouth lifted and ended in a wry smile. "Those are coveted by many more than I usually allow to attend, and he leaped at the chance to dine and talk with my men before their day on the sand."

A deep breath was followed by Aulus's huge sigh of relief. "Let's go get her."

Brutus leaned forward. He rested an elbow on the desk and rubbed his lips. "The problem is the man who bought her."

Marcus inhaled sharply beside Aulus. "Too politically well connected? Or too low class but wealthy enough to want that kind of woman?"

"More the latter. His name is Claudius Ursus. His father was an imperial freedman who amassed a fortune after Emperor Claudius freed him. Ursus has at least doubled that fortune, and he has no qualms about how he spends it."

"So, what do we do?" Aulus hovered between relief and worry.

"You and Marcus will go to see if it's Julia, and if so, you'll ask him to release her."

"Where is he? We'll go right now."

Brutus cradled his chin, his hand over his mouth. When he pulled it aside, he was frowning. "The dealer said she was loaded into a raeda and taken south to Ursus's villa. It's on the coast, about two miles west of Ardeo."

Aulus stood. "That's not too far. If we leave now, we can get there before nightfall. He'll have to release her when he knows who she is."

Brutus's frown shifted toward a smile. "I knew you'd be eager, but you underestimate the man. He's not to be trusted, and I'm not sending you there without some protection. Africanus and Rufus will go as your bodyguards." He smiled at Africanus, who returned a nod. "Africanus will also guide you in how to deal with him if your reasonable request is denied."

Brutus stood. "I've had my cook pack rolls, cheese, and fruit for your meals so you won't have to stop before Ardeo. Spend the night there, and go to see Ursus tomorrow morning."

He tossed a purse to Africanus. "Take care of the local arrangements."

Africanus snatched the purse from the air and nodded.

Brutus came around the desk and rested one hand on Aulus's and Marcus's shoulders. "May Fortuna smile on your journey and bring your sister home safely with you."

Rufus and Africanus left the room, with Africanus pausing in the doorway. "Let's go."

Brutus flicked his hand toward the door, and Aulus and Marcus followed the gladiators to the stable yard.

When Aulus took the reins and prepared to mount his mare, Africanus approached. "We have a long way to ride before nightfall." His voice was deep and unexpectedly quiet for such a big man. His eyes scanned Marcus's stallion and lingered on Aulus's mare. "You ride her long distances?"

"No. Mostly a few miles to Marcus's townhouse and some other friends' estates around Rome."

A frown barely formed before Africanus straightened his mouth. He pointed to one of the waiting horses. "You'll take mine."

A flick of his hand summoned the stable slave. "Saddle the master's stallion for me." He walked away to exchange soft words with Rufus that Aulus couldn't catch.

Marcus came to his side. "Amazing. No slave of mine would presume to take my horse without asking."

Aulus shrugged. "No one seems surprised, so Brutus must not mind."

As soon as Brutus's solid black stallion was saddled, they all mounted. Africanus rode first through the gate. He led them past the Amphitheater and the end of the Circus Maximus to pass through the city wall at the Porta Naevia.

He reined in just past the gate. "It's about twenty-four *milia passuum* to Ardeo down the Via Ardeotina. We'll stop half way to rest the horses a while."

Before Aulus could respond, the big Nubian kicked Brutus's horse into a trot and headed south.

Aulus followed, and the feeling of a stallion's power between his legs drew a smile. The black stallion he'd bought three weeks earlier would someday give him the same pleasure as this animal...if someone ever finished gentling it.

He hadn't seen the stable slave who was making good progress with that for several days. Vilicus must have him working somewhere else. But after Julia was safely back home, he'd tell the overseer to leave that slave in the stable until the stallion was tamed enough for him to ride. What good was it having a slave who was skilled with horses if he never did the job for which he'd been bought?

Ardeo, south of Rome

It was late afternoon when Aulus and his party rode into Ardeo. It was barely more than a village, much smaller than Aulus expected. Africanus reined in and scanned the small shops that lined the road.

Aulus rode up beside him. "How do we find Ursus's villa?"

Africanus swung his leg across his horse's neck and slid off. "Leave that to me."

He handed his reins to Rufus and strolled over to the nearest shop. Aulus couldn't hear his words, but whatever Africanus asked, it made the man nervous. Africanus moved from shop to shop, and at each, the shopkeeper looked like he wished he hadn't been questioned.

There were some children playing with a ball in a grassy area across a low stone wall. Africanus vaulted the wall and approached them, his movements relaxed and his lips smiling.

He crouched down beside a small girl who stood watching the older boys toss the ball. "Is one your brother?"

His voice carried a fatherly warmth with it. Not what Aulus expected from one of Brutus's best fighters.

She nodded and pointed to the biggest one.

"He's good with the ball. Has he taught you?"

She nodded. "He says I'm too little when he plays with his friends, but when it's just us..." She shrugged.

"You might not be as big, but I bet you watch things better. I bet you see things he doesn't even notice."

She smiled as her head bobbed up and down.

"We're trying to catch up with someone who drove a carriage through here yesterday. Did you see them?"

She tipped her head as the smile faded.

"I'm looking for a friend who might have been in that carriage. Did you see anyone inside it?"

"Maybe." She shifted her feet.

"Maybe is good. Tell me what you saw, and maybe I can tell you if it's her."

"Her?"

"Yes. A young woman, maybe three times as old as you. She's pretty like you, and very nice."

The smile disappeared from her lips, and she dropped her eyes to look at the ground.

"She's the daughter of a friend, and he's sick with worry that something bad might have happened to her. Did you maybe see her?"

Her eyes turned up, and she bit her lip.

"Your father would feel sick if you'd gone away and he couldn't find you. He'd be afraid you were in trouble and needed his help. Can you help me find her? She might be hurt and need help really bad."

"I did see someone. In the big carriage from the villa west of here. She leaned out the window and asked for help. But a man covered her mouth and pulled her back in. Then the curtain dropped, and I couldn't see her anymore."

Africanus's eyes warmed as his smile returned. "That's her. She'll be so grateful to know that you told me so I can help her get home to her father." His index finger pressed against his lips. "But let's keep it a secret between you and me, what you just told me. Secret friends who help each other are the best kind."

Her shy smile and quick nod broadened his smile.

"Is there an inn where we can stable our horses and find a good dinner tonight?"

She pointed down the street.

Africanus stood. "Thank you for my friend and for her. I'll tell her you're her secret friend now."

A bright smile, and the girl turned back to watch the boys.

Africanus vaulted the wall and took his reins from Rufus. A quick jump, and he threw his leg across the stallion's rump to land in the saddle.

When he nudged the horse into a walk and headed for the inn, Aulus rode up beside him. "Why aren't we going to get Julia?"

"It's not the right time."

Marcus nudged his horse to come up on the other side of Africanus. "Of course it's the right time. Why would we wait?"

Africanus looked at Marcus but turned his face toward Aulus before answering. "We wouldn't be allowed close enough to the villa to see anything this late, let alone to do anything. We'll go in the morning during the salutation time. As the son of an ex-consul, you'll request an audience with Ursus. Your family name will be recognized instantly, and you'll be granted admittance."

"But we know she's there now." Aulus's breaths came faster. "What if he does something to Julia tonight?"

Africanus rested his hand on Aulus's shoulder. "I understand men like this one. Nothing will happen tonight that didn't happen already. Tomorrow we won't just find her. We'll take her home."

As much as Aulus hated to wait, the calm certainty in the gladiator's eyes persuaded him. He drew a deep breath, and as he slowly released it, he could see the wisdom in Africanus's plan.

Tomorrow they would find Julia, and then he would bring her home.

Chapter 33

Life Was Good

Gaius's Farm, Day 23

It was mid-morning, and Leander's eyes kept drifting to Mistress Calantha as she worked at the big loom. Tying the warp yarns to the hanging weights, weaving the shuttle back and forth through them, tapping the yarn with a comb to push it up against the last strand to make the fabric—there was something both fascinating and soothing about the way her hands moved. When his mother and Ariana worked at the loom, he'd loved watching when he was a child.

His lips tightened. That had been so long ago, and he'd forgotten so much. But sometimes memories of what had been lost hurt too much to hold onto them.

Then, as if she felt his eyes upon her, she turned, and her smile lit the room. She placed the shuttle on the small shelf at the top of the loom and came to the bedside. He shifted to make more room, and she sat beside him.

"You look like something's hurting. Can I get you anything?"

He forced a smile. "No, but thank you."

"Are you feeling better today?"

"Yes, mistress. Much better."

Her eyebrows arched. "Be more careful what you say. Don't forget I'm Calantha now, and you're Leander." Her eyes warmed. "What's my name?"

"Calantha." It was becoming too easy to say it.

"That's right. And you are..."

"Leander."

She pushed his hair back from his forehead. "Tawny like a lion, but I wouldn't dare do this if you really were one."

His lips twitched, and then a real smile leaked out. She could charm a lion into letting her pet it like a house cat.

She rose and pulled up the blanket to cover his chest. After running her fingers through his hair one more time, she returned to the loom.

The mistress started humming, and he closed his eyes. As the music wrapped around him, he drifted off to sleep.

When Marcella came into the cottage carrying a bucket of water, Calantha placed the shuttle on the shelf and joined her at the counter.

"I never spent any time in our kitchen. I know almost nothing about cooking, but may I help?"

As Marcella poured some water into a large bowl, the corners of her mouth curved. "My girls loved watching when they were little. When they got big enough to help, they weren't quite as eager to keep me company."

She picked up the pot she'd filled with lentils and water at lunch time. "While I drain and rinse these, you can wash the carrots."

When Marcella returned, Calantha had the purple carrots cleaned and lined up on the countertop. Marcella lifted a cutting board from a peg on the wall. Then she took a carrot and cut a few slices. "For the stew, this is the way you want to cut them."

Calantha looked over her shoulder at Leander. His eyes were closed, his breathing slow and regular.

"It's a good thing he's sleeping." She silenced the chuckle that wanted to escape. "What he doesn't see, he can't tell me his mistress shouldn't be doing for him."

Marcella's smile broadened. "Sometimes it's better if my man doesn't know what I'm doing, too."

She handed her knife to Calantha and took another from the rack on the wall. "I'm glad you want to help. Many hands make for light labor."

"I'd love to help and learn all I can. If I'm pretending to be Calantha, I need to know how."

Marcella slipped her arm around Calantha's shoulders and gave her a quick hug. "And I'll enjoy every moment of teaching you."

As they worked together, their knives tapped out a rhythm against the cutting board. It was like music washing over Calantha. It was almost a month until Father would come back from Sicilia and she could return to Rome, but every day with Marcella made this cottage feel more like home.

It was early evening and almost time to eat. As Leander watched Marcella and Mistress Calantha getting the supper ready to serve, memories kept floating up from where he'd left them long ago. Memories of his mother's gentle instructions and Ariana's laughter when she tried something for the first time and it didn't turn out as she'd hoped.

Sweet memories of the happy times before the legions came and everything he'd known was destroyed. When everyone he'd loved was killed or dragged off to fates maybe worse than death.

So many times, he'd asked God why, and he never got an answer. But even though the questions remained, God's warm presence never faded. God was there in the dark hold of the slave ship that carried Leander to Rome. He was there at the auction where Leander was bought by the Crassus estate. God was there through the years of working with the Crassus horses, when being a slave had let him do what he loved most and he could almost feel free.

An even though he never would have prayed for any of what had happened the past three weeks, God's hand was still upon him.

His gaze settled on Mistress Calantha's beaming smile as Marcella wrapped her arm around the mistress's shoulders and hugged her.

Thank you, Lord, for putting me where I could save her from Ariana's fate.

Gaius came through the door and straight to his bedside. "You're looking much better. Ready to join us at the table tonight?"

"More than ready."

Marcella joined her husband. "But first I need to rig a sling for that arm. It's too soon for you to be using it."

She disappeared down the hallway and returned with a folded piece of fabric. Gaius helped him sit up, and Marcella draped it around his neck and tied a knot. Then she slipped his arm into the loop. "How's that?"

"Just right."

She patted his good shoulder. "Please bring our young man to the table, Gaius."

Leander stood, and with Gaius as his crutch, he hobbled over and sank into a chair.

Mistress Calantha brought the blanket from the bed and folded it in half before wrapping it around his shoulders. "We don't want you getting cold."

Cold was not the problem when she smiled at him like that. "Thank you, Calantha."

She joined Marcella to carry the stew bowls to the table, then sat next to him.

Gaius lowered his head. "We thank you, God, for this day and this food. And especially for Dacius being healed enough to join us. In the name of our Lord Jesus, amen."

Leander's gaze shifted to the mistress when her voice joined the amen.

She picked up his spoon and held it out for his left hand to take. "He's not Dacius anymore. He's Leander."

Gaius's mouth curved up. "A much better name for him, and I will remember to use it tomorrow."

Mistress Calantha's head tipped, and her brow furrowed. "Tomorrow?"

He was already raising a steaming spoon to his mouth, but he stopped halfway. "Tomorrow is *Solis*, and a few of our Christian friends will be coming to share a fellowship meal and worship."

Leander's grin was so big it almost hurt his face. "Nothing could be better. The estate that bought me when I first came to Rome had been owned by Gaius Licinius Crassus. Not long before I got there, he'd been forced to flee just ahead of the Urban Cohort arresting him as a Christian. The estate passed to his cousin. He wasn't a Christian, but he didn't change much about how the estate was run. He was wise enough to see it was treating slaves like people that made everyone work hard to grow good crops and make him wealthier. Life was good there.

"They didn't shackle the feet of field slaves while we worked. The overseer didn't chain us or lock us in the *ergastulum* at night. If we were really good at something, he tried to put us doing that, at least some.

"I was barely twelve when I got there. But my family had raised horses in Dacia, so he put me in the stables. He saw my skill with horses and mules and let me use it every way I could."

His eyes focused on the past, and that brought a smile. "I truly enjoyed the work. Seeing a new foal struggle to its feet and nicker for the first time. Gentling a young stallion so the master could ride him.

Watching a team of mules I'd trained work like they had a single mind. You should see the wild beauty of chariot horses in a field, racing each other for the sheer pleasure of it."

The memories brought a happy sigh.

"We had plenty of food and a half-day of rest on Solis. There were some other Christian slaves, and we met for a short time while the others rested." The big grin returned. "Getting to worship with brothers and sisters again...nothing could be better."

Gaius rubbed his mouth. "How did you come to be with Calantha?"

Leander's smile faded. "The master who loved the horses so much died, and his son decided to sell the racing stock to buy a townhouse in Rome. With the chariot horses gone, they didn't need a trainer like me anymore."

◆

The happiness in Leander's voice as he described where he served before Gallio bought him...it drove little daggers into Calantha. He'd been nothing more than a slave, but he spoke of so much that was good there, and none of what was bad.

What could he say if he were to describe life at the Secundus estate? That she'd never spoken to him or known his name before he almost died to save her? That she'd let him be whipped for simply speaking to her when all he wanted to do was spare her from harm?

Tendrils of regret wrapped around her heart and squeezed. No words on her part could make up for what had been done to him.

Leander's gaze settled on her, and his smile dimmed. "Life was good at the Crassus estate, but it's also good that God placed me at the Secundus estate in time to protect Mistress Calantha from her brother."

Marcella lifted the plate of bread and offered it to Calantha. "It's a very good thing that He did. I'm so thankful you were there."

Calantha took the plate, glad to have something to look at beside Leander's eyes.

Marcella patted Calantha's arm. "I'm thankful you found Servilia and that she got Gaius. It's such a pleasure having you both here with us."

◆

Mistress Calantha offered the plate to Leander, but he shook his head. "No, thank you, mistress."

She stroked his left hand as it lay on the table, and he liked it more than he should let himself.

"You look tired. As soon as you eat, you should lie down and rest again. And you're supposed to call me Calantha, not mistress."

His lips twitched before he replied. "I'll try harder to remember which I should say."

She leaned close to him and adjusted the blanket around his shoulders. But it wasn't the blanket that made him feel warmer.

"Perhaps you need more practice. You're Leander and I'm..."

"Calantha."

"Try to think of me more as a beautiful flower and less as a mistress. That should make it easier for you to remember."

"Perhaps."

But thinking of her too much as a mistress wasn't his real problem. It was thinking of it too little.

Chapter 34

SAVED FROM A LIVING HELL

Estate of Claudius Ursus, Day 24

Aulus and the others rose early for a quick breakfast before riding to the Ursus villa. While Marcus and the gladiators ate the herb-seasoned porridge and Rufus pronounced it delicious, Aulus couldn't eat a bite. Julia was only two milia passuum away, and there would be plenty of time for eating after he had her back under his protection.

When they finally left, Africanus kept their party at a trot, so it was less than half an hour before they arrived at the sprawling villa overlooking the sea.

As Africanus had told him, Aulus informed the slave organizing the salutation that Aulus Julius Secundus, son of ex-consul Tiberius Julius Secundus, current proconsul of Sicilia, was seeking an audience. There were five people waiting ahead of them, but Aulus and his companions were ushered into the reception hall as soon as the current visitor left the room.

Ursus was a flabby man in his forties, richly dressed in a fine linen tunic and toga with embroidered borders that blended gold and silver threads.

He sat on a throne-like chair that was embellished with carved scenes of frolicking satyrs and nymphs framed by gold filigree. He rose and held out both hands to Aulus. "It's both a surprise and an honor to receive the son of Julius Secundus in my home. To what do I owe this great pleasure?"

His smile felt as greasy as the scented oils he had worked into his hair.

Aulus cleared his throat. "We're looking for a young woman you purchased in Rome a few days ago. We have reason to believe she was kidnapped and is not really a slave."

Ursus's flattering smile stiffened. "You've been misinformed. I never buy unless I know the paperwork is legitimate."

Marcus took one step forward. "Be that as it may, we know you bought a girl who claimed she'd been kidnapped."

As his head tipped back, Ursus's eyelids lowered, letting him look down his nose at them. "Slaves often tell that lie. It's not true."

Aulus stepped up beside Marcus. "My sister Julia was kidnapped five days ago. The time of your purchase is perfect for it to be her."

"While I'm grieved to hear of your sister's plight, I can assure you the slave I purchased is not her. I personally inspected her papers and know them to be valid."

Marcus crossed his arms. "If that's the case, you should have no objection to letting us see the girl to be certain it isn't Julia."

"She's a mere slave, not your missing sister." Ursus's sneer shifted toward a patronizing smile. "But I have no objection to you seeing her. I'll soon be sharing her with all my friends."

He snapped his fingers, and a boy who'd been standing like a statue by the wall trotted over. "Bring the new girl."

Aulus glanced at Marcus. Would he ever be able to project the aura of calm superiority that came so naturally to his friend?

A door opened at the side of the room, and a girl was dragged in. Her tunic was expensive linen, but she wore no jewelry. Her hair hung loosely down her back, and her eyes were puffy from crying.

But the moment her gaze settled on Aulus, she rammed her elbow into the stomach of the man holding her other arm. She wrenched free and ran to Aulus. With both hands, she clutched his tunic.

"Please help me! I'm Pompeia Lenaea, a free woman and citizen of Rome. I was kidnapped." One hand released him and swung to point at Ursus. "He doesn't own me. He refuses to believe two thugs knocked out the slave escorting me home after dining with the sister of one of my father's students."

Marcus touched her arm. "Who's your father?"

"Gnaeus Pompeius Lenaeus, and his student is Valerius Flaccus. If you'll just send for either of them, they'll tell you I'm not a slave."

Marcus fixed steely eyes on Ursus. "I know Flaccus. Pompeius Lenaeus is his tutor. She's telling the truth, and you should release her immediately."

Ursus's lip curled as a laugh rumbled in his chest. "I paid good money for her, and I have papers to prove she's mine. Why should I care about the opinion of a mere youth?"

Marcus looked at Aulus, eyebrows raised.

Aulus's back straightened as he lifted his chin. "You should want to do what's right. Sending her home to her father is the only right choice. Roman law and Roman honor both demand it."

Ursus snorted. "I have every right to keep a slave I've legally purchased."

Africanus took a step forward. Ursus raised his hand and flicked his fingers. A pair of gladiators moved into the room through the side doorway.

Ursus's nostrils flared; then fury lit his eyes as they bored into Aulus. "Chain your guard dog and go."

"I'm not his guard dog." Africanus's deep voice was calm as his hand wrapped around the handle of his gladius. "I'm many times a champion in the Flavian Amphitheater and the special agent for an ex-consul of Rome who has Hadrian's ear. You know you're guilty of *plagium* now, even if you didn't know it when you bought her. Do you want to risk the anger of Julius Secundus and Emperor Hadrian himself over a mere girl that you had no right to bring here in the first place?"

Rufus shifted to keep both Ursus's bodyguards and the door to the atrium in view. His fingers tightened on the hilt of his sword.

Ursus's gaze bounced between Africanus and Rufus and finally settled on the girl. "Take her. Get out of my house and off my land."

Aulus wrapped his arm around Pompeia as she clung to him. "I thank you, Ursus, for choosing to do the right thing and release her. We'll get her back to her father, and my father will hear of your generosity in setting her free."

With venom in his gaze, Ursus flicked his hand toward the door behind them before marching past his bodyguards and leaving the room.

When his gladiators turned and followed him, Aulus blew out a long breath. "Let's leave before he changes his mind." He grinned at Africanus. "I can see why Brutus wanted you with us."

Africanus shrugged, but the hint of a smile tugged at the corners of his mouth.

They returned to the stable yard and reclaimed their horses. Aulus mounted, and Africanus lifted Pompeia to sit behind him.

She wrapped her arms around his waist and rested her cheek against his back. "There aren't enough words in the whole Empire to say how much I thank you, Julius Secundus. I'll remember what you just did forever."

"It's no more than any man should do." He patted her hand. "Hold on tight. It's a long ride, but we'll have you home before midnight."

When the rest were mounted, he nudged his horse into a fast walk.

They hadn't found Julia, but at least they'd saved Pompeia from a living hell.

Then the smile Pompeia's words had drawn faded.

Who had his sister? Another man like Ursus, or someone even worse?

His heart pounded, and even several deep breaths couldn't slow it.

Was she chained, caged, terrified of what the future held for her? Would he find her in time to save her?

Or was he already too late?

Chapter 35

FORGIVING THE ENEMY

Gaius's Farm, Dies Solis, Day 24

As Leander swallowed his last mouthful of Marcella's breakfast porridge, Gaius rose from the table.

"Dacius." He glanced at the hallway where Mistress Calantha had disappeared. "I mean Leander. Come join me in the sunshine. I need to prepare for our visitors."

"I can think of nothing better."

Marcella turned from the counter where she was cutting cheese slices. "Be careful with him, dear."

"I will."

When Gaius rolled his eyes after Marcella turned away, it took all Leander's self-control to keep from laughing. As Gaius headed out the door with his chair, he pressed one finger to his lips. Leander took a deep breath and managed not to chuckle.

He'd settled his mouth into his usual slight smile by the time Gaius returned. With Gaius's arm wrapped around him and his own good arm across his friend's shoulders, hobbling outside wasn't so bad.

As soon as Gaius lowered him into the chair, Gaius's mouth curved into a wry smile. "Shall I tell her I didn't break you when I get the next chair?"

Leander lowered his voice so no one inside could hear. "I wouldn't." Then his own grin broke free.

Two poles leaned against the wall, and Gaius dropped one end of each into the holes at the edge of the stone patio where he'd placed Leander's chair. Then he unrolled a canopy and stretched it from the hooks on the wall to the two poles, making an island of shade.

Leander cradled his arm and moved it in the sling to find the least painful position for his shoulder. "Maybe I can help with setting everything up next week."

Gaius patted his good arm on the way back to get another chair. "I made a crutch, and you can try it tomorrow. We'll see how much you've healed by then, and if Marcella thinks you're doing well enough, you can." He grinned at Leander. "I'm not going to put you to work too soon and risk a scolding for letting you hurt yourself."

He carried out the other three chairs from the kitchen and unstacked some benches that were stored by the wall.

Leander shifted in his chair and stretched out his bandaged leg to get more comfortable. "I always enjoyed helping get ready for the house church that met at our horse farm. One of the older men had grown up in a church in Thessalonica that had a copy of the gospel of Luke. He'd memorized it as a child, and he helped me memorize it, too. Then he'd lived in Ephesus, where he'd learned from Apostle John. He also had copies of several letters from Apostle Paul. So after I learned everything he knew of what Luke and Apostle John wrote about Jesus, I memorized the letters as well."

Gaius set one chair beside Leander and two across from him. "Do you still remember any of it?"

That triggered a soft chuckle. "How could I ever let myself forget the words of my Lord? Or the teachings of Apostle Paul that helped me understand what it means to follow Jesus as my Savior and Lord? On the slave ship, we were punished if we talked. But I recited them over and over inside my head, and they drove back the darkness that tried to swallow me."

His gaze drifted to the low hills that rose behind Gaius's vineyard. "Once I reached Rome and the Crassus estate bought me, I clung to them as my lifeline to the world I left behind. When I worked by myself, I'd recite them and then think about what they meant. How I could live as a slave and still please God." The corner of his mouth turned up. "Even more so since I was sold to the Secundus household. If I had a sestertius for every time I've had to remind myself of Apostle Paul's command to serve my master as if serving Lord Jesus, I'd be as rich as an imperial freedman."

Gaius moved two benches to complete the circle. "Would you be willing to share something you know with us today?"

The grin that split Leander's face was as big as the one when he'd heard Gaius could take them in. "There's nothing I would enjoy more."

Calantha came back from her room to find Leander gone. "Where is he?"

Marcella looked over her shoulder. "Gaius took him outside. He's fine." She arranged the last slices of cheese on the plate and turned.

"I should tell you something about the people who are coming. Publius Aelius Mestrius and his wife Lucillia own a taberna and private bath in the village just up the road from where you turned off to come here. They're about forty. She'll bring her lyre for our singing. Quintus Sertorius Festus and his wife Petronia are about Leander's age. They have a boy, Quintus, and a little daughter, Sertoria. They're expecting their third baby in less than a month. Mestrius brings a wagon, and he picks up Petronia's family on the way here."

She tucked a loose strand of hair behind her ear. "Then there's Sextus Valerius Genialis. His wife died a few months ago. I'd love to see him remarry when his grief has passed, but he doesn't know any other Christian women. He raises sheep and some vegetables on his farm just east of us. Gaius takes his produce to Rome when he takes ours. Sextus usually walks through our vineyard to get here."

The jingle of mules in harness grew louder, then stopped. Calantha's heart began to race. Strangers posed a risk. What if they told the wrong person they'd seen her and Leander?

Marcella wrapped her arm around Calantha. "Let's go meet your newest friends." She gave Calantha a quick hug. "Don't worry. We'll only tell them your new name, and none of them would betray you even if they knew the real one."

As Marcella introduced Julia as Calantha to each person in turn, Calantha found her eyes drifting to Leander. One arm in a sling, his other hand resting on his thigh, he looked as relaxed and happy as he did at the table with just Marcella and Gaius. If her protector saw no danger, there probably wasn't any.

As soon as the food was carried into the cottage, they all gathered under the canopy. Gaius took the chair by Leander, and Marcella took the other empty chair by Lucillia. Petronia patted the bench next to her and smiled, so Calantha sat beside her.

Lucillia plucked her lyre, and all began to sing a song of praise to their god. A surprising happiness brightened each face. Not all sang well, but even with the off-key notes, there was a beauty to the song.

Calantha's gaze shifted from Lucillia to Leander. He sat with his head tipped back and his eyes closed while the smile that was always hovering on his lips alternately broadened and relaxed.

After several songs, Gaius stood. "Leander will be with us for a few weeks, and we're truly blessed to have him here. He's memorized some of Paul's letters to the churches in Asia and Greece and much of the gospels written by Luke and John. He'll be sharing those with us."

Calantha fought to keep the surprise off her face. How had a farm slave had enough free time to do that? But maybe it was from before he was a slave.

With his left hand, he pushed himself up and shifted on the chair. His mouth twitched with a tiny grimace. "Normally, I'd stand to share God's Word, but that's a little hard for me today. Maybe next week."

His smile reappeared. "I have no words to tell you how special it is to worship here with fellow believers. My father led a house church, and one of the elders had lived in Thessalonica and Ephesus before coming to us. He even knew Apostle John. He found great joy in teaching what he knew to anyone in our fellowship who wanted to learn.

"As a child, I never realized how much that would mean to me in the years after I left home. But God knows what's best for us, and I've been blessed by Him giving me all I need and more."

His gaze traveled around their circle, pausing for a fleeting moment on Calantha's eyes. All the tension drained out of her. Her protector would never reveal something to endanger them.

"He blesses us so we can share our blessings with others. So, let me tell you about one day when Lord Jesus was in Galilee of Judaea, in a flat area where many people had gathered to hear Him teach. He taught them many things that day, but I want to share part of what Lord Jesus said that has carried me through hard times."

He closed his eyes, and tilted his face skyward. His smile broadened, and when he opened his eyes, the warmth in them was just like the love in Father's eyes when he drew her into his arms after a long journey.

His gaze rested on each face, including hers, and her cheeks warmed before he looked at Petronia, who sat beside her.

"Lord Jesus said, 'But I say to you who hear, love your enemies, do good to those who hate you, bless those who curse you, pray for those who abuse you. To one who strikes you on the cheek, offer the other also, and from one who takes away your cloak do not withhold your tunic either. Give to everyone who begs from you, and from one who takes away your goods do not demand them back. And as you wish that others would do to you, do so to them.'"

Calantha straightened. She'd loved Aulus...until he betrayed her. Surely Leander's god couldn't expect her to love him now or give him another chance to hurt her.

"'If you love those who love you, what benefit is that to you? For even sinners love those who love them. And if you do good to those who do good to you, what benefit is that to you? For even sinners do the same. And if you lend to those from whom you expect to receive, what credit is that to you? Even sinners lend to sinners, to get back the same amount.'"

He paused, and his eyes captured hers. "'But love your enemies, and do good, and lend, expecting nothing in return, and your reward will be great, and you will be sons of the Most High, for He is kind to the ungrateful and the evil.'"

Calantha bit her lip. Leander's god asked too much. She'd never forgive Aulus for what he'd done. And what kind of god would choose to be kind to evil men?

Leander paused, and his smile turned sad. "Things happen to all of us that make it hard to follow this command. Some of what happened to me and the people I loved hurt so much that I wondered how I could ever obey.

"But the answer is in the very next thing Jesus said to the people gathered around Him. 'Judge not, and you will not be judged; condemn not, and you will not be condemned; forgive, and you will be forgiven.'"

Calantha dropped her gaze to the foot of his chair, but she still felt his eyes upon her.

"Before we can love anyone who hurts us, we have to let go of the bitterness that keeps us from forgiving, that makes us want to strike back. When I let bitterness take hold of me, it chains me like the shackles on the legs of a farm slave."

Calantha's eyes flicked up to his face, but he was looking past them all toward the vineyard. How many times had real shackles clamped around his ankles?

"But forgiveness for those who hurt us isn't a feeling that comes naturally. It doesn't even start as a feeling. It's a decision we have to make. A decision to let go of hating those who hate us. A decision to forgive the ones who hurt us, like Lord Jesus forgave the Roman soldiers who crucified Him, even as He hung on a cross.

"Sometimes I still struggle with it, but when I do, I remember what

Jesus told me. Love my enemies. Forgive those who hurt me. However many times my anger rises, the Holy Spirit will give me the strength to turn that anger away. And each time I forgive, part of me is set free."

His regular smile returned, and he shrugged. "That's all God has given me to say today."

Gaius stood. "Thank you, Leander." He held his hand out to Lucillia. "Now let's lift our hearts to God again."

As the first notes rang out, Calantha wasn't sorry Leander had stopped. He'd said many things that she needed to think about, and some of them struck very close to the sore places in her own heart.

When the songs finished, Marcella shepherded the group into the kitchen, where the food was arranged on the table. Each had brought something, with Lucillia bringing a large pot brimming with a pork stew that filled the room with its savory aroma. Sextus had brought some vegetables cut up and mixed together as a salad. Petronia had brought a loaf of bread. Marcella had added the sliced cheese, some dried dates, and some more bread. She set a pitcher of watered wine on the side counter with enough cups beside it for everyone to drink.

Calantha stepped into the line beside Petronia. "Let me help you with your children."

Petronia's eyes lit. "I'd love to have your help. My baby should be born in about a month." She patted her swollen stomach. "It's not so easy to bend over to pick up my daughter now. My mother is coming to help with the children for a little while after the birth."

Calantha rested her hands on the shoulders of Petronia's five-year-old son. "That should be a great help."

"It will, but I've been doing a lot of weaving to finish making some things to sell before the new baby needs so much of my time. Standing on my feet for too long every day...it makes me so tired."

They would all eat outside, and Gaius was carrying a bowl and plate out to Leander.

Petronia's gaze followed him. "It's so good to have Leander here to teach. I've heard Greeks are some of the best teachers, and the elder from Thessalonica certainly did a wonderful job teaching him." Her brow furrowed. "Leander's a Greek name, but he doesn't look Greek to me. He looks more Germanic, or maybe Dacian. There are many Dacian slaves on the estate next to our farm."

Calantha bent to pick up Sertoria to avoid looking into Petronia's eyes. "I think he did mention once that his family was from Dacia." She propped the little girl on her hip. "How long have you known Marcella?"

Petronia's eyebrows rose; then a smile broke out. She placed Calantha's free hand on her stomach. "The baby's kicking. It's like having a little mule in there."

"My sister's babies were the same. I love feeling them." She withdrew her hand. "You were about to tell me about Marcella."

"I met Gaius and Marcella when they became Christians maybe ten years ago. I've met their two daughters, too, but their sons had joined the legion when they were old enough. They both died in the Dacian war."

Petronia's eyes sought out her son. "I pray my son never wants to do that. I can't imagine anything worse than him going to war and someone killing him. I would try to forgive, as Jesus commands, but whether I could truly do it...well, I hope I never have to find out like Marcella has."

Calantha turned her eyes back to the little girl on her hip so Petronia wouldn't see her astonishment. Leander had only been eleven at the time, but how could Marcella and Gaius treat any Dacian like they would their own sons? Could Leander be so happy to be with them if he knew their sons died conquering his homeland?

She glanced out the door and let her gaze linger on him. Even with his arm in the sling, he looked like he hadn't a care in the world as he talked with the Roman men whose armies had taken everything from him.

When he thought he was dying and she asked him why he risked everything to save her, he'd told her about Jesus commanding that he love his enemy. His god had commanded it, and he had obeyed.

Since Leander could forgive all that Vilicus and the kidnappers had done...and all she'd failed to do, not the smallest doubt of his willingness to forgive lingered in her mind. Leander wouldn't treat these men as enemies, even if Gaius himself had been the one who destroyed Leander's family and made him a slave.

Chapter 36

The Secundus villa, morning of Day 25

It was after the sixth hour of the night when Aulus and Marcus rode up to the Secundus stable gate and found it barred. Aulus dismounted and pounded with his fist, but no one came to open it.

"You should tell Gallio to make sure someone is here when you want in." Annoyance colored Marcus's voice. "Even if your overseer uses that stable slave for other work during the day, there's no excuse for him not to be here to open the gate at night when you return."

Aulus remounted. "Stay here. I'll be right back."

He rode around the corner of the building and knocked on the front door. The viewing portal opened before he struck the wood the fifth time.

"Send someone to open the stable gate."

"Yes, Master Aulus." The face disappeared, and the portal closed.

By the time Aulus returned, Marcus had already ridden into the stable yard.

Aulus was met by a glowering Gallio. "I told Canis to fetch me the moment you returned. Where have you been?"

Gallio rammed his fists into his hips. "You disappeared without telling me where you were going or when I could expect your return. I sent Julia's litter slaves all over Rome searching for you today—to the Drusus townhouse, your sister's estate, and the homes of six of your good friends. I already had to send a message to Master Tiberius about Julia's kidnapping. You had me worried sick that I'd be sending another that you'd been killed."

178

Aulus swung his leg over the stallion's neck and slid off. "I'm sorry. I hadn't planned to leave Rome when we went to the ludus, but Brutus heard that a girl who might have been Julia had been sold and taken to Ardeo. We went to find her before anything worse could happen. It wasn't Julia, but we did rescue the girl. She'd been kidnapped, too. We're so late because we were taking her home. Next time I'll send you a message."

Gallio's anger faded to be replaced by a sad smile. "I would appreciate that more than you realize. You're all like my own children. When I think about what might be happening to Mistress Julia..." His jaw clenched, and his eyes looked too moist.

Aulus rested his hand on Gallio's arm. "I'm going to find her. I won't stop looking until I do."

"Whatever you do, be careful. I don't want to lose you both."

Gallio's deep sigh before he returned to his room twisted the dagger in Aulus's own hurting heart.

As he and Marcus headed to their sleeping chambers, Aulus glanced back at Gallio. The steward's shoulders drooped, and his steps were slow. Gallio had seemed a man in his prime, but the last week had aged him. One more consequence of his stupid choice.

Aulus ran his fingers through his hair. Why hadn't he just asked Gallio for the money and let Father's anger blaze? Nothing Father would have done could be worse than the misery he'd caused himself... and too many others.

Wherever Julia was, whatever was happening to her—it was all his fault, and nothing he could do would ever make amends for what he'd done.

The Ludus Bruti

When Africanus left Aulus and Marcus at Pompeia's house, he'd told Aulus to come to the ludus first thing. So the early dawn found Aulus mounted on Africanus's stallion and heading back to the ludus with Marcus.

As they rode into the stable yard, Aulus spotted his gray mare being brushed. She was a good horse, but two days on the stallion had reminded him of what he was missing. Until the young black stallion he'd bought was gentled enough for him to ride, maybe Marcus could lend him one of the Drusus horses.

He and Marcus had barely dismounted when Africanus strode through the gate. He carried a cloth sack, and the aroma of fresh rosemary bread wafted toward them as he approached.

Aulus inhaled deeply. "I thought barley porridge was usually served for breakfast here."

The corner of Africanus's mouth turned up. "Master Brutus will be waiting for you in his office. I'll join you as soon as I give this to Rufus. My wife sent it to him. He loves her bread whenever he can get it."

He disappeared through a doorway.

Marcus's brow furrowed. "His wife? I thought he lived in the slave quarters."

Aulus shrugged. "I guess not. I wouldn't want to live here if I had a choice." He tapped Marcus's arm. "Let's go. Brutus is waiting."

Brutus sat at his desk with several wax tablets open before him. He glanced at Aulus and waved his hand toward the two empty chairs across from him, inviting them to sit as he continued writing.

When Africanus entered the room, Brutus closed the tablet in front of him and leaned back in his chair.

"Africanus told me what happened in Ardeo. Not quite what we'd hoped for, but you did well freeing the tutor's daughter." His gaze settled on Aulus. "Is your steward still sending a slave to the Castra Praetoria every day?"

"Yes." The muscles in Aulus's neck tensed at that question

"Good. He should keep doing that as a precaution." Brutus leaned forward. "Relax, Aulus. The longer they go without finding her body, the more likely it is that she's still alive. If she was dead, I think they would have found her by now. A fresh grave in an unexpected place or the smell of an unburied corpse is usually reported. And if she's alive and still in Roma, we will find her."

He tapped the tip of his brass stylus on the desk top. "While you were gone, I visited the rest of the special dealers I thought might handle her. I found nothing, but they know I'm in the market now. I expect I'll hear if someone tries to sell her."

Aulus rubbed the back of his neck. "I don't want to just sit and wait and hope she shows up."

Brutus's smiling frown appeared. "And you won't have to. Since we don't have any good leads for where Julia might be, we'll try to find the man you hired and make him tell us where she is."

He rubbed his jaw. "So, what do we know about him? Marcus, do I remember correctly that his name is Gaius Faltonius Callidus."

"If he gave us his real one." Marcus ran his fingers through his hair.

"I think he did. He spoke with pride of serving in the XIV Gemina, and he said he was discharged in Carnuntum. That legion is headquartered there. He'd expected to find his father still alive and running the family taberna. He said that taberna is gone, but that could mean it's been closed or someone else owns it now."

Marcus nodded. "That's what I remember, too."

"So, let's assume his father died within this past year. His death might not have been reported and recorded in the Tabularium. But if the taberna was seized and sold to pay outstanding debts, there will be a court record. That could tell us what part of Roma he comes from and where he might be hiding out if he still has your sister.

"I know someone who can check into that for us. But I have something for you boys to do while he does. Callidus came to me to sell himself into a ludus."

His eyes turned on Marcus. "How much did you pay him?"

"Only 150 denarii."

"Too bad it was so much. That buys him time to decide what to do, but he still might have gone to another ludus that took him on. I'm going to send you to find out. Africanus will go with you. He's well known as one of my men, and any lanista in Roma will speak truth to you when he knows you're asking for me."

Brutus stood. "There are no games this afternoon, so you should find the lanistae training their men if you hurry. After the baths open to men at lunchtime, you might not find them at their ludi."

Africanus glanced back over his shoulder as he strode through the doorway. "Let's go. We have eight to visit. We'll start with the lowest ranked one. The best wouldn't sign him."

As they hurried to catch up, Aulus offered Marcus a hopeful smile. "Seems like a good plan."

Marcus nodded, but his lips straightened. "I'd like it better if Brutus went with us instead of his slave. That would guarantee cooperation."

"Africanus knew what to do in Ardeo. Besides, you and I know what to ask to find Callidus. We shouldn't need Brutus with us."

Marcus's only reply was a soft snort.

Chapter 37

RAZOR'S EDGE

Gaius's farm, Day 25

Pain surged each time Leander put weight on his bad leg, but he limped the few steps to the table and lowered himself onto a chair. When Mistress Calantha took a bowl of breakfast porridge from Marcella and brought it to him, she didn't move away after setting the bowl down. Instead, she drew a fingertip across his cheek. It had been seven days since his last shave, and his stubble had grown into a beard.

She stroked his cheek again. "I think you look better without your beard. Perhaps you can shave today."

Marcella looked up from stirring the porridge. "He can borrow Gaius's razor after breakfast." Her gaze shifted between the two of them. One corner of her mouth pulled up, and then a full smile appeared. "I like my man clean shaven better than bearded, too."

When the mistress stroked his cheek a third time, that was temptation beyond what a man should have to bear.

He leaned back in the chair. "If that's what you want, I'll shave, mistress."

She ran her fingers through his hair. One more thing he wished she wouldn't do because he enjoyed it too much. "You keep forgetting, Leander. I'm Calantha, not mistress, while we're here." Her fingers slipped through his hair again. "What's my name now?"

He tipped his head back to look into her gold-flecked eyes and saw the kindness she showed her nieces. "Calantha."

"And what does that mean?" The kindness slipped toward teasing. Her eyes were too entrancing when they sparkled with a tease.

"Beautiful flower."

"Very good. And you're my Leander, the lion who protects me." Her fingers petted his cheek. "But this beard is too much like a lion's furry face. I like my lions without fur."

She moved away from him to get her own bowl from Marcella. He sighed as he turned his eyes away. It was too hard when she touched him like that.

She's the mistress, not a beautiful flower for me to enjoy watching. God, help me remember that.

After breakfast, Leander placed the crutch Gaius had made under his left arm. With halting steps, he hobbled out to the bench by the table under the tree. He'd told Marcella he thought the brighter light would help, but with his right arm in a sling, he didn't want to make a mess inside. He was a right-handed man, unaccustomed to doing precision work with his left.

Mistress Calantha carried Marcella's footed brass mirror, a small towel, a bowl of water, and Gaius's razor.

He didn't want her to watch him. "Thank you for bringing it all out...Calantha. I can do it alone now."

"Are you sure?" She arranged the bowl and mirror on the table and twirled the razor between her fingers before setting it down.

"I'm sure." He nodded for emphasis. Having her close was too distracting. It would be hard enough as it was not to cut himself.

He scooped a little water from the bowl with his left hand and wet his beard. He waited to pick up the razor until she started back to the house.

The mirror was too low, so he scrunched down until he could see his jaw. He twisted the razor handle until he thought he had the blade at the right angle for cutting.

It wasn't. The first swipe of the razor didn't cut any hair at all. It just slid across his beard. He turned the handle, and the next try started to nick him where he first pressed it to his cheek. This was harder than it looked.

He set the razor on the table and bent over to splash a little more water on his beard. As he drew the blade across his face, the first half inch scraped away, but then the blade skittered across the hair again.

He pulled a breath and blew it out. This was going to take a while. If she hadn't commanded he shave, he'd give up and just grow the beard. For a long moment, he twirled the razor and stared at it. He'd been shaving for years with his right hand, usually without a mirror. No reason he couldn't figure out how to do it with his left.

He set the razor down and splashed on a little more water. Then he reached for the razor handle.

Mistress Calantha's hand on his left shoulder made him jerk. Her left hand touched his, and he froze.

"This won't do, Leander. I don't want a half-shaved shaggy man or one with cuts all over his face serving me, so I'm going to shave you myself."

He turned his eyes up to hers. "You shouldn't be shaving me, mistress. That isn't something a noblewoman should do for her slave."

"Nonsense. And you're supposed to call me Calantha. I want you to feel better, and I always feel better when I look my best."

He started to open his mouth, and she mock-glared at him. "You're not going to argue with your mistress again, are you?" The fake glare flipped into laughing eyes and a warm smile.

"No, m...Calantha." A smile started to lift the corners of his lips; then he stopped it.

Mistress, not Calantha. Mistress.

"I used to love watching the slave do this for Father. I'm sure I can remember how to do it for you. Now, turn and face me."

He swung his legs out from under the table, and she moved closer. Too close.

She rested her left fingers on his right cheek to steady his face as she began to draw the razor across his left cheekbone. "Now hold perfectly still. I don't want to cut you."

He held his breath. She leaned in, her eyes serious as she focused on where the blade touched his cheek, her lips parted a little as she concentrated. He tried not to look at her lips.

She finished the first sweep of the blade and moved back to rinse it off in the bowl. "Not bad for a start. Much better than you were doing, anyway."

Her gaze shifted from his cheek to his eyes. "You're a very trusting man, letting a woman who's never done this before so near your throat with a razor." A laugh bubbled out of her as she leaned closer to his face. "I don't see the slightest trace of fear in your eyes, but I guess nothing really frightens you. My fearless lion, that's what you are."

Little did she know! The razor didn't frighten him, but her closeness was unnerving.

He forced some air to push his cheek out to make a smoother, tighter surface for the second stroke. She bit her lip as the laughter bubbled up again. "You look so funny. I guess Father did, too, now I remember."

Again, her fingertips on his right cheek steadied his face but made his pulse gallop. She drew the razor across.

"There, not a drop of blood yet. That's good for us both. You don't need to lose any more, and I don't need to faint on top of you." Teasing eyes met his. "You'd catch me, though." Her eyes flipped to serious. "I can always count on you for that."

She was right. He'd do anything he could for her. "Yes, m—."

It was hard not to say it aloud. She'd scold him again if he did, but she wouldn't mean it. The kindness in her eyes even when she did—it was almost like Ariana's, except with his sister he never had to fight against thoughts about what he longed for that kindness to mean.

She finished shaving his first cheek. "So far your trust has been justified. But now, I need to get your top lip. So, stretch your lip down." Her own upper lip lengthened and she tipped her head back slightly, just like he'd have to do.

He'd seen himself do that in front of a mirror, and he'd be the first to admit it made him look worse than normal. When she did it—she was just as beautiful as ever.

He did as ordered, and she placed the blade at the base of his nose. "Hold that face, and I don't think I'll cut you."

She slowly drew the razor down several times, and his mustache was gone.

Her fingertips skimmed up his shaved cheek and across his upper lip. Her touch was a feather-light caress. He'd never imagined how good that could feel, and for Calantha to be doing it—it was a blend of warm delight and hot distress for him.

He closed his eyes. *My mistress, not Calantha. She's only the mistress trying to help me until I don't need help. She means nothing more by it.*

But try as he might, he couldn't quite force her back into the mistress box when each touch was a caress, even if she didn't mean it to be.

"What do you think?"

He opened his eyes to find her holding the brass mirror before his face.

"Do you like yourself better with a beard or without? I can't quite decide myself. Maybe I should leave it half of each until I'm sure."

"Whatever you want." If she wanted him to look absurd, that was up to her. He'd lost any right to vanity when he was made a slave.

"I'm only teasing. I won't leave you looking silly, even though you'd let me without a single complaint."

She drew her fingertips across his clean-shaven cheek again. Without the beard, the tingling where each finger touched was even harder to ignore.

Her hand moved to the unshaved side and applied gentle pressure. "Turn your head a little and hold still so I can get the other side."

He obeyed. She seemed in no hurry to finish, but he wished she would. The mistress box he tried to keep her in was shrinking with every gentle touch. Why did she have to be so kind? Why did she have to be so pretty? Why did she have to look at him like he was a free man instead of her father's property?

He closed his eyes and puffed out his cheek. The blade slid across it several times. Five more sweeps and she'd finished his chin. She was working faster.

God, let this temptation be over.

It was easier with his eyes closed. Her laughing eyes were almost as bad as her touch.

"Are my lion's eyes closed because he's afraid I'll cut him?" She drew her fingertips across both cheeks and his chin. "I think I've done a good job so far. Be brave and look at me."

He suppressed a sigh. The mistress's order must be obeyed, even when it made things harder. His eyelids opened, and he looked past her.

"Look at me, Leander." He obeyed, and her eyes moved closer as she peered deep into his. "That's better. No, I don't see any fear, so maybe you're just tired. I'm almost done. Tip your head back, and I'll get the beard under your chin."

He complied, and that forced his gaze onto the lovely face that enthralled him. She leaned over to dip her hand in the water. Then she drew her wet fingers across his throat. That was worse than touching his cheek.

"I saw you wetting your beard, so I guess that must help. Hold still."

She placed the blade against his throat and began to pull it up.

He watched her eyes as they focused on the blade. As it neared his jaw, she glanced up. She looked deep into his eyes.

And then it happened. The blade nicked the edge of his jaw, and he started to bleed.

"Oh! I'm so sorry. And here I promised I wouldn't cut you."

He threw his left hand up to hide the blood. "It's nothing. I've done it many times myself."

She grasped his wrist and pulled. He resisted. "Let me see what I did." He still resisted. "Really, Leander. Let me look. I'm not going to faint on you."

He relaxed, and she lifted his hand away from the cut.

"It's not much, really." She wet a corner of the towel and wiped the blood away. "You've been very good for me, you know. Since I helped Marcella tend your wounds, I can look at a little blood without fainting. But now I've mastered that, I don't want to see you bleeding ever again."

She dabbed at the nick again with the wet towel. "It's stopping." She set down the towel and picked up the razor. "I'll try not to cut your throat any worse as I finish."

"I trust you."

The warmth in her eyes almost set him ablaze. "I know, but not as much as I trust you. I would trust you for anything."

She rested her fingertips on his forehead, pushed lightly to tip his head back, then left them there. "Now don't move."

He closed his eyes and felt the several sweeps of the blade needed to shave his throat. At long last, it was done.

"Open your eyes." She was holding the mirror for him again. "If something happens to Father and we have to stay here forever, do you I think I can earn a living shaving men? Don't *tonsores* make good money?"

"You won't have to do that, mistress. I'll take care of you."

She rested her palm on his smooth-shaven face. Her thumb stroked his cheekbone. "I know you will. And it's not mistress it's…?"

"Calantha."

She turned and gathered up the mirror, towel, and razor. After flinging the water out of the bowl, she flashed him a smile before strolling toward the cottage.

As she walked away, the smile her touch had pulled from him drooped. He'd take care of Calantha until he returned her to her father, and then he'd once more be only a litter bearer for Mistress Julia. He closed his eyes and shook his head.

God, give me strength to be content with what must be.

Chapter 38

MORE THAN THEY TOLD HIM

Late morning of Day 25

The back of Marcus's neck tingled as they approached the entrance to the first ludus. There was no reason someone would be following them, but he glanced over his shoulder anyway.

What if they found Callidus here? Would he say something in front of Africanus and the lanista that could implicate Marcus in the kidnapping plot? How much did Brutus's slave know already? He and Aulus were alone with Brutus when they revealed what they'd done that got Julia kidnapped.

Was there a risk if Africanus learned too much? Brutus must trust the big Nubian since he was sending him everywhere with them, but Marcus didn't. Only deep friendship made a man trustworthy, and Brutus's favorite gladiator did not like him.

The feeling was mutual.

Marcus's gaze settled on the back of the gladiator's head as he walked several paces ahead of Marcus and Aulus. He froze his face so Aulus wouldn't ask why he was frowning.

Every time Africanus looked at him, there was disapproval in his eyes. He never said anything he shouldn't, but he never seemed to speak to anyone without a particular reason. Even then, his words were few and to the point.

Those words were almost always addressed to Aulus, even when Marcus asked the question or made the comment that provoked Africanus to speak. Such disrespect from a slave was not something he normally tolerated.

But the gladiator was almost friendly toward Aulus. Anything Af-

188

ricanus might say that would get Marcus into trouble would drag Aulus right in with him. Maybe that would be enough to keep him from saying or doing anything to cause them problems.

Africanus stopped at the ludus doorway and waited for them to catch up. "It's enough to ask if a new man has joined the ludus. Don't explain why you're asking the question. The lanista here knows me, so he'll know Master Brutus wants you treated well. That should be enough to get an honest answer. If it's yes, ask to see the man." His unreadable eyes focused on Marcus. "You met him, so we'll find him even if he's using another name."

What Africanus said was the wisest way to proceed, but it still felt wrong for a slave to be telling them what to do.

"I did, but it might put him on his guard if he sees me. I'd rather he remain ignorant of his discovery until we can have the Urban Cohort pick him up for interrogation. He hasn't seen Aulus, so it's safe for him to go in and ask."

"I can ask, but I won't know if it's him." Uncertainty clouded Aulus's eyes.

Marcus's gaze flicked to Africanus, then back to Aulus. "Africanus saw him."

When he looked at Africanus again, he raised his eyebrows. "You do remember what he looks like, don't you?"

Africanus's mouth twitched. "Of course."

"I'll wait out here. Pretend you don't recognize him if he's there. Then come out here, and we'll decide the next step."

Aulus drew a deep breath and held it before releasing it. He directed a shaky smile at Africanus. "Let's go."

The two men went inside, Aulus leading.

As they disappeared from view, Marcus weighed the options. Perhaps they could tell Callidus there would be no legal charges if he'd tell them where they could find Julia and they got her back unharmed. The safe return of his sister would be enough to satisfy Aulus. But how much would it cost for a lanista to make sure Callidus died during practice before he could tell anyone who hired him?

◆

Tribune Titianus kept his nose from scrunching as he led his troop of eight men from the Forum through the edge of Subura closest to the Amphitheater, but he let his mouth turn down. This was the shortest route to the Baths of Titus and Trajan, but the stench of this part of

Rome was sometimes enough to make even a slave who tended the sewers gag.

His frown deepened when he spotted a familiar figure lounging in front of a third-rate ludus that provided arena fodder for stingy sponsors unwilling to pay for good talent.

Marcus Drusus straightened as Titianus approached.

"Drusus. I would not expect to find you in this part of Rome."

Drusus's mouth smiled, but his eyes stayed too cool. "I don't come here often."

Titianus crossed his arms. "So why today?"

A tic at the corner of Drusus's mouth was replaced by another smile with warmer eyes. "I'm waiting for a friend."

"Who's the friend, and what is he doing here?"

"Aulus is looking into hiring a bodyguard."

Titianus raised one eyebrow. "Why now?"

The tic returned, this time followed by a frown. "I would think that's obvious. With Julia kidnapped, he's concerned he might be next."

The door of the ludus swung open, drawing Titianus's gaze. Aulus Secundus and a tall African with impressive muscles entered the street.

Secundus's head bounced back. "Tribune. I didn't expect to see you here."

Titianus's gaze locked onto the gladiator. "You fight for Antonius Brutus, don't you?"

The big man crossed his arms. "Yes."

With his hand fingering the handle of his gladius, Titianus stared into Secundus's eyes. That flicker of unease should not be there. "What were you doing?"

"Africanus was talking with the lanista about something for Brutus." Secundus's stiff smile didn't match his eyes.

Drusus's voice came from Titianus's left. "Brutus sent Africanus with us to help pick out the right bodyguard for Aulus."

Titianus blanked his face. "One of Brutus's gladiators should be a good judge. I trust you'll find the right man."

With a curt nod to the two senatorial sons and a flick of his hand to signal his men to follow, he turned and continued toward the Amphitheater.

With his back toward Drusus and Secundus, he let the mask fall away.

His eyes narrowed. Julia Secunda had vanished without a trace, and he'd be willing to bet two months' wages that Drusus and Secundus knew more than they'd told him.

Much more. Nothing would keep him from learning what they didn't want him to know. And if they'd broken the laws of Rome, he'd make certain they paid for it.

Chapter 39

GRIEF AND HOPE

Gaius's farm, evening of Day 25

Calantha stepped outside, carrying two pillows. When Gaius had come in from the vineyard, he'd helped Leander outside for a change of view and some conversation while she and Marcella finished the dinner preparation.

Leander sat on a bench, resting his head against the wall. Gaius sat beside him.

She set one pillow down and clutched the second to her chest. "I've brought a pillow for Leander to sit on."

When she raised her eyebrows at Gaius, he mimicked her. "Did Marcella send you, or is it your own idea to make him stand up before you'll let him sit and relax?"

He chuckled, but he also helped Leander onto his good leg so she could place the pillow under him. As Gaius lowered him back onto the bench. Calantha slipped the second pillow behind his back.

She gave them both a smile. "It's a good idea, no matter which of us thought of it first."

Leander tipped his head to look up at her. "Thank you."

"*Salve.*" The voice behind her made Calantha spin.

Sextus stepped out from between the rows of grapes. Gaius walked over to meet him. After a quick hug and a slap on the shoulder, Gaius settled on the second bench with Sextus beside him.

One corner of Gaius's mouth turned up. "You can tell her he has two friends to take care of him now, so she needn't worry."

With a wave, Calantha stepped back inside.

As Marcella placed the last slices of cheese on the serving plate, she looked over her shoulder. "Is Sextus here?"

Calantha leaned on the counter beside her. "He just arrived." She picked up a sliver of cheese and popped it into her mouth. "The other day, I noticed how sad he looked when he watched the wagon leave. Is there a reason?"

Marcella's lips straightened. "It reminds him of what he lost. His wife died six months ago. I've been inviting him for dinner a few times each week since then. He and Favonia were very close. Jesus tells us that two become one flesh in Christian marriage. When one is suddenly gone, whoever remains feels like their own heart died with the one they loved. It's not something we get over quickly. Sextus was always such a cheerful man, but he's only now coming back to his old self. It's hard to be alone."

"Is his farm like yours?"

"It's bigger. He grows vegetables and fruit, but he also raises sheep. He makes very good money selling their fleece to women living in the city."

"If he's a successful farmer, there must be fathers with older daughters or widows who would be delighted to have him as a husband."

"They would." Marcella's eyes softened. "But that's not the problem. Christian men only marry women who love God and follow Jesus. He doesn't know any Christian women who aren't married."

Calantha looked up from rearranging the cheese slices into a pattern. "Servilia looks like she might be close to his age. Have you thought about introducing them? She was so kind to Leander, just like you, and so brave the way she took us in and hid us from the kidnappers. She'd make a wonderful wife for him."

Marcella's smile turned into a chuckle. "I hadn't thought about that, but it's definitely worth thinking about."

◆

When Marcella called out that dinner was ready, Leander gripped Gaius's arm to help him stand. With the crutch under his left arm, he hobbled back into the house and lowered himself onto a chair. Sextus followed with the pillows.

After leaning Leander's crutch against the wall, Gaius disappeared down the hallway and returned with an extra chair.

Mistress Calantha moved behind him as Gaius shuffled the chairs to make room for five. He jumped when her hands settled on each side of his neck and gently squeezed.

"Would you rather have me sit on your left or your right to help you?"

"Whatever you want." He'd rather have Gaius on one side and Sextus on the other, but how to tell her that?

"Maybe to your right so I can be your extra right arm when you need it."

He twisted to look up at her and nodded.

When all had seated themselves, Gaius led them in prayer. Sextus and Gaius sat to his left, and that's the direction Leander kept his gaze while they ate.

He'd scraped the last bite of stew from his bowl when Sextus leaned forward to rest his elbow on the table and cradle his jaw.

"It was good having you share on Solis. Before we pray and I head home, would you share something again?"

Leander placed his spoon in the empty bowl. "Something from the gospels or from Apostle Paul's letters?"

Sextus shrugged. "I don't care. Something to think about tonight when I'm alone. It's nighttime when I miss Favonia most."

Leander rested his good arm on the sling. "Apostle Paul wrote something to the church in Thessalonica that I often thought about after my parents died and I was coming alone to Rome."

He straightened in the chair and closed his eyes. "'But we do not want you to be uninformed, brothers, about those who are asleep, that you may not grieve as others do who have no hope. For since we believe that Jesus died and rose again, even so, through Jesus, God will bring with Him those who have fallen asleep. For this we declare to you by a word from the Lord, that we who are alive, who are left until the coming of the Lord, will not precede those who have fallen asleep.'"

When he opened his eyes, he leaned forward and placed his hand on Sextus's arm. "'For the Lord Himself will descend from heaven with a cry of command, with the voice of an archangel, and with the sound of the trumpet of God. And the dead in Christ will rise first. Then we who are alive, who are left, will be caught up together with them in the clouds to meet the Lord in the air, and so we will always be with the Lord. Therefore encourage one another with these words.'"

Leander lowered his gaze to the table and drew a deep breath before looking straight at Sextus. "I watched both my parents die the same day. And when grief was hardest upon me, I kept reminding myself of what Lord Jesus said. 'For this is the will of My Father, that everyone who looks on the Son and believes in Him should have eternal life, and I will raise him up on the last day.'

"Lord Jesus has promised, so we know it will come. And on that day when the trumpet sounds, the joy of that reunion with those we love..." He closed his eyes, and the warmth of God's presence surrounded him before he reopened them. "Words can't even describe what I can imagine, and the reality will be so much greater than that."

Sextus's smile started small, then grew as the fire in his eyes kindled. Then he whispered, "Yes!"

Gaius's beaming smile swept around the table. "Let's pray. We thank You, Father, for the gift of eternal life through the blood of Your Son Jesus, and for the joy and hope that gives us even here on earth. Thank You for Your word that can't be broken, and for bringing us Leander to share it with us. May Your peace be with us all until we meet together again. In the name of Your Son, Jesus our Lord, amen."

◆

When Sextus spoke of his wife, Calantha heard the pain-wrapped wistfulness in his voice. That same pain had colored Father's voice when her stepmother died.

Her own mother had died when she was barely four, and she had a few treasured memories of the smiles on her mother's face. Faint memories also remained of lullabies and laughter and an arm wrapped around her as she sat in a lap. Apicula had held her as she sobbed, then dried her tears when Mother's body was carried away to be burned. But when Father remarried and brought Trebonia Procula and her daughter Antonia to the Secundus estate, she had again been showered with love, and she drank it in until the desert place in her heart was lush with flowers again.

Father had shown both his wives warm affection as well as respect. She'd hoped for the same from Metilia's brother. That was rare among senatorial men, who married for political alliances, not love, and asked only that their wives run their households well and never do anything to cause embarrassment. But what woman wouldn't grow to love Father, no matter how she felt on the day of their marriage?

It had been four years since Trebonia's death, and a whiff of lavender on a passing woman was still enough to trigger memories of special times together and that hollow feeling of loss.

Father told her Trebonia awaited them in the Elysian Fields, but the deadness of his eyes as he spoke those words was nothing like the hope that danced in Sextus's. Like the certainty in Leander's as he spoke of his parents and the new life together his god would give them all.

Calantha massaged her neck. The god of Leander had the power to heal a dying man. But did he have that much power over death itself?

Chapter 40

MAKING THE FIRST CONNECTION

The Secundus villa, Day 26

As Marcus strode through the Secundus atrium on the way to Gallio's office, his mouth turned down. When he put his stallion in the empty stall he always used, there was no water or feed waiting for him. He'd stuck his head through the garden archway and yelled at Vilicus. The overseer had hurried over and then promised to have someone take care of the horse immediately, but Marcus had his doubts.

When he entered the office, Gallio sat behind his desk, elbows on the desktop, forehead resting on his palms. Aulus held a stylus, tapping restlessly on the arm of his chair.

"Sorry I'm late. I had to stable my horse myself. Any news?" Marcus took the second chair by the desk.

Gallio shook his head.

Aulus stopped drumming. "That stable slave never seems to be where he should be. I'm tired of riding the mares while I wait for my stallion to be trained. Vilicus should stop using him for other work until he finishes what we bought him for."

Gallio's head snapped back, and he stared at Aulus.

Aulus returned the stare. "What?"

"How could you not know that stable slave is the same one who disappeared when Mistress Julia did? Vilicus put him on the litter when your stallion killed her bearer. Now he has another slave feed and water the horses and occasionally clean the stalls, but that's all. That stallion lets someone into the stall with food and water. He'll sometimes let them clip a lead to his halter, but he doesn't let them touch him."

The slaps of scurrying sandals grew louder until the boy stuck his head in. "Steward, Tribune Titianus is back."

Gallio perked up. "Bring him immediately." As the slave hurried away, he smiled at Aulus. "Perhaps he has some news about where Mistress Julia might be." His smile dimmed. "But perhaps that news is bad."

The rapid click of hobnails on marble announced the tribune before he stepped into the room, red cape hanging from his shoulder, red-crested helmet still on his head.

He tipped his head toward Aulus. "Secundus." Another quick tip to Marcus. "Drusus." When the slave offered him a goblet, he waved it away. Then his gaze settled on Gallio.

"I have several questions and a few things to report. First, the questions."

Titianus crossed his arms. "Was there anything unusual going on with Julia? She deliberately went into a bad part of Rome. Subura is not an area where young noblewomen..." He shifted to face Aulus squarely. "Or young noblemen would normally go."

Aulus tensed. Marcus shifted in his chair, trying to draw Titianus's attention, but it didn't work.

"Was there any reason to suspect she was meeting someone other than her grieving friend?"

"No." Gallio's voice turned the tribune's head toward him. "The man who came for her said he'd come from Metilia Neposa. Julia was expecting her to return to Rome that week. I'd never seen him before, but the Nepos household has more than a hundred slaves, so that didn't seem odd."

"Aulus." Gallio leaned forward. "You two ate together the night before. Did she say anything?"

Aulus shook his head.

Arms still crossed, only Titianus's torso turned toward Marcus. "Are you aware that the house from which she disappeared is the property of Lucius Claudius Drusus? A strange coincidence that it belongs to your father, Marcus."

"Really? Father does own rental property all over Rome, so I'm not surprised he has some in that part of Subura. As you say, a strange coincidence, or perhaps a twisted sense of humor on the part of the gods."

A soft snort accompanied the downturn of the tribune's mouth. "The neighbors said it had been empty, presumably waiting for a new renter. But several reported a man had been living there for at least four days before her disappearance. He'd been seen eating in the local taberna several times. Three days before the kidnapping, he'd eaten with a thin man. The thin one wasn't a regular customer, but the proprietor had seen him in the area before. Neither man has been seen at the taberna since the night before the kidnapping."

Marcus leaned forward. "What did the men look like?"

"The one living in the house looked mid-forties and had the haircut and bearing of a soldier. The other, a thin man about the same age who looked Roman."

Aulus had been sitting on the edge of his chair, rocking slightly while Titianus talked.

Marcus rose and turned his back to Titianus before he rested his hand on Aulus's shoulder. "I told you Titianus would be the man to figure out where she's gone."

With his eyes and one quick squeeze, he signaled his friend to calm down. The rocking stopped.

Marcus turned to face the tribune. "Let's go ask the bearers if that sounds like the man who led Julia into the house." He faked an optimistic smile as he faced Titianus. "Finding that man is the first step to finding Julia. Let's go see if we're on the right track at last."

Near the Flavian Amphitheater

Late afternoon found Aulus, Marcus, and Africanus on a backstreet half a mile from the Amphitheater. As the door of the eighth and final ludus where Callidus might be closed behind Aulus, his shoulders sagged. No sign of Callidus, so no trail to Julia.

Africanus stepped up beside him. "We're not through looking yet."

Aulus rolled his eyes. "But where? If we can't find him, we'll never find her."

"Master Brutus and I talked about this last night and planned the next step."

Grim-faced, Marcus joined them from his place leaning against the wall. "No Callidus?"

Aulus tightened his lips and shook his head. "No." He glanced at the gladiator. "But Africanus says there's a plan for what to do next."

Marcus's eyes narrowed. His gaze swept over Africanus before switching to Aulus. "Then let's go talk with Brutus. The sooner we move to the next step, the sooner we find her."

Marcus slapped Aulus's arm and started up the street toward the Vicus Sandaliarius and the Ludus Bruti.

Aulus trotted a few steps to catch up, then walked at Marcus's side.

Africanus's voice came from behind them. "He won't be there. Return first thing tomorrow with good horses, and we'll continue the hunt."

Aulus looked back over his shoulder. "Will my mare be good enough?"

"No. It will be a hard day in the saddle."

Marcus's voice drew Aulus's eyes. "I can send to the eastern estate for my other stallion."

Africanus cleared his throat. "If it can't get here so we can leave the ludus before midmorning or isn't fit enough for the distance, I'll take the master's horse, and Aulus will ride mine."

Marcus swung around to face Africanus. "I only ride the best. And if you presume to take your master's horse, what do you expect him to ride?"

Africanus's shoulders squared. "I'll judge the fitness of the horse for how far and how fast we must ride." His mouth twitched. "When I take Master Brutus's horse, he uses Rufus's."

Aulus placed his hand on Marcus's arm. "I don't care what I ride as long as it helps us find Julia."

Marcus's lips tightened as his gaze raked Africanus. Then he turned and started up the street. "Let's go. Gallio is waiting to hear what we found today."

Aulus rubbed his neck before following. Brutus had been right when he said it would have been best to simply tell Gallio he'd lost the money. It would still have been all right if Marcus's father hadn't been too afraid of Sabinus to help. Using the ransom money had sounded like a good idea, and it would have been if the ex-legionary had been an honest man.

He glanced at Marcus, striding at his side, and the corners of his mouth turned up. When Fortuna frowns and things go from bad to worse, a man is lucky to have a friend who'll do whatever it takes to make it right.

Chapter 41

THE SAME BUT DIFFERENT

Day 26

Since breakfast, Calantha had been working on the cloak for Leander, but it was time for a break. She needed to move and stretch. Standing while reaching up over and over as she used the comb to control the selvedge loops and push the weft yarn up to the growing sheet of fabric was tiring. Plus the width of the cloak made her slip the weaving sword in from both sides to push the yarn firmly into place as she opened the space between the two sets of vertical warp yarns for the next pass of the shuttle.

When she stepped outside, Leander awaited her on the bench, sitting on one pillow and leaning back against the other like she'd made him.

She sat beside him. "How are you feeling?"

His head turned toward her. "Better every day." Then his eyes turned toward the vineyard.

She'd told him not to say "mistress" or "yes, Calantha" every time he spoke to her. It had taken a few reminders, but he seemed comfortable with that now.

"What are you watching?"

He glanced at her, then shifted his gaze back to the vines.

"Gaius. He's checking the leaves for caterpillars and removing any he finds." His mouth straightened. "I should be helping him."

Calantha's eyebrows rose. "I see how much it hurts even for you to come out here. You certainly aren't ready to work."

He shrugged. "I can do it. It's a one-handed job, and I'd just be standing on my good leg."

201

"Running with an arrow in your leg when we might get killed if you stopped was one thing. Using your leg too soon when it isn't a life-or-death matter is quite another. That's not something I want you to do."

He glanced at her and nodded before turning his eyes back to Gaius. "I'm not used to doing nothing."

She stood. "Well, you'll just have to get used to it until I think you're well enough to do more than rest."

His mouth twitched. "Yes, Calantha."

She rose. He mostly remembered not to say it. "Now I have weaving to do."

His steady eyes looked into hers, and his mouth relaxed into that trace of a smile.

"Don't even think about going out there to help him. Even lions rest when they need to."

The way his hair fell across his forehead made her want to push it back. It had the same effect on Marcella and Servilia. There was something about it that made a woman want to mother him.

Her fingers swept his hair to the side. "Call me if you need anything."

His smile broadened, but he didn't say anything. He nodded, but did that only mean he heard her, not that he'd actually do it?

◆

As Mistress Calantha's fingertips brushed his forehead, Leander felt his smile grow. The same thing happened when Marcella did it. The same thing, yet not the same.

Marcella's touches reminded him of life before the Romans came, when his mother's fingers used to tousle his hair and squeeze his shoulder as she passed. Ariana had done the same, and her touch spoke of the love that flowed within his family. Love that helped him understand the unconditional love of God.

But the touches of Mistress Calantha weren't like those of his sister or mother. They were nothing like the kind attention from Marcella and Servilia, his sisters in Christ.

She meant them to be, but they weren't. Touches that were meant to comfort stirred feelings he didn't welcome.

Smiles like she bestowed on her nieces felt like the smiles of a woman who liked him.

But the last thing he expected, the last thing he wanted, was for the mistress to look at him through the eyes of a woman and see a man she had feelings for.

The corner of his mouth turned up. Mistress Calantha had been a kind woman since the first day he carried her. Kindness plus gratitude for saving her could look like affection to a man who wanted to believe it.

But he never wanted to believe what wasn't true. And everyone knew the daughter of a consul of Rome would never let herself think of a slave as a man worthy of her love.

Chapter 42

Expanding the Hunt

Ludus Bruti, Day 27

When Marcus and Aulus rode into the stable yard at the Ludus Bruti, Africanus's bay was saddled and waiting. Brutus's horse stood in the stable yard, unsaddled and being brushed.

Africanus turned from a conversation with the slave brushing the stallion. His swift appraisal of Aulus on Marcus's chestnut stallion made the trace of a smile curve his mouth before he turned his eyes onto Marcus. He raised one eyebrow, then nodded.

Africanus spoke words too soft for Marcus to hear. Then the slave brushing Brutus's horse led it into its stall.

Marcus's teeth clenched. Brutus's slave had assumed he couldn't provide his friend with a mount worthy of a senatorial son.

The gladiator approached Aulus, who still sat astride Marcus's spare stallion. He ran his hand down the horse's foreleg, then slapped its shoulder. "This one should do well. Master Brutus is sparring with Rufus." His gaze shifted to Marcus and cooled. "Follow me."

Marcus expected to enter the arena where he trained with Fortis, but they walked past to a smaller one where only Brutus and Rufus were sparring.

When they stepped onto the sand, Brutus looked first at Africanus. A silent nod from the slave triggered Brutus's smiling frown. He snatched a towel from the bench and wiped his face and chest. He pitched it to Rufus, who did the same.

Brutus pulled a plain tunic over his head and flipped a leather belt around his waist. "My office, and I'll explain what we do next."

After a short walk down a narrow hallway, Brutus dropped into his chair and, with a wave of his hand, invited Marcus and Aulus to do the same.

"Since you didn't find Callidus at the Roman ludi, it's time to expand the search."

Aulus rubbed his neck. "But where?"

Brutus leaned back in his chair and crossed his arms. "I told him he wasn't good enough to stay alive fighting in Roma. I suggested Luna, but it's a twelve-day journey on foot. Too soon for him to have arrived even if he decided to take my advice. But there are other ludi less than a two-day walk from Roma, and he might have gone to one of those."

Leaning forward, he rested his crossed arms on the desktop. "You can visit the most likely ones. Africanus has been with me when I've shopped for talent there, so the lanistae should recognize him as my agent.

"This time, ask if anyone has sought to join their ludus in the last week. If yes and they didn't take him on, ask if they know where he might go next. Then ask them to let me know if he shows up later." The corner of his mouth turned up. "They'll think they can make some quick money if they sign him and then sell his contract to me at a profit."

Brutus rose. "You have a long way to ride. My cook packed some food for your trip."

Africanus had been standing against the wall. He started toward the door until Brutus flicked his hand.

"You boys go mount up. Africanus will join you momentarily."

As Marcus stepped through the door, he glanced back at Brutus. He was handing a purse to Africanus and speaking too softly for Marcus to catch his words.

Africanus glanced his way, and a soft snort accompanied a smile. A smile like Marcus's own when he laughed at a man, not with him.

With jaw clenched, he followed Aulus into the hallway and toward the stable.

Perhaps he should ask Father to buy the Nubian. He'd soon learn how a slave should behave, and that didn't include laughing at a Roman senator's son.

Alban Hills south of Rome

Mons Albanus rose behind the amphitheater in Alba Longa. On the summit of the volcanic hill, the gleaming white columns of the sanctuary of Jupiter Latiaris were silhouetted against an azure sky.

But neither the temple nor the amphitheater held Aulus's gaze. The drab brick walls of the first ludus they would visit that day fronted the road ahead.

The first ludus—and hopefully the last.

Africanus nudged his horse to move up beside Aulus and Marcus. "Ask three things. Did anyone sign on this week? If someone tried and was rejected, ask where he went next. Also ask the lanista to send a message to Brutus if someone comes after we leave."

Marcus's mouth curved down. "We heard Brutus's instructions."

Aulus swung his leg over his horse's neck and slid off. "Three things. I'll remember."

Marcus slipped from his stallion's back and handed his reins to Africanus. "The villas in this area have been home to consuls and senators for generations. I'd expected something more impressive for the amphitheater and higher quality gladiators, but I guess it's not that far to Rome for a better show."

Africanus dismounted and held out his hand to take Aulus's reins. "Some good fighters gain their skill in this arena. Master Brutus shops here for Class 4 and 5 who might improve to Class 3, like he does in Luna and anyplace else he attends the games."

As the big man led the horses toward the stable across from the ludus, Marcus rubbed his hands together. "Let's go see if Callidus is here."

Aulus watched Africanus as he talked with the stable slave. When the gladiator reached into his purse, his gaze returned to Marcus. "We need to wait for Africanus. Brutus said the lanista would be more inclined to help if he saw Africanus with us."

Marcus blew his breath out through his nose..

As soon as Africanus rejoined them, Aulus squared his shoulders. "May Fortuna smile upon us so we find Callidus here."

With Marcus at his side and Africanus right behind, he opened the door and stepped inside.

As the door of the Alba Longa ludus closed behind him and he stepped into the street, Aulus's shoulders sagged. He startled at Africanus's deep voice just behind his ear.

"Don't get too discouraged. We've only begun looking. We still have five more ludi to check."

"So many?"

An encouraging smile accompanied Africanus's nod as they walked to the stable. "One more today, maybe four more over the next three days if we don't find him in Tusculum." He pointed northeast, across Lacus Albanus. "Maybe half an hour to the ludus there. Enough villas of the rulers of Rome around that town for an amphitheater."

Aulus took the chestnut stallion's reins from the stable slave. "I've been there a few times. My father was consul of Rome. He's governing Sicilia right now."

He jumped and swung his leg over the horse's rump.

"I know." Africanus stroked the horse's neck. "Master Brutus says he's a man of honor." His gaze flicked to Marcus, then returned to Aulus. "Such men set good examples for young Romans." The corner of his mouth turned up. "Including their own sons."

Aulus's mouth tightened as he nodded.

The gladiator mounted. "We'll take the shorter way along the lake." He nudged his horse into a slow trot.

As Aulus followed, he glanced at Marcus beside him. Marcus was a loyal friend, a man he could rely on, no matter what. But the solution to the debt he'd suggested, the solution Aulus had willingly embraced, was only clever, not honorable.

Africanus kicked his horse into a canter, and Marcus's spare stallion matched the pace.

As they sped along the lakeside, one thing was clear. Loyalty and cleverness in getting out of trouble were poor substitutes for the honor that kept you from getting into it in the first place.

Lacus Albanus

As his steel-gray stallion guzzled the lake water, Marcus watched Africanus beside him.

The gladiator felt his gaze and returned it. "Did you need something?"

"No. Just observing. I didn't notice before with you on your master's horse, but Brutus likes to match horses and people. His stallion matches his hair, the chestnut Rufus rode to Ardeo matched his hair, and the bay you're on...you match well enough it's hard to tell where the horse ends and you begin."

Africanus's full-throated laugh merely confirmed Marcus's suspicion that the gladiator's mind didn't catch subtly, even in an insult.

Crinkles remained by the gladiator's eyes. "When we cross the Alpes to the estate in Germania Superior, I ride a steel-gray horse like the one you're on. A perfect match for my gladius and dagger. Perhaps that draws attention to how dangerous it is to make me angry." The laughter in his eyes dimmed, and Marcus felt it shift toward scorn. "But it's a foolish man who lets someone make him angry. It's the cool-headed man who leaves his opponent dead on the sand."

With a shrug of one shoulder and a wry smile, Africanus led his horse away.

Marcus rubbed his lip. Brutus's favorite slave wasn't as stupid or as tame as he'd thought. But even if he wasn't joking with that veiled threat, the gladiator probably wouldn't do anything. No cool-headed man would risk crucifixion for murdering a senatorial son.

But would anyone who lived to spill blood in the arena always act as a cool-headed man?

Porta Capena on the Via Appia, Rome

Marcus and his party wove their way through the line of wagons and carts waiting to enter Rome through the Porta Capena. Aulus slumped in the saddle beside him. Their failure to find Callidus in Tusculum meant another long day in the saddle tomorrow.

The wide stone arch cast a cooling shadow, but the sunlight that warmed them once they rode through was dimmed by a familiar voice.

"Drusus."

Before it could rub his neck, Marcus stopped his hand. The tribune of the Urban Cohort was the last man he expected to find waiting for them. Titianus stood with arms crossed, his troop of eight in two rows behind him.

Marcus reined in. "Tribune Titianus." He faked a friendly smile. "Is there some immediate threat to Rome that has you guarding a city gate?"

A smile twitched, then disappeared. "There is always some threat to the peace. Sometimes from the least likely sources." His head cocked. "What have you two been doing?"

"I was attending to some private business for my father. Since there was nothing Aulus could do as we wait for you to make progress in your investigation, I thought it would be good for him to get away from the Secundus villa for a while."

Titianus's head straightened. "You're a thoughtful friend." His gaze moved past Marcus. "I see you still have Brutus's favorite gladiator with you. Haven't you found the right bodyguard yet?" His cool eyes refocused on Marcus. "I heard you visited a number of ludi since I last saw you."

Marcus's neck hairs rose. "We haven't, and Brutus is kindly lending us Africanus until we do. We just came from Tusculum, and we'll be looking at some of the other ludi near Rome."

The tribune's skeptical smile failed to warm his eyes. "In my experience, it's not that hard to find a decent bodyguard. Almost any gladiator or ex-gladiator should do."

Marcus forced a grin. "Perhaps, but when we find what Aulus needs, we won't have Africanus anymore."

Titianus's mouth curved into a smiling frown. "No one wants a cart horse when they have the stallion from a championship team. Brutus might regret that loan before you're through."

He flicked his hand and strode away, his troop of eight following.

Aulus nudged his horse into a walk. Marcus followed, but his eyes remained on Titianus's back.

Being a good friend of Lucius should have made Titianus kindly disposed toward his younger brother. But this tribune was too much like his own big brother—a man who would do his duty without regard to what friendship demands.

He sucked in a breath and released it slowly. A game of cat and mouse was only fun when you were the cat.

Chapter 43

ALPHABETS AND ATTRACTIONS

Gaius's farm, Day 27

Leander swung his legs off the bed and arched his back to limber what had stiffened overnight. Not a good idea. The dagger wound had closed, but he still felt a pull and a pain if he moved his shoulder too much.

His leg was the same story. The wounds had sealed, but the deep tears the arrowhead had made in his muscles still made his stride more of a hobble. Still, a man who'd almost died should thank God he was even walking.

His first step was more of a lurch, but by the second, he'd settled into a rhythmic limp as he headed toward the door.

Marcella looked up from stirring the porridge. "After you've washed up, I have something special for you."

"Just being here is special enough. I don't want to make you extra work."

She offered a motherly smile. "Having you here is like having one of my sons home again. I enjoy making a young man happy. And you don't have to worry about it being extra work. I just have some fresh berries to go with the porridge."

The thought of berries bursting with flavor rolling around on his tongue drew a huge grin. "That's worth hurrying back for."

"Take the crutch Gaius made you." She shook her head. "Men. Never wanting to take care of themselves like they should."

Leander hobbled back to the bed to get the crutch. It didn't help as much as she thought. But Gaius had gone to the trouble of making it, so he would use it. It helped more when he got tired, but the thought of fresh berries would keep that from happening.

Mistress Calantha floated through the doorway as he reached it. "Leander, I just had a wonderful idea." Her brown-and-gold eyes flashed with a tease. "I feel like being a lion trainer today."

She slipped past him before he could answer.

Lion trainer. What was she planning to do to him? He suppressed the sigh. Something he'd probably regret, but whatever the mistress wanted, he'd let her do it.

With Gaius's crutch under his arm, he limped out the door.

Leander popped the last berry into his mouth and savored the explosion of sweetness as he bit into it. Then he turned to Gaius.

"While we're here, I'd like to work to pay for what we're costing you. I'm well enough to start."

Gaius leaned across the table and rested his hand on Leander's forearm. "I'll be glad to have your help, but I don't think you're quite ready. Besides, this morning I'm helping Sextus with his sheep." He rose. "I'm heading over there now."

Marcella also rose, and she held his hand as she followed him out the door.

Mistress Calantha leaned one elbow on the table and rested her cheek in her palm. "Gaius is right. You really shouldn't be trying to do any work with your leg or arm yet, but I have the perfect thing for you to do."

A teasing smile lifted the corner of her mouth when he said nothing. "Well, don't you want to know what it is?"

Leander was afraid to ask. It probably had something to do with her being a lion trainer. "What you want me to know, you'll tell me."

Her light laugh rippled across the room. "So true. I do want you to know things. Can you read and write Latin?"

"A farm slave has no use for that. My time is spent working, not reading."

"Well, that's about to change. I'm going to teach you. You speak Latin well, so it shouldn't take me long. First, I'm going to teach you the letters of the alphabet so you can sound out words and read. Then I'm going to teach you to pick the right letters so you can write. I'll train my lion to be a scholar. Then maybe you can do something other than dig in the garden or clean out the stalls. Wouldn't you like that?"

"Cleaning stalls isn't so bad. Nothing gives me more pleasure than working with horses. I'd do it all the time if I could choose what I do. You don't need to bother teaching me Latin letters for that."

He shifted his gaze from her face to the table. His thumb traced a swirl in the grain of the wood. He would like to learn, but she would stay too close to him as she taught.

"It's not a bother at all. I want to do it, and there really is nothing else for you to do right now."

His eyes stayed focused on the table. She'd see his desire to learn if he looked at her. "Not this morning with Gaius gone, but I want to start helping him to pay for all he and Marcella have done for us. There's probably something I can do when he gets back."

Mistress Calantha's voice sharpened. "It's perfectly obvious to me and to Gaius that you aren't strong enough to work yet. You probably won't be for at least a week, and even then, you shouldn't work for too long at a time. There will be plenty of time for me to teach you even when you start helping."

She rose and stepped closer to him. "Don't forget you're mine, and I'm the one who will decide when you're well enough to start helping Gaius. I won't have you hurt yourself by working too soon."

As he tipped his head back to look at her face, her lips relaxed into a smile. He saw her fingers coming, but there was nothing he could do. She ran them through his hair, and the smile he could no longer control when she did that broke free.

"I'm well enough to pick off caterpillars." His smile broadened. "I'm used to handling spirited horses and stubborn mules. A caterpillar won't give me any trouble."

She returned his smile. "That may be, but you should want to learn to read and write, if only because I want to teach you."

He drew a deep breath. She was the mistress, so he had to do what she told him, even if that meant sitting close to her at the table. He should be able to keep her hand from guiding his in the right way to make Latin letters on a wax tablet.

A slave had no right to disobey an order from a mistress who wanted something to do with her time. And a man who could already read and write Greek would learn so quickly he wouldn't have to suffer her closeness very long.

"If you want to spend your time teaching me, I'm willing to learn."

◆

"Good." Calantha handed him his crutch. "We'll work outside

where the light is brighter, and sharing the bench should make it easier for me to help you. I'm not sure if Marcella has a spare wax tablet, but we can start with something simpler."

She took a plate and spoon from the cupboard. Filled with fine dirt, it would serve as a good practice surface. He could trace the letters she made with a stick.

When she turned, he'd risen, but he still stood by the table, his brow furrowed.

She flicked her fingers at him. "Go out to the table. I'll be with you as soon as I get the dirt."

As she followed him out the door, it was obvious he would soon be able to help with one-handed chores. But it was important for him to learn to read before they returned to Rome. Surely Father would agree when she asked him to free Leander, and a freedman could do so much more if he could read and write.

She bent over and filled the plate with powdery dirt. When she straightened, Leander was sitting on the very edge of the bench. Ready to escape, like Aulus when his tutor had him writing poetry and he wanted to come play with her. The smile that memory triggered faded quickly.

Her teeth clenched. Aulus, the brother who once enjoyed her company as much as she enjoyed his, had betrayed her. Where would she be now, if not for Leander?

Then her jaw relaxed. When she got home, Father would make Aulus pay. And even though Leander almost died, he'd become a free man because he rescued her.

A free man who could read and write. She found two sticks the length of a stylus under the tree and joined her student on the bench.

She gripped one as if she were writing and offered the other to Leander. When he took it, he held it exactly like she did.

Her lips curved. If he could follow her example as closely when he copied what she wrote, he'd be a quick learner.

"Watch what I do carefully. I'll write a letter; then you can try to copy what I did below it. There are three sets of letters called *alphabeta*. The set you use depends on what you're writing. The square capitals are easy to carve into stone because they use straight lines and simple curves. The rustic capitals are what you'll see in scrolls and codices of history, philosophy, and poetry. The cursive *alphabetum* is what people use for ordinary writing. That can be a little hard to read when someone doesn't take time to write the letters carefully, so we'll work on those most."

He rolled the stick between his fingers as his eyes stayed focused on her face.

She rubbed her lip. How could she make it easier for him?

"I think the easiest are the square capitals, so we'll try those first."

She moved the plate of dirt in front of his right hand so he could reach it without taking his arm out of the sling.

When she slid next to him so she could reach it, too, his back straightened and his eyes dropped to look at the dish.

"I promise this won't be hard, and we won't go any faster than you're comfortable with."

With great care, she traced an A into the dirt. "This is the letter A. It's only three straight lines." She made another A. "Now you try."

Faster than she'd written herself, he made a perfect A.

"Very nice for your first letter. Now here's how you make a B."

She traced it slowly to let him see how she made the curves join the straight line. The moment she finished the second example, he made a perfect copy.

Her head snapped sideways, and she stared at him. Her brow furrowed. "You said you didn't know how to write."

"I don't know how to write Latin. I learned to read and write Greek as a child." He shrugged. "These letters I've seen on monuments and buildings almost every time I carried you."

"Then we'll just write them once as I tell you their names and move on to cursive."

"Whatever you want, I'll do."

She smoothed the dirt with the side of the stick. "Then let's proceed."

◆

For a man with a bad shoulder and his arm in a sling, writing small letters in the dirt was harder work than plucking caterpillars from grape leaves, but that wasn't something Leander could tell Mistress Calantha.

She beamed at him each time he learned a new letter and moved eagerly to the next one.

But his shoulder hurt, and it was getting harder to sit up straight.

He startled when her hand rested on his as he formed a letter.

"My lion's getting tired. You need to rest." She rose. "Come with me."

He slipped off the bench and placed the crutch under his arm. He turned toward the house, but the mistress headed toward the short grass under the carob tree.

His brow furrowed. He'd planned to lie down inside for a while. But what was the mistress planning?

When he joined her in the shade, she held out her hands. "Let me help you sit down."

As he lowered himself to the ground, he kept his eyes from rolling at what he feared was coming. When she sat beside him and patted her lap, no doubt remained.

"Lie down and put your head in my lap, like you did in the wagon."

"But it's not right for—"

"You have to stop telling me that." She tightened her lips and shook her head at him. "You're supposed to do whatever I want without all this arguing. You're going to take a nap, and when you awaken, we'll work on your writing again."

He wanted to say more and convince her he'd rest better inside, but she was the mistress. When she ordered him to do something, he had to obey, as long as it didn't put her in danger.

"Yes, Calantha."

As soon as his head rested in her lap, she began playing with his hair and humming.

Her fingers running through his hair or stroking his cheek as she teased him about lion fur…it gave him more pleasure than he should let it.

He let his eyes turn to watch her. She was looking at him like she looked at her nieces when she played with them. She was only being kind because she appreciated how he risked himself to save her.

Then he closed his eyes because looking at her gentle smile made it so much harder to remember she was only his mistress taking care of a slave who served her well.

◆

Calantha watched Leander's breathing slow and deepen. He was asleep.

She stopped fingering his hair, and her hand slipped down to rest on his cheek. It was prickly again. The stubble pressed into her palm. She almost stroked his cheekbone with her thumb, but that might awaken him. He needed the sleep.

Her head tilted as her gaze swept his peaceful face, finally resting on that hint of a smile that curved his lips, even when he slept. He'd shaved only a few hours before, but there was already more hair on his upper lip than Aulus could grow in a week.

His beard grew so fast he had to shave every day to stay like she wanted. He rested his elbow on the table and shaved quickly with his right hand now, but it must hurt some. Maybe she should shave it for him tomorrow. Her lips curved at that thought. She fought the urge to stroke his cheekbone again.

It wasn't easy for him to shave, but he didn't mind. He'd do anything for her, and he only objected when she told him to do something he thought showed disrespect for a mistress.

Her lips curved up. Mistress. He still tried to call her that sometimes, but that wasn't how she wanted him to see her.

Friend. That was how she thought of him. Not slave, but friend.

After all he'd done, she could never see him as a mere slave again, and she'd make sure he didn't stay a slave after they returned. Surely Father would free him and be glad to do it. How could he refuse to free the man who'd saved his daughter from slavery and death?

Tiberius Julius Leander. It would be a good name for him once he was freed.

Her thumb brushed the stubble below his cheekbone. He didn't stir.

It would be wrong to name him Dacius, after some place where he'd been enslaved, or even Diegis, like he'd been born. No, he'd always be Leander, her own lion, the man who fought the kidnappers to keep her from becoming a slave and took an arrow so she wouldn't die.

Chapter 44

A Man of Proven Worth

Day 28

When Marcus and Aulus rode into the ludus stable yard the next morning, Africanus was lounging on a bench, his arms stretched out along the back. His saddled bay stood by a manger, munching hay.

Marcus let his gaze sweep the gladiator, then raised one eyebrow. Yet again, the slave was acting like his own master.

Africanus rose and approached Aulus. He patted the shoulder of Marcus's chestnut and turned a smile on Aulus.

"Water your horse, and we'll leave. It will be a half-day ride out to Tibur."

With the Nubian walking beside him, Aulus steered his stallion to the water trough beside Africanus's horse. "Tibur?"

"The amphitheater there is popular because of all the villas of the elite. We'll pass near one that belonged to Emperor Augustus."

Marcus rode close enough that the space between him and Aulus was too small for a big man.

Africanus stopped walking and let them pass. When he mounted the bay, his tightened lips looked too much like they held back a laugh.

When the horses finished drinking, Africanus headed out the gate. He guided their party through the milling pedestrians to the Clivus Suburanus, which led to the Porta Esquilina and the Via Tiburtina beyond. When they cleared the line of wagons already forming to await evening access to the city, he urged his horse into a trot. After a quarter hour, he reined back to a walk.

Aulus nudged his horse up beside Africanus, leaving Marcus to ride alone. "Does Brutus have property near Tibur?"

Marcus joined the pair on the side away from the gladiator. "That's not likely. The best estates belong to the senatorial families, and Brutus is equestrian."

Aulus glanced at Marcus, then turned back to Africanus. "Does he?"

Africanus's mouth started to curve into a smile as his gaze rested on Marcus before moving back to Aulus.

"No. Master Brutus buys land for what it can earn him, not to impress other people. His six estates are north and south of Rome in prime wine country and in Germania Superior, Narbonensis, and Sicilia."

Marcus leaned forward to catch Africanus's eye. "Does he buy gladiators for the same reason? Have you made him a good profit?"

Africanus's eyes crinkled. "I've returned my cost to him a hundred times over, and I'd bring more than you could pay if he sold me." His mouth curved into a skeptical smile. "Some of us can prove our worth. For other men, you can only take their word, if you trust it. A man who sets his own value by that of his ancestors...perhaps he'll be worth something someday."

His head turned toward Aulus. "The horses have walked long enough."

The gladiator kicked his bay into a trot, and Marcus wasn't sorry. He had low tolerance for arrogant men. For arrogant slaves, he had none at all.

As Aulus and his party approached Tibur, they climbed a steep hill. In less than a mile, the distant roar of the falls on the Anio River reached their ears. By the time they rode onto the bridge that spanned the river before it plunged over the falls, Aulus had to almost shout at Africanus.

He reined in half way across the bridge to look down the valley. "Impressive. I was a child when I last came here with Father. He talked with several friends about some vote in the Senate."

Africanus's mouth curved into a wry smile. "The last time I came, a man who wanted to be consul hired men from my ludus to impress his friends. The arena isn't large, but it suits the men who live here to avoid the heat of the city. The local ludus is decent, but not up to the standards of Rome. Callidus might be good enough to sign with it."

Aulus pointed at a round building surrounded by marble columns across the ravine from the bridge. "The Temple of Vesta. After we visit the ludus, we should eat our lunch over there. It's not every day I get to watch such wild water, and I'm already hungry."

"I was a little younger than you when I saw the cataracts of the Nile." Africanus's nose twitched. "I hated them then. Perhaps I'd enjoy them now." He nudged his horse into a walk. "First we visit the ludus. If Callidus is there and tells us where your sister is, your lunch can be a celebration instead of a meal."

The ludus was housed in a brown brick building across from the amphitheater. Aulus bounded up the steps and pushed open the door. Inside, the clack of wooden sword on wooden sword met them. Africanus stepped past him and led them down a narrow hallway that opened into the practice arena.

The lanista stood with his back toward them until Aulus cleared his throat.

He turned, and his face darkened with a scowl. "What do you want?"

His eyes widened, and his face relaxed when he looked past Aulus. "Is Antonius Brutus with you? I have some fighters who might interest him."

Africanus's voice came from behind Aulus. "Not today, but he would like you to help this young man if you can."

The scowl flipped into a smile. "Anything for Brutus." His gaze returned to Aulus's face. "So, what do you need?"

"We're looking for a retired legionary who plans to sign on with a ludus. We were hoping he'd come to Tibur to join yours."

The lanista shook his head. "No one has applied here for several months. I could use new blood." He craned his neck to see past Aulus to Africanus. "I suppose Brutus could, too." He lowered his voice. "Is Africanus on the market? Brutus hasn't put him in a bout lately. Has he been injured? Lost some of his edge? He'd still be a draw here."

Aulus's head bounced back. "Not at all. He's Brutus's best trainer and only works with the finest of the students. He's the sparring partner Brutus uses himself. He always takes Africanus when he travels, and he chose Africanus to help us with a thorny problem. I can't imagine Brutus wanting to sell him. I can't see how anyone fortunate enough to own him would want to part with him."

The lanista shrugged. "You can't blame me for asking. Fighters like him are hard to find. Tell Brutus I'll keep my eyes open for the man he's looking for. If he comes to me, Brutus can have first chance to buy his contract."

◆

Marcus's eyebrows lowered. Aulus spoke too glowingly of their companion in the hunt. To make it worse, the gladiator was standing close enough that he must have heard.

Africanus had been useful for getting cordial receptions at the different ludi, but anyone recognized as belonging to Brutus would have made clear Brutus's interest in finding Callidus. The big Nubian had known how to handle Ursus when the too-rich freedman started to threaten them, but any well-trained bodyguard should have done as well.

It wasn't good for a slave to think you admired him. He might misinterpret it as permission to speak too freely and act as if he were more than property. And Africanus was already taking those kinds of liberties with both Aulus and himself.

After they finished the tour of the ludi, whether they found Callidus or not, it was time to trade Brutus's pet lion for a bodyguard that belonged to Aulus or him. One who knew both his duties and his place.

Chapter 45

THE FIRST QUESTIONS

Gaius's farm, Day 29

Calantha leaned closer to Leander as she examined his first attempt at the cursive letter b. "That's not bad. Even a child beginning to read would recognize it."

Out of the corner of her eye, she caught the amused lift of the corner of his mouth.

"I meant that as a compliment, and you know it. The cursive letters can be hard to read if someone writes them too fast. And there are two other forms of this letter that you might see."

He rubbed his mouth with his left hand. "One, three...it doesn't matter. I'll learn them all if you want to teach me."

She rested her hand on his arm. "You're getting tired."

He shook his head and looked away.

"Yes, you are." With her fingers on his cheek, she turned his eyes back onto hers. "Your eyes tell me the truth, even when your nods and head-shakes don't." She stood. "Time for a rest, like we did yesterday."

"I'm not tired." He made no move to rise.

She moved behind him and rested her hands atop his shoulders. A gentle squeeze, then she leaned across his shoulder to look into his eyes again. "But I see you are."

She handed him his crutch. "Follow me to the carob tree."

◆

With the mistress's help, Leander lowered himself to the ground. She sat beside him and patted her lap. There was nothing he could do except rest his head in her lap...again.

221

Was she going to make him do this every time she taught him?

Her fingers slipped into his hair. That felt good...too good.

Mistress Calantha's smile felt good, too. "If you're not sleepy yet, will you tell me one of the stories about your god, like you do at dinner when Sextus joins us? After seeing how he healed you, I've added him to the gods I already worship."

Leander's breath froze. That request was so far beyond anything he'd expected that it was hard not to break into a grin that would make her think he'd suddenly gone crazy. But his delight probably showed in his eyes.

"Marcella will be as happy to know that as I am, but God wants something more. Zalmoxis, the god worshiped by most Dacians, and the Roman gods aren't real. They only live in the minds of people. They're just stories passed down from our ancestors. Superstitions, not reality."

Her head tipped, and her brow furrowed. But it was curiosity he saw in her eyes, not irritation.

"Only the God we worship is real, and He demands that His people worship only Him."

"But Father says it's important for us to perform the rituals that keep the gods' favor toward Rome. They smile on us, and the Empire grows bigger and stronger."

Her fingers remained in his hair, but they had stopped moving.

His smile turned sad. "I've seen how the Empire grows. It's not by the favor of the Roman gods. It's the training of Rome's armies and ruthless determination that crushes weaker foes and makes conquered people slaves."

Her eyes softened, and she stroked his cheek. "I'm sorry they killed your parents and took your sisters away. I'm sorry you've suffered so much." Her fingers swept the hair from his forehead. "But I saw your god heal you. If he could do that, why did he let you become a slave?"

Her question...so many times he'd asked that himself when Rome crushed his world.

"Sometimes God allows things I don't understand, but He never leaves me without hope. He brought me to the Crassus estate. Like Apostle Paul said, I served my new masters as if I was serving Lord Jesus. It mostly didn't feel like slavery. I enjoyed working with the horses. I was content there."

She stroked his cheek again. "And then we bought you, and I almost got you killed."

"But God put me in your household, too, and I thank Him that He did."

Her head bounced back. "How can you say that after all the horrible things that have happened to you?"

How to explain giving thanks in all things? She wasn't ready to hear that.

"You're here, safe, and I'll get you home. That's worth giving Him thanks."

"But why did you care so much about what would happen to me? After I let Vilicus lash you, you owed me nothing but pain, like I'd let him give you."

"But I owe Lord Jesus everything. I only did what He tells me to do."

"What did he tell you?" That question lit her eyes.

"Jesus told us, 'If anyone loves Me, he will keep My word. My Father will love him, and We will come to him and make Our home with him.' And He went on to say, 'This is what I command you: Love one another.' That love He talks about—it's agape love. Unconditional love. That kind of love is something we do, not how we feel. He also said, 'No one has greater love than this: to lay down his life for his friends.'

"Jesus's death bought my freedom from sin and gave me eternal life. Like I told you before, death holds no terror for me. It only opens the way to a better life with Him. It would have been worth my earthly life to keep you free."

She looked away from him and bit her lip. When her gaze settled on him again, her smile wrapped him in its warmth. "Well, I'm glad you didn't die. I like you here with me. But it's time for you to rest, so close your eyes. When you awaken, I'll teach you how the letter d looks like b even though it's different."

He shut his eyes, as ordered. Sometimes her commands were as easy to obey as those of his Lord. Showing Mistress Calantha the love Jesus commanded had become the easiest thing in the world.

And if she was already praying to God, surely He would claim her heart. In Servilia and Marcella, Leander had found Christian sisters once more. Before he returned Mistress Calantha to her father, would he have the joy of seeing her become his sister, too?

◆

Leander's face was peaceful, but Calantha's mind wasn't. His words rattled around her head, knocking into what she'd always taken as fact, threatening to topple her long-held beliefs from their pedestals.

The Christian god was real. She'd seen proof the night the prayers of Gaius and Marcella instantly stopped the infection that was killing Leander. But was it possible that he was the only real god?

Both her mothers had been faithful in their daily worship of the family gods and the gods of Rome. She'd been too young to remember what Mother said, but Trebonia had never talked about any of the gods like Marcella did. She never talked to them in prayer as if they were real people in the room who might answer.

But everyone who came to worship on Solis shared in such prayers. They all spoke as if their god cared about them. And when they met together, there was something…a presence that she couldn't describe, but she felt it.

And Trebonia had never told Calantha any god loved her. What would a god's love even feel like? There were many stories of a god loving a woman, but that wasn't love, only sexual attraction. If a god truly loved her, wouldn't it be more like how Father loved her and wanted what was best for her?

Her gaze rested on Leander's eyes. They twitched, like he was dreaming, and that smile that always played at the corner of his mouth grew, then relaxed.

The way Leander's face glowed when he recited what he said were the words of his Lord Jesus…she'd never seen that on any other man.

What did he mean when he said Jesus's death bought his freedom from sin and gave him eternal life? Why did that make his own death not matter as long as he could save a stranger? That's really what she'd been to him. Worse than a stranger, because she'd caused his lashing.

She rested her hand on his cheek. He didn't awaken, but his smile seemed to broaden.

So many questions swirled in her mind. But there would be many writing lessons and many chances to cradle his head in her lap while he answered them.

Chapter 46

NOT AN EMOTION

Morning of Day 30

The morning sun streamed through the window, warming Leander with its beams. It would be a beautiful day.

He turned to Gaius. "I'm ready to help you pick off caterpillars."

Gaius swallowed his mouthful of porridge. "You seem to be getting around better. You can help, but only until you get tired."

Mistress Calantha sucked in a breath. "I'm not sure he's ready."

Marcella, who stood behind the mistress's chair, placed her hands on her shoulders and squeezed. "Let him do it for a little while. Men turn into grumpy bears if they don't do something useful."

The mistress tipped her head back to look at Marcella. "Do you think he's healed enough to work?"

Marcella squeezed once more before lifting her hands. "I do. Let him work this morning; teach him after lunch." She moved over to Leander and brushed his hair back from his forehead. "You'll promise Calantha you'll quit as soon as you start getting tired, won't you?" She picked up Gaius's empty bowl. "Would you men like another serving?"

Leander nodded and held out his bowl.

Mistress Calantha leaned on one elbow. "Does that nod mean you'll quit when you should or you want more porridge?"

He felt the grin leak out. She knew him too well now. "Both."

As Marcella set the steaming bowl before him, Leander glanced at Mistress Calantha. Having her safe at the table beside him was worth every drop of blood he'd lost to give her a future.

And if she kept asking him questions until she decided to follow Jesus, that future would be eternity with his Lord.

Afternoon

Leander finished the ten copies of the three different versions of the letter n, and the dirt on the plate now looked like a bird had been dancing on it.

Mistress Calantha leaned over and inspected the last line. "You've done an excellent job. That's twenty-three letters in square script and twelve in cursive. I think thirty-five are enough for one day."

She rose. "Time for you to rest."

He tipped his head back and caught her smile. "But I'm not that tired. Sitting a while on the bench by the wall—that will be enough."

"Simply sitting is not enough. I want you to sleep a while. But only after you explain something you said yesterday."

"Yesterday?"

"Yes, under the tree. And as soon as we get settled in there, you can start."

She handed him his crutch, and waited for him to rise.

With his first step, his heart rate ramped up. Apostle Paul had said to always be ready to explain the hope God gave him, but would he find the right words to open Mistress Calantha's heart and mind to Jesus?

Holy Spirit, show me the way.

Mistress Calantha helped him sit, then sat beside him and patted her lap.

His head in the mistress's lap—the last thing he wanted, but if that was how she wanted to listen to his words about God... He lowered himself onto her lap and rolled on his back to watch her face.

She smiled down at him. "So, you're the teacher now, and I have many questions." She looked away, then back at his eyes. "You said Jesus's death bought your freedom from sin and gave you eternal life. How does that work?" Again, her eyes focused on the distant hills, then returned to him. "What is sin? How could a man's death buy your freedom from it?"

Leander drew a deep breath and held it. She needed someone like Apostle John or Apostle Paul, who could explain everything. She only had him.

As he pondered his first words, the warm presence of God surrounded him, and he relaxed. Jesus had promised the Spirit would give the right words when standing before governors and kings. Mistress Calantha was only a person whose heart was responding to the call of God. No reason to fear saying the wrong thing.

"I'll try to explain, but tell me if I start to confuse you. I'm not a teacher of the faith, so I can only tell you what I've heard and seen and felt myself."

She pushed his hair back from his forehead. "I don't want a scholar's explanation. I want to understand what you and Marcella and Gaius believe."

"You asked the right first question. What makes me a Christian is that I know I've sinned, and I also know Jesus paid for my sins so I wouldn't have to. Sin is anything that separates us from God. It's doing things that God says I shouldn't. It's also not doing things that He says I should. And it's thinking about things in a way that's not how God wants me to think about them."

Her brow furrowed. "But how do you know what your god thinks you should or shouldn't do?"

"He told us through the messages He gave to the Jewish people hundreds of years ago through Moses and His prophets."

"But you're Dacian, not Jewish."

"Yes, but when Lord Jesus came, He told His Jewish followers that the good news of His coming and paying for sins was for all people everywhere, not just Jews. As Apostle Paul told us, there is no Jew or Greek, slave or free, man or woman…we're all one in Christ Jesus."

"No Roman or Dacian?"

"Exactly."

Mistress Calantha rubbed her lip. "So, what did he say was sin?"

"The short answer…when we fail to love God with all our heart, soul, mind, strength, and when we fail to love others like we love ourselves."

"Is that why you only worship him and no other gods?"

"Yes."

Her gaze shifted from his eyes to the distant hills. "I see. But if he is the only real god, like you say, then it would be silly to worship any others."

"It is."

"And because they love him with all their heart, mind, and

strength...that's why his followers let themselves be killed rather than offer a sacrifice to the genius of the emperor and the Roman gods."

"Yes."

When her eyes refocused on his, her fingertips stroked his stubbled cheek. "Would you?"

"I would. Death holds no terror for me, although I'd rather not die in the arena. Denying Him to save my own life...I wouldn't really be saving it. I'd only be losing eternity with Jesus and those I love who died before me."

"And Marcella and Gaius."

He nodded. And her, if she would only decide to follow his Lord.

She massaged her neck. "And the other part...loving others. Do you have to love everyone?"

"Yes. But it's not an emotion, like your love for your father and sister and nieces. It's choosing to do what you can to help someone, wanting what's best for them even if it costs you. It's forgiving someone when they hurt you."

Her head bounced back. "Like Aulus, after all he tried to do to me? After him causing what happened to you?"

"Yes. Even our enemies. Like the Roman who stabbed my father even though he wasn't armed and the one who slit my mother's throat when she ran to him." He turned his eyes on the hills. Even after twelve years, that memory still hurt.

Her soft gasp drew them back to her face.

"Even the ones who dragged my sisters away."

"But how can you do that? I'll never forgive Aulus for what he tried to do." Her eyes flared. "I'll make certain Father punishes him for it, and I'll love every moment watching him suffer."

"That will cost you more than it's worth. Jesus told us to forgive, just as we've been forgiven. He even said if I refuse to forgive, I forfeit the forgiveness of my own sins that His blood bought for me. No vengeance is worth eternity in hell, separated from God."

Her lips tightened, and she shook her head. "That's too much to ask. It's beyond what anyone can do."

"You're right. No one can do it alone. But God's Spirit within me helps me do what I could never do myself. And when I try, the forgiveness comes."

She bit her lip and looked away.

◆

Calantha tried to wrap her mind around what Leander said about love and forgiveness, and she couldn't. It wasn't the Roman way. Vengeance on your enemies, justice instead of mercy...she'd never questioned that before.

When she looked down at him again, his smoke-gray eyes were fixed on hers. He was waiting for her next question, but she had more than enough to think about for one day.

She ran her fingers through his hair. "My lion must be tired. Time for you to sleep a while."

"But there's so much I haven't told you."

"I know." She forced a smile. "But I need to think about what you said a while." Her smile turned real as his calm eyes drew her in. "I'll have more questions tomorrow. Close your eyes."

"Whenever you want, just ask." His eyelids shut, as ordered.

As his weight settled into her lap, his breathing slowed and deepened. After only a few moments, he was asleep.

Calantha's brow furrowed. His god's most important commands were to love. Love without limits, and Leander had that kind of love. Love that inspired forgiveness, not vengeance. Love that was something you did, not what you felt. Love that would make a man she'd never called by name take an arrow so she wouldn't die.

Was that kind of love possible...for her?

Chapter 47

NEVER TIME TO DESPAIR

Via Salaria north of Rome, Day 30

Aulus arched his back and shifted on his saddle. It was only mid-morning, but he was ready to quit for the day. Alba Longa and Tusculum three days earlier, Tiber two days ago, Ostia yesterday, and Fidenae today. No sign of Callidus in any of them.

Already more than a hundred milia ridden, and thirty more to go before they reached their final destination in Trebula Mutuesca. At least Father had a cousin with an estate just outside the town, so there would be a hot meal tonight, a soft bed, and a good breakfast before having to ride another forty back to Rome.

His back was tired, his legs were tired, and his mind was exhausted. He'd be willing to ride to the Alpes and back if he knew he'd find Julia there, but the longer they looked, the less likely that seemed.

Africanus rode a short distance ahead. It was better that way. Aulus glanced at Marcus, who rode in silence beside him. Marcus couldn't resist trying to bait Africanus, and every time the gladiator ignored the taunt or turned it cleverly back on Marcus, Aulus's best friend seethed.

When Africanus reined in by the bridge over a tree-lined stream, Aulus drew a deep breath and drained his lungs with a deeper sigh. It was time for lunch, but there would probably be more verbal sparring for dessert.

Marcus might be eager for that contest, but all Aulus wanted was to get off his horse, flop on the grass under a tree, and rest.

As they rode up beside Africanus, Marcus raised his chin. "Why are you stopping?"

Africanus swung his leg over his horse's neck and slid off. "This is the halfway point. The horses need a rest." A smile started on one side of his mouth, but not the other. "They're not the only ones."

Marcus's mouth twitched. "If you're too tired to ride a few more miles, I suppose we'll have to stop to rest you as well."

Aulus slipped off the chestnut stallion. "Well, I welcome however long the horses need."

Africanus took Aulus's reins and headed toward a clump of trees just upstream. "We'll eat first. Then sleep if you wish. I'll watch the horses until it's time to ride again."

Aulus walked beside Marcus, who didn't dismount until they reached the trees. His friend's eyelids drooped. He must be at least as tired as Aulus felt.

When Africanus pulled the rolls and cheese from the sack tied to his saddle, Aulus took one roll and waved the rest away. "Cousin Quadratus will serve a good dinner tonight. I'd rather sleep."

After wolfing it down, he pulled the cloak that hung off his shoulder over his head and rolled it into a pillow. Then he lowered himself to the ground, placed his cheek on the cloak, and closed his eyes.

Aulus awoke with a start to find Africanus squatting beside him.

"Time to ride again." The gladiator's deep voice spoke the words quietly.

When Aulus sat up, his gaze settled on Marcus, who lay flat on his back, eyes closed, mouth open. "Let him sleep a little longer. We were both about to fall out of our saddles before you stopped." He patted the ground. "Sit, and let's talk."

With the grace of a hunting cat, Africanus shifted from squatting to sitting. "About what?"

"How you came to be Brutus's man for solving problems. He consults with you before we do anything."

Africanus shrugged, but the corners of his mouth also lifted. "Marcus would tell you a gladiator's history wasn't worth knowing."

"Well, he'd be wrong."

The gladiator's mouth curved more. "Ask what you want to know. I might tell you."

"Where are you from? How did you come to Brutus's ludus?"

"I'm of the Nuba people in the mountains south of Aethiopia. Slavers from Aegypt attacked our village when the fighting men were gone. I was fourteen years then, just learning the ways of war. They took me down-river."

"Past the cataracts of the Nile? Is that why you hated them?"

Africanus tipped his head once. "In Alexandria, I was sold and sent to the arena in Cyrene."

"And you learned to fight there?"

"I learned to kill there." His mouth twitched. "I learned to stay calm in a fight, to give the crowd a show, and to see the moment of weakness when it's easiest to end it. The lanista sold me for many times what he paid for a Nubian boy."

"Did Brutus buy you there?"

"No. That buyer took me to Liternum on the coast north of Neapolis. One of the Brutus estates is near there. It has large vineyards and a winery. His father built a merchant fleet sailing out of Puteoli, so Master Brutus loads his own ship in Liternum to bring the wine to Rome."

A flick of Africanus's hand chased away a fly. "He was checking on the fleet and estate for his father when he saw me fight." A wry smile curved his mouth. "His father had given him control of the Ludus Bruti when he turned twenty. When Master Brutus sees something he wants, he knows how to get it at a good price."

"So, you've fought for him for ten years?"

"Almost fifteen."

The fly moved to Aulus's arm. When he swatted at it, he missed. "If you earn your freedom, will you go back home?"

A laughing snort answered the question. "My life is in Rome. I have a wife and family: a son and daughter and another one coming. I have the respect and friendship of the man I work for. After so many years, nothing in Nuba would be the same. Where I came from is no longer home."

Marcus stirred and rolled onto his side.

Africanus stood. "Wake your friend." His eyes lit with silent laughter. "He won't draw a dagger on you."

Aulus's head bounced back. "He wouldn't draw on you, either."

The amusement spread from Africanus's eyes to his mouth. "A wise man wouldn't, but wisdom is not something your friend has learned yet. Perhaps he will in time, if he lives long enough."

Aulus rubbed his neck as Africanus headed over to the horses. Wisdom wasn't something he'd learned yet either. One of the philosophers his tutor often quoted said wisdom came from experience.

With the way things were going since their stupid plan to get ransom money for Julia twisted out of control, he'd be a much wiser man by the time this nightmare ended.

Roma, Day 31

After ten hours in the saddle, Aulus and his party rode through the Porta Collina and followed the Vicus Longus off the Quirinal Hill into the heart of Rome. Africanus had kept them at a walk because the chestnut stallion Aulus was riding seemed too tired after trotting a distance that hadn't been a problem for it three days earlier.

That decision was good for the horse, but not for Marcus's temper. An off-hand comment by Africanus that they should have used Rufus's horse for the longest ride had pricked Marcus's pride. That led to verbal jabs about slaves and gladiators that Africanus either ignored or silently laughed at. And each time Marcus didn't get the response he wanted, his mood soured more.

Aulus had never seen a more welcome sight than the gate of the ludus stable yard. But four days and 160 milia passuum had brought them no closer to finding Julia than they'd been the morning she disappeared.

Where was she? Was she locked up somewhere, frightened or hurt? Was she still alive? Aulus sagged as he rode through the gate. If they couldn't find Callidus, how could they ever find her?

Africanus reined over beside him. "It's not time to despair. The fight isn't lost until you stop fighting. We've been waiting to give Callidus time to reach Luna before we go. He's more likely to be there than anywhere we've looked."

Aulus slumped more. "Another six days on the road?" Then he straightened. "Whatever it takes." He patted the chestnut's neck. "But this one's not up to it without a good rest."

"He doesn't need to be. We'll go by sea. Only three and a half days from Portus to Luna."

Aulus's eyebrows rose. "I've never been on a ship. Neither has Marcus."

Marcus rode up on the other side of Aulus. "But it should be an interesting voyage along the coast. I've heard the views are magnificent." He crossed his arms. "It should be a novel experience for you, Africanus. You'll get to travel on the deck of a ship. You should find it more enjoyable than being chained in the hold."

One corner of Africanus's mouth lifted "I've gone north and south along the coast of Italia more times than some Roman youths have been thirty milia from Rome." His whole mouth curved into a smile. "But you needn't worry, even if this is your first sea voyage. I'll get you safely to Luna and back."

Marcus's eyebrows plunged. "I'm not some child who needs a guardian."

Aulus nudged his horse forward so his body broke their eye contact. "But I could use one." He smiled at Africanus. "It's good we have you as guide and bodyguard."

Africanus slipped from his horse and handed the reins to the waiting stable slave. "Master Brutus shares your opinion."

His gaze shifted to the man holding his reins. "Has the master left for the night?" The man nodded before leading the horse toward its stall.

Africanus rested his hand on the chestnut's neck as he looked at Aulus. "Rest tomorrow. Come back early the next day. Bring what you'll need for eight, maybe nine days away, but pack light."

Rufus appeared in the hallway that led to Brutus's office and signaled Africanus to come. After a final pat on the chestnut's shoulder, he joined Rufus. The words they exchanged were too soft for Aulus to catch. Then Africanus looked over his shoulder at Marcus before they vanished down the dark corridor.

"You can spend the night at my house." Marcus's voice behind him sounded as exhausted as Aulus felt.

"But I want to send someone to tell Gallio we're back as expected." A deep sigh drained his lungs. "It's bad enough he has to worry about Julia. I don't want him worried about me as well."

"Of course." Marcus reined his horse toward the gate and nudged it into a walk.

As they rode under the archway and the gate closed behind them, the words of Africanus played in Aulus's mind. The fight wasn't lost yet, and he and Marcus would keep looking until they found Julia...one way or another.

Chapter 48

A Faithful Friend

Gaius's farm, Solis, Day 31

When Gaius rose to take his chair out to the patio for the weekly gathering, Leander stood, too. "Can I help set up today?"

Gaius's soft snort was the unwelcome answer. "As long as your arm is in a sling, you're still a one-armed man. You can't use a crutch and move furniture, too." He slapped Leander's good arm. "It will be enough for you to share more of the Word of God with us. But I could use your company while I set up."

Leander hobbled outside and stood watching as Gaius carried out the four chairs, set them up two by two, and moved the two benches into place to make a square.

He turned at the jingle of harness. When Publius climbed down, Leander moved over by his mules and stroked one's neck. When it turned to look at him, he rubbed its nose before sliding his hand up to scratch between its ears.

"Hmm." Publius moved beside him. "He doesn't usually let strangers touch him like that."

Leander stroked the mule's neck again. "I used to train mules. Once they trust you, they'll do almost anything you ask. They just have to think it's safe. I also worked with horses. I liked training the stallions. I could gentle even the wildest ones to where I could ride them." He grinned. "But sometimes the men who wanted to buy them couldn't."

"Publius." Lucillia's voice drew Publius's gaze. "Would you please carry in the stewpot, dear? I have the wine."

Publius tipped his head toward Lucillia. "The mules do what I want, and I do what she asks." He winked at Leander. "But it's worth it to have a happy wife."

Mistress Calantha's laughter as she lifted Petronia's little girl out of the wagon and swung her in the air drew Leander's gaze. Some lucky man would someday have her as his wife.

He looked away. He shouldn't let it, but that thought bothered him. He'd risked himself so she could have a happy future. And one thing was certain. He wouldn't be part of it.

The group gathered under the canopy, and everyone sat where they had the week before. After several songs with Lucillia playing the lyre, Gaius rose and stretched his arm toward Leander.

"Leander is going to share the Word of God with us again."

With his crutch for balance, Leander stood and bowed his head. "Lord, I thank You for Your love that saved us and Your words to guide us. Guide me as I speak today."

He opened his eyes after the soft chorus of amens.

"I've been thinking this week about sin, the forgiveness bought for us by the blood of Lord Jesus, and what that means for how God wants us to treat other people."

Mistress Calantha's gaze locked on him.

"What Lord Jesus tells us is very clear. 'Be merciful, even as Your Father is merciful. Judge not, and you will not be judged; condemn not, and you will not be condemned; forgive, and you will be forgiven; give, and it will be given to you. Good measure, pressed down, shaken together, running over, will be put into your lap. For with the measure you use, it will be measured back to you.'

"Lord Jesus tells us we have two choices when someone hurts us: condemn or forgive. But He wants us to forgive.

"Sometimes it's not that hard to choose the way that pleases God. Other times, it is. When the one who hurts us is someone we know, someone we care about who should care about us, too, we often guess at the intent of their heart. But only God knows the full thoughts of anyone, and what I think is malice might simply be foolishness."

He looked at the mistress. A tiny furrow appeared between her eyebrows.

"Lord Jesus tells me what I must do. 'If your brother sins, rebuke him, and if he repents, forgive him, and if he sins against you seven times in the day, and turns to you seven times, saying, 'I repent,' you must forgive him.'"

The furrow had deepened.

"There have been times I hurt someone, not meaning to but because I didn't think through what I was doing before I did it. And I pray that I'll be forgiven, just as Lord Jesus tells me I must forgive."

Her lips had tightened.

"With the measure I use, it will be measured back to me. I want that measure to be generous and guided by love.

"When someone repents and tells you so, forgiving isn't that hard. But when the person who hurt you isn't sorry, when they would do it again without a moment's thought if they had the chance...I've had to struggle with that."

The corners of the mistress's mouth dipped, and Leander shifted his gaze to Petronia beside her. Mistress Calantha didn't like what he was saying, but he had to say what he felt the Spirit guiding him to speak.

"But not forgiving isn't a choice that Lord Jesus left open to us. When His disciples asked Him to teach them how to pray, He made that clear. He told them, 'When you pray, say: 'Father, hallowed be Your name. Your kingdom come. Give us each day our daily bread, and forgive us our sins, for we ourselves forgive everyone who is indebted to us. And lead us not into temptation.''

"It couldn't be clearer that He expects us to forgive if we follow Him. And He promised a blessing when we obey, even when it's hard. Especially when it's hard."

A quick glance at Mistress Calantha revealed a deeper frown. But obeying the Master was more important than pleasing the mistress.

"Lord Jesus said, 'Why do you call me 'Lord, Lord,' and not do what I tell you? Everyone who comes to Me and hears My words and does them, I will show you what he is like: he is like a man building a house, who dug deep and laid the foundation on the rock. And when a flood arose, the stream broke against that house and could not shake it, because it had been well built. But the one who hears and does not do them is like a man who built a house on the ground without a foundation. When the stream broke against it, immediately it fell, and the ruin of that house was great.'

"I want to live like the wise man who built on solid rock. I want to always listen to God's words and do what He tells me. And His great command is this: love one another. As Apostle Paul told us, 'Aim for restoration, comfort one another, agree with one another, live in peace; and the God of love and peace will be with you.'"

He closed his eyes, and God's peace wrapped around him. When he opened them, his eyes turned on the mistress. Her head had tilted, and though her brow was still furrowed, a slight smile curved her lips.

"That's all the Spirit gave me to share today."

Leander lowered himself into his chair beside Gaius.

When Gaius stood, he squeezed the top of Leander's good shoulder. "Thank you for sharing God's Word with us. Now let's lift our voices in praise."

Lucillia strummed her lyre, and their voices blended in song.

And when Leander let his eyes return to Mistress Calantha, he was greeted by her smile.

◆

While the men filled their plates, Calantha held Sertoria on her hip, swaying as the little girl played with the brooches holding her tunic closed along her shoulder. Leander filled his plate, then hobbled out the door behind Gaius, who carried Leander's food as well as his own.

Lucillia held out her arms to take Sertoria so Calantha could serve both of them. "Leander seems much stronger today."

"He is." Calantha ladled some savory stew into her bowl. "He's helping Gaius a little in the vineyard now, and I've started teaching him to read and write Latin. He already writes Greek."

Lucillia chuckled. "It's important for a man to be doing something so he doesn't get bored. Whenever Publius seems to have nothing to do, I always have some small chore waiting that will make him feel useful."

She set Sertoria down to fill her own plate, and Calantha herded the girl out the door and over to the bench. Sertoria clambered up, and Calantha handed her the plate as soon as she settled in.

As Calantha seated herself, her eyes were drawn to Leander's laugh. Determined to be useful—that described him well. But useful wasn't the first word that came to mind when she thought of him. Faithful fit him better. Faithful to his god and what his god commanded. Loyal to her, even when she hadn't deserved it, because he chose to forgive.

His head turned, and his gaze met hers. His eyes warmed as his mouth curved into the smile of a friend. Then he turned back to respond to Sextus.

Her gaze lingered on him. After Father freed him, she'd miss the warmth of his smiling eyes.

Chapter 49

The Unexpected Scribe

Morning of Day 32

Leander hummed to himself as he plucked another caterpillar off a grape leaf. He tipped his head back and let the sun's rays warm his face. As long as he didn't move too much, he could forget he'd had a blade in his shoulder and arrow in his leg. It felt good to be alive.

The braying of one of the mules drew his gaze to their corral. Beyond it, a man on a trotting mule topped the low rise and raised his arm.

Leander returned Publius's greeting and turned back to the vines. The hoofbeats drew closer, then stopped behind him.

"Good morning, Leander." Publius slid off his mule. "I see Gaius has put you to work, but I hope you'll have time to do something for me as well."

"If I can. What is it?"

"Lucillia tells me Calantha said you can read and write."

"Only Greek, not Latin." Leander shrugged. "Calantha is teaching me, but the way I write with this sling..." He tapped his right arm. "She says it looks like a chicken walked across the plate of dirt she has me practice on."

"Even bad handwriting is better than none at all, and I can read Greek. My eyes are always open for opportunities, and when I see one, I seize it. You present an opportunity I never dreamed we'd have."

Leander's brow furrowed. "How?"

"When God blesses us with a man who has the writings of John and Luke and Paul in his head, that's something too good to waste."

Publius lifted the strap of his shoulder bag over his head and handed it to Leander. "I have papyrus, pens, and ink in here. Will you write down what you know for us to have after you leave?"

Leander flipped back the cover, peered inside, then handed it back to Publius. "There's nothing I'd rather do."

Gaius joined them. "To have the Lord's words and teachings even after you leave would be a great blessing. You should start right now."

He slapped Leander's good shoulder. "Marcella will be out any moment to tell me you've worked more than enough. Let's surprise her by you quitting before she makes you."

Gaius handed Leander the crutch, and he and Publius matched Leander's slow pace as they started toward the house.

When Leander tried a step without leaning on the crutch, his jaw tightened. Not quite ready to free up his second arm, but it wouldn't be long.

"What would you like first, in case there isn't time to write it all before we must return to Rome?"

Publius stroked his lip with his thumb. "What do you suggest?"

"The writings by Apostle John. He wrote so many things that Lord Jesus told His disciples in private. It's almost like being one of the blessed who sat at His feet and listened."

Publius's usual smile broadened. "Then that's what I want."

Marcella and Mistress Calantha were weaving when Leander walked through the doorway.

The mistress's brow furrowed. "Are you hurt?"

Gaius chuckled as he stepped inside. "Would I let him do something to hurt himself? Marcella said to be careful with him, and I have been."

Marcella left her loom to hug her husband. "It's a wise man who listens, and I married one."

Publius set the bag on the table. "Leander is going to write down the gospels and letters he knows." He placed his hand on Leander's shoulder. "We have our own walking library here."

He patted the bag. "If this isn't enough papyrus, I can get as much as you need. I also have some fine leather we can use for the cover."

As soon as Leander settled into a chair, Marcella took his crutch to its place against the wall.

Publius took three ink bottles from the bag and pulled the plug from one. He unwrapped a cloth that held three pens. Then he placed a single papyrus sheet in front of Leander.

"Now you can write the words from God." He patted the sheet. "I'd like to watch, but I need to get back before the lunch customers come."

"And I need to remove more caterpillars before they lunch on my grapes." Gaius followed Publius out the door.

As the women returned to their looms, Leander slipped his arm out of the sling. He could rest his arm on the table and only move his fingers to write on the plate of dirt, but dipping a pen into the ink bottle meant lifting his hand and reaching. The sling held his arm too close to his body.

Pen in hand, he closed his eyes and took several deep breaths. As they had so many times before, whether nestled at his mother's side, chained in the stinking hold of the slave ship, or lying on his pallet at the Crassus estate, the beginning words of Apostle John's gospel filled his mind.

He dipped pen in ink and began to write. *In the beginning...*

He hadn't finished the first sentence before he had to dip the pen again.

...and the darkness has not overcome it.

Barely five sentences, and his shoulder was protesting.

Mistress Calantha placed her shuttle on its shelf and came to stand beside him. "Your Greek letters are better than your Latin cursive."

He tipped his head to look up at her. "But that doesn't mean my Latin teacher isn't as good as my mother was. I'll get better with practice."

She swept some hair off his forehead. "I see your face when you dip the pen. It hurts to do this."

"Not much. But even if it does, I'm going to do it anyway. I might not finish before we leave if I wait."

"But I don't want you hurting. So..." She pulled out the chair next to him and lifted the pen from his fingers. "You're going to recite like you do on Solis, and I'm going to write down what you say."

Her smile turned teasing. "Your Greek letters are better than your Latin ones, but no one would ever hire you as a scribe." She scrunched her nose. "I, on the other hand, have been praised many times for the beauty of my letters." Her hand rested on his arm. "Let the writing be my small gift out of gratitude for all we've been given here."

Leander opened his mouth to say he could manage, then closed it. Publius always seized an opportunity, and God had just given him one.

When she'd asked what sin was and how another man's death could buy his freedom from it, he'd wished she had Apostle John or

Apostle Paul to answer her questions. Who would have thought that the truth of God captured in the apostle's words, spoken through Leander's mouth, written by the mistress's own hand, might become the path to lead her to God?

"As you wish." He slid the papyrus in front of her.

Before she wrote the last word from Apostle John, surely God would claim her as His own.

After lunch Calantha got the plate of dirt from its storage place in the corner. "It's time for you to write instead of me. I think we can finish the cursive alphabet today."

Leander rose from his chair and took three halting steps to where the crutch rested against the wall.

As she walked past him, she shot him a fake glare. "You should have let me get that for you."

His reply was a sheepish smile.

She led him to the table and waited for him to sit before sliding onto the bench beside him.

It took half an hour to show him the remaining eight cursive letters and have him review all the letters she'd taught him before.

She rose. "I think that's enough for today. It's time for you to rest under the tree."

He tipped his head to look up at her but made no move to rise. "I'm not tired. I've healed enough I don't need the rest."

"How you think you feel isn't the point. It's whether I think you need to rest, and I'm sure Marcella would agree with me." One corner of her mouth turned up. "I'm not certain you'd tell me if you were tired, even if you were about to drop, because you don't want your head in my lap."

He opened his mouth as if to answer; then closed it into another sheepish smile.

She handed him the crutch. "Besides, I have some questions about what I wrote this morning, and sitting under the tree is our usual place for such conversations."

He followed her to the carob tree and lowered himself beside her.

His head settled into her lap. "What are your questions?"

"You said the Word came from God, that he was God, and that he became the man Jesus. That Jesus is both the son of God and God himself. That confuses me."

Leander drew a deep breath and blew it out through pursed lips. "I've wrestled with that, too, and I don't have a good answer. I try to understand the things of God, and some of them I do. But I'm only a man. When I was a child, I didn't understand many things my father said, even after he explained them.

"I don't know how it works, but I do know what Lord Jesus said. Soon you'll write down what I'm about to tell you. He said, "I and the Father are one," and later He said He was in the Father and the Father was in Him. He told His disciples the night before His crucifixion that since they'd seen Him, they'd seen the Father. They should know that was true because they'd seen Him do the Father's works. So somehow the two are different and yet the same."

"I still don't understand. What does it mean to be in each other?"

His eyebrows lowered. "I'm not sure, but Lord Jesus said something else I do understand. If I obey His commands, He'll ask the Father to send the Spirit, and the Spirit will be in me."

"I've seen how you obey his commands. Did he do what you just said?"

He looked past her, as if someone stood behind her. "Oh, yes. And sometimes I feel wrapped in a love so perfect, a peace so overpowering, that...well, I have no words to describe it. Gaius and Marcella have felt it, too." The start of a smile tugged at the corner of his mouth. "Women are better with words than men. Maybe she could explain it."

The glow on Leander's face—she'd seen the same on the others when they sang on Solis. And sometimes she felt a presence when they prayed together in the evening.

She swept some hair off his forehead. "Maybe I'll understand better after I hear more of what John wrote about Jesus. My questions can wait until then. Now, close your eyes and try to sleep a little. And when you awaken, you can recite more for me to write."

He obeyed, and even though he'd told her he wasn't tired, his breathing slowed as soon as his eyelids closed.

His eyes twitched; he was dreaming. His smile broadened, then relaxed. He looked peaceful, like her younger niece when she napped.

She rubbed her lower lip as her gaze rested on the distant hills. Overpowering peace and perfect love. Would the spirit of his God give the same to her?

Day 33

Leander finished writing the cursive alphabet, each letter in order, and set his stick down. He'd helped Gaius some before beginning to recite midmorning. Calantha wrote fast, so by lunch time, they were more than half way through the gospel of Apostle John. A good lunch, some practice at writing Latin, and now it was time for her questions.

It was also time to change where she asked them.

Mistress Calantha rose. "A few questions for my teacher, and then you can rest." She handed him the crutch.

"If you don't mind, I'd like to stay at the table for your questions. Each day I'm less tired, and a man heals faster when he's up and doing something worthwhile. I don't need a nap."

"Answering my questions isn't worthwhile?"

His ears heated. "That's not what I meant. Anything you want me to do is worthwhile."

"Except resting in my lap."

"That's not something a—"

"Slave should do with his mistress. But you forget, while we're here I'm Calantha, not mistress, and you're the lion who protects me, not my slave."

"Yes, but—"

She patted his arm. "It's all right, Leander. I won't make you do something you really dislike if you don't need the rest." Her eyes teased. "But I'm going to watch to make sure you don't, and if I think you do, then you'll do it without arguing."

"Yes, Calantha."

She moved from their shared bench to the empty one beside it. With her elbow on the table, she cradled her chin in her palm and focused on his eyes. "So, my first question is this."

Before she could ask the question, a gust of wind ruffled his hair. And as he brushed it back, part of him wished the fingers touching his forehead were hers.

Chapter 50

Rough Waters

Ludus Bruti, Day 33

When Marcus rode through the stable gate of the Ludus Bruti, his jaw clenched. Rufus's chestnut stood saddled beside Africanus's bay. Marcus had sent his own over-tired stallion back to his mother's estate and had a spare stallion of his father's brought back for Aulus. But Brutus's arrogant slave had presumed he'd be unable to supply his friend.

The stable slave bowed before taking Marcus's reins. "Master Brutus awaits you in his office."

With Aulus beside him, he walked down the hallway that led to Brutus. When they entered the office, Africanus sat at the desk opposite Brutus, playing tabula.

"You boys have come in good time." Brutus leaned back in his chair. "You should reach Ostia early enough to have no problem booking passage for your trip up the coast."

Marcus moved close to Africanus and stood looking down at him. The gladiator rose and took his appropriate place by the wall.

After Aulus dropped into one chair, Marcus took the one vacated by Africanus.

From a side drawer of the desk, Brutus took a purse and pitched it overhand to the gladiator. "Africanus will take you up the coast to Luna. I have some hope Callidus will have already signed a contract with the ludus there. It's three and a quarter days one way by ship, so sailing early tomorrow should get you there mid-morning on *Saturni*. You should find Callidus at the ludus."

"What do we do if he won't tell us anything when we get there?" Aulus rubbed his neck.

Brutus tipped his head toward Africanus. "That's why my best man is going with you."

"When we find him, I'm sure he'll tell us what he knows." Marcus stood. "I'm ready to run our quarry to ground, and nothing will keep us from learning what we need."

After sweeping the tabula game pieces into an ivory-inlaid box, Brutus rose. "If you don't find Callidus in Luna, Africanus will buy some horses. Then you can work your way back to Roma, checking every ludus you pass."

Aulus blew his breath out through pursed lips. "But what if we don't find him?"

Brutus patted Aulus's arm. "Don't look for trouble before it finds you on its own. I think you'll find him."

He pointed at Africanus. "And I'm sending Africanus with you to make sure you do."

As Africanus's mouth curved into a smile, Marcus's shifted toward a frown.

Brutus returned to his desk and opened the wax tablet from the top of a tall stack. "May Fortuna smile upon you and bring you back knowing where Julia is."

Africanus straightened. "First stop, Ostia. Let's go."

He strode down the hallway ahead of Marcus and Aulus. When he reached the stable yard, he stopped six feet from Marcus's spare stallion and crossed his arms.

Marcus's jaw clenched as the gladiator appraised the horse. Then Africanus ran his hand down the horse's foreleg before slapping its shoulder.

"Only fifteen milia today. This one should be fine." He turned to the stable slave. "Rufus's horse can go back to his stall."

Aulus gathered the reins, seized the mane, and jumped to swing his leg over the black stallion's rump. "He belongs to Marcus's father. I bought a young one with the same sire. Niger isn't ready to ride yet, but when he is, I'll bring him for you to see."

One corner of Africanus's mouth curved. "A good man deserves a good horse."

He mounted. With a flick of his hand, he headed out the gate with Marcus and Aulus behind.

Ostia, port of Rome

After four days of riding more than thirty milia, the fifteen milia from Rome to Ostia seemed like nothing to Aulus.

As they entered the city along the Via Ostiensis, Africanus dropped back to ride beside him.

"We'll leave the horses with Master Brutus's wine agent. You can rest while I go to the docks to arrange passage tomorrow morning. We'll spend the night at Galbius's house."

Marcus nudged his horse to ride on the other side of Aulus. "It's only late morning. Can't we find one leaving this afternoon?"

"The coastal ships unload cargo at several ports along the way. Many don't sail at night. The ones that do leave early. With night sailing, we'll be there midmorning of the fourth day."

Africanus led them into a stable yard through an archway wide enough for large wagons. Teams of mules were harnessed to several wagons filled with brown amphorae. He tipped his head toward one with cream-colored amphorae. "Master Brutus's private vintage from Liturnum. He mostly keeps it for himself and his close friends. He sells it only to a select few willing to pay his price. If your fathers are among them, you want to try it." His eyes warmed. "It is extraordinary...a taste fit for Hadrian or the Roman gods, if you believe in them."

Aulus turned to Marcus to find him frowning. "We can ask Gallio and Malleolus when we get back." A wry smile pulled at the corner of Aulus's mouth. "I'm not certain Gallio would give me a taste even if I begged right now, but your father's steward probably will."

A stable slave approached, and Africanus swung his leg over his stallion's neck and slid off.

"These three will need to be stabled until we return. Seven days, maybe more."

The man tipped his head. "Yes, Africanus."

Africanus summoned Aulus and Marcus with a flip of his hand. "Come. First a word with Galbius about spending the night at his house. He'll have someone escort you there. I'll join you after I book our passage."

Brutus's agent entered the yard with a raised arm and a smile directed at Africanus. As Africanus stepped forward to meet him, tension drained from Aulus's shoulders. No matter what awaited them in Luna, Brutus had given them the right man to handle it.

On the Mare Nostrum

As the rowboats pulled the ship away from the pier, Marcus leaned on the railing. He was more than ready to escape the faint odor of dead fish that had plagued him since they boarded. The bundle of blankets that Africanus had carried aboard promised three nights on deck with little rest. Why the gladiator didn't find a ship with a cabin for wealthy travelers...

Aulus stood beside him, that contented smile on his face. His friend's hand shot out, pointing at the ship docked just upriver. A bay stallion dragged the slave back down to the pier after the third attempt to walk it up the gangplank.

"That horse is going to hurt a leg if they're not careful. Niger is still too wild to ride, but our stable slave can get him to follow anywhere like a puppy." His smile dimmed. "They say horses are good judges of character, but I don't believe it since he helped kidnap Julia."

Marcus patted Aulus's arm. "As soon as we find Callidus, we'll learn where they took Julia. When you get that slave back, you can see how well he handles lions on the sand."

When the ship was pulled past the lighthouse and out of the Tiber into the *Mare Nostrum*, the waves lapping at its sides grew larger. And with the larger waves, the ship began to rock. Slow and gentle, but a strange sensation started in Marcus's stomach.

The rowboats released the towropes and moved away. The sail on the central mast dropped, and the small sail opened on the angled mast at the front. The sails billowed as the wind filled them, and the ship leaped forward.

And as the ship rose and fell on the waves, Marcus's stomach leaped, too.

He swallowed hard, and the first rising of his stomach contents settled back into place. He took slow, deep breaths, willing the gyrations in his gut to settle. But as the ship picked up speed, the wild dance in his midsection spiraled upward, and he lost his breakfast over the side.

Aulus stepped back, his nose scrunched.

Marcus closed his eyes and breathed deeply. That only made the up and down sensations worse. With elbows leaning on the rail, he clasped his head. And the next time the ship rose, his stomach rose with it.

He felt rather than heard Africanus move beside him, and Marcus glanced at him.

"Many get *nauseabundus* on their first voyage. I'll get something that should help."

Marcus's lips tightened at the sympathy dripping from the gladiator's deep voice.

"It will pass. I've celebrated with too much wine. This is no worse."

Africanus's eyebrow rose. "Once, and it's over when you drink too much. This won't end quickly."

Marcus flicked his hand to send him away. Africanus shrugged and moved off.

Eyes closed and more deep breaths...but still his stomach churned.

"Marcus." Africanus's voice drew his glare. "Take a sip or two of this." He held out a cup.

"What is it?"

"Half wine, half water. A little might help, but not more. Go to the middle of the ship where it moves less. Lie down on your back. Or stay at the rail, but keep your eyes on where the water meets the sky."

Marcus's eyebrows lowered. "How do you know? You're no physician."

The corner of Africanus's mouth turned up. "No, but as I told you, I've been up and down the coast of Italia more times than you've ridden twenty milia from Rome. You're not the first I've seen with this."

The bow tipped up on a large swell, then dropped, slapping the water as the swell passed.

As Marcus's stomach heaved again, his forehead broke out in a cold sweat.

And he reached for the cup. Two sips, and he gave it back to the gladiator with a nod and a slight smile. The smile Africanus returned mirrored his own before the big man walked away.

With his gaze locked on the horizon, Marcus began counting the hours until his feet could be on steady ground once more.

Port of Castrum Novum

As soon as the captain ordered the gangplank lowered to the pier in Castrum Novum, Marcus hurried down it and up the ramp from the pier to the road. At least for the hour or so it took to offload some cargo from Rome and load some that waited on the Castrum Novum pier, he'd have his feet on solid ground.

Another two full days and part of a third on that accursed sea lay ahead of him. His gaze settled on Aulus, still leaning on the railing and watching the slaves carrying cargo. Only a friend like Aulus was worth that much misery.

Africanus strode down the gangplank and up the ramp toward him. With a nod but no words, he continued past and disappeared into the crowd. In less than a quarter hour, he returned and boarded the ship.

Too soon, the captain signaled Marcus to board. His stomach had settled, but would everything start swirling and tossing as soon as they returned to the sea?

After the rowboats pulled them out of the harbor and the sails unfurled, the pitch and roll had Marcus clutching the rail again, eyes riveted on the horizon as his stomach heaved.

Africanus appeared beside him. "Here." He held out two fat roots. "Ginger root. Suck on it, and it should help. And licorice root. In case the ginger doesn't work."

Marcus's eyebrows rose as he took the roots. "Perhaps a new job awaits when you tire of killing people. You can ask Brutus to let you heal them instead."

Africanus's mouth curved into a full smile. "Master Brutus values more than my skill on the sand. If I wanted that change, he'd give it to me."

As Africanus walked away, he moved in unison with the ship. Marcus's eyebrows dipped. The gladiator seemed to know what to do, no matter where they were or what was happening. It was a good thing Brutus had sent him with them, but Marcus would still rather have his own slave, not Brutus's favorite, as bodyguard in the hunt.

Chapter 51

ONE OF GOD'S OWN

Gaius's Farm, Day 34

Calantha watched Leander as he followed Gaius out to the vine-yard. Each day he moved a little faster. Soon he wouldn't need the crutch.

She turned back to her loom and stroked the fabric she'd already woven. It wouldn't be long before she could present the cloak to Leander. A smile leaked out. She already knew what he would say: "That's not something a mistress should do for her slave."

But he couldn't be more wrong. He deserved more than everything she could do for him, and the cloak was just the beginning.

Marcella joined her at the looms. "You do nice work. He'll enjoy wearing it."

Calantha flashed a smile. "After I convince him I made it for my own pleasure, not just for him. He doesn't realize how much I enjoy helping him."

"It took me years to teach that to Gaius." Marcella made the first pass of the shuttle through the warp yarns. "I'm so glad you're helping Leander write everything down. It will be so good to be able to hear the Lord's words even after you two leave."

Calantha's brow furrowed. "May I ask you something? Something very personal."

Marcella's head cocked. "Of course. What is it?"

First Calantha looked at the floor. Then she raised her eyes to Marcella's smiling face. "Petronia said you only became a Christian about ten years ago. Why did you decide to do that?" She glanced away, then back at her friend. "It's against Roman law, and you could die for it."

252

Marcella's eyes softened as her smile broadened. "I was dying on the inside before I did. I only came alive again when I accepted Jesus as my Lord.

"I was mourning the deaths of both my sons in the Dacian war." She shook her head. "They'd been so eager to enter the legions to see the world. They didn't want to stay on the family land and be farmers like their father and grandfather. They wanted travel, excitement, the feeling that they were part of something bigger than themselves. Gaius's uncle had been a legionary, and he told the boys so many stories about army life."

Her mouth turned down. "But only the good things. All about victory and marching in a triumph behind the emperor in Rome. Nothing about watching his friends cut down beside him or the smell of death so thick it made him gag."

A sigh escaped. "They pestered Gaius until he gave his permission to enlist in the IV Flavia Felix. They wrote us with cheerful stories about Moesia Superior. And then came the Dacian war, and both my boys died in the first assault on Sarmizegetusa."

She tightened her lips. "Killing and dying for the glory of Rome... what was that worth? Nothing! Everything seemed so pointless."

Her lips relaxed into the start of a smile. "Then a few months later, I went to the bath just down the road from Lucillia's taberna. I'd seen her there many times, but we never spoke. But that day she came and sat beside me. She said I looked too sad and asked if I wanted to talk about it. I don't know what came over me, but I told her both my boys had been killed and started to cry. She put her arm around my shoulders and asked me to come home with her to try a new herb bread before she served it to customers.

"I felt so desperately lonely that I would have done anything just to have someone to talk with. Gaius had pulled into a shell like a snail with his own grief, and my girls lived too far away in their husbands' homes."

"We sat at her table, and she just listened as all the pain came gushing out." Her smile broadened. "And when I finished, she took my hand and asked if she could pray for me."

Marcella closed her eyes, and when they opened, their warmth drew a smile from Calantha. "And when she prayed to God in the name of Jesus, it was like a bucket of cool water on the burning pain in my heart. I'd heard all the bad things about Christians. I wanted nothing to do with them, but when God poured His peace over me...Lucillia spent the rest of the afternoon telling me about Jesus, and I decided to follow Him, too."

"But that's so dangerous." Calantha massaged her neck as her gaze stayed locked on Marcella. "Weren't you afraid you'd be killed for your faith?"

"I'm in no hurry to die, but it's like Leander told you. Death isn't the end. It's the beginning of eternal life with Jesus." Marcella shrugged. "I'd never forfeit that just to live a little longer on earth."

Calantha bit her lip. "I can't explain it, but as Leander is telling me what Jesus said, it feels as if he's calling me to follow him, just like he called his disciples."

"He is calling. That's the Holy Spirit drawing you toward Him."

Calantha's mouth turned down. "Part of me wants to answer that call, but part of me is afraid of what that would cost. My father...he's Tiberius Julius Secundus."

"Wasn't he a consul a few years ago?" Marcella's smile vanished.

"Yes, and he's governing Sicilia right now. We're waiting for him to return to Rome before I can go back home."

Marcella drew air between her teeth. "That's a big problem."

"I know. I'm expected to marry a senatorial son who'll follow the *cursus honorum* to someday govern a province, too. That kind of man can't have a Christian wife. There are so many acts of worship of the Roman gods that I'd be expected to take part in, and Leander tells me God demands his followers worship only him."

Calantha cradled her face in both hands. "I love Father, and he loves me dearly. I don't want to hurt him. And if I become a Christian, I'll hurt him badly. But God is calling louder and louder, and I want to say yes."

Marcella wrapped an arm around Calantha's shoulders. "I didn't want to hurt my husband, but I couldn't say no to God calling me. Gaius was angry when I became a believer because he didn't want me killed, too. But I got him to talk with Publius, and then he heard God calling him as well."

"What did your father say? As paterfamilias, did he approve?"

"He was already dead. But it wouldn't have mattered, not after I chose to follow Jesus and the Holy Spirit came."

Calantha's shoulders slumped as she sighed. "I don't know what to do. I can see how much I'll lose, but when I look at you and Leander, I can see how much I'll gain."

Marcella pushed a strand of hair behind her ear. "You have many more days before you'll be leaving us. You don't have to make your choice today. I'll be praying for you, and you'll know what to do before it's time to leave."

She gazed out the open door. "It's probably time for you to check on Leander. Men are no good at knowing when they've worked enough."

"I'll fetch him. He can rest while he tells me what to write."

As Calantha headed out the door, she longed for rest. But it wasn't the kind of rest that would speed Leander's healing that she wanted. It was rest from the turmoil in her heart.

Leander leaned back in his chair and blew out a deep breath. "That's the end of the gospel Apostle John wrote."

Mistress Calantha added the final papyrus sheet to the stack and straightened the pile. "You were right when you said it was almost like sitting with his disciples, listening to Jesus himself." She placed her elbows on the table and covered her face with her hands. When she pulled her fingers down so he could see her eyes again, they swam in tears.

"I wonder how many crucifixions Father has ordered." She sighed. "Once the Jewish leaders said Pilatus was no friend of Caesar if he didn't execute Jesus, he really had no choice. It was Jesus's death or his own. I've read the histories. Emperor Tiberius was killing so many good men he thought were his enemies. He killed my great-grandfather's brother." She wiped at the corner of her eye.

He leaned forward. "Jesus's death or my own—that's true for everyone. Without Lord Jesus dying to pay for my sins, I'd spend eternity in hell instead of eternal life with my Lord."

"To watch him die, like John did..." The first tear trickled down her cheek. She flicked it away. Her lips quivered; then they curved into a smile. "But when he saw Jesus alive again, and he knew for certain that everything Jesus had said was true..." She sniffed, but her eyes lit up with her smile. "I'm glad we've written it all down."

"*Salve* and God's peace to you." Sextus entered the cottage, a bag slung over his shoulder. "Marcella said you were doing some weaving, so I brought some fleece for her to replace the yarn."

He sniffed the savory aroma of the stew that already filled the room. "Gaius should thank God every day that Marcella is such a good cook. If he didn't work so hard, he'd look like Publius. Not that Publius is fat, and maybe a taberna owner should advertise how good his food is by eating plenty of it." His eyes lingered on the stewpot. "Favonia made such delicious stews."

Gaius entered and slapped Sextus's arm. "She did." He patted the bottom of Sextus's bag. "What have we here?"

"Wool for Marcella and Calantha."

Marcella emerged from the storeroom and set a pitcher of wine on the counter. "Why, thank you." She took the bag and hugged it. "We'll put it to good use."

Leander freed his arm from the sling and rested his elbow on the table. He was eating right-handed again, but the mistress still tried to help him more than he liked. With Sextus joining them, he'd have a less interfering neighbor beside him.

Or so he'd thought.

Sextus took the chair beside Marcella, and Calantha sat beside him.

Mistress, not Calantha. With her writing down what he said for hours each day, too often he slipped into thinking of her with the name Marcella used. One gospel written, one to write, and then the letters of Apostle Paul—they were maybe a quarter of the way through. Another week and a half should finish it.

His eyes followed her as she helped Marcella carry the bowls of stew and platter of salad to the table.

Watching the mistress write perfectly formed letters so quickly and then nod for him to speak the next sentence...he could stand another week and a half of that.

He closed his eyes when Gaius began the prayer, and his smile broadened as they finished. Another good meal in the company of believers—what more could a man ask?

With a full stomach and enough conversation with friends to satisfy any man, Leander closed his eyes as Gaius ended their meal with prayer.

"We thank You, Lord, for this blessed time together. Keep us in Your peace until we gather again. In our Lord Jesus's name, we pray."

Even Mistress Calantha said amen with feeling.

"Leander." Sextus leaned forward. "Before I walk home, give me something to think about tonight. Something about being with Jesus, like Favonia is."

When the mistress leaned forward as well, Leander rubbed his lip. What would God choose for both of them to hear?

"When I was a child, our sheep didn't graze in a field by our house, like yours do. A shepherd took the sheep of several families to roam the hillsides. Sometimes he let me go out with him. When I tried to drive the ewes, they scattered and circled around behind me, back to where they'd been. But even when there were several flocks in the meadow, all he had to do was call, and his whole flock came. When he walked, they followed him.

"I still think of him when I hear Lord Jesus's words. 'My sheep hear My voice, and I know them, and they follow Me. I give them eternal life, and they will never perish, and no one will snatch them out of My hand. My Father, who has given them to Me, is greater than all, and no one is able to snatch them out of the Father's hand.'

"He also said, 'For this is the will of My Father, that everyone who looks on the Son and believes in Him should have eternal life, and I will raise him up on the last day.'"

His gaze was on Sextus, but from the corner of his eye, he saw the mistress draw back.

"For those we love who have gone before us, those whose faith we heard spoken and saw lived, we can be certain we'll be with them again. It's like Apostle Paul told us, 'If you confess with your mouth that Jesus is Lord and believe in your heart that God raised Him from the dead, you will be saved. For with the heart one believes and is justified, and with the mouth one confesses and is saved.'"

Sextus released a deep sigh, but it wasn't a sad one. "I remember the day I stood with Favonia and we made that confession together." His smile matched the peace in his eyes. He slid his chair back. "Someday the Shepherd will call me home as well, and we'll be together again."

Leander startled when Mistress Calantha's fingers touched his arm. He turned his gaze on her and raised his eyebrows.

"As I've been copying what John wrote, I've been thinking about everything he said. About all the things you told me before and about what I used to believe. And I've made a decision."

She squared her shoulders, and Leander's pulse ramped up. He'd taken the arrow so she wouldn't die unsaved. His blood had bought her time.

"I reject the gods of Rome. They're only stories, and I want to worship a god who is real. I reject the idea that the emperor can join the gods after he dies. I believe in God the Father, and I believe Jesus is the Son of God. I believe when Pilatus executed Him, He died for all our sins, and after that, the Father raised Him from the dead."

Her eyes glistened with a brightness Leander had never seen before. Jesus's blood had just bought her eternity, and Leander's heart pulsed with joy.

She took a deep breath. "I'm ready to confess and be saved." Her brow furrowed. "But how do I do that?"

Marcella slipped from her chair and wrapped Mistress Calantha in a motherly hug. "You have to believe Jesus died to save you, confess your sins, and ask forgiveness. Then thank God for making you His child."

At the word "forgiveness," Mistress Calantha's eyes turned to Leander. "I've been thinking about what Leander said the first Solis we were here, about how we have to forgive others if we want God to forgive us. I've struggled with that. I loved my brother Aulus, and I thought he loved me. But then he did something horrible that would have destroyed my life, something that almost killed Leander. And he did it only because he wanted money. I wanted to see him punished so badly I could taste it. I didn't want to forgive.

"But Jesus forgave the soldiers who crucified Him. What Aulus did was nothing compared to that. And if he hadn't done what he did, I wouldn't be here to learn about Jesus. I would never have known He paid for my sins, and I would never have known God wanted me as His child."

She closed her eyes. "God, I used to be content to live the Roman way, worshiping false gods, thinking only of myself. Please forgive me for all I did that was wrong. Forgive me for all I didn't do that I should have. I know Jesus paid for all my sins. Thank You for forgiving me because He did. I'm ready to follow Jesus. Thank you, God, for making me Your child. I'll try to love You with my whole heart and mind. I'll try to obey You and love others for the rest of my life."

And as her smile grew brighter until her face shone, Leander closed his eyes and reveled in the presence of the Spirit as He claimed Mistress Calantha as God's own.

Chapter 52

What to Believe?

Luna, Day 37

It was mid-morning when the ship arrived in Luna. With Aulus beside him, Marcus fidgeted at the rail as the rowboats pulled them toward the pier. The ginger had stopped the worst of the nausea, but he wouldn't be entirely free of it until the surface beneath his feet was once more solid ground.

Africanus finished tying the blankets into a bundle and carried it to the rail. He started to lower it to the deck beside Marcus, but he paused with it at knee level. When he straightened and carried it to the far side of Aulus, Marcus's eyebrows dipped.

"You could have left it beside me. My stomach isn't that weak."

Africanus held his mouth straight, but his eyes revealed his true thoughts. "Your stomach is far from the weakest I've seen." His lips tightened as he fought the grin, but his eyes crinkled. When he forced his face to relax and appear serious, his eyes still laughed. "You threw what was in your stomach much farther than most women can."

Before Marcus could frame a cutting reply, the gladiator turned and walked away to get their small bags of food and personal belongings.

Marcus crossed his arms. While Africanus stoically received the gushing praise of one of the passengers who recognized him, Marcus rehearsed a strong reprimand for forgetting his place. Then Aulus's hand rested against his shoulder.

"He didn't mean anything disrespectful by that." Aulus's mouth curved into a grin. "And you have to admit, it was funny. We can use it on someone else if we have to take a ship to our first tribune postings.

Now that you know to use ginger root, you shouldn't have a problem yourself."

Marcus blew his breath out through his nose. "I guess I can let it pass this time."

With the straps of the bags draped over one shoulder, Africanus returned to scoop up the blankets. "First, we'll get a room at an inn where I've stayed many times with Master Brutus. We can leave all this there. The doors lock, the beds are clean, and the food is good. Then we go to the ludus."

He inhaled, and his nose scrunched. "There's a bath just down the street, and the innkeeper will appreciate us visiting it before sleeping in his beds."

When Africanus took his first step toward the gangplank, Aulus fell in beside him. "If Callidus isn't here, then what?"

Africanus glanced down at Aulus but kept walking. "We'll work our way back to Rome. The fight isn't lost—"

"Until you stop fighting." Aulus's frown relaxed. "Since Marcus and I won't quit until we find her, we'll have to win in the end."

Aulus paused at the edge of the gangplank, and Africanus walked ahead with his bulky burden.

Marcus joined Aulus. "You're right. We won't quit until Julia is back by your side and Callidus pays for his betrayal."

He waved his hand for Aulus to go down before him. With Aulus's back toward him, Marcus's frown deepened. They would make Callidus tell them where he'd taken Julia, and then he'd have to die before he could tell anyone they hired him in the first place.

The Ludus in Luna

Marcus walked beside Aulus as Africanus led them past the stone amphitheater. No decorative arches or relief sculptures of fighting men and animals made it a pleasure to behold. It was only a functional building where a few thousand could enjoy a day of bloodletting. The ludus was a fortress-like brick building just east of the arena.

No one guarded the door. Once inside, they followed the crack of wooden swords down a hallway to the practice arena. The lanista stood, arms crossed, watching a dozen men striking either wooden stakes or each other.

Aulus tipped his head toward Marcus. "Do you see him?"

"No." He rolled his eyes. Three and a half days of nausea, and their quarry wasn't even in Luna.

"This is only part of the men here." Africanus stepped farther onto the sand. "Salve, Victor."

The lanista turned, and a gap-toothed grin appeared. "Africanus." His head tipped to look past Brutus's gladiator at Marcus and Aulus. "If those two weren't in purple stripes, I'd say Brutus's standards have dropped for new fighters. I might have one or two that would interest him this time."

"We're looking for one in particular. He would have just come from Rome. Ex-legionary looking for a contract."

Victor's grin relaxed into a friendly smile. "And I might just have what you're looking for. I made a contract with such a man two days ago."

Africanus swept his hand toward Aulus. "We're not in the market today, but these two would like to talk with him."

Victor pointed at a hallway beside the armor room. "Down there with the weightlifters. His contract is for sale if Brutus wants him, but talk is free."

Africanus flicked his hand to summon Marcus and headed down the hallway.

Marcus's stomach tightened as they walked past a row of small cells, mostly empty. But one held a man lying on a cot, arm draped across his forehead, with each breath ending in a soft moan.

And as they stepped into the light of the next arena, Marcus released a sigh. There, with a yoke bearing buckets of sand draped across his shoulders, stood Callidus. Africanus waved Marcus and Aulus forward and stepped back behind them.

"Callidus." Marcus used his lowest voice.

The ex-legionary's eyes saucered. His gaze bounced between Marcus and the doorway. Africanus moved to block the exit. With spread legs and crossed arms, his face hardened into warrior coldness. "First, he wants to talk to you. Depending on what you say, it might stop there."

Callidus swallowed hard, then nodded. "Let's talk."

Marcus tipped his head toward a corner away from the other gladiators. "Over there."

When Callidus reached the corner, Marcus, Aulus, and Africanus fanned out in front of him.

"You didn't come to meet me." Marcus raked him with his fiercest glare. "We found the dead escort. What did you do with Julia?"

Callidus raised both hands. "I didn't do anything with her. One of the litter slaves took her."

With arms crossed, Marcus shifted his frown toward a scowl. "Tell us exactly what happened. No lies."

"I did exactly what you told me. I waited at the house until that morning when the girl came in her litter. The old man told her bearers to leave, that her friend would get her home. She followed me into the house, the escort, too. Then out of nowhere, one of your litter slaves jumped him and killed him. Broke his neck. Then he came after her. I fought him, but he knocked me down, almost knocked me out."

He rubbed the back of his neck. "I tried to follow. I even asked another man to help me chase them. Your slave dragged her through a passageway into the next street over. We went up and down asking if anyone saw where they went. A shoemaker said they went through another passage into the next street. We searched that street, too, and never found a trace."

His gaze bounced from Marcus to Aulus and back. "She seemed to go with him willingly. Maybe they're living together somewhere because they fancied each other."

An energetic headshake accompanied Aulus's frown. "Julia would never do something like that to bring disgrace on Father. She's a proper Roman maiden. She wouldn't run off with a slave even if Father didn't care."

Marcus lowered his eyebrows. "If that's what happened, why didn't you come tell me right away? When it would have been easier to find them. You knew I'd come to the taberna to pay you."

Callidus scraped his lower lip with his teeth. "I didn't complete the job, so I didn't earn the money. I'm an honest man." His hand headed toward the back of his neck, but he stopped it and dropped it to his side. "Besides, I was afraid you'd think I was in on it with that slave."

Aulus's forehead furrowed. "Tribune Titianus said you ate with a man at a taberna near the house. You talked for a long time. Who was he?"

"Ate with someone?" His eyes scrunched. "Oh, yes. I was eating, and an old friend from childhood just happened to come eat there, too. We only talked a while about old times."

Africanus took a step toward Callidus, frowning. "Your friend's name?"

Callidus ran his tongue over his teeth. "I don't remember."

The gladiator moved one step closer. "How could you talk about old times with a friend without knowing his name?"

"A man's memory is a funny thing sometimes." He shrugged.

Africanus's head tilted before he crossed his arms. "It would be good to get your memory working without having to talk with the tribune of the Urban Cohort. You signed into a ludus. That makes you a slave until your contract is fulfilled." He tilted his head more. "You do know slaves are questioned with torture?"

The blood drained from Callidus's face. "I think his name was Gaius something." He rubbed his mouth. "I can't remember the last name."

Africanus's head pulled back. "One Roman in five is Gaius something. You can do better than that."

Callidus's eyes darted between the three of them. "I think maybe it was Bassus."

"Are you sure the first name was Gaius?" Africanus made a cutting motion across his throat with his hand. "Tribune Titianus has the eyes of a lion, and he's hungry for a kill since it's the daughter of a consul who's missing."

Callidus's eyes saucered. "Now that I think harder, it might have been Gnaeus."

Africanus squinted one eye. "You're a trained warrior, and you expect us to believe a litter slave beat you in a fight?"

"He took me by surprise. He knocked me down before I realized what he was planning."

"He had time to kill the escort. That took long enough for you to expect his attack." Africanus shook his head.

Marcus held up his hand to silence Africanus. "What the slave did to him doesn't matter." He turned an icy stare back on Callidus. "All that matters is that you tell us enough for us to find Julia. The passageway they went down. How far from the house was that? Left or right from the gate?"

"Right as you walk toward it, and maybe a thousand feet."

Aulus nudged Marcus. "Where we found the litter." His face turned grim. "The blood in the atrium." He took a deep breath. "Whose was it?"

"Mine." Callidus rubbed his nose. "He hit hard."

"Did he hurt her?" Worry colored Aulus's voice.

"Not that I saw. Like I said, she seemed to want to go with him."

"Why would she want to go with a man who'd just killed her escort?" A thick layer of doubt coated Africanus's words.

"Maybe she fancies red-haired men. Maybe they planned to run off, and the escort just got in the way."

Marcus held up his hand to Africanus before focusing again on Callidus. "Is there anything else you can think of to help us find her?"

"No. All I know is her slave took her with him, and they disappeared before I could get her back. It's been twenty-five years since I lived in Rome. I have no idea where they might be hiding."

With his eyes focused on Callidus's face, Marcus rubbed his lip. The old soldier hadn't told the full truth, but he believed the Secundus slave had taken Julia. Her other litter bearers told Titianus the same slave was one of the kidnappers. It might be a web of lies, but it would be enough to keep Titianus from discovering Marcus's own role in it. Perhaps he wouldn't have to arrange Callidus's death after all. Four years in the arena was likely to take care of that for him.

"It would have been better if you'd come to tell me this right away instead of waiting for us to hunt you down. But knowing she's with that slave should help us find her." Marcus summoned a fake smile. "*Vale*, Callidus. May Fortuna smile upon you with victories."

As he walked away, Aulus stepped up beside him. "Except for the part about Julia wanting to live with her litter slave, do you believe him?"

"Yes. He has no reason to lie to us."

They entered the hallway and once more passed the moaning gladiator. Too bad it wasn't Callidus.

As they cut through the practice arena on their way to the exit, Africanus detoured to the lanista's side.

The lanista turned from the fighting pair. "Did you hear what you needed?"

"He told us enough for now." Africanus's eyebrows dipped. "But don't sell his contract for a few months."

"Brutus might want him?"

"Master Brutus decides what he wants when he sees it. After you've trained Callidus for a while, if you think he might be good enough for Rome, let us know. Then...maybe."

The lanista turned back to his fighters, and Marcus led them to the exit.

When they reached the street, Marcus leaned against the sun-warmed wall. "It was a long hunt, but we finally learned what we need. Now back to Rome."

Africanus's brow furrowed. "I don't believe him. If that had really happened, Callidus would have met you and told you what Julia and her slave had done. If Callidus never held her captive, he never broke Roman law. There was no reason for him to run. You should tell the tribune we found Callidus and let Titianus get the truth out of him."

"Well, I do believe him." Marcus's lips tightened. "He was afraid no one would believe him, and that's reason enough to run. I don't want Titianus to get his hands on him when Callidus hasn't done anything that would hurt Julia."

Aulus's eyes flipped between the two of them. "I can't imagine Julia taking up with a slave, but he did disappear, and he could be holding her somewhere."

"How long had you owned the slave?" Africanus crossed his arms.

"About a month."

"Was he from Rome?"

"I don't think so. He'd been a farm slave working with chariot horses for several years. We bought him for the stable to get my stallion trained for riding. I think he'd been taken in the Dacian war."

Africanus shook his head. "Farm slaves don't leave the farm to make friends. It's chains during the day and the ergastulum at night for most of them. How could a man with no money or local friends find a place to hide and keep her prisoner without anyone reporting him?"

"That's why we need to go back to Rome and get Titianus looking for the slave and where he might be holding her." Marcus crossed his arms as his gaze raked Africanus. "You seem too eager to find a different culprit. Are you just one slave lying about an innocent man to protect another guilty slave from the full force of Roman law?"

Africanus's arms shot out and his palms hit the wall on either side of Marcus. With the big man towering over him, Marcus pressed back against the wall and swallowed hard.

"No man calls me a liar. Not to my face, not where I'll hear of it." The near-whisper of the gladiator's icy words only sharpened the threat. "You're still a boy, too young to know the full danger of attacking a man's honor." He dropped one arm, and Marcus slipped past him.

The gladiator's eyes smoldered. "There are those who would kill you for less than what you said."

He crossed his arms, and his fingers tightened around his biceps. "There was a lion handler at the amphitheater in Cyrene who used to torment the lions that were used to kill criminals. One day, the latch on a cage broke, and the lion had a good meal before they came to take it to dine on some Christians." His grip relaxed, and his arms dropped to his sides. "A wise man can learn many useful lessons from the animals."

He took a step toward Marcus. "When you question my honesty, you question my master's wisdom in trusting me. You question his integrity as well as mine, and I won't tolerate that."

Aulus stepped between them. "I mostly believe him. Marcus is right that we should sail for Rome tomorrow and tell Titianus what we learned."

Africanus's glare vanished when his gaze shifted to Aulus. "We know where Callidus will be for the next four years. He can be made to tell the truth later."

Africanus's eyes relaxed into that irritating expression that felt like he was laughing when he looked at Marcus. "Back to Rome for us. You should get a good meal and a good night's rest. Tomorrow won't be an easy day."

Marcus cringed. Another three and a half days of a rocking ship and a churning stomach. "Can you find a ship that will get us home faster than we came?"

The corner of Africanus's mouth lifted. "Maybe I'll find a way that takes longer." He shrugged. "Master Brutus entrusted your safe return to me. Whatever I find, you'll survive the trip. The bath near the inn—I'll meet you there after I arrange our way home."

He turned and walked away.

Marcus's eyes narrowed as he watched the gladiator. "He shouldn't act so free. He does whatever he wants without asking permission."

"But he knows more than the two of us put together, and Brutus told him to take care of everything. I'm glad he does."

Aulus slapped Marcus's back. "I, for one, can hardly wait to get four days of travel grime off me and relax in some hot water for a while. The baths await."

Marcus glanced down the street. He could see the back of the big Nubian's head above the rest of the throng. Brutus's man might be doing exactly what his master told him, but that didn't mean Marcus had to like how he did it.

Chapter 53

Only a Sister

Gaius's Farm, Solis, Day 38

The last songs of praise had been sung, and Calantha joined the other women preparing to serve the fellowship meal.

Petronia stood beside her and wrapped one arm around Calantha. After a big squeeze, she patted her bulging stomach. "Another three weeks or so and I should be able to give you a good two-armed hug. My mother will be coming so she'll be here when our little one is born. She'll help me with Sertoria and little Quintus for a while."

Lucillia hugged her with both arms. "When Gaius announced that you've joined us following Jesus, I couldn't think of anything that could bring us more joy."

Calantha beamed at them both when Lucillia let her go. "I owe it to Leander for telling me about why he believes and to Publius for bringing the papyrus so I'd hear everything while I wrote what Leander recited."

A playful smile curved Petronia's lips. "And now that you follow Jesus, that could open another door."

"What do you mean?" Calantha placed the loaves of bread on the table.

"Christian men only marry Christian women." Her smile grew into a grin. "Leander's such a nice man. You two would do well together."

Calantha felt the heat to the tip of her ears. "He is a nice man, but he doesn't think of me that way."

Petronia raised her eyebrows. "I wouldn't be so sure. I've seen him watch you when you're not looking, and I'm sure there's more than brotherly affection in his eyes. The moment he thinks you're looking back at him, have you noticed how he looks down or away. He's noticing you. Quintus looked at me that same way before he ever said anything." A light laugh escaped. "Or rather I should say he tried not to look at me that way."

"I don't think so. He's the lion who protects me, but he treats me no differently than Marcella."

Lucillia and Petronia exchanged knowing smiles.

"Tell me this." Lucillia pressed her lips together to stop a grin. "When you move close to him, does he tense up? Maybe move back a little? Find something he needs to go do right away?"

"Well, sometimes." Calantha lowered her eyes and pushed the bread plate a little to center it between the stew and salad. She knew how to control her smile, but her eyes could reveal too much.

They had described Leander perfectly. She'd always thought he was uncomfortable being close because she was mistress. He'd often said something wasn't right for a mistress to do for her slave. And everything he said that about involved her touch.

When Marcella walked through the door, Lucillia waved her over.

"Don't you think Leander and Calantha would make a wonderful husband and wife?"

Marcella's eyes focused on Calantha. Her smile started small and grew. "I can't think of a better pair. But it's God who brings people together to make them one flesh, and He might have other plans."

Calantha could have hugged Marcella for her words. Then that teasing smile Marcella used with Gaius was directed toward her, and her ears heated again.

The men's voices approached the door, and Calantha picked out Leander's above all others, even though it was the quietest of them all.

And every time she heard his voice, something inside her felt warm and safe.

He limped through the door with Gaius's hand resting on his shoulder. When his eyes met hers, his usual slight smile broadened.

She looked away. The women were watching her too closely, and Petronia was likely to say something if she saw how a smile meant just for her could draw one in return.

Sertoria tugged on her tunic, and she hoisted the little girl onto her hip. She kept her eyes off Leander by keeping them on the sweet child in her arms.

As he limped back out the door with his food, she let her gaze follow him. Little Quintus ran over and smiled up at him, and Leander balanced his cup on his plate so he could tousle the small boy's hair as he smiled back.

And a thought she'd never entertained thrust itself upon her. Before her stood the finest man she had ever known: brave, smart, selfless, kind.

Her friends would laugh and say it was ridiculous. Her father would scowl and declare her out of her mind.

She was the noble daughter of a consul of Rome, and Leander was a Dacian slave. Roman law and custom decreed they could never be bound in marriage. Yet her heart cried out that he was the husband of her dreams.

Since the day he rescued her, he'd treated her first as mistress, then as friend, and now as sister. Could he also want them to be so much more?

Too many years as a slave had trained him to hide his feelings. And every time she thought she caught a glimpse of him responding to her as a man does to a women, he'd look away or pull back or excuse himself to go do something. Was that because he felt nothing but friendship for her? Did he love her as a sister in Christ and nothing more?

Or was Petronia right? When his guard was down, when he thought she didn't see, did a glimmer of his real feelings show?

She kissed the top of Sertoria's head and sighed. Father would be angry when she told him she'd rejected the gods of Rome and given her heart to Jesus. What would he do if she rejected a senator's son because she'd given her heart to a slave?

◆

Leander offered the chair beside Gaius to Publius and sat on the bench with Sextus. He hadn't even taken his first bite when Calantha sat beside him.

"It's so wonderful to be here, worshiping God with everyone, knowing Jesus saved me. I remember when you said I'd spend eternity in hell if I died. You took the arrow to spare me from that fate. That's the bravest thing I've ever seen."

"Jesus allowed Himself to be crucified to spare me that fate, too." Leander shifted a little to face her. "An arrow in my leg is nothing by comparison."

"Don't make light of what you did. You didn't only rescue me from slavery. Your words led me toward Jesus. And having me write down all you'd memorized...those words have truly set me free." She took his hand and squeezed. "Having you in my life has been pure blessing."

His eyes widened. His mouth opened, but no words came. She had blessed his life, too, but he could never tell a mistress that.

Her light laugh wrapped around him. "I've made you speechless." She ran her fingers through his hair. "I rather like doing that."

When she moved away to sit with Petronia, Sextus grinned at him. "Having a Christian wife to share your love of the Lord...that's a blessing beyond measure." He nudged Leander with his elbow. "A wise man wouldn't miss what God has placed before him."

Leander nodded. But Sextus didn't know that soon he must return Calantha to her father to once more be Mistress Julia. That Leander the man must turn back into Dacius the slave. Calantha could never be more than his Christian sister, and her future happiness would come in the arms of another man.

And even as he smiled, that thought punched a hole in Leander's heart.

It was late afternoon, and Leander was ready for a rest, a good meal, and some conversation with dear friends. But first he wanted to clean up.

He pulled the tunic over his head and laid it on the table under the carob tree. His wounds had sealed, and Gaius had said they would all go in a few days to the small private bath that Publius operated next to his taberna. A good soak in hot water was the greatest luxury he'd known. But for now, the oil and scraper would do well enough.

"Leander." Her musical voice so close behind him made him jump. "Marcella said to tell you dinner is almost ready."

He glanced at the scars on either side of his thigh. Too often she told him they were her fault, and that brought a sadness to her eyes. But they were nothing compared to the one on his shoulder.

"I'll be there shortly." He answered without turning. What she didn't see wouldn't cause her grief.

Then her fingertip slowly traced one of the long scars that remained from the lashes the day he tried to warn her. He arched his back away from her touch.

Her breath caught. "Oh! I didn't think that would hurt you. I'm sorry."

Leander shook his head but didn't turn to face her. "They don't hurt. You only startled me."

"These are all my fault. I should have stopped Vilicus." Her finger traced another lash line. "Six of these when there shouldn't even be one."

"It's not your fault. You didn't tell him to use the lash."

"I know you've forgiven me, but it's still my fault. I didn't stop him, and I should have. You only wanted to protect me from Aulus."

"You didn't know that, and I frightened you."

"But he didn't need to whip you, and I should never have let him. I didn't even think about how much it hurt you. I only thought about myself and not wanting to see your blood. I never thought about you at all."

She started to trace another scar, and that slow caress was too much to handle. He spun to face her.

Mistake. His bare shoulder with the knife scar drew her gaze.

Then it drew her fingertips. "This is my fault, too."

She touched it as if he were made of gossamer glass—pressure so light it wouldn't even hurt a butterfly's wing. How could so light a touch make his heart pound like it would leap out of his chest? Why did she have to touch him at all? Even though it meant nothing but friendship to her, it tore him apart, with half of him wanting her to continue the caresses and half knowing those touches tempted him almost beyond endurance.

God, why do you let her do this to me?

He stepped back and snatched up his tunic. He dropped it over his head, and when it cleared his eyes, she was still too close for comfort.

The glistening tears of regret that moistened her eyes almost made him step forward to embrace her and tell her she should stop feeling so bad about things that lay in the past. The past couldn't be changed, and she'd apologized too many times when once was more than enough.

But that was a temptation, too. An even greater one than the prickling of his skin under her cool fingertips or the scalding of his heart by her warm tears.

After fastening his belt, he tipped his head toward the house. "We should go to the house if Marcella has everything ready. I don't like to make her wait. After you."

Mistress. You can never be anything but the mistress.

She took a step, then waited for him to start walking. After his first stride, she stepped close to walk beside him. Her hand brushed against his, and he jerked it back. For one unsettling moment, he thought she was going to hold his hand for the short walk to the house.

Both relief and regret surged through him when she didn't.

After dinner, Calantha leaned against the doorframe, gazing at the oranges and reds that flamed in the western sky.

The scrape of a chair was followed by Leander's limping footsteps. Then his voice right behind her. "Excuse me, Calantha. I need to check the mules for the night."

She turned and pushed a strand of hair from his forehead. "I'll only let you pass on one condition."

"What's that?"

"You'll sit on the bench with me until the sunset ends."

His back straightened. "I will, but why?"

"I love watching sunsets and sunrises. The way everything takes on the color of the sky, as if the whole world was in special harmony. The way each one holds the promise of a whole new day."

She took his hand, and his eyes widened. "Come on. We don't want to miss any of it. You can do what you need to do, and then we can sit and watch until the sky fire dies."

With his hand still wrapped in hers, she led him out to the bench by the table. "Hurry up with the mules. I'll be waiting."

She watched him as he checked the water and shook the gate to be sure it was securely latched. One of the mules sauntered over, and he paused to pet its nose and cheek and pull his fingers through its forelock. When the other walked over and demanded the same, he looked over his shoulder at her. His smile and shrug apologized for the delay, but he still gave the second mule what it wanted before leaving the rail.

The mules were lucky. What would the touch of his hand on her cheek feel like? His fingers pulling through her hair?

When he limped over to join her, he started to sit on the second bench. Then she patted the bench beside her. "Sit here, like when you were practicing letters."

When he lowered himself onto the edge of the bench, she twisted to face him. "Are you ready for a whole new day?"

His smoke-gray eyes gazed into her own. "I'm ready for whatever you want."

She turned her eyes back to the sky. Soon Father would come home from Sicilia, and they'd have to go back to Rome. But her home was no longer her father's villa. It was here with Marcella and Gaius and Leander. Somehow, she had to find a way to escape the future she'd been raised for, the one she'd always expected.

She felt as much as heard his sigh, and her own followed. The future she wanted sat beside her, but it would never be hers. Not in the ordinary way of things.

Her eyebrows rose. She worshipped a God not limited by the ordinary ways. He'd brought Leander back from the brink of death when Marcella and Gaius prayed. And even though she didn't follow Him then, He'd heard her prayer, too.

God, please don't let me be trapped by my past. Please give me a whole new day.

Chapter 54

Luna, Day 38

The sunshine streaming through the window woke Marcus from a fitful slumber. His face scrunched as he rubbed his forehead and swung his feet off the bed. They'd found Callidus and now had information to guide their next step in finding Julia, but at least three days of queasy stomach lay ahead before they could use it.

Aulus stuck his head in the door. "Coming down for breakfast?"

Marcus rubbed the back of his neck. "What's the point? I'm just going to lose it when we get out of the harbor."

"I don't think so. Africanus bought something that will solve your seasickness problem."

Marcus rose and ran his fingers through his hair. "His trick with the ginger helped, but it didn't stop it completely. He has something better?"

"Oh, yes." Aulus grinned. "He said he could promise you wouldn't be seasick on the way home."

Marcus followed Aulus down the stairs, but Aulus turned toward the exit instead of the dining room when they reached the lower hallway.

Aulus pushed open the door. "Follow me." He disappeared outside.

When Marcus stepped out behind him, his head bounced back. Three quality horses stood before him with the blankets and sacks tied at the rear of their saddles while Africanus stroked the neck of a proud gray stallion.

A smile spread across the gladiator's face. "I told you I might find something that took longer than three and a half days to get back to

Rome." The smile turned into a grin. "But I don't think you'll mind the extra three days."

Marcus crossed his arms. "You spent a lot of money on these."

"And Master Brutus will sell them for twice what I paid when we get to Rome." Africanus shrugged.

"No wonder he trusts you to take care of business for him." Marcus tipped his head to acknowledge Africanus's thoughtfulness.

Aulus appeared at his side. "Let's go eat so we can get started. The sooner we reach Rome, the sooner we find Julia."

Aulus entered the inn ahead of him. As Marcus followed, he paused in the doorway and turned.

Africanus glanced across his shoulder and smiled. Marcus responded in kind. Even if the gladiator sometimes forgot his place, it was good to have him along.

Alsium, north of Roma, Day 43

When Aulus jerked awake, his eyes took a few moments to adjust to the darkness. The soft sound of Marcus's breathing came from the bed above him. But between him and the stars outside the window was the large form of Africanus. The gladiator stood with arms crossed, leaning against the window frame.

Aulus slipped from his bed and joined him. "Something wrong?" He whispered so he wouldn't awaken Marcus.

A cloud blocked the moonlight, but Africanus's white tunic kept him from disappearing in the shadow.

"No. I like watching clouds cross the moon." For such a big man, his whisper seemed oddly quiet.

"We're almost back to Rome. I bet your family will be glad to see you. I'm sorry we've kept you away so long."

"Sometimes I'm gone for three or four months when Master Brutus visits his Germanic estate. But it will be good to get home."

"Does he always take you?"

"Yes, and often Rufus goes as well."

"Traveling so much together—is that how you became his friend?"

The cloud cleared the moon, and in its pale light, Aulus could see Africanus smile.

"Friendship grows out of respect. Antonius Brutus is a man anyone would respect. Honorable to the core. Devoted husband, fair master.

Brave and generous. He takes care of those he can…like helping you with your problem."

"He respects you." Aulus massaged his neck. "Except for Father, you deserve more respect than any man I know. Brutus is lucky to have you as a friend. I'd like to count you as one of mine, too."

Africanus's smile broadened. "You can." He glanced at the sleeping Marcus. "A loyal friend—a man can't set a price on that. But a wise man still looks closely at what his friend values. Even the most loyal friend can tell you to do something that isn't honorable, meaning it for good but causing bad."

Aulus's gaze settled on Marcus. "Like staging a fake kidnapping so I wouldn't have to tell Father the truth." His focus returned to Africanus. "I know I should never have agreed to the scheme. I should have just told Father and faced the anger I deserved. Marcus tried to get his father to give me the money, and when he refused, what started as a joke about faking my kidnapping turned into faking Julia's. We never thought through what could happen. But even if it had gone as planned, it would still have been wrong to lie that way."

Africanus placed his hand on Aulus's shoulder. "Wisdom comes from experience, and sometimes experience comes from mistakes. A good man learns to think first so he doesn't make those mistakes again." He slapped Aulus's arm. "You'll grow into a good man, Aulus Secundus." He glanced at Marcus. "And there's still time for Marcus Drusus to change into a good man, too."

Marcus stirred, and Aulus crept back to his bed. It creaked when he lowered himself onto it, but Marcus's breathing stayed steady. As he pulled the sheet back over himself, Aulus's gaze rested on Africanus, still watching the moon.

Loyalty and honor. Some men had both in abundance, and that was the kind of man he wanted to be.

Rome

It was midafternoon when Aulus and his companions rode across the Tiber on the Pons Aemilanus to reach the marble-and-concrete center of Rome. Less than a quarter hour, and they would reach Brutus's ludus. Then, with what they'd learned from Callidus, Brutus and Africanus could decide what to do next.

He glanced at Marcus. He was certain to have his own ideas on the best next step, but Aulus could get him to agree to the better plan. Since Africanus bought the horses, his friend had stopped the snide comments about Brutus's favorite slave. With Brutus's sage advice and the three of them working as a team, surely they'd find Julia, and he could finally bring her home.

"Secundus." The voice of authority in the body of Titianus rang out behind him. As he reined his horse to face the approaching tribune, Aulus's eyes sought Marcus. His friend read his plea and moved his own horse between them.

The tribune, in full armor with his red-plumed helmet on his head, held up his hand, and the eight soldiers stopped behind him.

"Secundus. Drusus." Titianus nodded toward each in turn. Then his gaze measured the three horses, and his eyes narrowed. "It's not often I see such fine horses with bridles and saddles fit for a slave." He glanced at Africanus before focusing again on Aulus. "Far below your usual standards."

"They belong to Antonius Brutus." Marcus's voice sounded relaxed. "We were just borrowing them."

The tribune's head cocked. "Where have you been with them?"

Marcus patted his horse's neck. "We went down to Brutus's wine agent in Ostia to see if the special vintage from his Liternum estate is worth its high price."

"Is it?" Titianus's mouth smiled, but his eyes didn't. "My uncle, Quintus Sabinus, always serves the best. He'll want some if it is."

"It is, indeed." Marcus's fake smile looked more genuine.

As Titianus's head tilted, his smile faded. "That would account for one, maybe two days of your absence from Rome, but not the ten days you've been gone. Where else have you been?"

Marcus straightened in the saddle. "Why are you wasting your time worrying about where we are and what we're doing? You should be looking for Julia, not watching us."

Aulus nudged his horse to join Marcus. Africanus reached over and gripped a rein. One shake of his head, and Aulus reined in.

Titianus's head tipped back as his gaze swung from Marcus to Africanus. "Brutus's man still with you? You've had more than enough time to find your own bodyguard." He rubbed his jaw. "I haven't seen this one with Brutus for at least ten days. He's been going around Rome with a red-haired bodyguard instead. Highly unusual for him."

Marcus shrugged. "You'll have to ask Brutus why he chooses one bodyguard over another. Africanus went with us to make sure we could find the wine agent."

Titianus's eyes bored into Aulus, but he tried not to fidget as he returned a relaxed smile.

"I may do that." He flicked his hand and moved off with his men following.

Marcus reined back beside Aulus, and the three continued their ride toward the Ludus Bruti.

Africanus's gaze locked on Marcus, and Marcus returned it.

"What are you looking at?"

Africanus's brow furrowed. "You lie easily. It almost sounds like the truth."

"But it was the truth." Marcus shrugged. "You did take us to Brutus's wine agent, and these are his horses. I just didn't tell him the rest of it. There's no reason for him to know. It wouldn't help him find Julia."

Africanus drew a breath and held it before responding. "Truth has value for its own sake."

"And it's best kept to yourself if telling it could get someone hurt. Like you said, Callidus is a slave now, and Titianus would interrogate with torture. He tried to keep Julia from being kidnapped, and he doesn't deserve that."

"If he did, I'd agree. But I don't believe him."

"Well, I do, and that's enough for all of us." Marcus kicked his horse and moved ahead.

When Africanus tightened his lips and shook his head, Aulus's gaze bounced between the two of them. Truth did have value in itself. Father and Africanus agreed on that, and perhaps it was time he joined them.

Ludus Bruti

The stable slave started over as soon as Aulus and his companions entered the gate, then froze with a furrowed brow.

"Our horses are with Galbius in Ostia. You can get them tomorrow." Africanus swung his leg over his horse's neck and slid off. "Is the master in his office?"

The stableman took his reins. "Yes, Africanus."

Africanus led them past the cells and small arenas to Brutus's office. When they entered the room, he stepped back against the wall and motioned them toward the two chairs in front of the desk.

With a snap, Brutus closed the wax tablet he was reading. "Was your trip successful?"

Aulus glanced at Marcus as he settled into a chair. "Mostly. We found Callidus in Luna, and he told us what happened. Her litter slave, Dacius, took her. Callidus tried to follow and get her back. He failed, but he did tell us where they disappeared, so we can start looking there."

Brutus shifted his gaze to Africanus and raised his eyebrows.

The gladiator's deep voice came from behind them. "Callidus only answered the questions when warned about torture, and what he did tell us was partly true, at best. He claimed her slave killed the escort and defeated him in a fight." A soft snort punctuated his words. "Even if her bearer had killed the old man, no legionary who could fight like he did would lose to a man not trained for battle."

He crossed his arms. "Her slave probably took her, but Callidus admitted she went willingly. So, was he kidnapper or protector?"

"Kidnapper." Marcus leaned forward. "The other bearers said he followed her into the house, and they never came back out. He must have been one of the kidnappers."

"But Taurus questioned that." Aulus rubbed his lip. "He's her regular litter escort, and he didn't think Dacius would do anything to hurt her."

With his elbow resting on the desk, Brutus rubbed his forehead. "Whatever his motive was doesn't matter. What matters is whether you have enough information to start the search here in Rome."

Aulus nodded. "We do, if we assume Callidus did chase them and try to catch them."

Brutus's eyes turned on Africanus again. "Your thoughts?"

"He would have chased them even if he was the kidnapper himself. She'd be worth a lot of money...a strong temptation for a man desperate enough to sell himself into the arena." Africanus tipped his head and nodded. "But what he said about where he chased them...it might be true. It's worth starting the hunt there."

"So, we will assume it's true and try to pick up their trail." Brutus's eyes focused on Aulus. "Is there any reason why she might be afraid to go home if her slave was only protecting her?"

Aulus sucked air between his teeth and looked at Marcus. "Dacius was bought to train my stallion. Marcus and I discussed the plan once when we thought no one was in the stable. If he was in one of the stalls…"

"And if he told her, they'd have good reason to be hiding until your father comes home." Brutus picked up a stylus and tapped the desk with it. "But you can set that straight when you find her, and if she's with him, she should be safe until you do."

He stood. "We'll keep checking the special dealers in case she shows up there, and tomorrow you three will start looking for someone who might know where they went."

"Something you should know." Africanus's words drew Brutus's instant attention. "Tribune Titianus of the Urban Cohort stopped us and asked where we'd been for ten days. He questioned why I hadn't been guarding you. He might come here."

"If he comes, I'll tell him the truth." Brutus shrugged. "I've lent you to Aulus until the matter of Julia's disappearance is resolved. You've been told to help in any way possible. That should satisfy him."

Brutus stepped past his desk and placed one hand on Aulus's shoulder and the other on Marcus. "Go home. Get a good night's rest, and come back early. Tomorrow you hunt, and when you find Julia, we'll celebrate."

Marcus left the office and headed down the hallway, but Aulus paused at the door. Brutus and Africanus were seated opposite each other at the desk, and Brutus was filling two silver goblets from a small, cream-colored jug.

Aulus's lips curved into a smile. If anyone deserved Brutus's best vintage, it was the man any Roman should be proud to call friend.

Chapter 55

Too Hard to Bear

Gaius's farm, evening of Day 44

Leander poured the last bucket of water into the mules' trough and hung it on the gatepost. When he turned, Calantha waited for him, elbow on the table, chin in her hand. For the last week, she'd insisted they watch the setting sun before retiring.

He wasn't sorry. The chirps of the crickets, the whisper of a gentle breeze stirring the carob leaves overhead—that was almost as enjoyable as the faint scent of roses from the perfumed oil that Calantha and Marcella had made together.

He breathed deep when she sat close, and with his eyes closed, he could once more see his mother's back as she gathered some blooms in her rose garden. But every time his mother turned, it was Calantha's teasing eyes that met his.

Calantha always worked a little rose oil into her hair when she let it down. It hung halfway down her back. Too long to comb herself, so Marcella helped her.

Marcella's hair was just as long, but Calantha didn't help her brush it. Gaius reserved that privilege for himself, and love flowed between them with each stroke. She'd tease him about pulling it, and he'd insist she needed a kiss to make up for that.

Calantha would laugh, and then she'd cast a glance his way, and that slow smile would curve her lips, and...then he had to look away before she could see her kind affection trigger his regret that the dreams of a slave remained only that...dreams.

Tonight, she patted the bench beside her, and he had just seated himself when Publius crested the hill.

Publius kept his mule at a trot and reined in beside them. "Lucillia sent me. Petronia's baby is coming early, and her mother won't be here for almost a week. She said I should fetch Calantha to help right away. Lucillia can take care of the delivery, but she needs to get back to the taberna soon. The little ones need someone to watch them, and Petronia could use a woman's help until her mother comes."

Calantha rose. "I'd love to help. I'll get a few things from the house, and we can go right now."

As she hurried toward the house, Publius slid off his mule. "I'll help you hitch the team and show you the way to their farm." He looked to the east and smiled. "Clear sky and the moon is rising, so we'll have plenty of light. A moonlight drive with a pretty young woman...I would have enjoyed that at your age."

"It's not that way with us."

Speaking that truth pricked his heart. But life was what it was. He was Dacius the slave, not Leander the free man. It was only play-acting, and the play would end when he took her home.

Publius's smile broadened. "Maybe not now, but things can change." The smile grew into a grin. "Lucillia likes delivering babies. Maybe soon she can deliver yours."

Marcella's farewell reached Leander's ears, and he turned to see Calantha hurrying toward them with something draped over her arm. Part looked like Marcella's cloak but the other...

She reached him. "Here." She offered what she'd been weaving since the day after she chose her false name and renamed him. "I made it to keep you warm."

He took it, then stood staring at it as he stroked the soft fabric. He opened his mouth, but the words didn't come.

That triggered her soft laugh. "This is the second time I've seen you at a loss for words. But maybe you'll have figured out what to say by the time I finish the tunic I'm making you."

"You should wear this. I won't feel the cold." Not with her sitting so close beside him.

"But I made it for you, and I want the pleasure of seeing you wear it. I have Marcella's."

"If you find pleasure in something, then I'll do it." He stroked the soft wool.

So many hours, so many days she'd put into making it...for him. But that could only be her way of thanking him one more time.

The music of her laughter drew his smile. "I won't forget my lion made that promise, and I'll hold you to it."

She lifted it from his hands and shook it open. Stepping close, she reached around his neck to catch one corner of it. Then she drew it around his shoulders and pinned it with one of the gold pins from the shoulder of her fancy tunic. When she patted the pin where it rested on his good shoulder, she left her other hand resting on his chest.

"It looks good on my lion."

Her hand—it was right above his heart. Surely, she must feel his heart rate rising beneath it. "Thank you. It does feel warm."

He stepped back. "Babies don't wait. Time to leave." He lifted her into the wagon, climbed aboard himself, and slapped the mules with the reins. The wagon jerked, and he followed Publius out of the farm yard.

He looked at Calantha so close beside him, and her excited smile lit her eyes as she returned his gaze.

Publius, Sextus, the women...they all expected a future he knew would never come.

It was not that way with them, and it never could be.

He turned his face away. What could he say if she asked about the heartache behind his smile?

◆

Calantha watched the moonlight play on the angles of Leander's face and fought a sigh. What she'd seen too often had just happened again.

A week of watching sunsets had given her plenty of time to watch him, but she was no closer to knowing whether Petronia was right. Sometimes Gaius and Marcella joined them. They would start the conversation, and it was as if the four of them had known each other all their lives. Leander smiled at Marcella's stories, chuckled at Gaius's jokes, and talked as much as Gaius about horses and mules and chickens and grapevines and all the things that seemed to fascinate men.

But when it was just the two of them, he responded when she spoke to him, but he was content to watch the clouds fade and stars appear in silence.

He sat on the bench beside her without being reminded, but always on the edge, and if she slid too close, she felt him tense.

But when she walked past him and slipped her fingers through his hair, that always drew his smile, and the warmth in his eyes when she had his full attention…how could a man look at her like that if he didn't care?

When she wrapped the cloak around his shoulders and placed her hand on his chest, his heart pounded beneath her palm, as if he'd been running. It took more than gratitude to do that to a man.

His eyes looked happy when he lifted her into the wagon and they began their trip to welcome a new life into the world. As they headed up the hill, he let his eyes meet hers. The heat behind them warmed her, and she let her own delight show.

Then he looked away, and the connection between them broke. He kept his eyes on the mules and never spoke a word.

And once more, she was left wondering whether the man who owned her heart saw her as a woman or only as a friend.

Gaius's farm, Day 45

It was midmorning, and Gaius walked through the vineyard, checking the growing clusters. He stopped to watch Leander, whose careful eye spotted every pest bent on reducing the yield.

His willing helper moved steadily down the row, but every now and then, Leander's shoulders would droop, his head would drop, and his eyes would close. Something was not right, and Marcella would have Gaius's hide if he let her favorite young man hurt himself.

When he reached Leander's side, he pointed at a log at the edge of the field. "Let's sit a while."

After they sat, Leander picked up a stick and drew in the dirt.

Gaius placed a hand on his shoulder. "What's wrong?"

Leander's gaze shifted to the distant hills, and when it returned to Gaius's face, his eyes were clouded.

"In less than a week, Calantha's father should be back from Sicilia. I'll have to take her home and become a slave in his household again."

He buried his face in his hands. After long moments of silence, he raised wounded eyes to Gaius.

"How am I ever going to do that? It wasn't so bad at the Crassus estate. The overseer there saw I was good with horses, and he used me to do work I truly enjoyed. I did exactly what Apostle Paul taught. I served my master as if everything I did was serving my Lord. The overseer treated me well because I did. I hadn't known freedom since I was a child, and somehow it didn't bother me that I belonged to the estate, just like the horses and mules.

"But it's different now. In the mistress's household, I was shifted around to do whatever the overseer felt like that day. I was only a talking tool in his eyes, only I knew better than to ever say anything.

"Since we came here, I've lived as if I were a free man. I'd forgotten life could feel so...full of possibilities." His shoulders sagged. "How can I go back to being no more than an animal serving the whim of the overseer?"

He ran his fingers through his hair. "And the mistress...I've grown so used to seeing her as Calantha...as a woman who actually sees me and talks to me and...maybe even likes me. Not as a woman likes a man, of course, but as a friend. When I take her home, she'll be Mistress Julia once more. I'll see her every day when I carry that litter, but I'll never get to talk with her again."

They stared into the distance together until the silence got too heavy.

Gaius blew out a deep breath. "You love her, don't you."

"Don't say that. It's not something I can even let myself think. If I say the words, it would make it too real. And somehow I have to make myself believe it isn't true. A future with her is impossible. If I'm ever going to be able to take her back where I become invisible again, I have to deny it, even to myself. And I have to take her back. It's where she belongs.

"She's the noble daughter of a Roman senator. Her father was a consul of Rome. He's just finishing his year as proconsul of Sicilia. We'd have no future even if I was free right now. Even if she wanted it, too. No senator's daughter can marry a freedman. Roman law forbids it."

Gaius wrapped his arm around Leander's shoulders. "The law of Rome is not God's law, and who knows what God may do to change what seems unchangeable?"

Leander tried to smile, but the pain in his eyes was undiminished.

"I know what Apostle Paul said. 'All things work together for good for those who love God.' I only wish I could see how that could be right now."

He stood. "I want to finish this row before lunch is ready." He tightened his lips as he slowly shook his head. "Thank you for listening."

As Leander limped back toward the grape vines, Gaius sighed. *Please help him, Father. Give him more than what he thinks is possible.*

Leander still had a tenth of a row to inspect when Gaius headed into the house. Marcella was humming as she set out bread, cheese, and dried dates for them.

She greeted him with a smile; then her brow furrowed. "Is something wrong?"

He ran his fingers through his hair. "Leander."

She straightened. "Did he hurt himself?"

"No. That would heal. There's no cure for his problem."

Her hand shot up and covered her mouth. "What happened?"

"He loves Calantha."

When her hand dropped away, it revealed a smile. "That's good. I've been watching her, and I think she loves him, too."

Gaius dropped into his chair. "It's not good. She's the daughter of a senator. Even worse, an ex-consul of Rome. He's a slave. But even if he was free now, they couldn't marry."

He placed his elbow on the table and rubbed his forehead. "He's going back to be treated like an animal while he waits for her to marry some Roman aristocrat. It's tearing him up inside."

She came to his side and wrapped her arm around his shoulders. "Has he told her?"

Gaius shook his head.

"Well, she needs to know. And if she loves him, too, we need to be praying for God to do something about it. I'm going to see Petronia and the new baby this afternoon, and I'll take care of that."

She craned her neck to look out the door. "He's coming. Not a word about me telling her until I know more."

He reached up and patted her hand where it rested on his shoulder, and she leaned over to kiss the top of his head.

And then he smiled. The prayers of a righteous woman were powerful things, and surely God would hear.

Petronia's house

When Marcella drove the wagon into Petronia's farmyard, Calantha went to greet her with a sleeping Sertoria on her hip.

"What a nice surprise. I'm afraid Petronia and the baby are asleep, but they should awaken soon." She kissed the little girl's head. "A little walk got this one sleepy, too."

"Where's Quintus?"

Calantha tipped her head toward the vineyard. "Helping his father look for bugs." Her mouth curved into a smile. "He's not as good at that as Leander, but give him some time…"

Marcella climbed out of the wagon. "Let them sleep. It's you I need to talk with first."

"Let's sit." A smile accompanied her glance at the toddler. "She gets heavy after a while."

They settled on a bench by the front door. Sertoria stirred, then went limp again.

"What did you need to tell me?"

"Actually, to ask you." Marcella cleared her throat. "About Leander."

Calantha straightened. "He's all right, isn't he?"

Marcella patted her arm. "Gaius is being careful with him. But he told Gaius something I think you ought to know."

"What is it?" Calantha tipped her head.

"He told Gaius he loves you."

"He said so?" Calantha's smile started small and broadened until she felt it stretching her face. "That's wonderful! Petronia told me he was starting to, but I couldn't tell for sure. He keeps his thoughts and feelings so well hidden. Too many years with masters who wanted it that way. I try to read his eyes and then tease the words out of him."

"That's why I came to tell you because I knew he never would." Marcella's smile faded. "Gaius said he thinks there's no hope of you ever being together."

Calantha drew a breath and released a deep sigh. "He's the best man I've ever known, and I want us to marry, more than anything. But he's right that there's a huge barrier between us. My father is Tiberius Julius Secundus. He's been consul of Rome, governor of Sicily, a leader in the Senate for as long as I can remember." She shoved some loose hair behind her ear. "It's stupid that Roman law won't let me marry Leander, even after he's a freedman. And I know Father will free him as soon as we go home. After what Leander did to save me from the kidnappers my brother hired, Father will do anything he can for him."

Her lips tightened. "But him being the finest man alive doesn't matter under Roman law. Only family history and political connections, and what Roman law requires, that's what Father will do."

"You know, there might be an easy solution." Marcella's brow furrowed, then relaxed. "You could just stay on with us. Don't go back to Rome."

Calantha closed her eyes and sighed as she smiled. "I'd love to do that, but he'd never agree to it. He's too honorable. He really would be a runaway if we did. Even if I told him he'd be serving my father best if he stayed and became my husband, he'd tell me I wasn't the one who owned him. Without Father's permission, he'd never stay."

Marcella touched her hand. "What are you going to do?"

"First, I'll go back to Father and get him to free Leander. I'm sure he'll do even more to reward him for almost dying to save me from Aulus." Her shoulders drooped. "But I still need to solve the problem of be being a Senator's daughter. There must be some way around that, if I can only find it."

She leaned toward Marcella. "Don't tell him anything about what I'm hoping for. I don't want him disappointed if it doesn't happen. But even if we can't be together, at least he'll be free to stay here with you."

Marcella placed her palm on Calantha's cheek. "As Gaius is fond of saying, the laws of Rome are not God's laws. If it's His will for you to be together, He'll show you the way."

A baby's wail drew Marcella's smile. "Time to go see the newest member of our house church."

As Calantha followed her through the door, she turned her face toward heaven.

Dear God, please give us a future where we hear our own baby's cry.

Chapter 56

FINALLY ON TRACK

Subura, Day 45

Aulus's stomach tightened as they once more approached the gate into the abandoned Drusus stable yard. It had been twenty-six days since Julia was taken from that house. Twenty-six days of worrying about what he had done to his sweet sister. His eyes shifted between Africanus and Marcus. If her bearer really had taken her somewhere, as Callidus claimed, had he protected her or hurt her? And what was he doing with her now?

Marcus strode past the gate, but Africanus paused. "Has this house been empty since the kidnapping?"

Marcus looked back over his shoulder. "Yes."

"Then we should search it. They might have circled back and hidden here."

Marcus frowned, then nodded. "Your point about the slave having no friends to hide him...probably well taken. If they stayed in Rome, here would be a good place."

They entered the atrium with its scum-coated pool. Aulus's eyes were drawn to the place by the wall where her tunic had swept the dirt away. The dust had returned; the last trace of her presence there was gone.

Africanus and Marcus each took a side and looked in the small rooms off the atrium and peristyle while Aulus climbed the stairs to search the rooms off the balcony. Nothing but dust and silence greeted him.

When he rejoined the others by the pool, Marcus slapped his arm. "Staying here would have been too risky. Titianus would have talked to everyone in this neighborhood. If it were me, I'd be afraid someone would report me."

Africanus moved toward the door. "But now we know they didn't, and it's time to find that shoemaker."

They reached the spot where the litter had been abandoned and followed the narrow passageway to the street beyond. To the left was a weaver, but across the street, a shoemaker was attaching the laces to a sandal.

Marcus pointed. "A shoemaker, just like Callidus said."

They approached, and he turned with a smile. "How can I help you?"

Aulus rested his palms on the counter. "We're looking for two people who would have come out of that passageway twenty-six days ago." He swung his arm toward the opening.

The shoemaker chuckled. "Twenty-six days? That's a long time to remember."

Marcus leaned in. "Try. It's very important."

A flick of Aulus's hand silenced him. "A retired legionary was trying to catch up with them. He asked you about a red-haired man in a red tunic and a young woman in green with jewels and fancy hair. You told him they went through another passageway, and he followed them."

"Oh, yes." The shoemaker rubbed his chin. "I remember the young couple, but it wasn't a military man who talked with me. It was a scrawny Roman who didn't look like he'd ever held a sword. He claimed he was chasing two slaves who had robbed their mistress. The man had been hurt." He pointed up the street to another passageway. "I told him they went through there, and he followed them."

Africanus's voice came from behind Aulus. "How badly hurt?"

"It couldn't have been too bad. He had hold of her hand, and they were running. But he was limping."

Africanus moved forward to lean on the counter. "Was she trying to get away from him?"

"No. She looked frightened, but not by the man with her. She could have tripped him and escaped easily if she wanted. She kept looking over her shoulder."

Africanus looked at Marcus, who tightened his lips, then shrugged. "What's beyond that passageway?"

"Mostly apartments and a few small shops. If you go left, the street leads to the farmers' market, like this one does. There's a cross street for wagons a hundred feet past that passage."

"Anything else to tell us?"

"No. May Fortuna be with you in your search."

"Thank you." Aulus flicked his hand, and the trio headed through the second passageway.

Servilia turned from the loom that had held her gaze while the two senatorial sons and giant bodyguard questioned her neighbor. She mouthed a silent thank you, and the shoemaker tipped his chin as he beamed at her.

She drew a breath and blew it out. It would be two days before Gaius came, and he usually came at dusk. She didn't know where his farm was, and she wasn't sure which street he used to reach the market. She'd have to make her best guess and wait some distance from the market to warn him they were hunting for Dacius and Julia.

And she would be praying that she saw Gaius before the hunters did.

Aulus took one side of the street, Marcus took the other, and Africanus switched back and forth. They worked their way up the street asking at each shop, but no one remembered seeing Julia and the slave. Then they returned to the passageway and worked their way down to the farmer's market.

"How is it possible that no one remembers a limping man dragging a wealthy girl?" Aulus massaged his neck.

Africanus raised an eyebrow. "In parts of Rome, it's safer not to remember what you see."

The street opened into a small forum filled with stalls and milling people. Aulus approached the first, where rows of fish carcasses lay with eyes that looked too long dead.

A woman who smelled too much like her fish offered a greasy smile. "Can I help you, noble sir?"

"Were you here twenty-six days ago?"

Surprise filled the woman's eyes; then they veiled. "I'm always here, ready to serve you."

"We're looking for a red-haired man in a red tunic with a limp and a pretty maiden in a green tunic."

"I did see them." She pointed to a fish, cloudy-eyed and with a distinct odor. "Did you want to buy something special for your cook to make for dinner before we talk?" She picked up the fish and waved it near his face. "Only one denarius."

Marcus took a step back, and Aulus fought against scrunching his nose. "Will you tell me where they went then?"

"Of course." Her mouth opened in a wide grin, and her breath was a fitting companion to the smell of the fish.

Aulus reached for his purse.

Africanus's voice came from behind. "Don't. Lies cost money. The truth is free."

The veil lifted from her eyes as anger filled them.

Africanus led them away from the smell of decay. "Let me do the asking. You reek of money, and that's a temptation to lie."

Marcus's tightened his lips. "But we might catch something you miss in what they say."

"Listen if you wish, but act like you're not with me." Africanus stretched to his full height and scanned the area.

He pointed at the main entrance to the market where several wagons were parked with some children playing around them. A girl of about eleven stood in one of the wagons, watching a cluster of little children play. But she was also looking around at what was going on nearby. "There's one worth asking."

They made their way over, and Africanus walked up to the wagon. "My daughter only watches her little brother. You watch them all?"

"Some, but mostly my brother and sister." She pointed at a little girl about three and two boys about four and six. "And that one on the days his father brings his cart to market."

"My son runs a lot. My daughter says he can be hard to keep track of."

That drew her smile. "They mostly stay where I tell them."

"That lets you watch everything else here, I bet."

She grinned and nodded.

"What's your name? I'm Africanus."

"Dercina."

"Maybe you can help me, Dercina. I've been looking for two people for a long time. A red-haired man in a red tunic with a limp and a rich girl in a green tunic. Did you see them three, maybe four weeks ago? They were looking for a wagon ride."

Her brow wrinkled; then she shook her head. "No, but I'm only here until the wagons start arriving. Then we go home." She pointed to a boy of about twelve who stood closer to the main road. "Sorex helps direct where the wagons can park, and he's here when they leave. He might have seen them."

A shy smile appeared. "He watches everything. He always waves back at me."

Africanus reached into his purse and pulled out four quadrans. "Thank you for helping me."

As he dropped them into her hand, her face lit up, and she pointed at a fruit stall. "I'll get a pomegranate for our lunch. Thank you!"

Africanus returned to Aulus and Marcus. As he walked past, he raised an eyebrow at Aulus. "Truth is free, but a gift for sharing it is always welcome."

As he sauntered toward the boy, Aulus and Marcus followed ten feet behind.

"Sorex?" A friendly smile warmed Africanus's voice.

The boy's eyebrows dipped. "Who's asking?"

"Africanus." He pointed at the girl. His wave received one in return. "Dercina said you might be able to help me."

The boy's face relaxed. "What do you want?"

"I'm looking for a pretty rich girl in a green tunic and a red-haired man in a red tunic. He had a limp. They were probably in a wagon with someone you usually see alone. It could be as long as twenty-six days ago, but it could be more recent, too."

Sorex's brow furrowed. "That's a long time ago and a lot of wagons since then."

Africanus tipped his head toward the girl. "I know, but Dercina said you see everything. I'm hoping you saw them."

Sorex rubbed his lip. "It's a long time but...maybe I saw something. There's a man who brings a wagon of produce and chickens twice a week. He usually unloads over there and leaves. Around the time you're asking about, he went farther." He pointed at a street leaving the far end of the market. "He was alone when he drove up that street."

It was one street over from the one they'd searched...the one the shoemaker was on.

"Then he came back down that street." He pointed at the one they'd just searched.

"He didn't have a rich lady with him or a man in red. But when he drove out, a pretty girl in a plain tunic sat in the back. There was a man with his head in her lap, but his tunic was plain. The driver said something about a good meal waiting for them at home."

"The man in the back, was his hair red?"

"Maybe. The torches didn't light him well. His hair wasn't dark like mine. It might have been reddish."

"Did she look frightened?"

"No, only serious. She was watching the man in her lap and playing with his hair."

Africanus's mouth curved into a smile. "When will the driver of that wagon come again?"

"Tomorrow, probably. Or the next day."

"If I come back, can you point him out to me?"

"Yes. He usually comes about dusk and stays about a quarter hour."

Africanus pulled a dupondius from his purse. "With my thanks. I'll be back."

Sorex's grin was even bigger than Dercina's as he fingered the coin. "I'll be here."

Africanus strode past Aulus and Marcus without speaking, and they hurried to catch up.

Marcus reached him first. "Brutus could rent you out as an *inquisitor*. You can get anyone to tell you anything." The corner of his mouth lifted. "Even without scaring the truth out of them."

"He already does." Africanus shrugged. "And I try not to scare people. But that's easier with children. They only see a big man, not a gladiator." He glanced at Aulus. "We'll return tomorrow before dusk with horses. Your sister might be with you tomorrow night."

As they headed back to the ludus, Aulus's gaze rested on Africanus. Like the children, it was the man, not the gladiator, that he saw.

Chapter 57

ALMOST IN SIGHT

Farmer's Market, Day 47

Africanus leaned against the wall of a bakery, watching Sorex. Yesterday the man they were hunting hadn't come. But the boy had said it might be two days, and they were ready.

The aroma of yeasty wheat and barley breads, some laced with herbs, wrapped around him. A steady stream of locals came to pick up the loaves they'd left to be baked in the community oven. Too often, one stopped to talk so they could brag about meeting the famous Nubian who had retired undefeated from the sand. Normally, he didn't mind, but today he wanted to blend in, a difficult task at best for a man as tall and muscled and dark as he was.

Perhaps he should have brought Rufus or Fortis or even one of the kitchen slaves to watch for Sorex's signal. He glanced toward the side street, where Aulus and Marcus waited with the horses. At least he didn't look as out of place as the two senatorial sons who drew even more stares and whispered comments than he did. He'd convinced Aulus to trade his purple-striped tunic for a plain one at the ludus, but not Marcus.

A wave snapped his attention back on the boy. A gray-haired man had just driven past, and Sorex raised his hand high before pointing down at him. Africanus raised one hand in response and tipped his head. The boy waved once more, then turned away.

Africanus would find Sorex later to give him some coins for his help.

He glanced at his companions in the hunt, but he didn't signal them. If they approached the wagon man too soon, he might change his destination to protect the fugitives. He'd talked about feeding them, so he wasn't giving a ride to strangers. Best to follow at a distance until they knew where he lived. But Marcus would never have the patience for that. He'd want to corner the man in the market and force him to talk.

The corner of Africanus's mouth curved. Marcus had yet to learn that the battle didn't always go to the one who went for the quick kill. It was better to let the steady loss of blood weaken the strong and slow down the swift. The man who waited usually finished the fight with a sword still in his hand.

The gray-haired man had unloaded his vegetables and was moving the last of the chickens from his crates to the vendor's. Africanus drew one last deep breath of the bakery's aroma, then strode toward the boys and the waiting horses.

One hour, maybe two, and Aulus's hunt could be over. But even if it wasn't, their quarry was almost in sight, and it wouldn't be long.

Hill overlooking Gaius's farm

Aulus reined back his horse and moved off the crest of the hill. The wagon had pulled into a farmyard three hundred feet ahead of them. Africanus had signaled a retreat, and even though Marcus jerked his head to demand they go forward, Aulus followed the wiser lead.

They tied the horses to a tree just below the crest. Bent over, Africanus led them to lie on the ground where they could see but not be seen.

It was almost dark, where shapes and movement are clear, but all colors fade to shades of gray. The wagon stopped by a corral. As the wagon man jumped down, the door of the house opened. A second man came out and limped over to the mules. He unhitched one and led it to the corral. As he took off its harness, the wagon man unharnessed the other. The mules were turned into the corral, and the second man closed the gate. Then the wagon man rested his hand on the limping man's shoulder, and they walked into the house together.

Marcus rolled off his stomach and sat up. "We found them. Let's go get Julia."

Africanus held up his hand. "We might have found them. We'll come back in the morning when we can see everything going on around us when we ask for her. I'll speak first. She might run when she hears your voices. It's too easy for someone to sneak away in the dark."

He rose and swept the dirt and bits of grass off his tunic. "I've ridden the main road many times with Master Brutus. There's an inn where we can stable the horses while we eat. Then I'll come back and stand guard in that grove we passed just before we got here."

"I saw no horses, so if they leave, it will be in the wagon." Africanus untied his horse and mounted. "You can go home if you wish and return early tomorrow. Or you can stay at the inn that's next to the taberna."

Aulus looked at Marcus, who nodded. "We'll stay."

As they retraced their path, Aulus looked back. The sister who'd always been his friend had been hiding for a month. Did she know what he'd done? Was she too afraid of him to come home? When they found her tomorrow and he begged her forgiveness, would that friendship ever be restored? Or would the love she once had for him be forever replaced by hate?

Publius's taberna

It was late when the two young men, one in purple stripes, entered the taberna with their bodyguard.

Publius met them at the door. "Welcome." His hand swept toward a table in the rear with two chairs. "Follow me, and we'll get your dinner started."

As the senatorial son and the other young man seated themselves, the bodyguard pulled a third chair from the adjacent table and sat down with them.

"Three glasses of wine, cut two to one with water." The deep voice of the large man left no doubt he was in charge.

Publius smiled at all three. "Right away. We have an excellent stew and fresh bread for dinner tonight."

"That sounds good, and make the servings large." The young man in white placed the order.

When Publius returned with the drinks on a tray, they were in deep conversation.

"Her bearer must have been hurt much worse than the shoemaker said if he's still limping that badly after a month." The man with purple stripes took a sip and nodded his approval.

Publius got a washcloth from behind the counter and returned to clean two tables away from theirs.

"Sorex said she had his head cradled in her lap when they left the market. He thought the slave was sleeping, but maybe he'd passed out. Any of our slaves would know not to take that liberty if he was conscious." The man in white ran his fingers through his hair.

"The blood in the atrium might have been his." The bodyguard took a sip. "Even bleeding badly, a man can run a long way if it matters enough. Protecting her must have been important to him. We'll find out tomorrow when we go back for her."

Publius's stomach flipped. Limping man, heavy blood loss, protecting her...it was Leander and Calantha they were after.

He stepped into the kitchen. "Lucillia." With a flick of his fingers, he summoned her from her talk with their baker.

"What is it?"

He dropped his voice to a whisper. "Three men out there are looking for Leander and Calantha."

Her hand flew up to cover her mouth. "Which?"

"The three at the back table."

She leaned to glance out the door. "They need to know tonight. I'll keep an eye on these three. You go now to warn them."

He kissed her on the cheek before heading out the door to the stable. He'd never taken a night ride before, but the moon was out, and his mule was surefooted. God would be with him as he rode to warn his friends.

Gauis's farm

The pounding would have been enough to wake Leander, but Publius calling his name snapped him to attention. He swung his legs out of bed and hurried to the door.

Gaius came out of the hall behind him and they stood together as Leander swung the door open for Publius to enter.

"Leander, you need to leave right now. There are three men at my taberna who will be here in the morning looking for you and Calantha. They know you've been protecting her, and they're coming after her. One said you were his slave and her litter bearer."

"Her brother has found us." Leander ran his fingers through his hair. He looked down, then at Publius. "It's true. Her brother and his friend tried to kidnap her for ransom and then sell her, and I stopped them. We've been waiting for her father to return before I took her home. He's supposed to be back in two days. I was going to wait two more weeks to be sure he made it. But if they've found us, I need to return her as soon as he might be there."

Gaius wrapped his arm around Leander's shoulders. "I'll take you day after tomorrow. But we can't have you here in the morning when they come. You'll go right now to Sextus's house."

Publius nodded. "Have you ever been there before?"

Leander shook his head.

"Then I'll go with you to make sure you get there all right. Lucillia is keeping an eye on them until I get back." The corner of his mouth turned up. "There's not a woman alive who's better at listening than my Lucillia. Nothing they say will get past her ears."

Marcella stood in the hallway. "And I'll take the wagon first thing to tell Calantha she should stay with Petronia until you come get her for the trip to Rome. They'll never think to look for her there."

She scooped his cloak off the end of his bed and draped it around his shoulders. "Here. She'd want you to wear this so you won't get cold."

"I shouldn't stay away too long, in case they ask for me." Publius opened the door. "Let's go."

Marcella hugged Leander, and Gaius slapped his back. "We'll convince them you aren't here. They'll give up, and then you can come back for your last night with us."

Leander nodded, but he knew that wasn't true. Anyone who would hunt them for a month and find them when no one except Servilia even knew they were with Gaius wasn't going to give up. She didn't know the way to Gaius's farm, and she would never have told anyone, even if she did.

There were too many eyes in Rome, and some must have seen Gaius rescue them. But it didn't matter who or how. The hunters had found them, and now his only hope to keep her safe was to get her back to her father before her brother came.

A few steps and Leander and Publius were out of the half-circle of light coming from the doorway. The moon's silver glow was enough to see where to put their feet as they walked through the vineyard, leading Publius's mule.

But Leander's mind wasn't on his own escape. Tiberius Secundus should be back from Sicilia in two days. If they could keep Calantha hidden from her brother until then, he could take her to her father. Then she should be safe.

His thigh felt tight, so he still limped. But it no longer hurt much when he was helping Gaius. Walking any distance was another matter. It was less than a mile to Sextus's house, but by the time they were half way there, his leg ached.

So did his heart. After so many years, he had family again. Now he faced the pain of goodbyes.

At least he wasn't cold. He drew the cloak she'd made him closer. The faintest scent of roses lingered. Her hands must have had rose oil on them when they took it from the loom and finished the edges. He inhaled the trace she'd left behind.

The joy in her eyes as she'd wrapped it around his shoulders. Her laughter when he couldn't find the words to thank her. They'd brightened that night like a full moon shining. But what can a man say when the woman he loves is as far out of reach as the stars in the night sky? When she's spent hours and days making him something just for him? When her looks and her smiles invite him to dream of a future, even though no future could ever be possible?

She'd told him he'd know what to say when she gave him the tunic. But it was only half done, and she'd never finish it now.

Lingering traces and half-finished plans, but they were still memories to cherish.

Two more days, and his life as Leander would be over. He'd be a slave in her father's house once more. He'd hoped for two more weeks as a man among friends, living free, hearing her laughter, seeing her smiles that were meant for him.

But the last month had only been play-acting, and the time to stop pretending had come.

Chapter 58

THE LIMPING MAN

Day 48, Gaius's farm

Pale pink clouds floated in a mostly gray sky as Gaius hitched the mules. Marcella, wrapped in her cloak, hurried toward him.

"I won't be gone long. As soon as I tell Calantha you two will come for her tomorrow afternoon, I'll come back."

He helped her into the wagon. "Stay a while and hold that new baby. I can handle any visitors."

Leaves rustled behind them, and they turned to see Sextus walk out from among the grapevines. He was limping.

Marcella gasped. "What happened? Is Leander all right?"

He grinned. "He's fine. I never knew a man with more women to worry about him." He slapped his thigh. "The men who are coming expect to find a limping man. Here I am."

"If I didn't need to leave right now, I'd come down and hug you."

Gaius handed her the reins. "Go, and God be with you."

She slapped the reins, and the mules started walking. Another two slaps, and they picked up the pace to a trot.

"Is Leander fine?"

"Yes, just worried about getting Calantha away before they find her. I had some harness that needs mending, and he's going to take care of that while I help you here. So, put me to work."

"Come inside. The breakfast porridge Marcella left for me is enough for two hungry men. The least I can do is feed you before they come."

As Sextus limped toward the house at his side, Gaius scanned the hill flanking the road. The men hunting his friends were coming soon. Were their eyes upon him even now?

Petronia's farm

When Marcella reined in her trotting mules by Petronia's house, Quintus came from the vineyard.

His welcoming smile dimmed when he saw her face. "What's wrong?"

Marcella looped the reins around a stick beside the seat and climbed down. "I need to talk to Calantha right away."

He pointed at the house. "In there, feeding the children."

When he gripped one mule's halter, she patted his arm. "They might like water, but I won't be long."

Calantha's eyes widened when Marcella entered the room. "What's happened?"

"Last night, Publius rode out to warn us. Your brother and two friends were at his taberna, and he overheard them saying they saw Leander and were coming today to find you."

Calantha's hand flew to her mouth. "Where's Leander? They'll do something horrible to him if they find him."

"Don't worry. He's over at Sextus's house, and Sextus is pretending to be the limping man they saw last night. After they visit, they should think they were mistaken about what they thought they saw and leave."

"How long do you think that will take?"

Marcella shrugged. "Gaius thinks one visit will do it. Leander thinks they won't leave until they find you, so he's planning to take you back to your father tomorrow. He said your father was supposed to be back then. He and Gaius will come with the wagon a couple of hours before dusk. You'll ride back to Rome when Gaius takes the produce and chickens in."

"But what if Father's not back yet?"

"Leander said you two could ask Servilia to let you stay with her until he does return."

Calantha cradled her face in her hands. "Oh, Marcella. I want to go back, but I also don't want to."

Marcella rested her hand on Calantha's arm. "Because of Leander?"

"Partly. I wish we could stay here and marry. Just forget about the laws of Rome. But I know that's not possible. Leander tells me God gives him strength to be content with whatever must be. He says that gets easier with time. And I guess he knows. He's lost so much and come through it so strong. I love being with him, but I know we have no future together.

"Father's the only reason to go back. I love him, and I want to see him. He's probably been worried sick, thinking I must be dead or worse. And I plan to ask him to free Leander as soon as he can, which I'm sure he'll do after everything Leander did to save me. I'd love to be with my lion forever, but I still can't see how. But once he's free, he can come back to you."

She rubbed her forehead. "But now that I follow Jesus, I can't do what Father expects of me. I'm supposed to make a brilliant political marriage to a man who will someday become consul of Rome. But I'd have to worship the gods of Rome and the genius of the Emperor. I'd have to entertain men who want to do things God condemns and act like that was perfectly fine. I can't do that anymore. Father's going to be so upset when I tell him. He'll think I've betrayed everything he taught me, everything he values." She squeezed her lips tight, but tears swam in her eyes. "Betrayed him."

"So, what are you going to do?" The pain in Calantha's eyes brought tears to Marcella's.

Calantha squared her shoulders even as her jaw quivered. "I'll go back. After I get Leander freed, I'll ask God to show me how to free myself."

"My dear child, I am so sorry." With her thumb, Marcella stroked Calantha's cheek. "I'll join you in that prayer every day until you return." She took a deep breath, then released it. "But right now, I need to get back. I want to be there when your brother comes."

She hugged Calantha and left the cottage. Outside the door, she looked back. Calantha sat at the table, face in her hands, shoulders shaking.

And after Marcella climbed into the wagon and slapped the reins, tears washed her face, too.

Gaius's farm

Aulus's heart rate ramped up as he crested the hill by the wagon man's farm. He could see two men working in the vineyard. One was the gray-haired man they'd followed. The other's hair was dark. As the dark-haired one walked from the end of one row of vines to the middle of the next, he limped.

Africanus rode up beside him. "The one we saw last night had lighter hair."

Marcus reined in on the other side. "Maybe that was because it was moonlight."

"The mules and wagon are gone." Africanus glanced at Marcus. "Maybe the one we saw left and took Julia with him."

"There's only one way to find out." Aulus nudged his horse and started down the hill.

Marcus moved up beside him before Africanus's voice came from behind. "Keep your eyes open. They might be hiding in the house."

As they rode closer, Aulus scanned the large vegetable garden and the small house. No sign of anyone except the two men, who kept working as they approached.

"That's odd." Suspicion tinged Africanus's voice. "Usually people react to the arrival of strangers."

When they reached the corral, Aulus stopped with Marcus on one side, Africanus on the other. The gray-haired man looked up, and Aulus waved. He started toward them, but the other only glanced at them and kept inspecting plants.

The gray-haired man greeted them with a smile. "Can I help you?"

"Maybe." Aulus waved his hand toward the dark-haired man. "Are you the only people here?"

The older man looked around and made a sweeping motion with his hand. "As you can see."

"Fresh wagon tracks." Africanus pointed at the ground. "Where did it go?"

The man peered at the ground and swept his foot over the track. "It hasn't rained for several days."

Africanus tipped his head toward the garden. "You have a very large garden. How do you get it to market?"

A broad smile curved the man's lips as he nodded. "We do, and it's producing a good crop this year. Did you want to buy something?"

Aulus looked at Africanus's impassive face, then at the garden. "What do you have?"

"Peas, carrots." The man pointed toward some beehives at the edge of the olive grove. "Our honey is good, too."

Africanus raised an eyebrow. "The missing wagon. Is it yours?"

"Missing?" The gray-haired man's eye twitched.

The jingle of harness behind them caused Aulus to turn. A woman about the age of the gray-haired man snapped the reins, and the mules quickened their trot.

She reined in beside them. "Gaius, you should have seen Cominia's new baby. He is the most precious thing with his father's eyes and his mother's mouth. And little Lucius is so proud of his new brother. He kept telling me all the things he would be teaching him."

She turned her eyes on Marcus, then Aulus, then Africanus. "We have company? Did you offer a drink to refresh them?"

Gaius blinked before his smile broadened. "No. I was just telling them what we have for sale today."

The woman wrapped the reins around the stick by the seat and clambered down. "That's good, dear. Did they want anything?" She beamed at Aulus as she stared into his eyes until he squirmed.

"Maybe some honey?"

"Come inside. I'll get you some."

He glanced at Africanus, who nodded once. "That would be good."

He slipped off his horse and followed her into the house.

"Come into the storeroom, and you can pick the jar you'd like."

With a flick of her fingers to bring him closer, she led him into a short hall, talking the whole time about beehives and bees and the flowers they loved. On one side was a small bedchamber with the sheets rolled into a bundle at the end of the rope bed. At the end, he could see the bed she and her husband would use.

She pointed to a shelf that held a dozen small clay jars sealed with wooden plugs. "This is the finest honey in all Rome. Pick."

He pointed at the third from the end.

"That will be one sestertius." She held out her hand.

Aulus reached into his purse and withdrew the coin. After he dropped it in her palm, she flicked her fingers to urge him from the room and led him outside.

"Anything else you'd like to buy?"

"No." He shook his head before shrugging.

"Now that you have the finest honey in all Rome, I hope you have a lovely ride home." She waved her hand toward the garden. "Seeing the new baby made me late. I need to get to work now."

Aulus stared at her back as the force of nature marched away.

Gaius smiled at her retreating form before turning back to Aulus. "Enjoy your honey. I need to get back to work, too." He turned and strode into his vineyard, not stopping until he was ten rows away.

Aulus looked at the jar in his hand, then at Africanus. The gladiator's lips were squeezed tight as he fought the laugh.

Aulus handed him the honey and mounted. "I've seen what I need. Let's go."

As he nudged his horse forward, the woman's singing floated through the air. It was loud, but not in tune. He kicked his horse into a trot.

As they climbed the hill, Africanus moved alongside and offered him the clay jar.

He waved it away. "Take it for your children."

Africanus grinned. "Stop at the grove. The next step is clear."

When they reached the trees, Africanus dismounted. "What did you see in the house?"

"Almost everything, and she never stopped talking the whole time. That one's a force of nature. She took me into the store room to pick my own honey. There were two other rooms off the hall: their bedroom and another one with a bed no one was using."

"Anything unusual?"

"No, except maybe the rope bed frame in the main room. But there was nothing on it."

Africanus rubbed his lip. "They're hiding something. She made sure you saw the whole house to make you think they weren't. And the man with the limp...he wasn't the one we saw last night. You can go back to Marcus's house, but I'm going to stay here and watch for a while to see if the red-haired one comes back or a young woman shows up."

Marcus shook his head. "We should stay, too. You don't know what Julia or her slave look like."

"They've hidden here for a month. If they think we've gone, they'll return. When they do, I'll come for you. One man can see without being seen. One horse can blend into some trees. Three...that's much harder."

"You're probably right, as always. Let's go, Marcus." Aulus nudged his horse toward the road, then stopped. "Can we bring you some food before we leave?"

A smile tugged at the corner of Africanus's mouth. "No." He lifted the clay jar. "I have the finest honey in all Rome."

Chapter 59

Escaping the Watchers

Day 49

Leander was oiling the harness he'd repaired the day before when a familiar voice came from behind him. He turned to see Gaius approaching from the opposite direction of his farm.

"Good morning, Sextus. You're looking young and strong today. I thought I'd take the long way around to come see you, just in case we were being watched." Gaius's voice contained a chuckle as he switched his two friends' names. "Leander did a fine job helping me yesterday, despite his limp."

"It's good to hear I'm so easy to replace." Leander forced a smile. "Did Marcella tell Calantha we need to leave right away?"

"Yes, and she got back just in time to meet Calantha's brother and his friends. Dark-haired young man in purple stripes and a large Nubian built like a gladiator."

"That was Marcus Drusus, the one who came up with the kidnapping plan. The other...maybe a bodyguard?"

"The bodyguard asked most of the questions." Gaius's eyebrows dipped. "He was suspicious. Her brother..." He chuckled. "Marcella got back just as we started talking, and Calantha's brother was soft clay in her hands. I think he left convinced you'd never been with us, and she even sold him a jar of honey worth a dupondius for a sestertius."

"But it's still time to take Calantha home. Her father should be back, but even if he isn't, she'll be safer in Rome with Servilia with me guarding until he does return."

Gaius's face sobered. "Yes, it is time for you to leave. It's my regular night to take produce into Rome. I'll swing by here to get Sextus's chickens and you, and then we'll pick up Calantha. It's only a few blocks from the forum to Servilia's shop."

He pulled a small purse from inside his tunic. "There's a decent inn on her street. In case her shop's closed and she's not there, here's enough for one night."

Leander bounced the small sack in his hand. "I wish I could repay you. Maybe I can get some from Calantha, I mean Mistress Julia, after she resumes her place."

His gaze swept the low hill that rose between the two farms. He inhaled the sweet country scent...the scent of freedom. His eyes returned to Gaius. The scent of friendship and love.

"Before you go back, I have something for you." He stepped into Sextus's house and returned with the cloak Calantha had made him.

He held it out. "For you. If I take it with me, the overseer will just take it for himself. I'd much rather you keep it. It's my thank you for everything you've done for me. It will be good to know my best friend and second father has the most precious thing I've ever owned."

Gaius took it and stared at it. Then he turned sad eyes on Leander. "It will be here waiting for you when you come back to us. Somehow God will bring good out of this."

He stroked the soft wool. "Maybe I could buy you and free you... to become my son."

Leander shook his head. "I trained champion racers, and Gallio paid 3000 denarii for me."

Gaius's face fell, then brightened. "Maybe Publius can help me find that much. Or maybe Calantha's father will free you for saving her. We'll all be praying for that."

Leander summoned a smile he didn't feel. "Maybe he will. Apostle Paul said all things work together for good for those who love God. Nothing could be better than to come back to live with my brothers and sisters in Christ."

Nothing except bringing Calantha with me as my wife.

Gaius sniffed and clutched the cloak to his chest. "I need to get back in case her brother and his friends come again. Marcella would know what to say, but Sextus...maybe not. I'll be back late afternoon for you and the chickens."

As Gaius headed back into the olive grove to make his secret way home, Leander clenched his jaw. It had only been a month, but he'd grown to love Gaius like a father.

And as he watched Gaius walk away, a sword as sharp as the one that spilled his own father's blood in Dacia pierced his heart once more.

The sun hadn't yet risen when Africanus left his horse in the grove and climbed to the crest of the hill. He found some low shrubs a few hundred feet off the road and settled in. From there, he'd have a good view of vineyard, garden, olive grove, and house.

Shortly after dawn, Gaius entered his olive grove. He was gone a long time, and when he returned, he carried something folded. Something the size of a blanket or cloak. He took it inside and stayed for a while, probably listening to chatter of the woman he was married to.

Then for several hours that crawled by like caterpillars, Gaius and the dark-haired limping man worked their way along the rows of grape vines.

After the three disappeared into the house, probably for lunch, limping man returned to the vineyard while Gaius and the Force of Nature loaded boxes of vegetables into the wagon. Midafternoon, they put some chickens into crates, then loaded those plus a few more without chickens. It was late afternoon when he hitched up the mules. After the Force gave Gaius a hug, he climbed aboard and flicked the reins.

As the mules pulled the wagon up the road, the Force stood by the doorway, watching until the wagon disappeared over the crest of the hill. Then she went inside.

A quarter hour or maybe a half passed with limping man working in the vineyard. Then the Force reappeared.

The limping man started toward the house...without his limp. Just before he reached her, he started limping again.

Africanus's gaze flipped between the pair in the farmyard and where the road disappeared over the hill. As the pair entered the house, he sucked air between his teeth. He'd made a strategic error. The wagon had been packed to leave enough room for a person in the back. He should be following Gaius.

He slipped back from the crest before he stood. He broke into a trot, but it was more than a quarter mile back to where he'd tied his horse. When he reached it, he hurled himself into the saddle and nudged it into a trot. There were several side tracks that turned off the road. He slowed as he passed each one, but there had been enough wagon traffic on all of them that he couldn't tell if Gaius had gone down any one in particular.

He reached the main road into Rome without finding a clear sign that Gaius's wagon turned off the road to his farm as it crossed several small hills and valleys. Turning his horse toward Rome, he cantered far enough toward the city to catch up with a trotting mule team.

His jaw clenched. No Gaius. He must have turned off on one of the side tracks, but which? He spun his horse and cantered back. When he entered the road to Gaius's farm, he slowed to a trot between side tracks and a walk as he passed each, watching for the freshest wagon tracks. He narrowed it to two, and took the first to the right.

He rode out of an olive grove to find a clear view of a farmyard. A wagon was being unloaded, but the man unloading had chestnut hair.

Africanus spun his horse and trotted back to take the other side road. It went past olives and vineyards until it topped a rise. At the house before him, two mules stood in a corral with an empty wagon beside it. The road continued into a fenced pasture where sheep grazed.

Muttering under his breath, Africanus spun his horse and trotted back to Gaius's road. When he reached it, his gaze flipped in the two directions as his mind weighed two options. See if Gaius had driven away from Rome, or go back to his watching post and wait for him to return.

He rubbed his chin. The wagon was loaded for market. He must have gone to Rome but took some shortcut Africanus didn't know.

He nudged his horse into a walk. After leaving it once more in the grove, he climbed back to his shrubby lookout.

It was about as dark as when they trailed Gaius home when the wagon returned. Gaius reined in by the corral and hopped down. As he started to unhitch his mules, the man with the fake limp came out of the house, but this time he wasn't limping. He helped Gaius put up the mules, then slapped the older man on the arm before walking into the vineyard. Gaius entered the house, and soon the lamp was blown out.

Africanus's lips tightened. The man was heading toward the farm where he'd seen the other wagon and mules. Gaius and his neighbor were working together to hide Aulus's sister or at least to hide the litter slave.

He glanced at the moon. Plenty of light for his ride back to Rome. In the morning, he would bring Aulus and Marcus back to look first at Gaius's house, and then at the limping impostor's farm. Her slave would be at one or the other.

As he walked back down the hill to get his stallion, his eyes narrowed. It was past time to find the limping young man. He was the key to finding Julia, and Gaius and his friend knew where he was.

Tomorrow, Africanus would come armed and scary to get the information they needed to find her.

Quintus's farm and the road to Rome

It was late afternoon when they reached Quintus's farm. Leander helped Calantha into the wagon before climbing in himself. He snapped the reins, the wagon lurched, and they started the final leg of their return to Rome.

Tears brimmed in Calantha's eyes as she waved farewell to Petronia and the children. Petronia swept tears from both her cheeks before returning the wave.

He clucked as he flicked the mules with the reins a second time, and they broke into a trot. There was no point in prolonging the heartbreaking view for her. They pulled into the grove, and Calantha faced forward again.

Gaius leaned back against the wall of the wagon. "That shortcut through Sextus's pasture cuts a mile or so off the trip between Quintus's farm and ours. Publius usually comes that way. It's handy on Solis, but it's even better if someone's trying to follow you."

Calantha sniffed. "I wouldn't have minded you taking longer to reach us."

Leander kept his eyes trained on the mules' ears. It hurt too much to watch even silent tears trickle down her cheeks.

She settled into silence, but he still felt each time she drew a deep breath and sighed.

Too soon they reached the main road and turned south toward Rome.

"Gaius." Leander glanced back over his shoulder.

"Hmm?"

"Which road is this? I wasn't awake when we left Rome before."

"It goes by the Castra Praetoria and through the Porta Viminalis. It turns into Vicus Patricius and goes down into Subura."

Calantha shifted beside him. "I'm sorry you were hurt. I was so worried about you then."

He offered her a smile. "I'm not sorry. You're free, you're safe, and you follow Jesus. I couldn't ask for better."

They slowed to a walk as they entered a congested area. To the right was the Thermae Mestrii.

Calantha turned in her seat as they drove past. "That must be Publius's bath."

She swung to face Leander. "Can we stop for a moment for me to tell Lucillia goodbye?"

The palla draped over her head had slipped back, revealing her profile. Leander gripped one edge and pulled it forward. "We can't risk it. Your brother and Drusus might still be there."

With both hands, she adjusted the palla, then lowered her face to conceal it from a passerby's view. "I know you're right, but it's hard not to say goodbye." She slumped, then straightened as her eyes brightened. "But I guess there's no reason I can't come back after Father's home to visit now I know where she lives."

"That's true." Leander put on a smile for her sake. She would be able to come visit, but he never would. Rome lay before him like the slave ship in Dyrrachium after the long march from Sarmizegetusa.

They were approaching the turn-off to Gaius's farm when Gaius grabbed Leander's arm. "Stop."

In the distance, a large Nubian cantered along the road toward him. But he turned down Gaius's road and kept riding fast until he disappeared behind some trees.

Gaius grinned. "They left a watcher, like you said they would, and God has blinded the eyes of the enemies of His children. The path should be clear for us on into Rome."

Calantha turned worried eyes toward him. "Will Marcella be safe?"

That drew Gaius's warm chuckle. "You should have seen her with them yesterday. Your brother even paid her a sestertius for a small jar of honey. God gave me a wise women, and He will protect her."

He rested his hand on Leander's back. "And God gave me strong mules. They can trot most of the way to town. The sooner you're with Servilia and out of sight, the better."

Leander flicked the reins, and the mules settled into a quick trot.

He glanced at the beautiful woman seated beside him, her eyes scanning the countryside as they passed. Gaius had made him drive because he said it would be easier on Leander's leg than crawling into the back. But it was really to give him one more chance to sit beside her, one more chance to talk.

Gaius would hear everything they said, but even if he wasn't there,

Leander could never tell her what his heart longed to say. Words once spoken could never be taken back.

She felt too deeply the wounds he'd received trying to protect her. They weren't her fault, but she still felt responsible. If she knew how his impossible love for her was tearing at his heart, she'd blame herself for that, too. But it wasn't her fault she was the woman she was, the one who would take his heart with her when she left him behind.

Chapter 60

LAST NIGHT OF FREEDOM

As Leander drove deeper into Rome, the traffic slowed to a crawl. Slower than the caterpillars he'd plucked from Gaius's grapes. Stop and start and stop again. But at last, he turned into the farmer's market. Gaius inched to the end of the wagon and jumped off.

He walked past the clucking chickens to stand beside Calantha, offering his hand to help her down. And as her foot touched the cobblestones, nothing changed on the outside. But whether she felt it or not, Leander sensed the beginning of the end. If her father was home, by this time tomorrow, she'd be Mistress Julia, and he'd once more be "You."

Leander walked past the mules, rubbing each one's forehead for the last time. Then he took his place beside her, once more ready to serve.

"How do we get to Servilia's?" The words came harder than he expected.

Gaius pointed past a long row of stalls to the entrance into a street. "Up there about a half mile and on the right. It's just before a walkway to the next street." He glanced at Leander's leg. "Can you walk it? If not, I can take you after I get everything unloaded."

Leander tapped his thigh. "It's almost as good as new. I've been down that passageway before. I'm sure I can find it."

Gaius took Calantha's hands. "If you ever need it, you know you have a home with us."

She pulled free and threw her arms around his neck. With her cheek lying against his chest she whispered, "I love you, Gaius."

He wrapped his arms around her and kissed the top of her head. "You'll always be a daughter to me. Come visit."

Her eyes swam in tears as she stepped back. "I will."

Gaius spread his arms, and Leander exchanged a quick hug. As he stepped back, Gaius slapped his arm. "May God be with you, son."

"And also with you." The lump in Leander's throat was too big to swallow.

Gaius waved his hand toward the street. "Off with you. Give Servilia my greetings, and thank her for giving us this time with you."

Calantha nodded. Then she turned and walked toward her future.

And Leander followed.

Leander walked beside Calantha as they approached the last shops before the passageway. The hour in the wagon had made his thigh feel tight as he walked, but he tried not to limp so she wouldn't fuss over him. Servilia stood at her loom, passing the shuttle through, then tapping the weft yarn up against the finished cloth.

"Servilia."

She spun when he spoke her name, and a huge grin overspread her face. "I didn't expect you back quite so soon."

The corner of his mouth turned up. "The way I looked when you saw me last, you might not have expected me back at all."

She scooped up both his hands. "No, God brought you to me for a purpose, and I didn't think you'd be dying before you fulfilled it."

She turned gentle eyes on Calantha. "And it's good to see Julia again, too."

"We're Calantha and Leander now." Julia's words made Servilia's eyebrows rise.

"If you say so, then so will I. Help me put my weavings inside, and we can go eat to celebrate your return."

Leander dropped his voice. "Tomorrow, I hope to take her back to her father, but tonight we need a place to sleep."

"Say no more. Of course you'll stay with me. Jul...Calantha can share my bed, and if you don't mind a pallet of blankets on the floor..."

The corner of his mouth turned up. "The floor was good enough for me last time. It can't help being better this time."

"We'll eat, and then you can tell me everything when we come back here for the night."

She waved at a stack of blankets, and Calantha scooped them up.

After they carried everything inside, Leander helped her place the shutters and slide the iron bars into the rings to lock them in place. Servilia snapped the padlock shut and draped the key chain around her neck After dropping the key inside her tunic, she held out her hands to each.

"First a good dinner, and then you can tell me everything."

As they walked down the street to the taberna, Leander smiled. When they could tell Servilia in private that Calantha was a sister now, joy would fill the gentle eyes that had looked on him with compassion and love.

Servilia's response to her deciding to follow Jesus was exactly what Calantha expected: happy tears and hugs and smiles brimming with joy.

But the best decision she'd made in her life came with the biggest problem.

"It's been nothing but wonderful living with Marcella and Gaius." Her gaze rested on the man who'd made it even more wonderful, even though she didn't speak his name. "Worshipping with everyone on Sunday, praying together every day. But when I go home to Father..."

She rested her cheek in her palm as she sat with Servilia on the bed. "My father is Tiberius Julius Secundus."

Servilia's eyes widened. "The consul?"

"Yes, and that's a huge problem. I'm expected to marry a man who'll rise in the service of Rome, just like Father did. I'd be the *domina* of a senatorial household. There are so many religious duties in that position, not just at home but in public with my husband. I can't do them now Jesus is my Lord. I'll have to tell Father as soon as I see him so he won't be arranging a marriage that would force me to do them...or die."

Fear for her wrinkled Servilia's brow, and Calantha touched her hand.

"Father has choices that will protect me. He can let me remain unmarried in his household. It would look odd, but it does happen sometimes. And someday when he dies, my share of our family fortune will let me continue as I choose."

She turned her eyes on Leander, sitting on the floor, his bad leg stretched out and his back against the wall. His stone-gray eyes were fixed upon her, but the trace of a smile that usually curved his mouth was gone. If only being his wife were one of the choices.

"Father loves me dearly, and he won't put me in danger by telling anyone my secret. We'll figure out what's best for me to do."

The curves at the corners of his mouth that had become so dear to her returned.

Father would figure out what to do, but the future he'd plan wouldn't be the one she wished for. Leander was the only man she wanted for her husband. But she was a senator's daughter, and he was a slave. Even after Father freed him, the marriage she longed for was impossible. Roman law wouldn't let her marry a freedman, and her father would never let her break Roman law.

He massaged his injured thigh, and Calanta's brow furrowed. "It's a long walk from here to the baths and an even longer one from there to the villa. Are you healed enough for that?"

"It won't be a problem." His smile looked forced.

"But you were limping more when got here than you did at home."

"My leg stiffened a little during the drive. I limp more out of habit than any real pain. Tomorrow will not be a problem."

"If you say so." Something about his eyes said he wasn't telling her everything.

But she wasn't telling everything herself. She bit her lip. Tomorrow would be a huge problem for her.

Tomorrow, she would ask Father to set her lion free. Then he could go home to Gaius and Marcella. Roman law blocked her path to happiness with him, but he might find love in the arms of someone not chained by Roman law. That would be her prayer each night as she lifted those she loved up to God.

She turned her eyes away from him and smiled at whatever Servilia had just said.

A senatorial daughter was trained to hide emotions in public. She'd let herself be real in the house of her dearest friends. But it was time to use that training. She would never let him see her pain from losing a future with the man she loved.

Chapter 61

Nothing of His Own

Servilia's shop, Day 50

Calantha awoke to the sound of men arguing in the street. Servilia had managed to slip from the bed and open the shutter that served as a door without disturbing her.

She opened her eyes. A few specks of dust danced in the sunbeams that lit the room, and she wanted to dance with them. The problem she'd thought impossible the night before seemed so simple now.

She stretched and gave thanks to God. Servilia had opened the shutter to let in the light of day. In the final moments before waking, God had just shown her the door that might let in the future she longed for.

Energy pulsed through her as she swung her feet to the floor. Her gaze settled on Leander, still sleeping on the pallet in the corner where she'd once watched him bleed.

Her mouth curved into a crooked smile. Leander had certainly cured her of her weakness around blood.

His selfless courage had saved her from the selfish act of her brother. But that same hurtful act might prove to be the best thing her brother had ever done for her. A few more hours, and she'd know.

◆

The light of morning had entered the room, but Leander kept his eyes closed. For more than a decade, he'd slept on the ground. It had been comfortable enough and easy to sleep after a hard day's work. But last night, with what he knew lay ahead, sleep had eluded him.

He remained still when Servilia rose. She might want to talk, and

318

he didn't want to burden her with the thoughts that circled his mind like jackals, waiting for the end.

When the bed creaked as Calantha rose, he still kept his eyes closed. Then the faint scent of roses teased his nostrils, and the heat of her presence as she knelt beside him was more than he could ignore.

He opened his eyes.

"Are you ready for today?" Her voice was cheerful, and her eyes danced with anticipation.

He pushed himself into a sitting position with his left arm. "I will be." He wiped his face with his palm.

Her brightness dimmed. "You don't look like you slept well."

"I haven't slept on the ground for a while." He patted the floor. "It's not as soft as the straw in the stable. That's as good as Marcella's bed."

"Maybe I can arrange something better for you when we get home." She rocked back on her feet and stood.

He nodded. The softest bed in the Secundus household couldn't solve what disturbed his sleep. Aching thoughts of her riding in the litter, close enough to hear her words to others but forever silent himself. Bracing himself to once more being treated as an animal after living like a free man. None were things he could say without causing her pain.

Would her father believe the truth about what happened? That he only tried to protect her as a loyal slave should? But what had started as duty had turned to love, and love was something he didn't know how to hide. Somehow, he must find a way. They'd been gone much too long for anyone to believe her still virtuous if he didn't.

"Found it." Servilia entered the room, waving a blank sheet of papyrus. In her other hand was a pen and a bottle of ink. "I bought the sheet, but the scribe-for-hire four stalls down lent me the pen and ink."

Calantha held out her hands for the writing supplies. "When Leander thought he was dying, he said I should send a message to Father telling him to come alone to the Baths of Titus and to tell no one he'd heard from me. He said you and I could pretend to be mother and daughter while we waited for Father to come. That's still a good plan."

She flashed Leander a smile. "It's much better to have you here to deliver the message and make sure all goes as planned."

She headed out to the counter to write with Servilia behind her. When they returned, Calantha held a papyrus roll tied with three pieces of yarn.

Servilia took some rolls and cheese from the cupboard and dropped them in a small sack. "If we leave now and eat as we walk, the baths will be opening when we get there."

Calantha spread her arms and inspected her tunic. "I'm already dressed like your daughter, so I'm ready. It's maybe an hour's walk to the villa from the baths. Then Leander will need to wait his turn in the salutation. I think Father will want to come as soon as he reads my letter. So that would be another hour to two hours before he can return with Father. We can wait in the garden for a long time without drawing too many eyes."

She waved the rolled-up papyrus at Leander. "Father should want to come immediately after reading this. But it's important that you put it into his hand yourself. Don't let his secretary take it.

"For a week after Father returns, there are so many people wanting his attention that salutation lasts well into the afternoon. There should be plenty of time for you to join the clients and gain an audience today. There are some people who get his immediate attention, so we'll have you say you have a private message on behalf of one of them."

She tapped her mouth with her fingers. "Father was consul with Egnatius Marcellinus. Marcellinus always said I reminded him of his own daughter and told me if I ever needed anything, he'd be happy to help. He wouldn't mind us saying you've brought a confidential message on his behalf that demands urgent attention."

"Egnatius Marcellinus." Dacius wiped his lips with the back of his hand. "What if someone recognizes me before I can say his name and present your letter? They might not let me see your father."

"Father's private secretary screens the clients. He was in Sicilia with Father, so he shouldn't recognize you. Tell the slave at the front door that you've come for the salutation, and he'll have someone take you straight to the waiting area."

She leaned over and swept some hair off his forehead. "I wish you had your cloak here. It would make you look more...worthy to receive Father's immediate attention."

Servilia stood. "I have the perfect thing for him to wear. I just finished a special order, and they won't pick it up until next week." From a shelf next to the door, she picked up an off-white cloak with several bands of colored wool woven in. She shook it open and draped it across Leander's shoulders. From a small box on a shelf above her bed, she removed a brass brooch and pinned it on the cloak.

"There." She patted the brooch. "We'll add a new tunic." She got one from the same shelf and handed it to him. "Now you look like a man of business."

He glanced down at his well-worn sandals and lifted his eyebrows. "From the knees up."

Servilia tipped her head and scanned him head to foot. "My handiwork in the cloak will draw all their eyes." She grinned. "And a prayer to keep their eyes partly closed would be a good idea, too."

She took Calantha's hand. "We'll step outside for you to dress. Call us when you're done, and we can leave for the baths."

Leander stroked the soft fabric as they left the room. The cloak was skillfully made, and the colors were beautiful. But nothing could compare with his own cloak that he'd given to Gaius.

He stripped off the tunic that had belonged to Servilia's husband, slipped the new tunic over his head, and fastened the well-made belt he'd worn as Mistress Julia's litter slave. He flung the cloak across his shoulder and pinned it with the brooch.

A slave owned nothing, and it was fitting that nothing he wore as he returned to that life was his own.

Chapter 62

END OF THE HUNT

Gaius's Farm, Day 50

Aulus reined in at the crest of the hill overlooking Gaius's farm, this time wearing the purple stripes that declared his rank. Africanus waited to his left, wearing leather body armor over a blood-red tunic. Several dark patches where blood had soaked in and stained the leather declared the armor's purpose was battle, not decoration. Leather arm guards and the strap across his chest, holding the gladius at his side, completed the message that the time for friendly talking was over. Marcus, on his right, sat a stallion fidgeting as it sensed the tension of its rider.

Gaius was repairing a chicken crate, and his wife was hoeing in the garden. No sign of the limping impostor, but that might mean their red-haired quarry had returned and awaited them in the house.

Aulus nudged his horse, and they started down the hill.

◆

Cantering hoofbeats pulled Gaius's attention from the crate he was mending. Then his breath caught. Wealth and power bore down upon him, and the bodyguard who'd seemed only suspicious the day before radiated menace.

He closed his eyes, breathed a prayer for protection, then faced the approaching trio with a smile.

"Welcome back. Did you come for more honey?"

They reined in three feet from him, and the armed giant's shadow covered him.

"We've come for your limping friend. The real one, not the impostor." The young man formerly in white, now in purple stripes, glared at him.

Gaius's pulse raced as the big man in leather armor rested his hand on the handle of his sword. Leander and Calantha were in Rome with Servilia, but would they be safe if he said the wrong words? He glanced toward the garden. Would he and Marcella be safe, even if he said the right ones?

God, deliver us from evil, and give me wisdom.

"Salve!" Marcella's cheery voice boomed as she marched toward them. "We didn't expect you back so soon." She reached his side and stood beaming as her eyes swept the trio. "What would you like today? More of the finest honey in Rome?"

The young man leaned forward in his saddle. "I'd like the truth. My sister was taken by her litter slave, and we saw him here two nights ago with the limp he had when he took her. When we came yesterday, you'd switched in another man to fool us. But we won't be fooled to-day, and you will give that slave to us now."

Gaius opened his mouth, but before the first word came out, his wife's chuckle stopped him.

"Why didn't you tell us this yesterday? We could have saved you a trip." She rested her hand on Gaius's arm. "Sextus came to help because Leander isn't here. Sometimes Sextus's hip bothers him. He limps a little then but not all the time."

"Leander?" The young aristocrat's brow furrowed.

"Yes, he's a young man we took in to help with the work." She pat-ted Gaius's shoulder. "Gaius isn't so young anymore, and he can use the help, even when he doesn't like to admit it." She shifted her gaze to the bodyguard, then back as she smiled. "Even a young man like your-self needs help sometimes."

"Where is this Leander?" The bodyguard's voice was quiet, but there was menace behind the measured words.

"He went to Rome to help a friend."

"He's not the only one who's been staying with you. Where's the girl?" Ice coated the big man's voice as his eyes drilled first into Mar-cella, then Gaius.

Gaius swallowed. How long had they watched, and how much had they seen?

"Calantha? She went to town with him to visit her father." Marcel-la's chuckle drew Gaius's gaze to her face. "She plans for him to meet Leander. She wants to ask his permission for them to marry."

Gaius fought to keep the amazement off his face.

The young aristocrat's eyes focused first on the young man beside him, who shrugged, then on the bodyguard.

With eyebrows dipped and a frown curving his mouth, the bodyguard stared too long for comfort at Gaius, then even longer at Marcella.

Marcella's smile never wavered under his glare.

Finally, after a quick nod, the bodyguard turned to the young man. The corner of his mouth turned up. "Truth is free, and we just heard it."

The young man released a deep sigh. "So, we start over." He directed a weary smile at Marcella. "May Fortuna bless them with many children and a long life together."

Marcella's smile broadened. "I'll tell them you said so."

First the bodyguard, then the two young men turned their horses and rode away.

Marcella drew a deep breath and blew it out quickly. "Praise God that's over."

Gaius stared at her, his mouth open.

"Something wrong, dear?"

"I never expected my wife to be such a skillful liar."

"When we ask the Lord for wisdom in the face of danger, He guides us through." She bounced her eyebrows at him as she grinned. "But I wasn't lying at all."

After a quick kiss to his cheek, she marched back to the garden, singing to herself.

Gaius rubbed his chin. God had blessed him with the perfect wife, but even after more than thirty years, he didn't understand her.

Chapter 63

No More Time

As he trudged up the Clivus Suburanus toward the top of the Oppian Hill, where the Baths of Trajan and Titus overlooked the city, Leander's leg complained with every step. He fought to keep from limping worse than normal. He didn't need Calantha questioning his decision to take her home before he had healed enough. Sometimes a man had no choice, and he just had to bear whatever he must.

When the pain ramped up enough to win the battle, he slowed to let Calantha and Servilia move ahead of him, and he fell in behind.

Finally, they reached the hilltop, and the street leveled off. Coming toward them was a litter on the shoulders of four blond men. Its canopy and curtains were the same shade of red as the Secundus litter. The escort was a tall, muscled German who could have been Taurus's twin.

Leander glanced at the new clothes Servilia had given him. He looked like a man who might ride, not the ones on the poles. But he hadn't forgotten the weight on his shoulder and the long hours of boredom waiting to go back to his horses.

Still, a man must live where God had put him and choose to be content. *Slaves, obey your earthly masters with respect and fear and sincerity of heart, just as you would obey Christ.* That was what Apostle Paul had commanded. *Serve with your whole heart, as if you were serving the Lord, not men.*

He'd done it before. God would give him strength to do it again.

They were two blocks away when Calantha pointed to a townhouse with an intricate mosaic in the entryway.

"That was the home of one of my friends who married a few months ago. I was supposed to marry my best friend's brother. Father had arranged the match when I was twelve. Metilia always said he was a kind brother who'd make a wonderful husband, but he died in Britannia. I was on my way to console her when Leander stopped the kidnapping."

Leander's mouth curved down. How long would Calantha remain in her father's house before she married? Would her father find her another kind man who would love her, or would he only care about a political alliance?

He ran his fingers through his hair. What if the man her father chose was cruel or unfaithful? Would that man give her children to love?

Would he ever know if she was happy?

As a stable slave, he wouldn't be there to see her new husband place the iron band on her finger. He wouldn't be part of the procession to the house that would become her new home. But that was something to be thankful for.

"It's hard when a daughter marries and moves away. Gaius and Marcella must be missing you already. I'm sure I would." Servilia's voice was wistful.

"Marcella looked after Leander like a son. No woman could help growing fond of him." Calantha glanced over her shoulder and smiled at him before turning back to Servilia. "I want to keep him near me. I don't intend for him to remain a slave in Father's house."

Her words hit him like the arrow. She'd remain in her father's house until she married, and then she'd become domina of her husband's house. Keeping him near—she might mean it for his good, but she didn't understand a man's heart.

He'd been so careful to never let her see how he felt. She couldn't know how much it would hurt to watch her love another man. If he must, he would ask her to leave him in her father's house when the time came for her to marry and leave. Surely she'd grant him that request. Until then, he'd at least get to watch over her and know she was safe.

By the time they reached the concrete walls of the Baths of Titus, his leg was burning. But as long as he focused on each step, he managed not to limp any more than he had at the farm.

Calantha led them through an ornate arch into a rose garden. Small groups of mostly women strolled or sat on benches. That would change after lunchtime, when the bathing rooms opened to men, but there would still be enough women for them to blend in.

Servilia pointed to a vacant bench by the wall. "That should do for us while we wait." She led the way and sat before someone else claimed it.

Leander drew a deep breath. It was time for him to leave them and fetch her father. Time to return to what he'd been and forget what he longed to be. But he was still in charge of her safety, and he could still tell her what to do one last time.

"I should be back in two, maybe three hours, if all goes well. But if I don't return with your father by late afternoon, you need to go back to the farm. Servilia will get you to Gaius when he brings the wagon into town again. He'll help you figure out what to do next."

"You'll be back, and you'll have Father with you. We'll be praying for you." She handed him the papyrus roll. "Don't say anything to anyone about me being alive and waiting here. Don't let anyone but Father see what's in the letter. Everything depends on only Father knowing. I've asked him to come with you right away, and I'm sure he will."

He held out his hand for the letter that signaled the end of his time with her, the end of his time as a free man. She placed it in his hand, then stepped against him.

Leander's hand squeezed the rolled-up sheet when Calantha slipped her arms around him and rested her cheek against his chest. His heart raced like the stallions he once trained.

He should push her away, free himself from her arms. He was her father's slave, and it was wrong to let her touch him like that. But in that moment, he could no longer deny he loved her, no longer pretend she was only the mistress.

He enfolded her in his arms and rested his cheek against her crown. Her luxuriant hair caught on his stubble when she wriggled a little as she snuggled in, holding him tighter. He closed his eyes and inhaled deeply. The faint scent of roses entranced him and drew a smile.

God, I've resisted for so long, but just this once, for a memory to treasure until You take me home. He entangled the fingers of his free hand in her silken tresses. *If only she really was Calantha and I was Leander.*

His heart beat faster, and his chest ached. *Why did You let me fall in love with her?*

Smiling lips sagged into a frown. He stared past her at the marble statue of Venus, its reflection shimmering in the pool surrounding it.

Why couldn't she have been cold and remote instead of a flesh-and-blood woman with the kindest heart he'd ever known?

If only her brother had never tried to kidnap her and she'd never become more than the mistress he carried. But she had, and how was he ever going to bear seeing her every day but never speaking with her, never feeling her fingers swish through his hair, never gazing into the teasing eyes that drove everything but her from his mind?

She slid her hands up his back until her fingers wrapped over his shoulders. He felt the pulsing of her heartbeat in his own chest.

The sheer pleasure of holding her close—it was no danger to her, only to him, and the damage was done anyway. It was too late to turn back from giving her his heart. She would own it forever. They had no future, but at least he would have the memory of these precious moments wrapped in the arms of the woman he'd gladly die for.

She made no move to release him, even as the pleasure transformed into pain as he faced what must be.

God, help me do this.

He slid his hands to her upper arms and eased her away from him. "Mistress, I'm only Dacius, your father's slave."

The shackles of the past clamped around his heart as the future he longed for died. "And it's not right for me to hold you."

Her face glowed as gold-flecked eyes gazed into his. "Not so, Leander. You're the lion who protects me, and I'm Calantha, not mistress."

Her eyes still teased. Was it all only a game to her?

Did she not realize everything was about to change back to what it had been, that he had to become a thing again instead of a man? Her father had owned his body, but his heart and mind had been free. No more. She'd taken his heart captive as surely as the Roman soldier had taken his body, and he'd never be free again.

Dacius stepped back as he straightened his arms. She'd slip her arms around him again if he didn't hold her away. If he was going to return her, he needed to make the break now. Every moment together made it harder.

"I'll return with the master as soon as I can."

He spun and strode toward the garden exit. Each step was agony, but this time it wasn't only his leg that pulsed with pain.

It was his heart.

◆

Calantha watched Leander as he wove his way between several small groups of chatting women. He was favoring his right leg, and the farther he walked, the more pronounced the limp became. His shoulders drooped, and his head hung lower, too.

She pressed her palm to her cheek. He hadn't told her the truth when he said he was well enough to take her home. She should have believed her own eyes, not his words, but she hadn't wanted to wait another day to find out whether Father would grant her heart's desire for him...and for her.

She turned to Servilia. "When will he be like he was before?"

Servilia's eyes glistened. "Never."

Calantha's breath caught. "But you said you'd seen men hurt much worse go back to battle in only three months."

"Oh, his leg will heal, but he'll never be the same. I saw his face as he held you. When you came to me, he was your litter slave and content to be that. Now he's in love with you, and that's the worst thing that could have happened."

"Why do you say that? I can't think of anything better."

Servilia's eyebrows shot up. "Do you have any idea what's going to happen to him? No slave is permitted to love the master's daughter. Your father will know the moment he sees you together. Dacius is too honest to fool anyone, and he won't even try if your father asks. If you can't convince your father that he never touched you, he'll end up dead or wishing he was within the week."

Calantha shook her head emphatically. "No, Father is not that kind of man. I've never lied to him, and he'll believe me when I tell him what happened. I know what he's going to do to Leander because I'm going to ask him to do what he ought to. Father will agree with me, and then I'll ask him for what I really want."

Chapter 64

WORTHY OF TRUST

The Secundus villa

For the hundredth time, Dacius paused and massaged his throbbing thigh. It had taken half again as long as when he carried Cal...Mistress Julia to the baths, but at last, the ornately carved threshold of the Secundus villa stood before him.

He squared his shoulders and assumed the posture of master, not slave. With his jaw clenched against the pain, he focused on taking steady, even steps toward the doorkeeper.

The man bowed his head. "Welcome to—" His brow furrowed as he looked at Dacius's sandals. "The entrance for trade is that way." He pointed along the wall that led to the stable gate.

"I'm here for the salutation."

The doorkeeper moved to block his way.

"I'm here on behalf of Egnatius Marcellinus."

With eyes shifting between the sandals and Servilia's cloak, the doorkeeper took his measure, then stepped aside. "Speak with Master Secundus's secretary about your request."

Dacius assumed the proud look he'd seen so many times on Marcus Drusus and walked in.

His eyes swept the atrium with its mosaic floor of animal fights and battling men and its marble pool with statues on pedestals down its center. Paintings of mountains and gardens lined the walls. Everything declared the wealth and importance of its owner.

Ahead were more than forty men, some standing, some seated on the benches lining the walls. They were mostly in togas, several with purple stripes. So many...even if the master only spoke a few words with most of them, it could be hours before it was his turn. Not one looked less important than him.

It could be dark before he could give her father the letter and bring him to the baths. Would Mistress Julia be safe?

A middle-aged man with a toga and a harried expression approached him. "Your business with Julius Secundus?"

Again, he was inspected from cloak to sandals and came up lacking.

God, open the way for me. Let her father read and respond as she hopes.

He pulled the rolled papyrus from inside his tunic. "I have an urgent message on behalf of Egnatius Marcellinus, and I must deliver it in person."

The secretary reached for it, and Dacius raised it over his head. He assumed his best impression of Marcus Drusus. "I said in person. The matter is highly confidential. Marcellinus would not want me to be kept waiting."

The secretary blinked twice, then tipped his head. "Follow me."

As they walked past the clusters of clients to the first position by the closed door, Dacius fought a smile. Marcus Drusus would never know how he'd helped his friend's sister, whether he wanted to or not.

The door opened, and a man exited with head bowed and mouth grim. The hairs on the back of Dacius's neck quivered. Calantha called him the lion who protected her, but the father of Mistress Julia was a true lion of Rome, and he'd just taken a bite out of the man before him.

The secretary paused in the doorway and, with a flick of his hand, invited Dacius into the lion's den.

"A messenger from Egnatius Marcellinus." The secretary led Dacius forward and stopped ten feet from the man who had just ruled a province.

Secundus sat on a throne-like chair on a raised platform. The portrait masks of generations of Julii Secundii lined the walls.

The eyes taking Dacius's measure were emotionless. "If it's so urgent, why did Marcellinus send a messenger who can barely walk?"

Dacius stood as straight as he could while keeping some weight off his right leg. "It's a matter of extreme sensitivity for your eyes and ears only."

Secundus's eyes narrowed, and the long silence made Dacius's skin crawl.

"Flip back your cloak and raise your arms."

An odd command, but Dacius obeyed, holding the papyrus high.

The secretary stepped close and felt for a hidden dagger. "Unarmed."

"Then you may leave us."

The secretary left the room, and the door latched behind him.

With a face as cold as the masks on the wall, Secundus held out his hand. "The message."

Lightning bolts of pain ripped through Dacius's thigh with his first step. He placed the roll on his master's palm and stepped back.

After loosening the first yarn tie, Secundus glanced up at Dacius. "You can go."

Dacius drew a deep breath. "An immediate response is required."

Secundus's mouth turned down as he removed the second and third ties. As he began to read the letter from the daughter he must have thought dead, the mask of the politician fell away. She'd told Dacius what she wrote, and the contents of each line were written on her father's face. Joyful shock as he realized she was alive. Concern over her insistence that he tell no one before he came to see her. His eyes bored into Dacius when he hit the part about going alone with the man who brought the letter and he would bring Secundus to her.

When her father finished reading, he rolled the papyrus and waved it at Dacius. "Do you know what is in this?"

"Yes, and I'm ready to take you where you need to go."

Secundus's eyebrows dipped. "How far?"

"It took me almost two hours to get here."

Secundus slipped the papyrus inside his tunic. "With that leg, you can't make that walk again today. Can you ride?"

"Yes." Dacius's neck muscles tensed. If they rode, would they have to enter the stable yard? In his merchant's disguise, would anyone there recognize him?

He took a deep breath and relaxed. People see what they expect, and a litter slave who's considered a runaway wouldn't be expected to return walking at the side of the master. He was an ordinary looking man, except for maybe his hair color, and anyone seeing him would assume he was there on business. It should be safe enough.

Secundus rose from his chair and strode to the door. He opened it, and his secretary hurried over.

"An urgent matter has arisen. Send them all home." Before the secretary could speak, he closed the door. He walked to a tapestry of men in battle and pulled it aside to reveal a doorway.

"Follow me."

The short hallway led to a door that opened into the garden. Dacius was finally in a part of the villa he recognized. The new reflecting pool had been finished, and the bank of rose bushes had been planted on the dirt he'd helped move.

They entered the stable yard, and Dacius relaxed. The only person there was a stable slave he didn't recognize carrying a bucket of water toward Niger's stall.

As the man unlatched the stall door, her father's voice pulled his gaze away.

"There's a placid mare that should suit you."

"I can ride whatever you want to put me on."

The whinny from Niger's stall made him regret those words. With a loud thud, the stallion hit the door, knocking it open and sending the stable slave sprawling. As the man rolled into a ball, he screamed, covering his head as Niger thundered past.

The stallion paused, looking for the friend who belonged to that voice, then trotted over to Dacius. He nickered and bumped his head against Dacius's chest, demanding attention.

Dacius obliged by stroking his nose, then his blaze, but the damage was done. His disguise had failed.

Vilicus charged through the second archway to the garden. "What's going on?" His gaze locked on Dacius. "It's you!"

Two garden slaves entered behind him. Vilicus pointed and yelled, "Grab him."

As they ran toward Dacius, Niger shied away and started pacing the stable yard.

The two men grabbed Dacius's arms, and he offered no resistance. His leg wouldn't let him escape even if he tried.

God, deliver me. Please don't let me fail her."

The brass handle on Vilicus's whip glinted in the sun as he raised his arm to strike.

"Stop."

Secundus's single word froze Vilicus's arm. Then the overseer's fists rammed into his hips. "But this is the slave who vanished during the kidnapping. Tribune Titianus will take this one, and the torturers can get what he's done with the mistress out of him."

Secundus's hand clamped on Dacius's jaw and forced his chin up. Merciless eyes burned with anger, driving daggers of fear into him.

"Are you that slave?" The menace in Secundus's voice twisted those daggers, but he could only answer with the truth.

"I am, but I was not one of the kidnappers. The letter explains everything."

With eyes narrowed, Secundus released Dacius's jaw with a jerk. Then he rubbed his lip. Dacius met his gaze, desperately praying that he would believe the words of his daughter in the letter, not the accusation of the overseer standing before him.

A quick tip of his head, and Secundus stepped back. "If he'd been one of Julia's kidnappers, he would never return here. Release him, and get back to your work." He directed a frown toward Vilicus, who made no move to leave. "You, too."

The slaves shuffled back through the archway, and Vilicus followed.

Secundus turned his attention to the stable slave, who was keeping a good distance between himself and the pacing Niger. "Fetch Taurus and saddle my stallion and two mares."

With a frightened glance at Niger, he scurried off to get Taurus first.

Dacius clucked, and Niger trotted over for another nose rub.

Her father walked to a bench by the entrance to the villa. As he unwrapped his toga and piled the many feet of fabric on the bench, he glanced over his shoulder. "What's your name?"

"In your household, I'm called Dacius."

Still marked as a senator by the broad purple stripes on his tunic, Secundus returned to Dacius's side. Even wearing only a tunic, her father projected Roman power, and standing too close was unnerving.

"Gallio bought me for the stable. I'll get the horses ready."

The big stallion followed him like a puppy to the bay mare's stall. He led her out, and Niger nosed his back several times as he saddled her.

"You're a pest, you are." He rubbed the stallion's blaze, then slipped his fingers into his forelock and pulled them through.

When Taurus and the stable man appeared, Dacius pointed at the largest mare. "That one for Taurus."

The German paused at Dacius's side. His smile started small and grew. "Welcome back. I knew Primus was lying."

"Where is he?"

"Sold with the other two." He lowered his voice. "No mistress, no need for litter slaves."

Taurus reached to stroke Niger, and the horse backed off with a snort. "Still suspicious of me. I sometimes give him carrots, like you used to. He's almost friendly then."

The stable man led the master's stallion from its stall to saddle, and Niger's ears flattened. Dacius gripped his halter. "No fights for you today." He led him back to his stall and slapped his rump to send him in. As Dacius latched the half-door, Niger hung his head over for one more nose rub.

He turned to find Secundus and Taurus mounted. So he wouldn't have to swing his bad leg over the horse's rump, he mounted the bay mare from the right-hand side.

As soon as he settled into the saddle, Secundus moved beside him. "You know horses. They're all afraid of that black stallion."

Dacius nudged the mare into a walk and turned toward the baths after they passed through the gate.

"That's why Gallio bought me—to train Niger so your son could ride him."

"How did you end up carrying Julia?"

"A small fire in some straw frightened him. He trampled one of her bearers. Vilicus used me the next day because I was the right height, and Gallio decided not to replace the dead man."

Secundus's soft snort accompanied a half-smile. "A fortunate chain of events for her. I haven't seen my son since I returned. Can he ride that stallion?"

Dacius fought a smile. "Not yet, but I'll get Niger to where he can."

"Can you?"

"Yes."

"Can anyone else?"

"Not yet, but—"

"You'll get him to where they can." Secundus's half-smile grew to full. "You do have a way with horses."

Dacius's own slight smile was accompanied by a shrug. "And with mules, once they trust me."

Secundus eyed him. "Trust can be hard to earn."

"I earn a mule's trust by being trustworthy."

Secundus's voice hardened. "And how is it my daughter trusts you so much? She's been missing a month."

Dacius glanced over his shoulder at Taurus two horse-lengths behind them and lowered his voice to a whisper. "I earned her trust the same way."

"Hmph."

They rode on in silence.

The Baths of Trajan and Titus

As they approached the entrance to the Baths of Trajan, Dacius glanced at Tiberius Secundus. "We need to leave Taurus here with the horses."

Secundus turned cool eyes on him. "Since my daughter trusts you so much, perhaps I can dispense with the bodyguard."

Dacius reined in and slipped from his horse. "We walk from here."

Secundus snapped his fingers, and Taurus rode up. "Wait here." He dismounted, handed both their reins to Taurus, and turned toward Dacius. "Will we be long?"

"It's close."

One step, and his leg almost buckled. He'd tried to ride relaxed, not gripping too much with his knees, but it hadn't been enough for his thigh to recover.

"This way." With eyes focused on the entrance steps, he led his owner toward the reunion both father and daughter wanted. Secundus projected emotionless power, but Calantha loved him deeply. Beneath his haughty manner, there might be a man worthy of that love. A man whose love matched her own.

He took them in the front entrance, then out a back door that opened onto the space between the two bath complexes.

Almost there. He closed his eyes and asked God for one more measure of strength. Even with his jaw clamped, each step brought a grimace.

"You're in no shape for this. Walk slower." Secundus's tone had warmed. "Why didn't we ride back here?"

"I don't want to risk anyone but you seeing her. No one must know she's here."

Her father's head pulled back. "Her escort knows we came to the baths."

"If you tell Taurus to say nothing, he's a man who can be trusted with a secret."

A skeptical smile lifted the corner of Secundus's mouth. "So, you think you know men as well as you do horses?"

"Some men. Trust is earned by being trustworthy." He glanced at her father, then away. "But torture can force a secret from the best of men or make them tell lies to end it."

"If Julia is waiting for me, you won't have to find out which describes you."

Dacius's jaw clenched as he took the next step, but it wasn't the pain that triggered it. Then he caught the fleeting smile on her father's face. He was joking...maybe.

The garden archway loomed before them, and his grunt drew her father's glance. Ten more steps, and they would see her. Fifty more steps, and he would deliver her father to her.

One hundred more steps, and he might not be on his feet, no matter how hard he tried.

Chapter 65

Dead and Alive

When Julia saw her father and Leander step through the arch, she turned her back. "There he is. Tell me when he gets here."

She silently counted down the steps they would have to take, her heart rate rising as the number dropped.

"They're here."

Her smile burst forth at Servilia's words. She spun and slipped her arms around Father and burrowed into his chest. His arms wrapped around her and pinned her there.

"You need to sit."

Servilia's words popped Calantha's eyes open in time to see their friend lift Leander's arm onto her shoulder and wrap her arm around his waist. Her father's arms kept her from going to him. But after Servilia helped him sit, he smiled and waved her away.

Her lion was tired, but he'd be all right. Now to set him free.

"I'm so glad you came home on time. We've been hiding out for a month, waiting for your return."

Father's eyes veiled. "We?"

"Leander and me."

His eyes flipped toward Leander, then returned to her. "When I asked his name, he said Dacius. You say Leander."

"I renamed him. He fought like a lion to protect me from the kidnappers, and it fits him. Leander thought it might be too dangerous to use my real name, so I renamed myself, too. I became Calantha so Aulus couldn't find me."

Father's back straightened. He stepped back but left his hands on her arms. "Aulus? Your brother?"

"Yes. Leander overheard him talking about losing too much gambling, and he and Marcus planned the kidnapping to get the ransom to pay the debt without you knowing." Her eyes sought out Leander on the bench, where Servilia stood with her hand on his shoulder. "Leander tried to warn me, but I didn't let him. Then he stopped the kidnappers, and he almost died protecting me. Even when I thought he was dying, all he thought about was keeping me safe until you returned."

She turned to look at Leander, and her father's gaze followed her own.

Then he smiled at her lion as he sat on the bench with his head back against the wall, eyes closed. "He doesn't look like a lion now, but I've seen his courage."

"What you've seen is nothing compared to what he really is. He knocked out the first kidnapper. Then the second one stabbed him, and he knocked that one down, too. We were getting away when one of them tried to shoot me, and he deliberately took the arrow. That's why he's limping."

Father's eyes were focused on hers, and his smile wrapped around her like a warm blanket. It was time for her first request.

"He couldn't have been more loyal or taken better care of me until you returned." A deep breath, and she forged ahead. "The only fitting reward is to free him."

Her father rested his hand on her cheek. "Any man who would do what he did to bring you back to me deserves his freedom."

She beamed at him. "Promise me you'll do it as soon as possible? Even as soon as tomorrow?"

"I will."

She walked over to Leander and swept some hair off his forehead. He smiled without opening his eyes. "I knew you'd want to do the right thing for a man who risked everything to save me."

When she ran her fingers through his hair, her father's eyes narrowed. "Where have the two of you been for the last month?" He crossed his arms.

She stepped away from Leander so another touch wouldn't add fuel to Father's suspicions and moved within arm's length of her father again.

"Servilia helped us when the kidnappers were chasing us, and she asked a friend and his wife to let us stay at their farm until you returned. First Servilia, then Marcella took care of Leander and me."

His face relaxed. "I'll repay them for everything."

"You can offer, but they probably won't take it. They helped because we needed it, not for any reward."

Her pulse quickened. It was time for her second request. "I discovered something while I was with them, Father, and I hope you'll approve."

"What?" His smile warmed her like summer sunshine.

As she gazed on the face of the earthly father who loved her, she asked her heavenly Father for help.

"You know how much I love you. No one ever had a better father. I love being your daughter." A deep breath, a quick prayer, and she took the first step toward freedom.

"But I don't want the life I had. I've grown to love the life of a common woman. I love Marcella and her husband. They took me in and protected me, no questions asked. She's like another mother to me, and they've become my dearest friends."

His smile vanished.

Another deep breath, another prayer, and she forged ahead. "I want to stay with them as Calantha instead of returning to your house as Julia."

The frown he used so often on Aulus appeared.

"It all started as an act to keep me safe until you returned. But I've been so happy there, and I don't want it to end. I've been missing for so long everyone thinks I'm dead. Let them keep thinking that."

"That's foolishness." Father's mouth turned from frown to scowl. "You're a Julius Secundus. No one would choose to be otherwise. I thought you were dead. Now that I have you back, I'm not losing you again."

"You don't want to lose Aulus, either. After being gone so long, my return will raise so many questions. What if someone learns he had me kidnapped? He'd be in terrible trouble. It would end his political future. It would disgrace our family name."

Her father's eyebrows dipped. She had found his weak point, but victory was still not assured.

"Please, Father. I don't want my brother destroyed. I don't even want him getting into trouble over this. What he did was stupid. But if he hadn't been so desperate to hide what he'd lost from you, he would never have done anything that could hurt me. It was Marcus's plan, and you know how he follows Marcus's lead without thinking. I've forgiven him, and I want you to forgive him, too."

"Forgiven him?" Father snorted. "You haven't even seen him for him to ask it of you. No one forgives without the other person asking for forgiveness." His hand swept the thought of that possibility away. "And usually not even then."

She drew a deep breath and braced for Father's anger. It was time to expose the truth that might make her death reality. "Christians do, and I've become one."

Father's eyes widened. His jaw started to drop until he clamped it shut. His eyes scanned those around them. No one was listening.

"Do not say that. No Julius Secundus will ever become one. Not while I'm paterfamilias." His whisper-soft words hit her like a shout.

She lowered her voice to match his. "But I already have. And that means I can never marry the kind of man we'd planned. I won't worship the Roman gods ever again, and as soon as some enemy of yours tells Emperor Hadrian, I'll be killed." She took his hand. "But if you leave me dead, I can marry a man I love, and you can come see me and your grandchildren as often as you want."

A scowl blackened Father's face as he tipped his head toward Leander. "Is he one, too?"

"That's why he risked dying to save me. Jesus tells us there's no greater love than to lay down our life for another. Even an enemy. Even someone who only treated you like an animal...which is what I did to him before he saved me."

Father ran his fingers through his hair. Then he fixed icy eyes on Servilia. "Is she one?"

Calantha froze. Father was a magistrate of Rome, and Rome was an enemy of the followers of Jesus. Had her desire for her own freedom just brought death upon two people she loved? Could Father hunt down Marcella and all her friends and kill them, too?

Tears filled her eyes, and she turned to Servilia. "Run."

Before Servilia could move, Father seized her arm. "Stop. You saved my daughter. I'm not going to hurt you." She offered no resistance, and he released her. But she backed away to stand by Leander. He struggled to his feet and pushed her behind him.

Father massaged his neck as his eyes bored into Calantha. "This farmer and his wife who hid you and won't take anything for it, are they also what these two are?"

"Yes, Father. We all are, and what happens to them should happen to me, too. If you want them to die, you'll have to kill me." She squared her shoulders and stared at him with eyes both pleading and defiant.

Father's gaze swept the area around them before returning to her. "Stop saying that." He rubbed his forehead. "If this was a year ago, I would have shipped you to the estate in Gallia and disposed of your friends.

"But some things have changed while I was in Sicilia." Again, he checked that no one was listening. "Lucius Cordus has a farm there. He's the centurion who saved me when I was tribune of the I Minervia during Saturninus's rebellion." The anger drained from her father's eyes. "We met to discuss old battles and life since the legion." His lips tightened. "And he told me he's a Christian now. But there's no finer Roman or better man than him. So..." He released a deep sigh. "If you can keep it secret, I will allow it."

Calantha kept her smile from bursting forth. Father was on the edge...only one small shove was needed. "But how can I keep it secret if I come back to live as your daughter? Especially after I marry. Quintus Sabinus or some other enemy of yours will find out. He has spies everywhere, and I could never be careful enough. Please, Father, let the old me die so I can continue to live."

His shoulders slumped, and his eyes closed. When he opened them, resignation had quenched the fire. "You leave me no choice. I don't want to grieve your death a second time." A deep sigh drained his lungs. "I will allow you to stay dead...Calantha."

She slipped her arms around him and squeezed as hard as she could. "Thank you, Father."

A wry smile tugged at the corner of his mouth. "You say you don't want the senatorial life, but you just proved you would have played the political games brilliantly."

Two barriers down. Only one to go, but first she had to know for sure. She stepped back and took Father's hand. "One more thing."

He rolled his eyes. "What else could there possibly be?"

"I'll tell you in a moment, but first I need to ask Leander something. In private."

Servilia stood behind Leander, leaning out for a better view. She came from behind him and winked as she passed Calantha. "There are some beautiful roses by the fountain. Perhaps your father would like to look at them, too."

His eyebrows dipped as his gaze moved from Calantha to Leander.

Then, with the poise he displayed when he addressed the Senate, he followed Servilia.

◆

Leander took a deep breath when she moved within an arm's length of him. Her eyes lit with the teasing fire he'd come to love.

A slight breeze carried the scent of roses from her hair. "Does my lion know what just happened?"

"Your father agreed to free me and to let you go back to Marcella and Gaius."

She caressed his stubbled cheek. "Do you know what that means?"

He fought the grin. "That Roman law doesn't have to chain us when God doesn't want it to."

"Exactly...and where does that leave us?"

Her laughing eyes breached his defenses, and the grin broke free. "Wherever you want it to."

"You were willing to give your blood for me." She touched his tunic where it covered the knife scar. "Can you give me something else?" She placed her palm on his chest.

Again, his heart pounded like the hooves of a racing stallion. But this time, the finish line was in sight.

"You already own my heart. What else do you want?"

"All of you, if you want to marry me."

As he touched her cheek for the first time, she closed her eyes and leaned into his hand.

"There is nothing on this earth I want more."

She patted his chest. "In that case, it's time to tell Father."

"Tell? Don't you mean ask?"

Her fingertip traced his jawline. "As I'm certain Gaius will tell you, when a woman truly wants something, there's not much difference."

◆

Calantha's father stood by the fountain, arms crossed, watching them. She waved, and he strode to her side.

He lifted her chin and scanned her face with wary eyes. "What is your one more thing?"

"Now that Julia is dead and I'm only Calantha, I want to marry Leander."

His hand dropped. Then he rubbed his lips as his eyes bounced between the two of them. Finally, he snorted. "Why am I not surprised? What other bad news do you have for me?"

She wrapped both her hands around one of his and held them to her chest. "But it's not bad news, Father. There's no better man for me than him. As you get to know him, you'll see. Just because everyone else thinks I'm dead, that doesn't mean you can't come often to visit us."

His sigh was deep, but with his free hand, he stroked her cheek. "If you intend to marry this man, I can't just free him."

Her eyes widened. "But you promised."

"I did, and I always keep my word." He scanned Leander head to sandal and back. "How old is your Leander?"

Calantha looked at Leander with eyebrows raised, and he answered for himself. "Twenty-three."

"As I thought. Too young for citizenship under normal manumission." He blew his breath out through his nose. "I won't have my daughter married to a Junian Latin."

"I don't care what he is, Father. He'll be the best husband."

"Perhaps you don't care, but I do. Dead or not, I'm still your father."

He stood facing Leander, the corners of his mouth slightly down. "Where did you get your skill with horses?"

Leander shifted to face him head on. "My father raised them in Dacia, and I trained them at the Licinius Crassus estate before Gallio bought me."

"You trained Crassus horses? For the circus?" Father's eyebrows shot up.

"Yes, and for private drivers."

The corner of his mouth lifted, followed by another soft snort. "Then you're going to be my agent running my new training stable." His mouth curved into a crooked smile. "Then the Council of Ten will grant you full citizenship. No one will question my choice, despite your youth."

Calantha rested her hand on Leander's shoulder. "It needs to be near Marcella's farm."

Father crossed his arms, but this time he smiled at them both. "That should be possible. I can make anyone an offer they can't refuse." His smile turned wry. "Rather like a daughter I used to have."

His chin rose as he squared his shoulders, but the warmth in his eyes remained. "If you have no more surprises for me, it's time for you to return to Servilia's home while the streets are still safe. Have her send me word when you return to that farm you love so much."

"I know you have to keep Leander for a while to free him, but how soon will he join me?"

"The Council meets weekly. While we wait, we'll pick out the land and the first of the horses. I expect fewer than ten days."

She took Leander's hand and held it to her cheek. "I guess that's not too long. Marcella and Gaius will be so glad to get their new son back."

Leander stroked her cheekbone with his thumb. "And his future wife."

Father looked at their hands before rolling his eyes. Then he sighed. "I have several senators coming for dinner. It's time to leave."

As the four of them walked through the archway, Calantha released Leander's hand.

"The next time I see you, you won't belong to Father anymore." She rested her palm on his bristly cheek. "But you'll still be mine. You'll always be mine...and I'll be yours."

His beaming smile was all the answer she needed.

As she walked away with Servilia, Calantha looked back. Her father stood beside her future husband. Leander was smiling, and Father at least looked resigned. He'd granted the first desire of her heart by leaving her dead. Her prayers would now be for him to fulfill the second...that he'd turn to Jesus and join her in being fully alive.

After a slow-as-a-caterpillar walk back through Trajan's Bath, Leander and his future father-in-law found Taurus leaning against a wall, holding the horses.

Secundus took his reins. "Go back to the villa. Tell Gallio to start the banquet without me. I'll return as soon as I can to join my guests."

"Yes, master." Taurus dipped his head before mounting his horse and trotting away.

Once more, Leander mounted from the right-hand side. But this time, his thoughts were on the joy in his future, not the pain in his thigh.

They rode many blocks in silence. Then Leander cleared his throat.

Secundus raised his eyebrows. "You want to say something?"

"Thank you for freeing me." No words would be enough to speak Leander's full gratitude at that moment, so he kept it short. "And for everything else you're doing for us."

Secundus shrugged. "I love my daughter, and you kept her alive, even if I have to pretend she's dead. What one Roman took from you in Dacia, I can return in Rome, at least in part. And freeing you should be highly profitable. With your horse skills, I can make excellent money off those who want well-trained but spirited horses for riding or for their private chariots. A few well-placed stories about how you tamed a murderous stallion and letting them see you ride him should be enough. You'll take that beast with you when you leave. Aulus will never be able to handle him."

"Not yet."

"Not ever." Secundus's face softened. "Julia loves children. She'll be a wonderful mother, and I'll be expecting you to give me grandchildren." The Roman lion smiled at the prospect.

Leander's own smile broadened. "I'll do my best to make her never regret her choice."

"I trust you will."

Chapter 66

A Whole New Day

The Secundus villa, Day 51

It was midmorning when Aulus rode into the stable yard after a night at Marcus's house. He'd been tempted to drink himself unconscious, but that would only have given him a beastly headache without solving his problem. It was drinking too much that got him into the mess in the first place, and no amount of drink would get him out of it.

Africanus was going to try for a few more days to find someone who had seen anything in the area where she'd disappeared, but after so long, Aulus didn't expect success. The one good lead that had seemed so promising had turned up nothing. Africanus had suggested letting Titianus interrogate Callidus, but neither he nor Marcus could risk him telling the full truth. And Marcus was probably right that the soldier had already told them everything he knew that might lead to Julia.

The new stable slave trotted over to take his horse. "The master is home, and he said to tell you he wants to speak with you as soon as you returned."

As the slave led the horse away, Aulus closed his eyes and heaved a sigh. Then he strode into the house, not eager but ready for the confrontation. When they first told Brutus what they'd done, he'd offered to go with Aulus to speak to Father. He'd repeated the offer yesterday. It was tempting to have a man whose opinion Father respected come along to dampen his father's anger when he first confessed what he'd done. But a man should face the consequences of his actions, and to hide behind another man in an attempt to avoid them was no longer something he could do.

If he'd learned anything in the last month, it was that truth might be free, but it had the highest value. And honor was not just a matter of what others thought of him. It should define him as a man.

The salutation was in progress, and it would be better if the clients didn't hear Father yelling at him. So he told Father's secretary that he'd be in the library until the clients left and then he'd like to speak with Father before he went out.

He'd barely unrolled a scroll of Tacitus when Gallio entered. "Your father wants to speak with you in his private office."

Aulus sucked a breath through his teeth. For Father to suspend the salutation, to send Gallio, not his secretary, for him…that did not bode well. But he squared his shoulders and marched behind Gallio to face the man who both loved and scared him.

Father was sitting at his desk, tapping a wax tablet with a stylus. "You wanted to speak with me."

"Yes, Father." Time to confess, but how to start?

Father pointed at the chair across the desk from him. "Well, sit and speak." He set down the stylus and steepled his fingers.

Aulus perched on the edge of the seat, his back straight. "I've done two things while you were gone that I shouldn't have."

Father was like a marble statue, mouth straight, eyes unreadable.

"I lost 10,000 denarii gambling with Quintus Sabinus's son. I didn't want you to know I'd been gambling with bets that high when you'd told me not to." He took a deep breath to slow his racing heart. "So I planned to fake Julia's kidnapping and use the ransom to pay the debt without you ever knowing."

Father's eyes bored into him, but his flinty expression remained unchanged.

"But something went wrong. I got the money and paid the debt. But the old slave who was supposed to get her home after I had the money ended up dead. The man hired to hold the two of them said one of her litter slaves overpowered him and took her. He said he trailed them but lost them in Subura. But he vanished before telling me this. I started hunting for him and Julia. I found him, but I can't find a trace of her. I don't know if she's already dead or suffering somewhere as a slave."

He hung his head. "Because I decided to lie to you, I've probably killed my sister."

"Is that all?"

Aulus rolled his eyes. "Isn't that enough? I shouldn't have gambled. But after I did, I should have told Gallio and had him pay the debt. You would rightly have been furious with me, but Julia would still be safe here with us."

Aulus stared at his feet and waited for his father's explosion.

Instead, silence coiled around him like a snake, squeezing tighter and tighter until he could scarcely breathe.

He lifted his eyes enough to look at his father. He still sat with steepled fingers, watching him.

Then Father picked up the stylus and rolled it between his fingers. "When you say 'I', do you really mean 'we'? Was Marcus involved? Was this really his plan?"

"Yes, but it's my fault that we actually did it. It started as a joke about faking my kidnapping to get the ransom, and then when his father wouldn't give him the money, it turned into kidnapping Julia."

Aulus rubbed the back of his neck. "But you shouldn't blame him. It's not another man's fault when I choose to do something I know is wrong. Two men of honor have convinced me of that, and I take full responsibility."

"These men of honor, who are they and how much do they know?"

"Antonius Brutus and Africanus. They know everything."

"Africanus? His bodyguard?"

"Yes. Brutus told him to go everywhere with us and do what he could to help. He's as honorable as his master."

"Will they tell anyone what they know?"

"No. Brutus told me the first day that he would come with me to tell you privately, but a man shouldn't try to hide from facing what he's done."

Father closed his eyes and rubbed his face. Then he crossed his arms and stared at Aulus.

Aulus bowed his head and waited for the angry condemnation he deserved. When none came, he raised his eyes to his father's face.

"Well, Aulus, had you not come to confess like this, I would be saying something very different to you. But as you've owned up to everything you did, thinking I didn't already know..."

Father rubbed his lower lip. "What I am about to tell you is a family secret. You are never to tell Marcus Drusus or anyone else. Your sister's life and maybe your own depend upon it. Swear your silence in this matter."

Aulus took a deep breath. "I swear."

"The slave you thought kidnapped her actually saved her from the kidnappers. He's been protecting her while they waited for me to return. Protecting her from you because he heard you and Marcus talking."

"So you already knew everything I just told you?" Aulus slumped back in the chair.

"Yes, but it's good you told me yourself. Because of your honesty, I will tell you something."

Aulus straightened, waiting for the secret he could never tell.

"Your sister is alive."

Aulus closed his eyes and breathed a sigh of thanksgiving.

"But she has asked me to let everyone continue to think she's dead."

Aulus's eyes popped open. "But why?"

"She wants to marry the man who rescued her. I've freed him, but Julia Secunda, alive, couldn't marry a freedman. Dead, she can. And she wanted me to tell you she forgives you. She doesn't want you to suffer for your foolish choice. She's actually glad you did what you did because she expects a happier life with him than with us."

"Can I see her?"

"Perhaps. I'm setting up her future husband as my agent to train horses." The corner of his mouth turned up. "You've given your black stallion to them as a wedding present."

Aulus smile drifted toward a grin. "Good. I was never going to be able to ride him. He's too much horse for me."

His father rose and walked around the desk to rest his hand on Aulus's shoulder. "For the boy you were when you bought him, that's true. For the man I see before me now...I expect you'll do many things that will surprise us both."

Gaius's farm, Day 57

Leander sat with Calantha on the bench under Gaius's carob tree. Tomorrow would be their wedding day, and even the crickets were singing for joy.

The broken clouds that hugged the western horizon blazed orange and red before fading toward gray.

He wrapped his left arm around her shoulders, and she snuggled in. Then she reached up and stroked his stubbled cheek. "I like my lions without fur. Maybe I'll help you shave tomorrow before everyone comes."

"Whatever you want is fine with me."

She leaned her head against his shoulder. "I love sunsets. They mark the end of one day, and during the night, God prepares us for a whole new day. I went through my night before I came to know you, before I knew Jesus and the peace He gives." She stroked his cheek once more before kissing it. "I love you, Leander. You're my whole new day."

She slipped her arms around him, and the scent of roses in her hair made him smile.

And as he held Calantha close, feeling her heart beat in time with his own, Leander knew the words of Apostle Paul were true. Who would have thought, as he lay bleeding in the dark, that in only a month the God he loved would give him freedom and a family and a future with the woman he'd been willing to die for? All things did work together for good for those who loved God.

Finis

I'D LOVE TO HEAR FROM YOU!

If you enjoyed *True Freedom*, it would be wonderful if you'd post a review at the retailer you purchased it from. A good review is like a precious jewel set in gold for an author. Hearing you loved it makes all the hours at the keyboard worthwhile.

If you'd like to learn about my latest writing adventures and hear first about upcoming releases and special offers available only to newsletter subscribers, please sign up for my newsletter at carol-ashby.com. Leave me a note while you're there, too. I'd love to hear what you liked most about *True Freedom*.

MORE LIGHT IN THE EMPIRE

Dangerous times, difficult friendships, lives transformed by forgiveness and love

Honor Bound is the seventh volume in the Light in the Empire series, which follows the interconnected lives of four Roman families during the reigns of Trajan and Hadrian. Each can be read stand-alone. The eight novels of the series will take you around the Empire, from Germania and Britannia to Thracia, Dacia, and Judaea and, of course, to Rome itself.

Brutus and Africanus will return in *Honor Bound* in AD 122,
four years after *True Freedom*

For a preview of the opening chapter
of the seventh volume in the series,
coming in November 2019, read on!

Honor Bound

When the honorable path isn't clear, how do you find your way?

Marcus Brutus owns estates, ships, and gladiator schools that increase his fortune daily, but his greatest treasures are his honor and his wife. When she reveals her faith in Jesus before dying after the birth of their son, he's consumed by hatred for the unnamed Christian woman who led his beloved to abandon the Roman gods, making him lose her in this life and the next.

For fifteen years, Licinia's father hid her Christian faith. But now her father is dead, and a ruthless political enemy is hunting for anything to destroy her brother's career. When she becomes the target, her brother sends her to their estate in Germania. But is that far enough to protect her from an evil man who will stop at nothing?

When a carriage accident leaves Brutus injured and his best friend near death after rescuing Brutus's son, Licinia welcomes and cares for them. But her strange habits and his friend's unexpected recovery make Brutus suspect she's the Christian who corrupted his wife. When her brother's enemies come for her, does honor require him to protect her or turn her over as an enemy of Rome? And when Licinia's heart is drawn toward the pagan man who makes money off death, can she reconcile her growing affection with her love for Christ?

Chapter 1

GOODBYES

Rome, Fall of AD 122

The ring of steel on steel echoed across the practice arena of the *Ludus Bruti*, Marcus Brutus's gladiator school in central Roma.

When Brutus lowered his *gladius* and backed away from his favorite sparring partner, he wiped some sweat from his forehead with his forearm. "A good match, Africanus, but were you holding back today?"

The muscled, curly haired Nubian who was four inches taller than Brutus raised his eyebrows. "Holding back, Master Brutus?" He pressed his lips together to stop a guilty smile. "Don't you always want our best efforts, practice or combat?"

"So, the answer is yes."

Africanus shrugged. "You seemed tired today."

"I couldn't get to sleep, so I read most of the night. Camilla's time draws near."

"I found waiting for my first hard. By the third, it becomes easier."

"Your wife is strong and healthy. Camilla..." He chewed his lip. "The third try almost killed her."

"But all has gone well this time. Not like the others."

Brutus pulled a deep breath and blew it out. "True, but I'll have no peace until she hands me the baby and calls me 'Father.' I'll relax then, not before."

The rapid slaps of sandals drew Brutus's eyes to the hallway beside the armor room. His jaw clenched when one of the slaves from his villa trotted onto the arena sand.

"Stabularius. Why are you here?" His whole body tensed, fearing the answer.

"The mistress's labor started a few hours ago, master."

"A few hours? Why didn't someone come for me immediately?"

"Mistress Camilla said you'd be home soon enough anyway, but then the physician decided you should come as soon as possible...because of the mistress's problems in the past."

Brutus handed his gladius to Africanus. "Bring my stallion back to the villa."

He trotted down the hall to his office to snatch his tunic and belt. He pulled the tunic over his head as he strode toward the stable yard. He was still fastening his belt when he entered it.

The horse Stabularius had ridden from the villa lifted its head from the trough, water dripping from its muzzle. Brutus scooped up the reins, grabbed a handful of mane, and hurled himself onto its back.

"Open the gate."

The stable slave scurried to obey and held it open as Brutus trotted through.

Labor took many hours, and the first baby was the slowest to come. But the physician had said as soon as possible, and fear gnawed at him. What if as soon as possible wasn't soon enough?

◆

Africanus sucked air between his teeth as Brutus trotted down the hallway. Then his gaze shifted to Stabularius.

"Is the physician overcautious, or is something wrong?"

The villa stable slave shrugged. "I don't know. They only told me to get here quickly."

"Go saddle Master Brutus's stallion and my horse as well. I'll ride back with you."

Stabularius nodded and disappeared into the hallway.

Africanus turned toward the red-haired gladiator who'd been wielding a wooden practice sword against one of the heavy wooden stakes around the edge of the arena.

"Rufus."

Rufus turned, eyebrows raised.

"Go tell my wife I'm going out to the villa. I doubt I'll be home for dinner."

Rufus nodded. "Fortuna smiled on you, giving you such a good cook for a wife."

Any other time, Rufus's comment would have drawn a smile. "Tell her I want you to eat what she's prepared for me."

Africanus carried the steel *gladii* into the armor room and placed them in the rack. Then he selected two wooden ones that were used for practice by the gladiator slaves. Brutus would want to spar to relieve the tension as he waited.

They usually sparred with metal swords, but he'd rather not fight the master, even with dull-edged steel, when Brutus was distracted. He ran his hand down the weighted wooden blade. Wooden swords should be safe enough.

If the mistress did not survive the delivery and the master needed to fight in anger and grief, he'd rather not die as well.

It had been several hours. Brutus paced in the peristyle, staring often at her closed door on the balcony above. Africanus sat on a chair, tipped on its back legs, with the wooden swords across his lap.

Her every cry cut like a sharpened sword nicking him when his timing was off when sparring.

Then her scream blended with another sound, higher pitched and angry. A piercing, lusty wail.

Their child.

He slapped Africanus's shoulder as a grin split his face. Two steps at a time, he bounded up the stairs and trotted down the balcony to her door.

His palm pushed against it...and it didn't budge.

Why latched?

He knocked softly, but it didn't open. Several harder raps with his knuckles, but still it remained closed.

His fist pounded on the carved door panel. "Open this door. Now!"

A slow, scratching sound as the bolt was drawn back, then Camilla's maid, Capria, opened the door and stepped behind it.

Brutus stood in the doorway, taking in the vision of Camilla cuddling a tiny bundle at her breast. Her hair was soaked with sweat, and she seemed pale, but he'd never seen her more beautiful.

She tipped the baby to turn its face toward him. "See your father, Marcus?" Her lips brushed the baby's cheek.

Brutus strode across the room and sat on the bed beside her, grinning like a fool.

"Reach out your arms. Hold our son."

He took the tiny bundle and gazed into their baby's eyes.

Camilla lifted her hand to stroke his tiny cheek. "He has your eyes. Raise him to have your honor and courage, and he'll be the finest man."

He grinned at her. "We'll raise him to have your wisdom and humor, too."

His eyes locked on hers, and something changed. Their expression shifted from joyful to...wistful?

She shifted in the bed. "Capria, take our son. Everyone, leave us."

Her maid stood before him, arms outstretched, and he transferred the precious bundle to her.

Physician, maid, and two other slaves filed out of the room and closed the door.

Brutus's gut twisted. "Why did you do that?"

"I have some things to tell you that only you should hear."

He shifted on the bed to face her, resting his knee against her side and taking her hand in his. "What?"

"The bleeding isn't going to stop."

"You don't know that. It stopped last time. Why not—"

Her fingers rested on his lips, silencing him.

"I just know. I want you to promise to bury me by the olive grove, where we watch the sunset. Don't cremate me, and don't have the usual Roman burial ceremony." She drew a deep breath. "I'm a Christian, and I want to be buried like one."

He stared at her as his whole world crumbled. A Christian? It couldn't be. That would bar her forever from the Elysian Fields, the place of reunion in the afterlife, reserved for the good and pious. To lose her now would rip his heart out, but to never see her again?

Her fingers shifted from his lips to his cheek. "You haven't promised."

He forced his voice to sound calm, pushing down the surging anger. "I promise. But who convinced you to become one?"

"I won't tell you her name. I don't want her hurt. Don't try to find her."

"But what could she have said to turn you from the gods? I was the one who questioned whether they were real, not you."

"It didn't start with what she said. It's what she did. I told her I wanted to give you a son more than anything, but after losing three babies, I knew the gods were against me. Just before you came home from the Genava estate, she prayed to her god for me to conceive. Before the last words of that prayer, I knew something was different inside me. When I begged you to lay with me the night you returned and you gave in, I knew we would have a son."

"But that doesn't mean her prayer did anything. You conceived three times before."

"That was only the start. I wanted to know the God who has real power. She told me how much God loves me, that He came as Jesus to let me become His child if I just believed, that I would feel that love when I did. And she was right. God gave me love and peace and joy. I used to fear death, but not now. I'll be with Jesus when I die."

Her thumb stroked his cheekbone. "God truly blessed me because He gave me the son I always wanted for you. My only regret is I won't be with you to raise him."

Married for ten years, and he'd thought they kept no secrets from each other. How could she hide this?

"Why didn't you tell me before?"

"I wanted to. I almost did, several times. But then you'd mock the Christians who died for their faith in the arena, and I knew it wasn't the right time. But time has run out."

Her fingers stroked his hair. "I wish I'd told you. Then you'd know how wonderful it is, and we'd be together for eternity. I'll keep praying for you to come to Jesus, too."

He tried to hide the emotions from her as he oscillated between pain and anger. Come to Jesus? He would never want to worship the god who took her from him.

He'd told her again and again he didn't need her to give him a son. He could adopt one, and he knew several men willing to give him one of theirs. Nothing was worth losing her in childbirth. Why had some Christian convinced her it would be safe to try?

Her fingertips drifted down his cheek to his lips. "I don't want you to grieve too long. Promise me."

His jaw clenched. His nod drew her smile. "I'll try." *But the best part of me dies with you. How can I not grieve until death swallows the rest?*

A wave of shivers swept over Camilla. "I feel so cold."

Brutus lay down beside her and drew her trembling body against his own. "Better?"

"Much." She turned her head enough for their eyes to meet. "God has truly blessed me with you."

He kissed her forehead, and wrapped her tighter in his arms. As he willed the warmth of life to flow from him to her, her contented sigh was a dagger slicing into his heart.

Her breaths grew shallower...and stopped.

He held her for several minutes before he rose and strode from her chamber.

Africanus stood, grim-faced, in the peristyle below, his arms hanging, each hand holding a wooden gladius. Brutus charged down the stairs. His slave yet closest friend held one out as he neared.

Brutus's knuckles whitened as his grip tightened on the hilt.

The clack of wooden sword on sword echoed through the house until sweat soaked Brutus's hair and his arm was too leaden to raise the sword one more time.

And with every strike, he cursed the Christian woman who'd taken his beloved from him...in this life and the next.

Portus, seaport of Rome, that evening

Licinia's fingers gripped the ship's rail. The sun had vanished below the edge of the sea an hour earlier, but the wharves of Portus still swarmed with slaves unloading and loading cargo by torchlight. None of them wanted to be there, and neither did she.

A deep sigh drained her lungs. "I know you only want to protect me, Sextus, but to leave with only one day's warning? To be parted from almost everyone I care about like this?" She bit her lip. "I didn't even get to tell Camilla goodbye."

Her brother's brow furrowed. "It's too dangerous to delay."

She blinked hard to force back the tears she was determined not to shed where her brother could see. "You and Father have kept my secret for fifteen years. I still don't think his death has to change everything."

Sextus rested his hand on hers and squeezed. "I wish it didn't, but it does. Father let everyone think he couldn't bear to give you in marriage because you were so much like Mother. Some thought that foolish, but no one questioned his right to do it. But I've been *paterfamilias* for two months now, and I can't use that excuse. Eyebrows are already raised because I haven't arranged a marriage for you yet."

He withdrew his hand. "You're twenty-seven, and most women have half-grown children by your age. Many think marriage to a Licinius Crassus has great political value...and they're right. I've already had several inquiries about you."

"I could keep my faith secret from a husband. Camilla has."

Sextus's head drew back. "No, you couldn't. What would you do the first time he asked you to offer a libation to his household gods? Or go with him to one of the temple ceremonies? Or host a dinner with male and female slaves to entertain his guests?" A frown accompanied the shake of his head. "You'd never go against what your god commands just to make a husband happy."

He rubbed the back of his neck. "Gnaeus overheard one of Sabinus's allies asking one of my clients why I didn't want you to marry... what was wrong with you. That same client was fishing for information about you when he came to the salutation yesterday." His mouth turned down. "For enough money, he'll betray us.

"No one important is asking me dangerous questions...yet, but what can I say when they do? I'm not a good liar. Sabinus is looking for any way to undermine me. Even if that means getting you killed."

His eyes turned away from her. "As *praetor*, it's my job to judge and condemn the Christians brought before me. Imagine the scandal if it comes out that my own sister has been one for years." His jaw clenched. "Nothing would give that reptile greater pleasure than exposing you to hurt me. Emperor Hadrian wouldn't care about your religion if you were a slave or some shopkeeper's wife, but a daughter of one of the noblest families, the sister of one of his magistrates...he'll demand action against you."

Licinia's lips tightened. "And that would keep you from ever becoming a provincial governor."

The pain in his eyes at her words made her wish she'd never uttered them. She reached for his hand and squeezed. "I'm sorry I said that. I know that's not why you're sending me to the Octodurus estate."

His eyes clouded, but the pain was gone. "Uncle Gaius barely escaped his estate with Priscilla and his children before the soldiers came to arrest him. He was no more threat to Rome than you are, but that doesn't seem to matter to the ones who want you Christians converted back to worshiping the Roman gods...or dead." His eyes closed as his lips tightened. Sadness darkened them when he fixed them on her again. "I hate condemning them just because some Christians won't make a meaningless sacrifice to the genius of the emperor and the Roman gods, but I have no choice when that's the law."

She drew a deep breath, then let it out slowly. No more sighs...she didn't want to make sending her away harder for her brother than it already was.

"I only wish I could stay in Rome until Camilla's son is born. For years, it's been her deepest desire to give Brutus an heir."

A skeptical smile accompanied the shake of Sextus's head. "What if she has a girl?"

"She won't. When I prayed for her to conceive, God told me it would be a son."

His laughing snort was exactly what she expected.

"Laugh if you want, Sextus, but I know I'm right. You'll hear when the newest Marcus Antonius Brutus is born. When he is, I want you to deliver the special blanket I wove for him to Camilla. I promised her I'd be there for the delivery. I was going to give it to her then, but now..." A tear tried to escape again.

"I will, but it will have to be an anonymous gift. I don't want to draw Brutus's anger if he discovers you've corrupted his wife by getting her to become a Christian, too."

"It's not corruption. It's liberation from silly superstitions to freedom and joy in the presence of the only true God."

Sextus rolled his eyes. "So you've told me for years, but that's not how Brutus will see it. If he suspects you, he'll throw his support behind Sabinus. Brutus might only be an equestrian, but his network of connections makes him a political force. He's trained half the sons of the senatorial order before they take their first tribune post in the *cursus honorum*. He also rents out some of the best gladiators as bodyguards, enforcers, and fighters in the arena. I don't want him as an enemy."

He rested his hand on her cheek. "Time to bid you farewell, little sister. I don't want anyone to know which ship you're on, so I'd better leave before someone recognizes us. Stay in the cabin out of sight until you're out to sea." His thumb caressed her cheekbone. "I'll miss you. Don't forget to write to me as freedman Sextus Licinius Gratus. I can't be certain your letters won't be intercepted by one of Sabinus's agents, and he must not discover where I've sent you."

She shook the sleeve of the plain white tunic he'd borrowed from their steward. "You may think the famous Senator Crassus is recognized everywhere, but I think you can pass incognito without your purple stripes."

Her teasing relaxed the grim lines around his mouth, just as it always had.

"I'll write as soon as we reach the estate." She took his other hand between both of hers. "And I'll pray for you every day."

The corner of his mouth pulled up. "You can pray for my health and success, but I want you to promise you will not be praying for my conversion."

She stood on tiptoes to kiss him on the cheek. "That's one promise I will never make."

Their hands slipped apart as Sextus stepped back. Then he strode down the gangplank and wove his way through the cargo on the wharf. His pace quickened as he climbed the ramp to the road. He paused in a circle of light beneath one of the torches and raised his hand. Then his figure was swallowed by darkness.

Licinia clenched her teeth, but some tears escaped anyway. Would she ever see the brother who'd teased and taught and defended her again? *Please, God, protect him until you claim him as your own.*

She swept the teardrops from her cheeks and squared her shoulders. Father was dead, and life in Rome was over.

She glanced at the cabin door. Primula, her maid and sister in Christ, awaited her in the cabin, and the four male slaves traveling with them were brothers as well. The life she'd known was gone, but she wasn't completely alone.

She belonged to Jesus, and even though she couldn't see it now, maybe this was God's plan after all.

Historical Note

SLAVERY IN ROMAN TIMES: HOPING FOR FREEDOM WHILE LEGALLY CLASSIFIED AS A THING

In ancient times, slavery was a normal part of virtually all cultures surrounding the Mediterranean Sea. Slave labor was the engine that powered many segments of the Roman economy, and it underpinned the lifestyle of the Roman elite. While the Empire-wide slave population has been estimated at 15% during the early Empire, in Italy and Sicily it was as high as 30%.

Each time Rome's armies conquered a new area or reconquered a rebellious one, many of its men, women, and children were captured and sold to the slave traders who followed the legions. These men transported the newly enslaved to slave markets throughout the Empire.

By the time the Empire reached its greatest extent under Trajan in AD 117, more than a million people had been taken as slaves. While many Dacians from the region of present-day Romania were already Roman slaves, Trajan's two wars with Decebalus (AD 101 to 102, 105 to 106), injected as many as 400,000 newly enslaved Dacians into the Roman markets.

A slave was considered property to be treated however the owner wished. The Latin legal term for slaves emphasized their lowly status: *res* (a thing, an object, property). In the Digest, which compiled centuries of Roman law in AD 533, a slave was called a *res mortales* (mortal thing), and any injury was treated as damage to the property of the owner and nothing more.

When a person was first enslaved, it was customary for the first owner to rename him or her as part of stripping them of personhood. Names often reflected their place of origin (Dacius for a male slave who came from Dacia). They could be named after plants or animals, after a physical characteristic, or even a number. If a slave was sold, the new owner often changed the name again. Born Diegis in Dacia, the hero in *True Freedom* was renamed Dacius to reflect where he was born.

After he almost dies rescuing his owner's daughter, Julia recognizes his selfless bravery by renaming him Leander because of his courage as he fought to save her.

Owning many slaves was a way to flaunt a person's wealth. Although the private home of an average person in Rome might use five to twelve slaves, the elite might have up to 500 slaves in their urban townhouse (*domus*), even though a fraction of that number could perform the tasks. Many of these slaves had limited duties and ample free time while they waited to serve.

Owners often allowed their urban/household slaves (*familia urbana*) to go to the public baths, watch chariot races and gladiatorial games, and even run their own small businesses. Masters sometimes became friends with those who served them as stewards, secretaries, and in other duties that allowed frequent personal contact. It was common for some to be freed during the owner's lifetime or, more likely, in the will of a *paterfamilias* (legal head/patriarch of a Roman family who owned all the family property).

In contrast, life as a farm slave was one of constant toil. The *familia rustica* of a large estate might include two or three thousand slaves, and often they were treated worse than the estate's livestock. A slave or ex-slave overseer (*vilicus*) made them work them from dawn until dusk, seven days a week. Unless an owner decided to free a fraction of his farm slaves in his will, servitude was usually until death.

The Latin terms for farm equipment demonstrate the farm slave's subhuman status in Roman society. A farm implement, like a plow, was an *instrumentum*. The ox pulling the plow was an *instrumentum semivocalis*. The slave driving the ox was an *instrumentum vocalis*, a talking tool. Their lodging was an *ergastulum* (private prison), and on some estates, farm slaves might work and even sleep in chains.

Life could be brutal for a Roman slave, but for those who were freed, the future could be bright. When freed by a Roman citizen, some became Roman citizens themselves. New freedmen had limited political rights and specific obligations to the ones who freed them. But their children from a legally recognized marriage had the full rights of any freeborn Roman citizen. Publius Helvius Pertinax, the son of a freed slave, even became emperor.

When a Roman citizen freed a slave (manumission), the new freedman or freedwoman joined one of three classes: Roman citizens, Junian Latins, and those given the status of an enemy who fought against Rome and then surrendered (*peregrini dediticii*). If the owner was over twenty and the slave over thirty, a new Roman citizen was created. For slaves under thirty, manumission made them Junian Latins without citizen rights but with more rights than foreigners.

Under special conditions, a slave under thirty might get full citizenship. Natural children of their owner could be made citizens. A female slave being freed to marry her former owner also became a citizen so their children could be full citizens. For a male slave, citizenship was granted if he was to become an agent in business with his former owner.

For older slaves, the master and slave appeared before a *praetor* (judge), and the slave was declared free. The praetor touched the slave with a rod to officially free him or her. This manumission "by the rod" (*vindicta*) could occur anytime and anyplace, even while walking through the streets or relaxing at the baths. The freed slaves became Roman citizens, although they were barred from holding elected office. For slaves under thirty in Rome, a council of five senators and five equestrians convened to determine whether the conditions for citizenship were being met.

Once freed, the former master became the patron and the new freedman became his client. While the patron or his children lived, a freedman owed specific services to his former owner. The most significant was his duty to give his patron *officium*. This could consist of a specified number of days of work *(operae)* or their equivalent in money. Often the new freedman continued working for his patron as he had before being freed. Like other clients, freedmen often visited their patron during the morning salutation to express their respect and often to receive a gift of food or money from their patron.

When a male slave was freed, his name changed one more time. He took his former owner's first and clan names (*praenomen* and *nomen*) and added his slave name as his third name (*cognomen*). For example, when Leander was freed by Tiberius Julius Secundus, he became Tiberius Julius Leander. In essence, a freed slave became a member of the former owner's extended family.

In the polytheistic Roman society, it was not uncommon to allow a slave to worship gods different from those of his or her Roman owners. Some chose to become Christians, where they were welcomed as brothers and sisters even by wealthy Romans who owned many slaves themselves. The teaching of Paul the Apostle explained this unusual relationship in his letter to the Galatians: "There is neither Jew nor

Greek, there is neither slave nor free, there is no male and female, for you are all one in Christ Jesus." Galatians 3:28 (ESV).

Paul also told Christian slaves how they were to behave. "Bondservants (slaves), obey your earthly masters with fear and trembling, with a sincere heart, as you would Christ, not by the way of eye-service, as people-pleasers, but as bondservants of Christ, doing the will of God from the heart, rendering service with a good will as to the Lord and not to man." Galatians 6:5-7 (ESV). One can imagine how hard that must have been when a master was cruel and treated his slaves like livestock.

In *True Freedom*, Diegis is torn from his childhood home by Rome's conquering armies and sold as a farm slave to labor until he dies. Re-named Dacius, his faith gives him strength to bear what he must and serve without complaining. When he follows Jesus's command to love even his enemies and rescues his owner's daughter, gratitude for his loyal service brings the freedom he never expected, with all the benefits his Roman owner can bestow.

For more about life in the Roman Empire at its peak, please go to carolashby.com.

Discussion Guide

1) Dacius had a good life in a close Christian community in Dacia. Then when he was eleven, he saw his parents killed by Roman soldiers, and he and his sisters were sold into slavery. Yet he holds onto his faith in Jesus, always reminding himself that God can use all things for good. Have you ever been in a situation where your life felt like it was crumbling? What did that do to your faith?

2) Born to wealth and the highest social status, Julia is not unkind, but she doesn't notice those who serve to make her life comfortable. Do you ever find yourself taking the help of others for granted? How can we let those who serve know we appreciate them?

3) At eighteen, Julia's brother Aulus is old enough to be a responsible young man, but he isn't. After running up a debt gambling when his father told him not to, he takes the bad advice of a good friend on how to get money to pay the debt without his father knowing. Have you ever known someone who listened to bad advice to avoid a problem, only to make it go from minor to disastrous? What could have prevented that?

4) While trying to be a good friend, Marcus gives bad advice that involves lying to Aulus's father. Lacking honor himself, he draws his too-easily-led friend down a dishonest path. Have you known such people? How did they affect you?

5) Africanus was enslaved at fourteen, fought as a gladiator, and earned the respect and trust of his owner, who is also his good friend. He's an honorable man wise in the world's darker ways. Aulus and Marcus rely on his help in the hunt for Julia, but they respond very differently to a slave telling them what to do. Why the difference?

6) First Servilia and then Marcella and Gaius help Julia and Dacius and ask for nothing in return. How did that affect Julia? Why did she respond as she did?

7) When Dacius tells Julia she should change her name while they are

in hiding, she decides to change his name, too. Why? How did the name changes affect their relationship? Have you seen the power of a name to change people?

8) As the time when Leander must take Juila home nears, he knows he must return to his life as a slave, treated as no more than property. How did that knowledge affect him? Could you have done what he did?

9) When Julia's father Tiberius returns, he learns the daughter he'd thought dead is alive, but she no longer wants to be the young woman he knew. How did he respond? Would you have done the same?

10) When Aulus confessed to his father, did you expect Tiberius to respond as he did? How do you think the actions of both son and daughter will affect Tiberius in the future?

11) True Freedom is a story of faith when the future might seem hopeless, love to the point of sacrifice, and the power of faith and love to bring true freedom to all involved. What touched you most? What made you think about what your own choices would be?

WHO WOULD YOU LIKE TO SEE IN A FUTURE NOVEL?

I grew to love several of the characters in *True Freedom* while I was writing. That usually happens, and often the next story for a character takes shape in my head even before I finish. I knew Brutus would need his own story after introducing him in *Faithful*. Africanus and Brutus will be coming back in the next volume in the series, *Honor Bound*, in November 2019. But there are so many people in *True Freedom* that I would like to spend more time with, and I hope there are some for you, too. Who else would you most like to see in a future story? What was it about them that made you want more of them? I'd love to hear what you think. Please go to my website, <u>carol-ashby.com</u> and share your thoughts in the comment box. Looking forward to hearing from you!

Glossary

Alphabetum: alphabet

Auctoratus: gladiator who signs a limited-term contract to fight for a gladiator school

Aureus: (plural *aurei*) gold coin worth 25 *denarii*

Caldarium: the hot bath room in a Roman bath complex

Caupona: inn, canteen, tavern; sometimes a place to find prostitutes

Centurion: 1st level officer over 80 men; rises through the ranks based on merit

Cohors Urbana: Urban Cohort, a military unit serving as police force in Rome

Corbita: merchant sailing ship

Cursus honorum: the sequence of military and political offices held by men of the senatorial order

Denarius: (plural *denarii*) silver coin worth about one day's living wage

Dies Solis: Sunday

Doctor: teacher; in gladiatorial schools, a trainer who assists the *lanista*

Domina: female head of a Roman household.

Dupondius: brass coin worth 1/8 *denarius*

Equestrian order: 2nd highest class of Roman citizens; required personal wealth greater than 100,000 *denarii*

Ergastulum: farm prison where slaves were locked up at night, often with feet chained

Flumen: river

Familia: the Roman family unit consisting of the paterfamilias, his married and unmarried children regardless of age, and his slaves

Familia gladiatoria Bruti: members of the gladiatorial schools (*ludi*) of Brutus

Gladius: short thrusting sword used by the Roman military and some gladiators

Inquisitor: investigator, spy

Instrumentum vocale: A slave, a "speaking instrument"

Lanista: the head trainer of a gladiatorial school

Libra: Roman unit of weight equal to 328.9 grams or 0.724 pounds

Ludi: "games," especially public spectacles like gladiatorial contests

Ludus: a gladiator training school, which also rents bodyguards and professional "intimidators"

Ludus Bruti: the gladiator school, including all the trainers, fighters, and slaves belonging to Brutus

Mille passus: (plural *milia passuum*) Roman mile = 0.92 English miles = 1.48 km

Nauseabundus: seasick

Palla: rectangular cloth wrap worm by Roman women

Paterfamilias: oldest living male of an extended Roman family; the patriarch who owns everything

Peregrine: a person who is not a Roman citizen

Plagium: the crime of holding a Roman citizen against his/her will

Plaustrum: a wagon for carrying goods, often with 4 wheels,

Polenta: barley porridge

Praemia militiae: stipend awarded retiring legionary, money or equivalent in land

Quadrans: Roman bronze coin worth 1/64 denarius

Questor: Roman magistrate who oversees markets and financial matters

Raeda: a four-wheeled closed-in carriage

Res mortales: "Mortal thing." Official Roman legal term for a slave.

Salutation: daily ritual during which prominent citizens received clients and others seeking favors

Salve: Latin greeting, "hello"

Saturni: Saturday

Senatorial order: highest class of Roman citizens; required personal wealth greater than 250,000 *denarii*

Sestertius: (plural *sesterces*) Roman coin worth 1/4 denarius, also called sesterce

Solis: Sunday

Stadia: Roman units for distances: 1 English mile = 8.7 stadia; 1 km = 5.4 stadia

Stola: a long robe worn by married women fastened by clasps at the shoulder and worn over a tunic

Taberna: tavern or shop selling prepared food

Tablinum: the main office and reception room for the Roman master of the house

Tabula: popular Roman board game, often played with betting

Tabularium: the central official records office of the Roman Empire, located in Rome.

Thermae: Roman bathhouse
Thermopolium: a shop selling hot foods and drinks
Trireme: Roman warship with three banks of oars
Vale: Latin farewell, "goodbye"
Veneris: Friday
Vestibulum: short hallway between the entrance door and the atrium

Scripture References

CSB = Christian Standard Bible
ESV = English Standard Version
NIV = New International Version

Chapter 1: Ephesians 6:5 (NIV) and 6:7 paraphrased.
Chapter 35: Luke 6:27-37 (ESV)
Chapter 39: I Thessalonians 4:13-18 and John 6:40 (ESV)
Chapter 45: John 14:23 (ESV) and John 15:13, 17 (CSB)
Chapter 48: Luke 6:36-38, Luke 17:3-4, Luke 11:2-4, Luke 6:46-49, and II Corinthians 13:11 (ESV)
Chapter 49: John 10:30 (ESV) John 14:9-11, 15-17 paraphrased.
Chapter 51: John 10:27-29, John 6:40, and Romans 10:9-10 (ESV)
Chapter 63: Ephesians 6:5 (NIV) and 6:7 paraphrased.

Acknowledgements

First, I thank God for this opportunity to tell a story of how He can use any of us, no matter how powerless, to make a difference in the lives of others. I loved writing how God brought good from the bad for Leander and Calantha, giving them both a future they never thought possible. It was even more fun leading Aulus from irresponsible adolescence to honorable young adulthood under Africanus's and Brutus's influence. Those two men of honor will have a chance to become men of God in the next novel. Nothing gives me more pleasure than writing about lives being transformed by forgiveness and love.

No one can write the best book possible without the help of many others. I want to thank Andrew Budek-Schmeisser for being my critique partner and good friend. Despite serious health problems, he's given unstintingly of his knowledge of good writing, his spiritual insight, and his expertise with horses, combat, and low-tech field medicine. When I so often wanted to bounce something I'd just written off someone at 1:00 or 2:00 in the morning, he was usually online and willing to help. He's helped me with *The Legacy, Faithful, Second Chances, True Freedom, Honor Bound* (the next in the series), and many brainstorming sessions about characters in future volumes. This book wouldn't have been the same without him.

I'm especially thankful for my alpha beta and treasured friend, Lisa Garcia, who's a true kindred spirit and wise woman of God. She's also so good at spotting typos that I'll never need a copy editor.

My critique partner, Katie Powner, who's an award-winning author herself, helped me spot and fix things only an author would see. Ray Warters, a fellow author who also writes about the Roman empire, read and commented on the entire manuscript. Terry Shoebotham, my local writing buddy and prayer partner, also beta-read the full manuscript. Thanks also to Mesu Andrews for being my prayer partner for inspiration and meeting deadlines.

Special thanks to Anne Perrault, fellow author and expert on horsey matters, for checking the equine scenes to make sure Leander's four-footed friends remained believable.

Many thanks to my friends who read shorter sections, looked at draft covers, and gave me helpful feedback: Shelli Littleton, Brennan McPherson, Hy Tran, and Patti Stouter.

My line editor, Wendy Chorot, has once more blessed me with her skill as an editor and her insights for making the deep spiritual scenes reflect real life. She's a joy to work with as well.

Each time I think Roseanna White couldn't possibly design a better cover than the last one, and each time she proves me wrong. It takes amazing talent to start with a collection of separate images and meld them together to get something that looks like the Romans had color photography. Once more, she came up with a design that's attractive to both men and women. I can't wait to see what she does with the next one in the series.

I especially want to thank my wonderful son, Paul, and my beautiful daughter, Lydia, for their love and patience with my obsession with writing.

But my special thanks go to my amazing husband, Jim. It takes a special man to listen to the latest twist in a plot for the umpteenth time with only a slight eyeroll, always accompanied by a smile. He makes it easy to write about men who are smart, funny, kind, patient...in short, men who are so much like him.

About the Author

Carol Ashby has been a professional writer for most of her life, but her articles and books were about lasers and compound semiconductors (the electronics that make cell phones, laser pointers, and LED displays work). She still writes about light, but her Light in the Empire series tells stories of difficult friendships and life-changing decisions in dangerous times, where forgiveness and love open hearts to discover their own faith in Christ. Her fascination with the Roman Empire was born during her first middle-school Latin class. A research career in New Mexico inspires her to get every historical detail right so she can spin stories that make her readers feel like they're living under the Caesars themselves.

Read her articles about many facets of life in the Roman Empire at carolashby.com, or join her at her blog, The Beauty of Truth, at carol-ashby.com.

Light *in the* Empire Series

*Dangerous times, difficult friendships,
lives transformed by forgiveness and love.*

The Light in the Empire Series follows the interconnected lives of four Roman families during the reigns of Trajan and Hadrian. Join them as they travel the Empire, from Germania and Britannia to Thracia, Dacia, and Judaea and, of course, to Rome itself.

Now Available

Forgiven

Are some wounds too deep to forgive?

With a ruthless father who murdered for the family inheritance, Marcus Drusus plans to do the same. In AD 122, Marcus follows his brother Lucius to Judaea and plots to frame a zealot for his older brother's death. But the plan goes awry, and Lucius is rescued by a Messianic Jewish woman. Her oldest brother is a zealot and a Roman soldier killed her twin, but Rachel still persuades her father Joseph to put his love for Jesus above his anger with Rome and hide Lucius until he heals.

Rachel cares for the enemy, and more than broken bones heal as duty turns to love. Lucius embraces Joseph's faith in Jesus, but sharing a faith doesn't heal all wounds. Even before revealed secrets slice open old scars, Joseph wants no Roman son-in-law. With Rachel's zealot brother suspecting he's a Roman officer and his own brother planning to kill him when he returns, can Lucius survive long enough to change Joseph's mind?

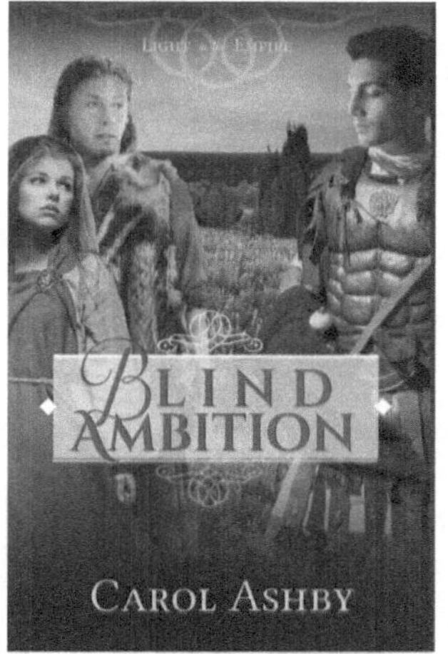

Blind Ambition

Sometimes you have to almost die to discover how you want to live.

It's AD 114 in the Roman province of Germania Superior, and being a Christian carries a death sentence. Tribune Decimus Lentulus is on the fast track for a stellar political career back in Rome. When he's robbed, blinded, and left for dead, a young German woman who follows the Way finds him. Valeria knows it's his duty to have her and her family killed, but she chooses to obey Jesus's command to love her enemy and takes him home to care for him.

It's not his miraculous recovery that shakes Decimus to his core. It's the way they love him like family and their unconcealed love for Jesus. In spite of himself, he falls in love with the Christian woman Rome wants him to kill. Can Valeria hide her faith to follow him into the circles of Roman power? Or should he abandon his ambition to help rule the Empire and choose to follow a different way?

The Legacy

When Rome has taken everything, what's left for a man to give?

Betrayed by a ruthless son who'll do anything for power and wealth, Publius Drusus faces death with an unanswered prayer—that his treasured daughter, Claudia, and honorable son, Titus, will someday share his faith. But who will lead them to the truth once he's gone?

Claudia's oldest brother Lucius arranged their father's execution to inherit everything, and now he's forcing her to marry a cruel Roman power broker. If only she could get to Titus—a thousand miles away in Thracia. Then the man who secretly told her father about Jesus arranges for his son Philip to sneak her out of Rome and take her to the brother she can trust.

A childhood accident scarred Philip's face. A woman's rejection scarred his heart. Claudia's gratitude grows into love, but what can Philip do when the first woman who returns his love hates the God he loves even more?

Titus and Claudia hunger for revenge on their brother and the Christians they blame for their father's deadly conversion. When Titus buys Miriam, a secret Christian, to serve his sister, he starts them all down a path of conflicting loyalties and dangerous decisions. His father's final letter commands the forgiveness Titus refuses to give. What will it take to free him from the hatred poisoning his own heart?

Join the people you met in *Second Chances* eight years earlier in this tale of betrayal, hatred, love, and forgiveness, where even bad things can work together for good.

Faithful

Is the price of true friendship ever too high?

In AD 122, Adela, the fiery daughter of a Germanic chieftain, is kidnapped and taken across the Roman frontier to be sold as a slave. When horse-trader Otto wins her while gambling with her kidnappers, he entrusts her to his friend and trading partner, Galen. Then Otto is kidnapped by the same men, and Galen must track them half way across the Empire before his best friend loses a fight to the death in a Roman arena.

Adela joins Galen in the chase, hungry for vengeance. As the perilous journey deepens their friendship, will the kind, faithful man open her eyes to a life she never dreamed she'd want?

A trip to the heart of the Empire poses mortal danger to a man who follows Jesus, especially when he must seek the help of an enemy of the faith for Otto to survive. Tiberius hunted Christians when he governed Germania Superior and banished his own son when he became one.

When Tiberius learns sparing Galen offers a chance at reconciliation, he joins the trio on their journey home. Can his animosity toward the followers of Jesus survive a trip with the Christian man whose courage and faithfulness demand his respect?

Follow the continuing saga of the people you met in *Blind Ambition* from the frontier of Germany to the heart of the Empire.

Second Chances

*Must the shadows of the past destroy
the hope of the future?*

In AD 122, Cornelia Scipia, proud daughter of one of Rome's noblest families, learns her adulterous husband plans to betroth their daughter to the vicious son of his best friend. Over her dead body! Cornelia divorces him, reclaims her enormous dowry, and kidnaps her own daughter. She plans to start over with Drusilla a thousand miles away. No more husbands for her. But she didn't count on meeting Hector, the widowed Greek captain of the ship carrying her to her new life.

Devastated by the loss of his wife and daughter, Hector's heart begins to heal as he befriends Drusilla. Cornelia's sacrificial love for Drusilla and her courage and humor in the face of the unknown earn his admiration...as a friend. Is he ready for more?

Marriage to the kind, honest sea captain would give Drusilla the father she deserves...and Cornelia the faithful husband she's always longed for. But while her ex-husband hunts them to drag Drusilla back to Rome, secrets in Hector's past and the chasms between their social classes and different faiths erect complicated barriers to any future together. Will God give two lonely hearts a second chance at happiness?

Join the people you met in *The Legacy* eight years later in this tale of hope and a future never imagined until God opens the door.

Hope Unchained

Can the deepest loss bring the greatest gain?

Rome's conquering army took Ariana's family and freedom, but nothing can take her faith in Jesus. When she rescues a tribune's wife from certain death, her reward is freedom and a chance to free her brother and sister. But first she must catch up with the slave caravan before they vanish forever, and tracking them from Dacia to the coast seems impossible for one woman alone.

Discharged from the legion with a hand crippled by a Dacian knife, Donatus faces a future without hope. When the tribune asks him to escort Ariana on her quest, it's the only work he can find. It means four weeks with a Dacian woman and a gladiator bodyguard, but it takes money to eat. A man without options must take what he can get.

But a lot can happen in four weeks. Even battle-hardened men can be touched by love and forgiveness, and it's easier to face an enemy with a sword than to face the truth. When his moment of truth comes, what will Donatus choose, and what will that mean for both of them?

Honor Bound

When the honorable path isn't clear, how do you find your way?

Marcus Brutus owns estates, ships, and gladiator schools that increase his fortune daily, but his greatest treasures are his honor and his wife. When she reveals her faith in Jesus before dying after the birth of their son, he's consumed by hatred for the unnamed Christian woman who led his beloved to abandon the Roman gods, making him lose her in this life and the next.

For fifteen years, Licinia's father hid her Christian faith. But now her father is dead, and a ruthless political enemy is hunting for anything to destroy her brother's career. When she becomes the target, her brother sends her to their estate in Germania. But is that far enough to protect her from an evil man who will stop at nothing?

When a carriage accident leaves Brutus injured and his best friend near death after rescuing Brutus's son, Licinia welcomes and cares for them. But her strange habits and his friend's unexpected recovery make Brutus suspect she's the Christian who corrupted his wife. When her brother's enemies come for her, does honor require him to protect her or turn her over as an enemy of Rome? And when Licinia's heart is drawn toward the pagan man who makes money off death, can she reconcile her growing affection with her love for Christ?

Join some of the people you met in *True Freedom* four years later in this tale of loss and discovery, anger and forgiveness, and the truth that sets people free.

I'd Love to Hear from You!

If you enjoyed this book, it would be a real gift to me if you would post a review at the retailer you purchased it from. A good review is like a jewel set in gold for an author. Other great places to share reviews are Goodreads and BookBub. If you've read others in the series, it would be great if you post a review of those, too.

I'd also love to hear from you at carol-ashby.com or directly at carolashbyauthor@gmail.com.

Want to hear about upcoming releases in the Light in the Empire series and free gifts only for newsletter subscribers?

For free gifts and other special offers, advance notices of upcoming releases, and info about my latest writing adventures, I hope you'll sign up for my newsletter at carol-ashby.com.

Carol Ashby